I0694163

THE LAST TIME
I RUN

THE LAST TIME

I RUN

Y.A. ROMAN

Moca Tree House

New York

Published by Moca Tree House, New York

Library of Congress Control Number: 2025918858

First Edition

Manufactured in the United States of America

ISBN 978-1-971132-00-6 (pbk)
ISBN 978-1-971132-01-3 (hardcover)
ISBN 978-1-971132-02-0 (ebook)

For my boys.
May your dreams guide you,
your purpose ground you,
and may my love walk beside you always,
in every step you take.

* * *

For every girl who has doubted her worth,
and every woman still learning to believe it.
You are enough.
You matter.
You carry purpose within you.

Author's Note

This story was written from a place of both ache and hope.

It explores trauma, healing, faith, and the courage it takes to believe in love again.

My greatest wish is that Amaya's journey reminds you that broken things can still bloom—that light can live alongside pain, and that healing is not about forgetting, but about learning to live fully again.

If any part of this story reflects pieces of your own, please know you are not alone.

There is no shame in seeking help, rest, or peace at your own pace.

Healing is not linear—it's holy work, and you deserve gentleness while you walk through it.

With love,

Y.A. Roman

Prologue

I have always believed in the kind of love that makes your soul feel
like a song.
The kind that steals your breath in the quietest moments.
That holds you captive in a glance.
That lingers like a favorite melody, long after the music has stopped
playing.
But I used to believe love was patient.
That it was kind.
That it found you when you least expected it.
Just like in the movies.
But love—real love—isn't a perfect story.
At least, not the kind they sell in books and movies.
Love is messy.
And dramatic.
And dangerous.
Love is that unreliable friend who swears she's on her way—
then shows up three hours late… if she shows up at all.
It's the *abuela* at the domino table,
sweet one minute and smacking you with a *chancleta* the next.
Some people find comfort in a partner.
I find comfort in my work.
In knowing my rent is paid.
The couch is mine,
and my peace is intact.
Love sounds nice in theory—
someone to share inside jokes with,
someone who knows exactly how I take my coffee

without a step-by-step guide,
someone who notices when my smile doesn't quite reach my eyes.
But being alone? That's not some tragic, unbearable fate.
It's safe. It's steady. And at the very least, it means I always get the last
bite of dessert.
Besides, love has never been particularly kind to me.
Love—or at least my experience with it—has always been
complicated.
Twisting itself into something unrecognizable before I even had the
chance to hold onto it.
Pablo Neruda once said, *"Es tan corto el amor, y tan largo el olvido."*
Love is so short, forgetting is so long.
And I know that truth too well.
Love has a way of making promises it can't keep—
slipping through your fingers before you even realize you were
holding it.
And the forgetting? That's the part that lingers.
The echo that stays long after the music has stopped. After the last
laugh has faded. After you're left standing in an empty room,
still waiting for something that isn't coming back.
Love is supposed to make you feel safe.
Like home.
But I learned a long time ago—home isn't always safe.
And sometimes, love is the thing you run from. Even when a small
part of you still hopes it chases after you.
Like a song that once meant everything, still playing faintly in the
background—even after you've stopped dancing

Chapter One

Seven years ago today, I, Amaya Lee, escaped and survived.

"Escaped and survived."

I say it out loud, letting the words hang in the chilly morning air—then again, firmer, because part of me still needs proof. The weight settles on my chest—heavy, grounding, and still somehow not enough. I stare at the calendar on the fridge.

Freebird.

I write it there every year. Sure, I love the FREEBIRD shoe brand—but this is about something else. A symbol of freedom, of rebirth—born out of chaos.

And every year, her face flashes in my mind—twisted in rage, knife in hand—and I wonder… did she ever feel even a whisper of remorse?

The morning chill seeps through the gaps of my worn cardigan as I step onto the balcony. My fingers wrap around the cold metal railing. Below, the Hudson River reflects the first blush of sunrise—calm, still, unbothered. A perfect mirror. Its peace mocks the storm inside me. I hug the sweater tighter, like that'll keep the past out.

Seven years ago, I promised myself I'd never look back. But how do you leave behind someone who never really leaves you?

The gurgle and hiss of my *greca* pulls me back to the present.

Yes, I still use a good old *greca*. There's something grounding about it—like a quiet rebellion in a world that moves too fast and forgets too easily. Walk into any real Dominican kitchen, and you'll find that metal pot standing proud—steeped in years of laughter, *chisme*, and the kind of tears that knew how to sit beside joy. Mine is small, dented, and worn like a story. But it still delivers—strong, hot, and just bitter enough to warn you not to underestimate it.

I step back inside, letting the view go. The warmth of my kitchen wraps around me, but the past still lingers in the corners like an uninvited guest. I grab my favorite black mug—the one with WORTHY printed in gold above a tiny heart. A reminder.

I take a sip of Café Bustelo—the only thing left that connects me to Soledad. She liked hers black with exactly three sugars—no more, no less—and a Newport menthol on the side. She'd stir in one spoon for health, one for money, and one for love, whispering, *"Salud, dinero, amor."* Then she'd take a long sip, cigarette already balanced between her fingers, exhaling smoke like a benediction.

But not once did she ever add a teaspoon for me.

Her coffee always came in the same chipped mug, painted with *muñecas de Limé*—those faceless dolls found in every Dominican home. A symbol of our island's pride and diversity. As a child, I used to trace their shapes, wondering why they had no eyes, no mouths—just smooth, blank ovals where expressions should've been.

Back home, they say the dolls are faceless because we come from everywhere—African, Spanish, Taíno—too many roots to be defined by a single feature. They're meant to honor our shared identity.

But in Soledad's house, those blank faces meant something else. Not pride. Not unity. Just silence. Like the rules I learned early. Swallow your words. Hide your feelings. Erase yourself. In a house where voices could spark storms, maybe being faceless was the only way to survive.

Half of Nyack is still asleep. The other half is probably lined up at Maison Madeleine, warming up cold fingers on buttery croissants and spiced lattes.

I wasn't supposed to have friends. Soledad made that clear.

But Yiyi didn't count. She lived next door. Her mom worked nights at a club, so sometimes Soledad babysat her. It was convenient. And Yiyi was quiet. She knew how to stay small. Knew not to make noise or take up space. She was the only girl my age Soledad ever let me be around—not because she liked her, but because Yiyi understood the rules. She never looked Soledad in the eye for too long. Sometimes I wonder what happened to her—if she ever got out, or if she learned to stay invisible.

Once, on our way to visit family in the Village of Haverstraw—a small river town just north of Nyack, basically Little Washington

Heights, with more hair salons and barbershops than parking spots, and Spanish rolling off stoops and open windows louder than the church bells—I mentioned, offhand, that one day I'd live in Nyack.

Soledad turned in the driver's seat, her venomous smile curling like smoke. "Hah. Dominican girls like you don't live in places like this, *querida*." She swept her hand at the upscale apartments, the perfect riverfront homes. "This neighborhood is for rich white people. Who do you think you are, Amaya? An Island Queen?"

I stopped mentioning Nyack after that. But that night, I wrote it down in my diary. And years later, I turned her mockery into a dream.

Let's be clear—I'm not rich. No marble countertops. No soaking tub. No doorman named Giuseppe. My apartment is a shoebox with a stove. The bathroom's so small I can brush my teeth while showering. But it has character. A view. And most of all? It's mine. As long as I pay the rent on time. Every morning, I look out at the Hudson and remind myself—I made it.

I take the last sip and let the bitterness linger, remembering the scent of Soledad's kitchen. I close my eyes, and for a moment, she's there—her spirit curling through the steam, impossible to wash away.

I grab the journal Basha gave me for my birthday—the one I promised I'd use. It's been years since I wrote to "Sofia," but maybe it's time to start again.

Life's been moving fast. And honestly… I think I got scared of what the page might say back. I used to write everything down—about Soledad, the dreams I never thought would come true, and the pieces of home I missed most. Then I stopped. Somewhere between survival and growing up, the words just… went quiet.

But right now feels like the right time to remember the noise I ran from—and the pieces I still miss. I flip open to the first clean page and let the pen hover—waiting to see if the girl who wrote her way through everything is still here.

Hey Sofia,

Remember how, back when I was a teen, I used to dream about living here? Funny how you can love where you are and still miss the place that tried to break you. Some nights, my heart still drifts back to the noise I swore I'd never miss.

To me, Nyack meant freedom—cobblestone streets, cute little shops, and no one yelling or slamming doors before breakfast. Just peace—and maybe a cute boy who said "hey, good morning" instead of "yo, ma." A whole different world from the chaos of Inwood.

But girl, I'd be lying if I said I don't miss it sometimes.

I miss Dyckman on a summer night—my block was further up, but that strip was where everybody poured out. Chimichurri trucks lined up like a parade, grill smoke tangled with *bachata* and *reggaetón* like the block had its own playlist. The *señoras in rolos* and *chancletas*, running errands like they owned the whole street. The bodegas blasting loud music—louder gossip.

Later, we moved deeper into Inwood—where I finally had my own bedroom instead of sleeping in the living room wedged between the plastic-covered couch and Soledad's stash of knockoff saint candles that always smelled like burnt plastic and broken promises.

The bodegas here in Nyack? Quiet as a library most days. Folks in there ordering "pass-tell-ittos" like it's fine dining. I swear I saw a man eat one with a fork and knife once. I almost cried.

I miss the sound of dominoes slamming on wooden tables. I'll never forget the day Don Chucho and Doña Marta almost threw down mid-game. Chucho swore Marta was cheating—said he counted her pieces.

"*¡Eso es trampa, Marta!*" he yelled, slapping the table so hard a domino flew onto the sidewalk.

Marta didn't miss a beat. She pointed her cigarette right at him and said, "*¡Cállate, burro, que tú no sabes ni contar!*"

The whole block erupted. Don Chucho tried to snatch her dominoes, and she smacked his hand with her *chancleta*. His son had to drag him upstairs, yelling, "Papi, it's just a game!"

But the next day? Same table. Same heat. Like nothing happened.

Inwood had this energy—raw, alive, in-your-bones kind of real.

But missing it doesn't mean I want to go back.

I don't miss the weight of her hands. Or the nights I prayed to be invisible. I don't miss waking up with bruises in places no one could see.

I love waking up now and knowing nothing's about to explode. That I don't have to read the air like a weather report, waiting for the storm. I love my morning runs by the river, where the water stretches wide and no one's yelling my name like it's a warning.

I love that I sleep. Deep. Dreamless. Safe. I love not having to guess if today will be a good day or a war zone. So yeah, I miss pieces of Dyckman and Inwood. But I don't miss who I had to be to survive them.

'Til next time,

xoxo, Amaya

I close my journal and exhale, fingers tracing the edge of the cover. Writing helps—but some thoughts are too heavy for paper. Some memories don't just live in your head. They live in your body. They settle into muscle and breath. They show up in the way my heart races at a slammed door, in how my shoulders tense without warning.

That's why I move. Jump rope. Run. Push. Sweat. Until the thoughts blur into motion. It's not about fitness—it's about control. About proving, every single day, that this body is mine. Not Soledad's. Not theirs.

I grab my Crossrope, throw on an old hoodie, and head to the Palisades Center Mall. Exercise is cheaper than therapy. And when your apartment's the size of a supply closet, the mall becomes your gym— echoes, tile, and all.

✳ ✳ ✳

The parking lot is mostly empty this early—just a few scattered cars from maintenance crews and fellow early risers. My sneakers scuff across the pavement. Overhead, faint holiday music drifts from hidden speakers.

"Jingle Bells." I freeze, staring up at the dull gray sky. It's October. I shake my head and laugh. Nothing says mall culture like Christmas in fall.

Inside, the silence hits harder. That rare kind of quiet that only exists before the world wakes up—before shoppers spill in, before registers beep and the food court starts smelling like grease and sugar. The air carries traces of floor polish and stale popcorn.

I weave past shuttered stores until I reach my usual spot—a quiet stretch outside the gated Barnes & Noble. And I start.

Jump. Jump. Breathe. Speed walk. Jump again.

The rope slaps the polished tile—rhythmic, precise. Like distant thunder before a storm.

My heart pounds. Muscles burn. For a few glorious minutes, there's only me, the rope, and motion.

Then I hear it—the squeak of sneakers on tile. Right on schedule.

The Mall Walkers have arrived.

Maria and Joyce lead the pack, voices calm and unhurried—like pages turning in a well-loved book. Behind them, Richard and Paul stroll at a more philosophical pace, probably solving the world's problems between laps—or at least debating whether oatmeal counts as breakfast or dessert.

Maria spots me first and waves, her purple tracksuit as cheery as ever.

"Well, look at that. Our favorite jumper is at it again!"

Joyce beams. "Yes! Our favorite jumper—with the energy of a squirrel on espresso!"

I pause mid-jump, resting the rope on my shoulders. "Are you just calling me your favorite because I'm the only jumper here?"

They laugh. Richard and Paul crack smiles too.

Maria steps closer, hands on her hips. "You're something else, Amaya. Always keeping us entertained."

"And motivated," Richard adds, nodding.

Paul raises a hand. "Motivated to stay in our lane—so we don't land in the ER."

Another round of laughter bounces through the quiet space.

Maria shakes her head. "Keep it up, girl. You're putting us to shame."

"And we're perfectly okay with that," Joyce adds with a wink.

I throw my hands up. "Okay, but you guys are missing out on this cardio-induced misery."

I watch them continue their loop, steps unhurried, rhythm steady as sunrise.

Some people think real friendships have to be deep. Messy. Complicated. But the Mall Walkers show otherwise. Sometimes, the best connections are the simplest ones. No heavy expectations. No emotional baggage. Just familiar faces, gentle laughter, and a reminder that not everything in life has to be a battle. Some things—like small, ordinary joys—are meant to be enjoyed.

✳ ✳ ✳

I barely make it through the door before my phone vibrates. I dig it out of my hoodie pocket.

The screen lights up with a photo of Basha and me at Maison Madeleine, our favorite French café. It's from last year's baguette-baking contest—we're laughing like maniacs, faces and clothes covered in flour like we went ten rounds in a bakery brawl.

I smile, remembering how we turned a friendly competition into a full-blown flour war. It's a miracle Mr. Nouel and Esperanza didn't ban us for life.

Before I can say a word, Basha beats me to it.

"Rise and shine, Freebird!"

Her voice blasts through the speaker, already at level ten while mine's stuck in neutral.

"You in one of your deep-thinking moods again?"

I laugh. She knows me too well.

"Basha, it's barely past eight, and I've already worked out and jumped rope at the mall. So technically, I'm ahead of you today."

She gasps like I've just joined the military. "Of course you have! You're a machine, Amaya. You make the rest of us look tragic."

Then she pauses. Which means she's about to drop a bomb.

"All right, well… be ready. I'll be there in thirty."

I look down at my oversized hoodie and leggings.

"Ready for what, exactly?"

"For MAX Fitness! Remember? You promised you'd try the class with me."

I groan, already regretting all my life choices. "Basha. You know I hate gyms. People in there are either staring at themselves or at each other—flexing like they're on some reality show called *Who Can Lift More and Look Angrier Doing It.* I want no part of it."

Basha sighs like I just crushed her dreams. "That's exactly why you need to come! You've been doing the same thing forever—jumping rope like you're training for a Rocky reboot. It's time to try something new."

I shake my head. "I like what I do. Besides, the last time I 'tried something new,' someone farted in the middle of Pilates, and I got kicked out for laughing too hard."

Basha howls with laughter. "That was epic! And completely not my fault."

I can hear the smile in her voice. "But I swear, this will be different. No farting gym-goers, I promise. Plus, MAX Fitness is upscale. Trendy. Full of hot, muscular men."

I groan. "Oh no. Don't even start with that."

Basha cracks up, but I can tell—she's not letting this go. "Come on, Freebird. Gotta live a little! You can't stay in your comfort zone forever."

I lean against the kitchen counter, eyeing my coffee mug like it might offer an escape. "I *am* comfortable. And I don't need a sweaty gym bro to feel good about myself."

Her voice softens—that dangerous kind of soft. The one that's talked me into karaoke nights, disastrous blind dates, and one very illegal midnight swim.

"I get it. I do. But just think about it—one class. One hour. If you hate it, I'll never bring it up again."

I pause. She's definitely bringing it up again. Then exhale.

"Nope. Still not happening. I'm good with my jump ropes. And you know today's my annual Day of Glorious Relaxation—commemorating the day I ran like hell and never looked back. I've earned this one."

She groans. "Ugh, you are impossible."

"*Adiós*, Basha. Love you."

Chapter Two

"I'm going for one class, Basha. *One*." I emphasize the last word like it's a legally binding contract.

"And you'll thank me later," she sings back. "See you in a few!"

I sigh, dragging myself toward the bedroom. Today was supposed to be a take-it-easy, messy-hair, rom-com, zero-effort kind of day.

Instead, here I am, pulling on a cute workout set because, as Abuela always said, *"Dios me libre de salir hecha un desastre."* She'd rather drop dead than be seen in public looking a mess. Abuela was a wise woman. I miss her so much.

I catch myself in the mirror. My curls look like I wrestled a leaf blower and lost. No amount of curl cream is reviving this situation. I rake my fingers through the mess and my hand gets stuck halfway. Of course.

By the time Basha pulls up, I'm seriously debating how convincingly I can fake appendicitis.

She rolls down the window, practically glowing. "Hey, Freebird! Ready to work those muscles?"

I groan. "More like ready to regret every life decision that led me to this moment."

She laughs. "Oh, you say that now. Just wait till you're addicted to the burn."

Sliding into her passenger seat, I sigh. "If I have to endure one guy flexing in the mirror and making sexy grunts, you owe me a croissant and a spicy latte."

"Deal," Basha shoots back, smirking. "But if you enjoy yourself, you owe me mimosas.

"Damn, girl, a mimosa sounds good right about now."

✱ ✱ ✱

We pull up to MAX Fitness—and it's not the grim, sweaty dungeon I pictured. It's sleek. Modern. The kind of place where water probably costs ten bucks a bottle.

"This is a gym?" I ask, eyeing the pristine black doors. It looks more like an Instagram museum for fitness influencers.

Basha hops out, annoyingly flawless in a neon pink workout set, high ponytail sharp enough to slice air, and glossy lips like she's headed to a photo shoot.

"Ready?" she asks, bouncing on spotless pink sneakers.

I sigh. "Not even remotely."

"Too late now," she sings with a wicked smile.

"First sexy grunt equals croissant, spicy latte, AND a *pastelito*—or an empanada, for you non-Dominicans."

"Girl, by then you might as well throw in Dominican cake," she teases.

Her laugh pulls out mine. Suddenly we're giggling like kids.

Inside, the gym smells like eucalyptus, citrus, and unattainable body goals. Mirrors multiply toned, confident bodies. I already feel out of place. This isn't Nyack Beach State Park or my quiet corner of the mall. This is… something else entirely.

Basha starts waving like she's guiding a plane in for landing.

And then—*he* walks in.

Tall. Broad-shouldered. Unfairly attractive. His fitted gym tee clings to a sculpted frame, his dark hair is annoyingly perfect and those deep brown eyes? Yeah. He's trouble.

"Maximiliano," Basha whispers, like she's revealing classified information.

"Maxi-who?" I say flatly.

She presses a hand to her chest like I just insulted her entire bloodline. "*The* Maximiliano. Owner of MAX Fitness!"

I try to play it cool, but my mind betrays me—wandering straight to places it has no business being.

"Oh. Him."

"Maximiliano," she repeats, this time with that scheming smile I know too well—as if she's already picturing our wedding hashtags.

"This is my best friend, Amaya. First class today. I've been hyping up your gym forever!"

"Thank you—but the only time someone calls me 'Maximiliano' is when I'm in deep trouble." His laugh is warm, rich. And somehow, worse.

Basha laughs like he's the funniest man alive.

Then he turns to me.

"Welcome to MAX Fitness, Amaya." He offers his hand. "Max."

His voice? Deep. Smooth. The kind that talks people into bad decisions.

I hesitate, then shake his hand. His grip is big, soft, warm—way too easy to notice. And that's the problem. Guys like him? Players. The kind who know exactly what effect they have. Not me. Not today. Not ever.

"Nice to meet you," I say, a little softer than I meant.

"First class, right?" he asks, watching me a little too closely.

"First and maybe last." *Great job, Amaya. Real subtle.* Men like him? Heartbreak in gym gear.

He smirks—like he read my mind. "We'll see about that."

"She'll love it," Basha chimes in confidently.

Max smiles again—cool, knowing. "Glad you're here, Amaya."

My pulse quickens. Annoyingly.

✱ ✱ ✱

The music hits—hard bass, fast rhythm. I feel it in my bones. For a second, it's like being back at Party Guayo Dance Club in Washington Heights.

Max shifts into instructor mode, voice low and commanding. "Today's class is strength and conditioning. Push hard but remember—form first."

I swear he's looking straight at me.

Basha and I move easily through the warm-up. For a moment, I almost feel like I belong here—loose, energized, a little too confident. And then the real workout begins. I throw a few hesitant jabs at the air. Basha? She's a pro. Fluid, controlled, like she's shadowboxing for a Nike commercial. Then she breaks into a playful Muhammad Ali shuffle, raising a brow like she's about to knock someone out.

I arch one back. *Dramática.*

She follows it with a slow-mo punch. "Dun-dun-dun… *pow!*"

I burst out laughing—loud and unladylike. Abuela would be horrified. Meanwhile, I'm over here fighting invisible mosquitoes. Very aggressive, very persistent mosquitoes.

Then Max appears behind me.

"Keep your guard up. Don't leave your chin exposed."

I spin too fast and almost punch him in the chest. He catches my wrist like it's nothing, eyes dancing.

"Easy," he says, cocky. "I'd prefer to stay conscious."

Heat climbs my neck. "Noted."

He moves on. I try to focus. Throw stronger punches. Add bounce. Look like I know what I'm doing. And of course—I get cocky. My wild swing nearly clocks Basha in the face. She ducks just in time, laughing.

"You training for the circus?"

"Nice enthusiasm, Amaya!" Max calls out, too amused.

I hate that I like the way he says my name.

I breathe deep. Reset. Regain my stance, my focus, my dignity. You got this, Amaya. Channel your inner Rocky. Move like you belong here. I manage a few solid combos—until my shoelace betrays me and I almost eat the floor. *Kill me now.*

Before I can pretend it didn't happen, Max is there. Fast. Close. *Too* close. His hand hovers like he's debating whether to catch me, that signature smirk already in place.

"You good?"

I flash a thumbs-up. "Oh yeah. Just adding some groundwork. Very intentional."

Basha's nearly in tears. "Girl, *Cirque du Soleil* awaits!"

"Nice work, everyone," Max calls. "Cool down, hydrate, and I better see you back soon."

I'm drenched in sweat. Arms like lead. Legs like overcooked rice.

Basha beams like she just watched me win gold.

"See? Didn't I tell you? You're a total badass!"

"If by badass you mean barely alive," I pant.

Something cold taps my shoulder. I jump.

Max.

"Figured you could use hydration after that performance," he says, smirking.

"Thanks. You didn't have to."

"Wanted to." His eyes linger—just long enough.

I go still.

Before I can make a graceful exit, he holds out a card. "Personal training. One-on-one. Customized to your needs."

Yeah. He definitely emphasized *one-on-one*.

Basha's trying—and failing—not to hit me with a look that screams, *Girl, take the damn training. And the man.*

I take it cautiously. "Are you… selling me a gym package right now?"

"Offering an opportunity," he counters. "You've got potential, Amaya."

My throat goes dry.

I twist the cap too hard, nearly send it flying, then take a long sip—maybe too long. Beside me, Basha is vibrating.

"I'll think about it," I blurt, too fast.

"Oh, she'll love it," Basha adds, smug as ever. I swear, if her sneakers weren't so cute, they'd be suffering right now.

"Oh no, my hair appointment," I lie, already walking off.

The second we're outside, Basha *loses it*. "Girl. You're so screwed."

"It was just water," I protest.

"Water, personal training, and that voice. *Fire.*"

I shake my head. "What fire? Oh please. He's polite. I'm sure he treats all new members like that. Especially the ladies. Classic gym move. It's good business."

"Mmhmm. Just wait till you start picking gym outfits based on who might see you. I'll be here. Front row. With popcorn and my one-pound pink dumbbell."

She hooks her arm through mine, smirking like she just unlocked a VIP pass to my future drama.

I look back—couldn't help it. And there he is, watching me. That infuriating smile on his face. Like he's daring me to look again. Why did I look back? Rookie move, Amaya.

Chapter Three

The second we step into Maison Madeleine, the sweet, sinful scent of cinnamon and fresh croissants hits me like a warm hug I'd gladly let suffocate me. If heaven had a smell, this would be it.

The bakery-café oozes charm—exposed brick walls, well-worn wooden tables that look like they've heard a thousand secrets, soft light filtering in like a staged rom-com. Despite the cozy, old-world vibe, the place is humming. People crowd tiny tables, sipping lattes like they're the last good thing today, debating oat milk versus almond like it's a political scandal.

Near the window, the town librarian—eternal queen of red lipstick—leans in close to the man across from her, rolling a sugar packet between her fingers like he just recited love poetry. Poor guy looks smitten and terrified in equal measure.

This place has always felt like home. Not in a childhood memory way, but in a butter-and-caffeine sanctuary way.

Basha inhales like she just found inner peace behind the pastry case. "Now this," she says, eyes locked on a pile of almond croissants, "this is what life is about. Forget the gym, forget my Oscar, forget Maximiliano and his stupid perfect smile—this is my religion."

I laugh, the last scraps of post-workout misery dissolving like sugar in hot coffee. "You're not wrong," I say, eyeing a golden croissant. "I could live off these." And I could. I got my sweet tooth from my dad.

From the back, Mr. Nouel appears like a pastry king returning from battle—apron dusted in flour, cheeks flushed pink from the ovens, wiping his hands like he just won *Top Chef Croissant Wars*.

"Amaya! Basha! *Mesdames préférées!*" His voice is warm and smooth, like honey over toast. He always makes you feel like the star of your own feel-good movie—even if you look like you just crawled out of bed.

"Mr. Nouel!" Basha practically sings, leaning halfway over the counter. I smile. "Good to see you, Mr. Nouel. How've you been?"

He waves a floury hand. "Busy as always! But never too busy for my favorites. And please—call me Marcel. You make me feel ancient with this 'Mr. Nouel.'"

Basha cuts in dramatically. "Have you and Mrs. Nouel decided to adopt me yet? I promise I'll only eat half your pastries."

"Half?" Marcel laughs. "Basha, *ma chère*, you'd put me out of business."

Behind him, Esperanza appears like sunshine in an apron—a dish towel slung over one shoulder, perfume warm with sweet cloves and sun-warmed guava. She beams, her smile as quick and generous as the way she pulls us into her arms.

"My girls!" she says, squeezing us before stepping back. "How's the Box of Beets, Basha?"

"Beets Beauty Box," Basha corrects, puffing up. "Thriving. People finally appreciate my genius. Though *someone* still won't let me give her highlights."

Esperanza laughs. "Maybe one day. But I'm not sure the world's ready for me with beet-colored hair."

"Oh, it's ready," Basha says, elbowing me. "Amaya's next. She just doesn't know it yet."

I hold up my hands. "No, thank you. I've got enough chaos without adding beet-red hair."

Esperanza softens, tilting her head. "How's the studio coming, *querida*? Tell me it's finally happening."

Warmth creeps up my neck. "Yeah… it's getting there. Still some things to figure out, but it feels real now. I used to stand right here dreaming about it when I was just trying to make rent."

Esperanza's smile is *café con leche* at dawn. "You've always been a fighter, Amaya. Even when things were rough, you never let go of what you love. That heart? It shows in everything you touch."

"Thank you." Even though it's nowhere near enough. Her words land like warm bread in an empty belly—exactly what I didn't know I needed. They always treated me like family—especially back when I was just trying to stay afloat.

"I was telling Ryan last night how excited you are. He was thrilled for you."

Heat flares up my neck. "Oh really?" I try to play it off. "How's he doing?"

Basha clocks me sideways. "*Of course* he was thrilled."

Esperanza shakes her head, smiling. "Oh, you know Ryan—always somewhere building something. If he keeps it up, they'll name streets after him."

I force a smile. "That's amazing. He's really… making a difference." I should leave it there. But the way his name sits in the air twists something low in my chest.

Esperanza pats my arm, turning back to her ovens. "*Ay, Virgen*! If these croissants burn, I'll be writing apology letters all week. Last time we ran out, I swear people almost started a riot."

I laugh, picturing caffeine-deprived regulars storming the counter.

"People take their pastries too seriously," Basha says, eyes dancing.

Then she flips the switch, as only Basha can.

"Girl! You *have* to come with me to Hudson River Tavern Saturday night—that new spot in Piermont. And guess what? Oscar finally agreed to check it out."

"Wait. Oscar agreed? Since when does he play nice with other bars?"

"Exactly!" Basha flashes a wicked smile. "He says he wants to 'support the scene,' but come on—he's dying to see the competition."

I hesitate. "I don't know, Bash. I've got so much to do for the studio. That workout alone nearly finished me off."

Basha throws her hands up. "One night, Amaya! You'll thank me when you're sipping a spicy cocktail instead of stress-browsing Pinterest. You *need* this."

I fight it, but my willpower's softer than *flan*.

She leans in, smug. "Don't act like you forgot about that black dress. The one you bought for a what-if night that still hasn't happened."

I sigh. "Fine. But only because I need to see Oscar walk into enemy territory."

"Yesss!" Basha claps like she just won a game show. "It's gonna be legendary."

We sink into a corner table—fresh pastries, steaming drinks, the hush of French melodies and soft voices weaving through the air like a cozy blanket.

Basha takes a dramatic bite of her almond croissant, powdered sugar everywhere. "So… how many times did you almost punch Max today?"

I narrow my eyes. "Just once, thank you very much."

She dabs her lip, smirking. "And he looked ready to catch you in slo-mo."

I roll my eyes, but a smile slips through. "Please. I've been catching myself since day one."

"Pfft." She flicks a crumb at me. "He'd *love* to be your hero. You're not some background noise, Freebird—you're the whole damn show."

"Yeah? This 'show' writes her own script."

Basha raises her cappuccino. "To Saturday nights—and the stories we'll deny in daylight."

I lift my spicy latte. "To spicy lattes now… and a spicier drink Saturday night."

The apartment welcomes me with quiet.

Sunlight filters through the windows, casting golden streaks across the hardwood. It's the first moment of calm I've had in days.

I promised myself a no-stress day. No work, just rest. But honestly? I'm terrible at doing nothing. Organizing my closet doesn't count as work. It's therapy. That's my story, and I'm sticking to it.

I hit play on my Girl Chill playlist and let the music settle into the air. As I move through my bedroom, folding sweaters and tucking away shoes, my mind drifts back to Maison Madeleine. Mr. Nouel's quiet kindness, Esperanza's laughter, Basha being Basha. The scent of fresh pastries still clings to me. It's the kind of day I don't want to forget.

I pull my ladder from the corner and climb up to the top shelf. One by one, I start rearranging my shoeboxes—by vibe, by heel height, by what-was-I-thinking. No one with two feet needs this many shoes.

Then I see it—tucked in the back, a too-familiar shoebox, its edges soft and slightly worn. My fingers graze the lid, careful, like touching an old photograph.

Sofia.

A soft smile tugs at my lips.

The originals. The ones that started it all.

I haven't opened this box in forever. Inside are the old journals—letters to Sofia from another lifetime. Pages written by a girl who hadn't yet learned how to survive the world but was already trying to understand it.

I used to fill these constantly, like breathing. Then life happened—work, school, survival—and the pages went quiet. I thought I'd lost her for good. But lately, since writing to Sofia again, I can feel her voice stirring back to life.

I pick up the stack, fingertips brushing their worn covers. The scent of old ink rises—nostalgic and grounding all at once. I hold them against my chest like they're holding pieces of me I'd forgotten.

When I finally pull one away, instinct takes over. I sit on the bed, tracing the slightly curled edges, the ink softened and blurred with time.

I flip through until a familiar entry catches my eye.

Hey Sofia,

OMG girl, I have the best news! Today I stopped by Maison Madeleine—you know, that cute French bakery everyone's obsessed with? I walked in nervous but determined, and guess what? They hired me on the spot!

I needed that second paycheck like yesterday. Between tuition, rent, and swiping my MetroCard like it prints money, I was this close to panic mode. I was about to cry in the bodega, no lie. Like, staring at the Induveca salami, wishing my budget matched my cravings. Tell me why survival mode never wants plain rice and beans—it always wants the good stuff.

Mr. and Mrs. Nouel (aka the sweetest people alive) said they loved my energy. I was shook. When they saw my resume, they were like, "Wow, you really hustle." I mean, facts. Dog-sitting, cleaning houses, doing makeup for guests at the B&B—I'm out here.

Mrs. Nouel smiled and said, "You remind me of myself at your age." And boom—job secured. And get this—her name's Esperanza, and she's Dominican. You know we clicked instantly.

I was already dreaming up ways to sneak island flavors into the menu. Like, imagine *coconetes* and *flan* sitting next to a croissant. Tell me that wouldn't be iconic. Look at me, already trying to turn this French spot into a Dominican bakery.

This feels like one step closer to something bigger. I don't know what yet, but I can feel it. You know me, Sof—always chasing something.

'Til next time,

xoxo, Amaya

I smile, shaking my head, remembering how excited I was back then. If only I knew that job would lead to way more than just pastries.

And speaking of things I wasn't ready for…

Hey Sofia,

You are not going to believe what happened. I finally met Mr. Nouel's son—from his late wife, Madeleine.

Oh. My. Gosh. This man is fine. Tall, built, dreamy coffee-colored eyes, and hair that makes you want to sin. And don't even get me started on that smile—it could melt butter in a snowstorm.

He walked in, said "hello," and I swear my heart did a little merengue.

But girl, he's not just fine—he's actually mad sweet. And smart, too. Like, where did this man even come from? Most guys I know just wanna party and talk big.

Okay, don't judge me, but I may or may not have overheard (fine, eavesdropped on) a convo between him, Mr. Nouel, and Esperanza. Turns out, he's graduating from Baruch soon, and they're throwing him a little bakery party because he refused a big one. A guy who doesn't need to flex for the 'gram? Is this real life?

Now I'm sitting here wondering—will they invite me? I mean, technically I just started working here, but I've already gotten friendly with everyone. And let's be real, I would *not* mind another excuse to see him again.

And girl, tell me why I suddenly turned into the world's most dedicated cleaner? I wiped the same counter three times like it owed me rent. I know Mr. Nouel and Esperanza were probably thinking, "Do we need to start paying this girl overtime?"

And when I finally talked to Ryan? Disaster. I was so nervous, I could barely get a word out. Me! Stuttering. I was like, "Uh, um, I... hi." Like, WHAT? I probably looked like I had a brain freeze without the ice cream.

But hey—at least I didn't spill anything or trip over my own feet. Gotta count the small wins, right?

Tomorrow, I need to get it together, because if I see him again? I refuse to go out like that. If I do, Sof, just bury me with a *pastelito* in each hand.

Wish me luck, girl!

'Til next time, xoxo, Amaya.

I finish reading and stare at the page, fingers tracing over my own words.

Ryan.

I can still see him—leaning on the counter, that easy smile, the tiny lines in his eyes when he laughed. The way his laugh always landed somewhere in my chest and stayed there.

I shake my head and let out a breath. I shouldn't be thinking about this. About him. It's been years. And yet... here I am.

I flip the page, ready to leave the past where it belongs. But part of me knows—I won't.

Hey Sofia,

Today was another amazing bakery day! I swear, people walk in like they haven't seen carbs since birth. Every time I hand someone a baguette, they look at me like I performed a miracle. One guy said, "Thank you, angel." Like, sir—it's bread, not a kidney.

Still working weekends at the Nyack Hideaway B&B. Some guests are super sweet. Others? Absolutely allergic to tipping. Like, I'm folding your towels, making your bed, vacuuming, wiping your crusty toothpaste off the sink—and you leave me a smile and a "thanks"? Sir, I'm not your mom. Tip accordingly. Straight-up stingy.

Still renting a room from Willow—the barefoot hippie queen of Nyack. Her hair? Bird's nest energy with no regrets. I don't think she's touched a brush since Y2K. The other day I showed her one of my Dominican conditioners (trying to be subtle), and she squinted at the label like I handed her radioactive slime.

"If it's not homemade, herbal, or blessed by the forest, I don't trust it," she said.

Girl. I love natural stuff, but these curls? They need a little extra chemical sometimes. Shea butter alone is not gonna detangle this battlefield.

And don't even get me started on her cooking. I wish Abuela were here to teach her what real seasoning looks like—and that not everything in the woods needs to be stew.

One time she made deer stew. And before you ask—absolutely not. I didn't eat it.

"But it's organic!" she said. Organic?! Ma'am, I'm pretty sure suspicious roadkill boiled with pine needles doesn't count. I left the apartment. Came back an hour later and made myself *mangú* with fried cheese, fried eggs, fried salami, and slices of *aguacate*—like a normal person.

And yes, I'm still daydreaming about Ryan. You knew that. But I swear, it's not just him. It's this place, this job, this chaotic little life—it finally feels like mine.

'Til next time,

xoxo, Amaya

I slam the journal shut and drop it back in the shoebox like it's burning my palms. The apartment's too quiet. My head's too loud. So, I grab my keys and go hunting for sugar.

Downtown Nyack's half-asleep—storefronts dark, string lights blinking lazy above Main. There's this tiny homemade ice cream shop wedged between a bookstore and an old record shop with a half-dead neon sign that hums like it's given up. Old blues drifts out the door, mixing with the crisp fall air. They've only got maybe a dozen flavors, and they close the last day of October, so everyone acts like they're rationing joy before winter. Bar crowds line up at midnight, half drunk and half pretending they aren't.

I order a swirl—vanilla and chocolate, stacked high in one of those still-warm waffle cones, dipped in dark chocolate that snaps when I bite it. Go big or go home.

I'm halfway through when I spot him.

Max.

Of course. Mr. MAX Fitness himself. The man, the brand, the last person I need tonight.

He's leaning against the brick wall by the record shop, hoodie up, joggers, clean sneakers—like he left the gym and drifted here instead of his bed. He's got that stupid grin that says he's been here *watching me* longer than I want to admit. Of course he'd be standing there now—right when I'm halfway to sticky-fingered twelve-year-old mode. Perfect.

He pushes off the wall, slow—like he's got all night to test my patience. He nods at my cone. "Didn't picture you as the midnight-ice-cream type."

I lick a drip off my knuckle, sweet smile fake as can be. "Didn't peg you as the stand-around-watching-girls-eat type."

He laughs—low, easy, the kind that slides in past every annoyed bone in my body.

"I'm not watching. I'm appreciating. Big difference."

He steps in closer, eyes flicking—of course—to my mouth. His voice dips. "You make that look way too good."

I arch a brow and lick my cone slow, just to annoy him. "It's called dessert, *Maximiliano*. You should try it sometime."

His mouth twitches. "Max," he says, voice low but playful. "Told you. Only my mom calls me that—or when I'm in trouble."

"Exactly." I bite down, slow on purpose, let him watch. "Feels right."

He laughs under his breath, like he can't help it. Moves in— warmth brushing away the chill on my arms.

"You're trouble," he says, like it's both a fact and a challenge.

I lift a shoulder, playing it off. "I'm dessert. Try and keep up."

He doesn't answer right away. Just watches me—eyes darker now, steady, unbothered, holding me like he knows I'm not going anywhere. My heart kicks, loud enough I swear he can hear it.

"You know," he says, voice dipping, "that offer still stands."

I tilt my head, fake clueless. "What offer?"

He leans in—close enough that clean, expensive cologne hits somewhere soft behind my ribs.

"Personal training. One-on-one. Could work on your form…" He lets it hang—lets the word do its job.

I bark a laugh—too loud, too sharp. "Smooth, Maximiliano."

"Max." Softer now. "You gonna keep testing me?"

I tilt my chin, pretend I'm winning. "I survived one class. Might retire undefeated. Legend status."

He tips in that last inch—close enough that my knees want to betray me for good.

"Retire?" His voice is lower now, teasing gone. "I haven't even seen you sweat for real yet."

That line fries my brain. I shove a bite of ice cream into my mouth before it betrays me.

He nods at my cone, eyes locked like it's a dare. "Last bite. Make it count."

I drag it out—slow, dramatic. He watches every second, shameless, like I'm the show he paid extra for. I toss the wrapper, swipe chocolate off my lip like, sorry, Max—show's over.

"You always this dedicated?" he murmurs—voice like a dare.

I step back—one, two—like distance helps. "Only when someone's watching."

He smiles, lazy, like he's filing it away like a promise. "You like it when I watch, huh?"

I roll my eyes so hard they nearly stick. "Goodnight, Maximiliano." I drag it out, poking him right where I want it to.

His smile deepens, darkens—like this is only the beginning. "Sweet dreams, Amaya."

And the way he says it? It doesn't just crawl under my skin. It stays there the whole walk home.

Chapter Four

Damn, girl, you look good.

I give myself one last once-over in the mirror, adjusting the straps of my black dress. It hugs in all the right places—sleek, elegant, dangerous. My curls bounce like they know they're the main character. For a second, I actually see the version of me I've been chasing.

I let out a breath, fingers tightening on the counter. *Okay, Amaya. Fun night. No overthinking. Just good vibes.*

A low rumble outside pulls me from my head. Through the window, Oscar's Jeep slides to the curb. A second later, Basha's voice cuts through the street.

"Girl, if you don't get your cute little self out here, I will drag you out myself!"

I laugh, grab my clutch, and step into the night.

Basha leans dramatically out the window, waving like she's parking a plane. "Oh. My. Gosh. Look at you! That dress should be illegal. Walk carefully—we do not have bail money."

I slide into the backseat smiling. "You're one to talk. You look like a Vogue cover."

Oscar glances at me in the rearview mirror, eyes amused. "You two are dressed to kill. Should I be nervous?"

"Please," Basha says, elbowing him. "Be nervous for your bar. Tonight's all about the competition."

They fall into their usual rhythm—her stirring the pot, him rolling with it like nothing rattles him. Somehow it works.

"Bar Barazo got soul," Oscar says, turning onto the main road. "Vibes you can't fake."

I lean forward. "We'll see. Maybe you'll pick up some tips—new cocktail menu, mood lighting…"

He smirks. "We don't need tricks. Our regulars hug the bartenders."

The ride blurs by—music blasting, Basha hyping us up, Oscar sighing like a dad chauffeuring two chaotic daughters. I don't go out much—too busy saving every dollar, every hour, pouring it all into my studio. But tonight? Tonight I get a break.

Hudson River Tavern glows against the water like a movie set. Glass windows, golden light, music spilling into the street.

Oscar parks, turning to us. "Ready?"

"Always," Basha says, flashing every tooth.

He hops out, opens our doors with a dramatic bow. "After you, queens."

Inside, the energy hits—warm light, exposed brick, bass under laughter and clinking glasses. Alive. Perfect.

At the bar, a bubbly bartender waves us over. Strawberry-blonde curls, smile bright enough to light the place.

"Well, hello there, gorgeous people! I'm Maggie. What can I get you?"

"Gin and tonic—extra lime, mostly tonic," I say.

"Manhattan. Extra cherries," Basha adds.

Oscar goes classic and local. "Hudson Valley Reserve. Neat."

Maggie lights up. "Strong choice for the gentleman. Aged just right." Then she winks at us. "And I love the ladies' picks. Fresh, bold, timeless. You all came to play." She spins away like she owns the room.

Basha leans close. "Tell me this place isn't perfect."

She's right. The energy hums easy, alive. Our drinks arrive, and Basha raises hers.

"To good vibes."

We clink.

"And nights we'll laugh about forever," I add.

Oscar's smile is crooked, easy. "And dance moves we'll blame on the alcohol."

We laugh—loud, unguarded, the kind that scrubs your soul clean. Then something shifts, static in the air. My skin prickles, and I turn.

Of course. Him.

Maximiliano. Dark jeans, black button-up, sleeves rolled just enough to show off forearms that do too much. A gold watch flashes as he moves. Confidence that doesn't shout, just exists.

And beside him? Perfection in heels. Tall. Glowing. The kind of woman who belongs in the spotlight. His hand brushes her back as they move to a booth, and something inside me twists.

I look away too late. He's already seen me.

Our eyes lock. Just for a second. Then he looks past me like I'm air.

"Hey, girl," Basha says, reading my mood instantly. "You good?"

"Yep," I say too fast.

She arches a brow. "Because it looks like you want to drown that gin and tonic."

"It's nothing." It's a lie. *It's everything.* I lift my chin like that might make it true.

The music pulls me back. I let my curls fly, moving loose, wild—like no one's watching. But I know he is. And then—his voice.

"Hey, Oscar. Basha. Amaya. This is Milania."

Milania. Of course her name is Milania.

She's polite. Perfect. Effortless. I paste on a smile that feels like glass. "Hello. Amaya."

Basha greets her with too much enthusiasm. "Heyyy, I'm Basha. Nice to meet you!"

Max claps Oscar's back like he hasn't just set me on fire. "Oscar, good to see you, man! Who's holding down the fort at Bar Barazo while you're here?"

Oscar laughs. "The place runs itself, Max. You know that."

"I'll be right back," I mumble, already heading for the door.

River air hits sharp and cool. Lights scatter across the water like broken stars. It should feel peaceful. So why doesn't it?

Basha trails after me, voice softer now. "Okay. Talk."

I sigh, arms crossed tight. "He was flirting at the gym. Then again at the ice cream shop. And now he shows up here—with her?"

"She might not be his girlfriend."

"Please. Did you see them?"

"Sounds like jealousy—with extra lime."

"I don't do jealous."

"Mmhmm. Keep saying that. So what's really eating you, then?"

I blow out a breath. "It's not her. It's guys like him. Smooth when no one's watching, then flipping it like it was all in my head. I hate that."

"So you're pissed."

"I'm annoyed. Big difference."

"Or maybe you're wrong. She could be his cousin."

"Right. And I'm Miss Dominican Republic."

Basha smirks. "I'd vote for you."

Her teasing cracks my mood. We head back inside. I duck into the bathroom, swipe on fresh gloss, whisper a quick pep talk to my reflection. Then I turn a corner—straight into a solid chest.

Hands catch me. His hands.

Heat floods my skin before I even look up.

Max.

"Careful." His voice is low, controlled. "You look… stunning tonight."

I cross my arms. "That your line for every girl, or just the ones you leave stranded?"

His smile slips. "Maybe you don't know me as well as you think."

"I know enough." I brush past, straight to the bar.

Oscar beams, waving down a busy Maggie. "I'm ordering shots for everyone! Max and Milania included."

"Wait—what?" I blurt, my voice pitching higher than I want.

Basha whips around to Oscar, eyes wide. "Oscar—no. No, absolutely not."

Oscar waves us off, casual as ever. "Come on, it's Milania's birthday."

I glance over at their booth—Max and Milania laughing together, totally in sync. My stomach twists.

Before I can object, Oscar adds, almost like an afterthought, "And yeah—she's his sister."

The words smack the air right out of me. My drink turns to ice in my hand. My entire theory, gone in two seconds flat.

Basha's smirk screams *I told you so.*

"Though honestly, he could've picked my bar. Best vibes in town, just saying," Oscar adds.

Basha leans in, bumping his shoulder. "Oh, come on, babe. We won't hold it against them—this time. Besides, you could turn a cardboard box into a club. You're the vibe."

Then she leans close. "See? Jumped to conclusions, *amiga*."

I try to laugh it off, but it comes out weak. "Yeah, well… happens to the best of us."

I lift my glass. "Happy birthday, Milania."

Across the room, Max leans back, laughing with his sister. I swallow down my pride with the rest of my mostly tonic gin.

Oscar's voice cuts through the haze. "Hey, Maggie! Five shots of your Hudson Valley Reserve, *por favor*!"

Maggie raises a brow, grinning. "Five shots? You trying to start the party without me?"

"Make that six. One for you," I say.

Basha lights up. "Yeah, Maggie, you're definitely part of this chaos now!"

Maggie laughs as she lines up the glasses. "Now this is my kind of crowd."

Oscar points at Maggie, then us. "Shots with the bartender? Don't blame me when we're dancing on tables."

We burst out laughing—the kind that makes the whole bar lean in like they want whatever we're having.

Oscar steadies the tray and carries it to Max and Milania. "A round for the birthday girl!"

Milania claps, eyes shining. "Oh my gosh, thank you, everyone! You guys are amazing!"

Max lifts his glass. "Thanks, everyone—to Milania, best sister in the world."

We all lift our glasses.

"To a wild night and stories we won't believe tomorrow," Basha says.

"To good trouble," I add, the whiskey hitting just right.

Milania turns to Max, practically glowing. "Alright, birthday tradition—you're up. Time to dance."

He groans, but he's already on his feet. No resistance. The music shifts, and suddenly we're all pulled in. Basha's spinning like she's in a music video, Milania's hips are criminal, and Oscar's doing that uncle-at-a-family-party routine—shuffle, shoulder roll, a bachata warm-up that's equal parts embarrassing and endearing. I can't.

The night loosens around the edges, soft and golden.

Basha turns to Milania mid-dance. "Alright, birthday girl—how about a game of pool? Oscar and I can take you down eyes closed."

Milania smirks. "You wish. I've been hustling pool since middle school."

They make their way to the pool table, full of smack talk and fake confidence.

As they head across the room, Basha tosses a look over her shoulder. "You two joining, or what?"

Max leans back, arms stretched across the booth, completely at ease. "I'm good."

"Same," I say, lifting my drink. "I'd rather watch the professionals crash and burn."

The noise fades just a notch. The lights feel warmer. The booth feels smaller.

I glance at Max. He's watching me with a look I can't untangle—quiet, focused, like I'm the only thing in the room worth seeing.

He nods toward the seat beside him. "What? You don't hustle at pool?"

I smirk, slipping into the booth across from him instead. "Trust me, if I'm going to hustle, it won't be at pool. I prefer a front-row seat to their… disastrous—I mean, creative—moves."

He laughs—low, unfiltered, the kind that starts in his chest and pulls you in before you realize it. One arm slides across the back of the booth, fingers brushing the leather like he owns it.

"I don't think I've laughed this much in a while."

I study him, letting the silence stretch just enough.

"Feels like a bit of a reset, huh?"

His expression shifts—softens, deepens. Like something unsaid just showed up in the space between us.

"Yeah. It does."

And for a second, I want to pause time. Crawl into that space between what he says and what he means. Before I can stop myself, I ask, "Back there… outside the bathroom. Did you expect me to just smile and play along?"

His eyes stay fixed on me. "No. I expected you to be exactly who you are."

I search his face for cracks. But there aren't any. Just steady confidence, like he meant it the second he saw me—and still does.

"Tennessee Whiskey" slides through the speakers, smooth and smoky. I hate how my skin notices every chord. I lean back, a teasing smile tugging at my lips. "So, Maximiliano," I draw it out, playful, "is your sister always this much of a firecracker?"

He glances toward the pool table, where Milania is mid-celebration over a lucky shot.

His laugh is easy. Affectionate. "She's wild. Every year we do something together. It's tradition. She takes it way too seriously, but honestly? I wouldn't change a thing."

His eyes drift back to mine.

"And please—call me Max. Unless you're trying to get me in trouble." He pauses, voice dipping, "but the way you say it…" My pulse skips. "I might not mind being in deep trouble."

"Careful. I might hold you to that."

His eyes spark. "Fair enough."

The air shifts again—warmer, deeper. I let the moment stretch. Let the silence say something, too. Then I exhale. "I might've misjudged you."

He leans in, brow raised. "Might've?"

I roll my eyes, but I'm smiling. "Fine. Definitely."

The music hums on, the crowd still there—but in this second, it's just us. Close, still—caught in our own quiet orbit.

Max tilts his head, voice low, teasing again. "So, Amaya… you really thought Milania was my date?"

I try not to cringe. "Look, you two looked pretty cozy. You can't blame me for assuming."

He arches a brow, glancing at the space between us—our knees almost brushing.

"Cozy?" A slow grin pulls at his mouth. "Nah. This is cozy."

I roll my eyes, fighting the smile threatening to break through. "Oh, shut up."

Without a word, Max signals Maggie over. His voice is measured. Decisive. "Two Hudson Valley Reserve. Neat. And a Saratoga with lemon—for the lady."

He doesn't ask what I want. I should be annoyed, but the quiet certainty in his voice slides under my skin, sparking something I don't want to name. I don't even realize how close we've gotten until Maggie returns, setting down the two whiskeys, a water, and a dish of perfect lemon slices. I slide back against the booth, casually—like I need space, but also kind of don't.

Max slips her a crisp hundred. "Keep the change."

"You trying to impress her—or me?" she teases.

"Can't it be both?"

Maggie winks and heads off, her smile trailing behind her.

He lifts his glass. "To unexpected company."

"To keeping you on your toes."

The whiskey burns warm. Not harsh—enough to steady something trembling inside me.

He leans in, close enough I feel his breath. "So, Amaya… what keeps you busy when you're not keeping me on edge?"

I smirk. "A little of everything. I create. I style. I read. I cook. I move. I live."

He watches me like I'm a story he's memorizing.

"Is there anything you don't do? What's your real passion?"

"I'm opening my own studio—photography, fashion styling, makeup. I couldn't choose one, so I didn't."

His brow lifts—impressed. "Ambitious."

"Or reckless. We'll see."

"What made you want to put it all under one roof?"

"I've always loved creating. Making people feel beautiful. Freezing a moment in time." I trace the rim of my glass. "Fashion was survival—turning hand-me-downs into something that felt like me. Makeup was connection—me and my cousins, pretending to be grown. And photography?" I smile. "That was magic. A way to keep a moment or create a different reality."

A quiet moment settles between us.

"But honestly? I'm freaking out. What if no one shows up?"

"That won't happen."

I raise a brow. "You sound pretty confident, huh?"

"I am. Women want spaces made for them. And you?" He nods toward my lips, then my eyes. "You're impossible to ignore."

His fingers brush mine. I don't pull away.

"So," I say, keeping my tone light, "are you from around here?"

"Grew up just outside the city. Moved to Nyack for work. This place pulls you in, doesn't it? What about you? Always been local?"

I nod, a bittersweet pang catching in my chest. "Not originally. I moved here from Inwood—uptown Manhattan—when I was seventeen. Nyack's… quieter. Softer. A reset."

"City in your blood, quiet in your bones," he says softly. "We should do this again. Just us."

"I'd like that."

His scent wraps around me—warm, spiced. The kind that lingers.

"How'd you end up running MAX Fitness?" I ask.

He leans back. "Always been into working out. Let's just say the gym kept me out of trouble."

"Trouble?" I repeat, letting the word hang there between us.

He hesitates—just for a breath, but I feel it.

"When you've got too much energy and nowhere to put it, you end up in places you don't belong." He stalls again, that second silence heavier than the first. "Working out gave me focus. Discipline."

There's weight in what he doesn't say—something raw tucked beneath all that polish.

But then he shifts, brushing it off like it's not that deep. "Eventually got lucky. Made a few smart investments. Saved up. Built something I love."

"Smart move." I tilt my head. "Inspiring, honestly."

"Like you. Going all in. Passion matters. I hope your studio takes off, Amaya."

"Thanks."

The way he says my name slides under my skin. His cologne wraps around me, dark spice and something clean, the kind of scent that pulls you closer without you noticing you've moved.

Suddenly every detail feels louder—the heat simmering between us, the soft give of the booth, his knee brushing mine and staying there.

He studies me. "So when's the big opening?"

"Soon. Very soon. I'm not announcing a date yet."

He nods, letting it land. "I like that you go after what you want."

I don't answer. I just look at him—slowly, fully. And smile.

Something changes in his eyes, the air thickening between us. His gaze dips to my mouth. When his fingers brush mine—slow, intentional, lingering—everything in me sparks alive. Then his lips part, like he's about to say something he shouldn't.

I twirl a curl around my finger, buying time I don't really want. "Go on, then. How's that?"

He leans in, his breath grazing my skin. "I'm usually the one in control." His voice dips lower. "With you… I'm not so sure."

Heat rolls through me, slow and unwelcome and perfect.

Before I can respond—before I can even breathe—Basha and the crew slide back into the booth, laughter cracking the moment wide open.

"Keep dreaming," Oscar says, voice easy. Milania laughs, light and carefree, like nothing in the world weighs her down.

The sound folds around me. A reminder to stay here, even when part of me is still caught in that quiet between us.

But I can't. My pulse is still racing. And when I look back at Max— he's still watching me. That same look. That same quiet dare. Like he's waiting for me to admit it too.

Water, Amaya. Water.

The opening chords of "Love on the Brain" melt through the speakers—slow and sultry. The bass hums under my skin, low and deep, like a heartbeat reminding me how to want again.

Oscar grabs Basha's hand and spins her into him. "Come on, Babe. Let's show 'em how it's done."

She laughs, head tossed back. "See? He can't resist me!"

Milania blows Max a kiss and heads toward the bathroom. "Be right back," she says with a wink.

I consider slipping outside, catching air, putting space between me and this pull I can't shake. But Max takes my hand. No words. No question. Just a touch. A pull. And I go.

The crowd blurs—color, sound, movement fading behind us. It's just us now. The music slows the air, stretching time into something soft and endless. He lifts my arms and drapes them around his neck. Suddenly, we're so close I feel every breath he takes.

He leans in again, his voice brushing my ear, low and warm enough to unravel me. "You smell amazing."

The words sink in—low, devastating. I swallow, not trusting my voice. He doesn't say another word. He doesn't need to. His eyes lock on mine, focused and hungry, like he sees everything I've never said out loud. His hands slip lower, fingertips grazing the small of my back. The way he touches me—warm, sure, claiming—makes the rest of the room disappear.

It's just this.

The slow rhythm we move to. The quiet pull between us. The way his body fits against mine like it was always meant to.

We don't talk. We don't need to.

My forehead brushes his, and for a second we just stay there, breathing each other in as the song winds down, every note stretched thin and aching. I lean in, almost falling.

Then the music stops. What's left is breath. Shallow, uneven. Mine. His. Ours.

I pull back slowly, peeling myself away from something I'm not ready to lose. His hands fall, but the warmth lingers. My body's still slow dancing with a song that's already over.

And suddenly—"Bad Romance" explodes through the speakers like a firecracker. Loud. Flashy. Ruthless.

The crowd roars, bodies surging, hands in the air. Everyone jumps in.

Everyone but me.

Chapter Five

The first thing I notice when I wake up is the pounding in my head. Not just a throb—a full-body drumline that refuses to quit. Great. I'm dying.

I feel nauseous—like my stomach's been thrown into a blender—and by mid-morning, I'm throwing up everything but my soul. At first, I blame the whiskey shots from last night. But then the chills hit. My body aches like I ran a marathon in stilettos. I check my temperature. Fever. Awesome. Just what I need with everything piling up at the studio.

Panic creeps in. I try to rest, but by afternoon I'm shivering under a pile of blankets, my head splitting open like it's trying to escape my skull. This is it. Death by poor life choices.

Still, something feels… off. Too off.

I drag on a hoodie, grab my keys, and drive to Nyack Urgent Care. Every red light tests my will to keep going. A coma sounds better. But what if it's serious?

In the waiting room, I collapse into a chair, hood low. The fluorescent lights? Violent. Every cough rattles me apart. When the nurse finally calls me in, I move like I'm wading through wet cement.

The door swings open. I blink. No way.

Maggie.

The bartender from Hudson River Tavern.

She smiles like she's been waiting for this plot twist. "Let me guess—one too many cocktails last night?"

I groan. "You've got to be kidding me."

She laughs. "I get that a lot. Nurse practitioner by day, bartender by night. Student loans don't pay themselves."

My head's spinning, but her energy steadies me while she checks vitals, runs tests, and taps her tablet to send a prescription to the pharmacy.

"And rest," she says firmly, giving me a look like she already knows I won't.

I force a smile. "Rest. Right. I'll put it on the calendar… sometime in 2045."

✳ ✳ ✳

I unlock the front door, keys still cold in my hand. I'm ready to toss the mail straight into the junk pile—then I see it. A thick, glossy envelope.

Riverview Lifestyle Magazine.

My heart skips. Is this it? THE article?

I bolt upstairs like it's Christmas morning and this envelope is wrapped in gold. I drop my keys, antibiotics, and the rest of the mail onto the counter.

I rip open the prescription first—priorities—then set the kettle on the burner. I make tea the Dominican way, with too much lemon, way too much honey, and absolutely no concern for seeds.

My phone buzzes.

> **Basha:** You okay?

> **Me:** Oh, totally fine. You know, just casually dying. Antibiotics, tea, and bathing in Vicks. Living the dream. Not gonna die, promise.

> **Basha:** Good, 'cause "Nyack's New Business Owner Dies BEFORE the Grand Opening" would be tragic. Also—what's up with y'all Latinas and Vicks?

> **Me:** Because it WORKS. Don't disrespect the sacred menthol. Anyway… guess what came in the mail?

> **Basha:** A new liver?

Me: Close—Riverview Lifestyle Magazine. Pretty sure the studio article is in it.

Basha: WHY ARE YOU NOT RIPPING IT OPEN WITH YOUR TEETH RIGHT NOW?!

I laugh, glancing at the magazine still untouched on the table. Like it might bite me.

Me: Because I'm sick. Obviously on my deathbed.

Basha: Girl, if I have to drag your half-dead body to the opening, I will. OPEN. IT. NOW.

Me: LOL, fine. Opening it. Bye.

Basha: Coming over later with soup. I'm amazing like that. If they make your photo look like a bad LinkedIn headshot or call you an "aspiring entrepreneur" like you're running a lemonade stand, I'm suing.

Me: You are ridiculous.

Basha: And if you pass out, the soup is mine.

I set my phone down, grab my tea, wrap myself in a blanket burrito. The magazine watches me from the table. I breathe in the steam, then reach for it with trembling hands.

The envelope tears. My photo stares back—me in front of the old tailor shop, paintbrush in hand, faded signage behind me like a ghost of what once was.

My hands shake; I flip the page.

COMING SOON

REFLECTIONS STUDIO

By Tom Riley

SOMETHING EXCITING IS stirring in downtown Nyack—a long-closed space is on its way to becoming a vibrant hub of creativity, led by a young entrepreneur with vision and grit. Reflections Studio, a soon-to-open haven for fashion, beauty, and photography, is expected to debut in the coming weeks, promising to bring a fresh, artistic pulse to the local business scene.

Located in what was once a beloved tailor shop, the space is currently undergoing a bold transformation under the hands-on direction of its founder, Amaya Lee. A talented photographer, fashion stylist, and makeup artist, Amaya isn't just launching a business—she's building a dream from the ground up, weaving new energy into the fabric of Nyack's history.

"Every corner of this studio will tell a story," says Amaya, who has been hands-on with the renovation process, often spotted with a paintbrush or broom in hand. "This isn't just about creating a workspace for me—it's about creating a space where everyone who walks in feels inspired and celebrated."

I set the magazine down. My hands are actually shaking. I take a sip of tea—and nearly set my tongue on fire. My nerves won't settle. I pace the room once, then grab the magazine again.

A LEGACY REIMAGINED

The storefront, long dormant, is becoming a symbol of resilience and imagination. Though renovations are still underway, the vision is already clear: a studio with deep character and personal storytelling. From a restored Singer sewing machine to a large, cracked mirror set to become a statement piece, Amaya plans to honor the space's past while crafting something uniquely hers.

"I wanted to keep the character of the space, but also make it personal," she explains. "One of my favorite pieces is a faceless ceramic doll from the Dominican Republic. It represents heritage, beauty, and identity—and reminds me where I came from."

According to Amaya, the doll will be part of a larger display meant to celebrate Caribbean culture and offer clients little touches of home, history, and warmth.

I sink back into the couch like my body just gave up. My chest? Still tight. My heart? Still racing. I close my eyes, but the words won't stop echoing.

A VISION FOR THE FUTURE

"Reflections Studio isn't just a business," Amaya shares. "It's a celebration of creativity and self-expression. I want every client who walks in to feel like they belong—and leave seeing themselves in a new light."

Nyack is watching with anticipation as the finishing touches come together. The excitement is growing, and though the doors haven't opened just yet, one thing is already certain: Reflections Studio is on its way to becoming a space where beauty, identity, and community meet.

My fingers trace the glossy page, slow, like it might vanish if I blink. That name. That photo. That girl.//
And that's when the tears come. Fast. Hot. Unstoppable.//
Because the woman in the article—grounded, visionary, fearless—doesn't feel like me. But she is. Somehow, she is.

✳ ✳ ✳

I call the one person who's always believed in me.

On the other end, I hear it. The low moo of cows, the crow of a rooster. I close my eyes and I'm back there—the little house in Moca, painted bright against endless green. Fruit trees sagging heavy. Chickens strutting like they own the land. My father's plantation, alive with rhythm and hard work, taught me more about wealth than any bank ever could.

An outsider might've looked at our life there and seen poverty. But that house—overflowing with fruit, with music, with love, had everything we ever needed.

I left too young to understand what I was walking away from. I didn't know I'd ache for it all these years—the soil, the sounds, the simplicity, him.

"*Hola*, Papi," I say, my voice already breaking.

"*Hola, mi tesoro*. So happy to hear your voice."

Only my father makes me feel like treasure. Always. How I wish I could hug him right now.

"You're not gonna believe this… the article came out."

There's a pause, then a soft sniffle. "*¡Mi hija. Qué bendición!* I'm so proud of you." I can hear the phone shifting in his hands. "*¡Marisol! ¡Ven acá!* Our daughter's in a magazine!"

Her voice rushes in, warm and bright. "*¿Qué pasa? Amaya, mi niña.*"

"The article. About the studio. It's out," I say, laughing through tears.

"*Mujer*, they wrote about her," Papi says, thick with pride. "Our girl's in a magazine. In *Nueva Yorr*!"

"*No me digas*," Marisol gasps. "*Ay, mi amor*, I'm so proud of you. When are you coming home? I'll make your favorite *sancocho*."

I close my eyes. Taste it already. That broth. Yuca. Corn. Plantains. Love in a bowl.

"Soon, I promise. How's everything over there?"

She doesn't miss a beat. "*Ay, mi niña,* the avocado tree is showing off again. I caught the neighbors sneaking some. But what can I do? At least knock on the door! The tamarind and mango trees too—you won't believe how much fruit we have this year. I'm gonna make so *mucho dulce* to sell."

Then, like it's a breaking news alert—"Oh—and guess what. Remember Carmelita? She almost lost a foot from diabetes… and a tooth!"

"A tooth? From diabetes?"

"No, no. The foot was diabetes. The tooth? That was from a fight with Rosalinda." She pauses, casual as ever. "They made up. Rosalinda's even doing payment plans for a new one."

I laugh so hard my chest aches. Only in Moca.

But then I soften. "Papi… do you want to try for a visa this time? Maybe come visit, you and Marisol?" He cuts me off with that little laugh. The kind that says, *we've been here before.*

"I'm not getting on one of those metal birds, Amaya. I like my feet on the ground, just like the good Lord intended."

I shake my head, laughing. Classic Papi.

"Of course you won't. Stubborn as ever."

Marisol jumps in, all logic.

"I'm not going without your father. Who's gonna feed him? He won't eat from just anybody's hand—you know how picky he is."

She's not wrong.

"Okay, okay. But if you change your minds, let me know. I'm putting together a few boxes for Christmas."

"Ay, *mija*, you're always so thoughtful. You don't have to—but we'll be waiting," Marisol says.

Papi laughs again, deep and smug like he's cracking a serious negotiation.

"Just don't forget the Café Bustelo—not that watery stuff from the little shop down the block you sent last time. That's for weak folks."

He pauses, like he's about to say something truly profound.

"And if there's room… maybe toss in a jar of those blended peanuts I like."

I blink, then burst out laughing. "You mean peanut butter, Papi."

He doesn't miss a beat. "That's what I said."

I wipe my eyes, grinning through the lump in my throat. "I got you, Papi. Extra creamy."

"We love you so much, *mi amor*," Marisol says softly.

"You make me proud every single day, *mi querida hija*. Don't forget that," Papi says softly.

"I love you both," I whisper, my heart heavy in the best and worst way. Their voices. Their warmth. That tiny, bright piece of home. It's everything I miss.

They weren't perfect. But they tried. Always.

Marisol did her best. And my father? He's always been a good man. Still is. Full of laughter, love, and stubborn pride. We say our goodbyes, promise to talk again soon. I set the phone down and stare at it for a while, the silence settling around me like a warm quilt.

But then it comes—the shadow, sharp and sudden. If only I had stayed. If only Soledad hadn't taken me.

I wasn't even allowed to call Papi alone. She was always there—hovering, listening, filtering my words like she could hear the truth trying to slip out. Because if I had said anything? If I'd told him what was really happening? He would've had a heart attack. He never would've let his little girl stay in that house. Not with what waited behind that door—hurt no child should ever carry.

Maybe my life would've been different. Simpler. Safer. Happier.

The phone buzzes again, pulling me back. I think of the Nouels. My second parents. They were there when I was putting myself through FIT, giving me work, guidance, and love. They poured their wisdom into me like I was theirs. If anyone understands what this moment means—it's them.

Esperanza answers, bright as ever. "*¡Hola, mi niña!* Almost ready for the big day?"

"Not even close," I laugh, choked up. "But… I have something to tell you."

Her tone shifts instantly. "What is it? Are you okay, Amaya?"

"No—it's good. Really good."

When I tell her about the article, there's silence—then shouting, then more shouting. My chest aches with love.

"Marcel! Marcel, come quick! Our Amaya's in a magazine!"

I hear Mr. Nouel's calm voice in the background. "What's going on, *mon amour*?"

"She's in a magazine, Marcel! They wrote all about her studio. Our girl is famous!"

I laugh, wiping tears from my face, still overwhelmed.

"I couldn't have done it without you two. You believed in me when I didn't even know what I was building yet."

"Amaya," she says, voice softening. "You've always had it in you. We just gave you a little push. We are so proud of you."

Then she yells again, "Marcel! Get the fancy wine! We're celebrating tonight!"

I smile into the phone. "I just wanted to share it with you both."

"You're going to change lives with that studio, Amaya. I feel it."

"Thank you," I whisper. "I love you both."

"We love you too, sweetheart! Now hurry down here so we can toast your success. Let's crack open the good stuff!"

In the background, I hear Mr. Nouel say, all dramatic, "Ah, so it's time to visit the cellar for the good stuff, then!"

"Thanks, Esperanza. I'll definitely pour some... tea, though. Doctor's orders. Gotta stick with the antibiotics."

"Tea for now! But once you're back on your feet, we're toasting properly—with that fancy bottle Ryan sent from California!"

And just like that, his name lands heavy as stone.

For just a breath, my smile falters. What would've happened if he'd stayed? If I'd followed him instead of chasing something of my own?

But dreams aren't meant to be borrowed. They're meant to be built.

And this one—this studio—is mine.

✷ ✷ ✷

I'm itching to run to the studio, but my body has other plans. I sink into the couch, Fire Stick in hand, scrolling aimlessly. *Resting won't kill you, Amaya,* I tell myself. Though honestly? It kinda feels like it might.

I hover over *The Holiday*—almost hit play, then decide to save it. I like my Christmas movies closer to December, when they feel like magic instead of background noise.

So instead, I land on *27 Dresses*. Again. I've probably seen it twenty-seven times, but at this point, it's tradition.

The opening credits roll, blanket tucked tight, but my mind won't sit still. It drifts—to the article, the studio, the girl I used to be. And the version I'm finally becoming. The one building something of her own. The one no longer defined by what she survived.

But the fever hums beneath it all like static I can't shake. I text Basha to say I'll nap until she gets here, then close my eyes. And that's when the name rises. Sofia.

I pause the movie, shove off the blanket, and walk to the closet. The shoebox isn't tucked away anymore—it waits. Heavy. Patient. I carry it back to the couch, balance it on my lap. My fingers tremble as I lift the lid. The smell of old paper rises up, familiar and sharp.

These journals carry a version of me no one else ever saw.

I pick one at random, flip through the pages, my breath catching on the tilt of rushed handwriting. One entry stops me cold. The ink slants like it's running from something.

Hey Sofia,

I'm so scared to close my eyes now. Had the dream again.

Adrian's hands all over me. Touching, grabbing, pressing into places I keep trying so hard to forget. I couldn't move. Couldn't scream. Just laid there like a broken doll while he did whatever he wanted.

And Fernando—just in the kitchen, laughing. Loud. Drunk. Like he couldn't even hear. Or maybe he did and just didn't care. His friend locked inside with a kid, and he acted like it didn't matter.

I tried to scream. I swear I did. But nothing came out. Just air. Panic. Like my throat didn't remember how to work anymore.

I woke up shaking. Sweat everywhere. Heart going crazy. But I still felt them. I still feel them. Even now, just writing this, I feel their hands. I hear their voices. My skin crawls.

I hate it. I hate them. And I hate that I can't tell anyone. I want to. I do. But who would even believe me? She'd just say I was being dramatic. Or lying. Or trying to make trouble.

Nobody's ever listened. So why would they now?

No one's ever helped. No one ever will.

Gotta go!

The words blur. My chest tightens. A sharp breath scrapes my throat.

I pause; my finger pressed to the page like I'm trying to steady myself. I flip further back—hoping for something softer. But there it is. Another bruise I carried in secret.

Hey Sofia,
Soledad says no more lipstick till college. She came home early and found me at the door with red on my mouth. I felt pretty for five minutes—that's all I get.

"AMAYA! What's on your face?" she yelled, voice too loud for our walls. Her eyes went wild. Before I could lie, she grabbed my arms so tight her nails left little half-moons. She shook me so hard my head snapped back.

She dragged me to the bathroom, shoved my face to the mirror like she wanted me to see what she sees—dirt. Shame. Something to be hidden. "Take it off. Now. You want the neighbors to say you're fast? You want them whispering you're just like—"

She didn't finish. She didn't have to. I knew what she meant. I always knew.

She always calls me *hija de la gran puta* when she's like this. Daughter of a whore. Funny how she spits it like poison but forgets she's talking about herself first.

She shook me again—so hard my teeth clicked. I just stared at the tile behind her head. I felt one tear slip out and panicked—she hates tears. I blinked it back fast before she could see.

Later, while I was washing her dirty dishes, she started up again. Called me cheap. Stupid. Said everyone's watching—waiting for me to open my legs, to prove them right. Said I'd ruin what's left of her name.

And today? She smiled like none of it happened. Held out a pale pink tube like a gift. The kind that smells like plastic and chemicals, cap cracked from too many purses. She said I could wear it *only* when I help out at the salon for free—so she looks like the good mother.

"See? I'm not so bad. I'm trying to protect you. So you don't end up with a criminal." She smiled so wide I almost fell for it—for half a second. Then I remembered how fast that smile can turn to teeth. So I nodded. Said "gracias." Pretended to be grateful. What choice did I have?

It's not about lipstick. It's about her making sure my voice never feels pretty enough to keep.

'Til next time,
xoxo, Amaya

I close the journal, thumb pressed tight to the cover like it might keep her in. That version of me—she didn't have a voice. But I do now. Still, the past hums under my skin, waiting for any crack to pour back through.

Chapter Six

I wake up feeling… human again.

Still a little hazy from the antibiotics, but the fever's gone, the aches have chilled out, and my brain isn't trying to claw its way out of my skull. Which means one thing—no more excuses. I can't sit still anymore. The studio is calling.

By the time I unlock the door, the air inside greets me with its usual welcome—stale dust, stubborn grit, and the soft hum of forgotten dreams. It used to be a tailor shop, back in the day. You can feel it in the bones of the place, the lingering chalk lines still clinging to the walls, in the pride stitched into every seam that once came to life here.

Now? It's mine. Still rough. But mine.

The faded sign above the door barely hangs on—too stubborn to fall, too tired to stand proud. Inside, it's a time capsule. A vintage Singer sits like a relic in the corner, a cracked mirror slouches against the wall like it's too ashamed to reflect anything at all, and bolts of fabric rest untouched, so brittle they might crumble if I breathe on them.

The floors creak. The air tastes like old stories. The back windows are veiled in grime and cobwebs thick as spun sugar. The walls are still a mess, but the new shelving is up, and I finally cleared a path to the back room. Small wins. The kind that stack up if you let them.

It's a battle. I wipe something clean, the plumbers or electricians stir up a fresh layer of chaos. I scrub, they drill; I sweep, someone tracks in more grit. Some days I walk in ready to conquer the world and leave wondering what I actually did. Some days it's too much. Still—

underneath it all, there's something real. Potential. Beauty waiting to be uncovered.

I grab the ladder Mr. Nouel loaned me—my noble, rickety steed—and get to work.

Halfway up, I'm dusting the ceiling vents and trying not to inhale the past—one wrong move and I'm probably breathing in 1979—when my phone buzzes in my back pocket. I shift my weight, balance on one foot, and answer.

"Surviving the chaos?" Basha bursts through the speaker—bright, teasing.

"Barely. But I'm back from the dead," I say, swiping sweat from my forehead. "Shoutout to Maggie the bartender-slash-nurse. And you, for that soup. I owe you my life."

"Anytime, Freebird. Want me to send Oscar to help out, or is this your audition for *Extreme Makeover—Studio Edition?*"

"I'm good. Got a lot done, actually. Mr. Nouel stopped by earlier to help, bless his soul. Now I think I need a shoulder replacement. Know a good orthopedic surgeon?"

"Well, you're not getting mine. These shoulders carry the weight of beauty—and bills."

We crack up. A few more jabs, then we hang up. I'm alone again with the ladder, the shadows, and my thoughts. I climb a few steps higher, swat at a spider web that refuses to die, and—like clockwork—my mind drifts to Ryan.

It would be nice to have someone for the heavy lifting. His arms. His hands. His—nope. Cut it out, Amaya. Focus. You've got YouTube tutorials, a borrowed ladder, and the stubbornness of someone who's survived worse. You don't need a man.

I'm mid-swipe when the front door creaks.

I freeze.

"Hello?" I call, leaning a little too far—absolutely not my brightest move.

The ladder shifts. My heart launches into my throat. A flash of what-if opens under my feet—empty studio, open door, me off balance and alone.

"Whoa!" A voice snaps from below—familiar, sharp.

Max.

What the hell.

He rushes in and grabs the bottom of the ladder, locking it down with those damn hands. I grip the rails tight, heart pounding like a nail gun.

"You trying to die today?" he says, looking up at me.

I blink down, thrown, breathless, and low-key annoyed that I'm not… annoyed to see him.

"Max? What are you—how did you even—"

He shrugs, still steadying the ladder. "Door was open."

I climb down, slower this time, pretending I'm not rattled. Not just from the ladder. From him. From the clean spice of black pepper and something reckless that clings to his skin.

"Didn't realize I was accepting visitors today," I say, brushing grit off my jeans.

"Didn't realize you were going for death-by-ladder," he says, that smirk curling like it has a mind of its own.

"I'm fine."

"You sure?" He reaches out and brushes something off my cheek—dust, probably. His thumb lingers a beat too long, like the dust wasn't the point.

I step back.

"Thanks," I say, eyes sliding away from his mouth. "Now I'm officially dust-free."

He lifts a shoulder. "Not quite. You've still got a little—" he waves at the air around me "—chaos everywhere."

I try to hold it in, but I laugh. Can't help it. And just like that, he rolls up his sleeves and starts helping—like it's the most normal thing in the world. I tell him what I'm trying to do on a tight budget, half-expecting him to toss out dumb solutions or take over. He doesn't. He listens. Really listens. Nods. Offers ideas like we're building something together. We move through the space, digging through what's left behind. Dust, dreams, and all.

"Vintage Singer sewing machine?" he asks, lifting it like it weighs nothing.

"Yep. This place came with its own memories," I say. "Was going to sell it, but I'm keeping it—for now. It's practically a museum piece."

We fall into an easy rhythm—cleaning, sorting, imagining. Then my stomach growls so loud it might've rattled the walls. He stops. Looks at me.

"Wok & Roll's next door. What do you want?"

"I'm good," I lie, stomach fully protesting.

He arches an eyebrow. "You're not. Be right back."

I open my mouth to argue, but he's already gone.

Fifteen minutes later he's back with a takeout bag in one hand and zero shame in the other. The smell hits like a hug from the inside out.

"Fried rice, dumplings, kung pao chicken, and spicy noodles," he says, holding it out like a bribe he knows I'll take.

"You didn't have to."

"Clearly, I did."

We sit cross-legged on the dusty floor, boxes and half-done dreams around us, cartons spread like a picnic in a ruin. The fried dumplings crackle at the bite. The chicken hits with heat that reminds me I'm alive. The noodles are comfort with a kick—a warm slap I didn't know I needed. I try to be cute with the chopsticks. Mistake. One slick noodle escapes, slapping the inside of the container like—nice try, rookie.

Max watches, amused. "Is that your signature technique, or—"

"This is advanced," I deadpan. "You just don't get it."

He leans back on his palms, that crooked grin doing things it shouldn't. He watches me the way he did at Hudson River Tavern— like I'm a puzzle he wants to keep unsolved a little longer. I don't trust myself with that look. Not sitting this close. Not with heat creeping up my neck. So I grab the safest distraction I can find.

"How's Milania?"

"Good. She's on her way home now," he says, popping a dumpling. "I just came from the airport."

"Wait—you came straight here?"

He nods like it's nothing. "Was thinking about the studio. And you."

The way he says you is casual—easy—but it lands warm and heavy in the center of my chest.

I don't answer right away. I'm too busy noticing the way his thigh brushes mine. How our fingers bump—again and again—reaching for the same bite. The silence stretches. Not awkward, just thick with something electric. I feel something unfolding—unspoken, slow, impossible to ignore. Like static right before lightning.

And the wildest part—I don't hate it. Not even a little. Which might be the most dangerous thing of all.

$$* \quad * \quad *$$

"I'll take you home, if you want," he offers, voice low and warm.

I shake my head, wiping my hands on a rag that's already clean.

"I live around the corner," I say. "By the time you hit the traffic light, I'll already be in bed. Plus, I'm still kind of gross."

I try not to read into it, but when his eyes drop to my collarbone—then flick back up—heat sparks low in my chest, quiet but insistent. The last thing I need is a distraction. Especially not from him.

He laughs—slow, easy, that chest-deep rumble that curls through me like smoke I can't clear.

It makes me want to punch something. Or kiss him. Or maybe both.

At the door, he lingers. Doesn't move. Doesn't speak.

He watches me like he's still deciding something. Like I'm a question he's not sure he's allowed to answer. The pressure coils tighter in my ribs—nothing, everything, all at once.

There's a pause—just long enough for my pulse to catch up to my thoughts.

His eyes dip to my mouth. Barely. But I feel it. Like a whisper across my lips.

I catch the faint trace of his cologne again—warm, peppery, dark—still clinging to the air between us. My fingers tighten around the doorknob like it's the only thing holding me together.

He doesn't lean in. But his body tilts, just slightly—like instinct pulling him forward and reason fighting to catch up. We are one breath apart. And the space between us holds perfectly still. Waiting.

And for a second? I almost let it happen.

But I blink, clear my throat, and step back—just enough to breathe. Just enough to remind myself how far I've come.

He doesn't push.

He tilts his head, a slow smile teasing his mouth. "If you ever need anything…" he says, letting the word *anything* hang there, thick with maybe.

I smirk. Because humor is safer than honesty.

"Anything?" I ask, tilting my head. "Even if I need someone to scrub toilets?"

A lazy grin spreads. "Especially then," he says, voice low and warm—but under it, something heavier thrums, unsaid.

He lets the moment linger. Then turns and walks out—with maddening calm—leaving the door ajar behind him. The air hums, warm and restless, like a touch that almost happened.

I close the door softly, press my back to it, and exhale.

Amaya, what are you doing?

Ugh. I hate how my body forgets everything I've survived the moment he looks at me like that. That grin should come with a hazard sign. And his voice? All warmth and danger—like striking a match and daring it not to burn.

It's not fair—how one word from him can melt my spine and strip away my good sense.

I push off the door, pacing once before stopping in front of the mirror.

"You're not doing this," I whisper to my reflection. Not again.

I turn off the lights, lock up, and walk away—one stubborn step at a time.

✳ ✳ ✳

I take a long, hot shower—letting the steam strip away the day and some of the heat still clinging to my skin.

I brew my coffee extra strong. No milk tonight. Most people would say *"Are you crazy? Coffee at this hour?"* But Dominicans are born with *café* in their veins. I want the flavor raw and sharp—bitter, earthy, curling through me like home.

Curled up on the couch, wrapped in an old hoodie and the kind of exhaustion that lives deeper than bone, I pull one of my Sofias from the shoebox and flip through pages scribbled by a girl who refused to stop dreaming.

Hey Sofia,

I know, I know—I've been MIA. Sorry. Well not that sorry, life's been nuts. Anyway, MAJOR lesson learned: never, and I mean never, say the word fashion around Soledad.

So the other day Ramona came over (love her). She asked what I wanna study in college and I was like, "fashion." She didn't even blink—just laughed and went, "Go for it." Ugh. I wish she was my mom. Ramona just GETS me. She's got real style, like every color of the rainbow—on purpose. Even her hair matches sometimes. And she's got this gold tooth that sparkles when she laughs. It's impossible not to smile around her.

She's fearless. Her voice is deep. Kinda surprising but it fits. And she smokes like it's nothing. I told her my health teacher said smoking takes years off your life and she just looked at me like, "men take more years off your life than these ever will, *princesa*. Never marry. Enjoy your freedom forever." I LOVE her.

You should've seen her face when I showed her my design. I was so proud. Like I couldn't stop smiling. It's this fitted dress, kinda simple on top (sleeveless, little sweetheart neckline, cute), but the bottom is where it gets magical. It hugs your hips and then flares out in these wavy layers that look like they're moving. Like leaves in the wind or something. And the back? Omg. Dips super low almost to the waist and laces up with ribbons.

I wanna wear it to prom. LOL. Like Soledad would EVER let me go. She'd be like, "You think you're a princess now?" And then remind me again how "dresses don't pay the bills." She'll probably make me mop floors that night just to be extra.

Ramona loved it though. Said it needed color. I was like "It's just a sketch!" but now I kinda wanna make it bold just for her. She even said she'd buy one of my dresses someday. As long as it's not boring or black. I can literally see her in it—each layer a different color. Loud. Proud. Totally her.

And then OF COURSE Soledad had to ruin everything. Storms in with a frying pan in one hand, cigarette in the other like she's about to fight somebody. Screaming, "What are you doing, wasting time when there's real work to be done?"

Her voice feels like a punch. Always. She looked me dead in the eye and I swear I thought she was gonna THROW that greasy pan at me. If she did, I'd be knocked out and smell like onions forever. Ugh, I hate onions.

She snatched my sketchbook and threw it on the floor. "This better be the last time I hear about fashion this, fashion that, fashion ANYTHING!" I nodded, pretending my hands weren't shaking. Picked up my sketchbook and looked at Ramona. She gave me this tiny smile like, I got you.

My heart was racing. That pan felt like a weapon. And yeah—she's hit me before. Whatever's nearby. *Chancletas, combs,* whatever her hand lands on. Nothing's safe.

Ramona—who's always cracking jokes—looked serious for once. I know she felt bad. But she also knows better than to fight with Soledad. Nobody wins that fight. Sometimes I don't even get why they're friends.

When Soledad stomped back to the kitchen, Ramona stood up quiet. Put a hand on my shoulder and whispered, "Don't let her take away your light."

And I swear—right then I promised myself. I can't give up. I won't. One day I'll be out of here. I'll live my life the way I want to. This isn't forever. I SWEAR it.

Before she left, Ramona looked back and said one last thing: "Sometimes the only way to survive is to hold on to what makes you feel alive."

'Til next time,

xoxo, Amaya

My thumb hovers over the words like I need proof they're real. But they are. They came from me. The girl who kept dreaming, even when it hurt. I close the journal. There's still dust in the corners. The walls still ache with old stories. But me? I'm not giving up. Not now. Not ever.

Chapter Seven

The air at Rockland Lake hits different this morning—cool, crisp, full of that earthy fall smell, like leaves and pine needles and fresh starts. Every breath stretches my lungs, scrubbing out the last of the antibiotics and studio dust. The trees are showing off—gold, crimson, fire. It feels like the whole world is in transition, shedding its skin just in time for something new. And maybe… me too.

By the time I finish my lap, my breath comes easy and my head's clearer than it's been in days. My body's still tired from all the scrubbing, lifting, and surviving Max's almost-kiss—but moving helps.

I've got a client shoot at The Harbors at Haverstraw this morning, and I'm so excited to turn her vision into something real.

The Harbors is all clean-lined townhomes and quiet waterfront elegance—the kind of place where the light hits just right from every angle and everything feels soft around the edges. Cobblestone walkways always get me. This community is a whole vibe.

Vivi Velasquez is already there when I pull up—standing by the water like she just floated out of a bridal editorial. Flowy dress. Wind-swept hair. That cool-girl energy that says she wins every argument—and considering she's a lawyer, she probably does.

We get right into it. She's easy—knows what she wants but lets me do my thing. I click away while she moves through poses, framing her against the Hudson like she belongs in Vogue.

Between shots, we talk about her engagement party, bridesmaids' dresses, and the kind of makeup look she wants. Timeless glam with a little edge. My favorite.

I make a mental note to text Basha later. She's the one who recommended me to Vivi—like she always does. We look out for each other, but lately, she's been the one opening doors while I've been buried in invoices and renovation dust. She always sees the big picture when I'm tangled in the small stuff.

While I'm packing up, my phone buzzes.

I stare at the screen longer than I should. I don't answer. Just slip the phone into my jacket and load the rest of my gear into the trunk.

But the question—jazz in the city with Max—lingers, low and steady, like a bass line I can't shake.

The whole drive home, I'm stuck in a loop. The studio. The almost-kiss. The way he said, *"I was thinking about the studio… and you."*

I've always been careful with my heart. Ryan taught me that.

He made the future sound so easy—until Nyack felt too small for his dreams. He wanted more. Bigger. Elsewhere. I wanted something solid. Something here. And just like that, we became a what-if.

But Max? He's different. Solid as a promise, grounded. But there's something electric under the surface—like if I'm not careful, I won't just fall. I'll crash.

✷ ✷ ✷

By the time I park in front of my building, I've replayed Max's text at least twelve times.

I send Basha a message:

I toss my phone on the couch and start flipping through my closet like I've already said yes. Silk. Black lace. Something red.

Why am I even doing this? I haven't responded. Yet.

My phone buzzes instantly.

Me: Because I'm playing it cool.

Basha: Girl. Playing it cool is one thing. Missing out on jazz with a man who smells like black pepper and sin? That's just poor judgment.

I laugh out loud. She kills me.

Basha: Also—he's not playing it cool. He's making moves. Don't overthink it.

Me: I might.

And I don't just mean overthinking. Another buzz. This time, not Basha.

Max: Let me know if you're up for a little adventure. You won't regret it.

I stare at the words. *You won't regret it.* Regret? I know regret. I've lived it. But this…this feels different. Like maybe saying yes could lead somewhere I don't already know the ending to.

✳ ✳ ✳

Back at my apartment, the quiet hits different. No noise. No edits. No filters. Just stillness. I hang my jacket, kick off my boots, and sink onto the edge of the couch. No mood for TV. No mood for cooking. No mood for background noise.

Across the room, the Sofia shoebox waits—right where I left it. I don't plan it. I just get up, cross the room, and open it. Maybe I'm looking for a reminder. Or maybe I just miss the girl who kept believing when the world gave her every reason not to.

I flip through until I find the one with *Mrs. Brown's* name scribbled in the corner. I wonder if she's still teaching—or if she finally packed her bags and disappeared into one of those glossy pages she used to lend me. Paris, maybe. Or Oxford. Somewhere that smells like old books and new beginnings. A place where someone like her could finally breathe.

If Soledad knew half of what I'm dreaming about, she'd probably throw more than just her frying pan at me. Whatever. I don't care. I'm not staying stuck in this dump forever. I'm gonna get out. I will get out. I'm gonna live a happy life and do things Soledad wouldn't even believe are possible. She'll still be yelling about cigarettes, her man, or money—and I'll be at FIT studying fashion, then traveling so far she can't find me.

She keeps saying my fashion dreams are trash. Like I better start thinking about being a doctor or an engineer or a lawyer. Please. I swear—she'd lose her mind if she knew how deep I am in this. How clothes are everything. How you can put on a jacket or a skirt and feel like a whole different person.

Most of what I wear is hand-me-downs anyway—cousins, neighbors, random bags from Soledad's "connections" at the Salvation Army or whatever agency feels sorry for girls like me. Daughters of immigrants with nothing lined up but cleaning or cooking. But those "trapos"? They made me creative.

Sometimes when girls at school ask where I got something, all excited, expecting me to say Pink Tree or American Eagle, I just smile and say, "Oh, it's from a cute little shop upstate." Like they'd ever guess it's from dead people's closets. So what.

Tía Julia gave me this old church dress from, like, 1975. I cinched it with that red leather belt from Tía Lola and boom— retro chic. Why does every Latina girl have an aunt named Lola? It's a rule, I swear. And her name's really Dolores, but if you call her that she'll clutch her chest and act like you just said the worst cuss word in church.

One day I'll travel. For real. Walk through Paris—no clue what anybody's saying but I'll still feel at home. Or maybe Tokyo. I thought I'd try sushi until I realized it rhymes with Poochie, that cross-eyed dog our neighbor owns. Ugh. Never mind. Scratch Tokyo. Or maybe not.

And I wanna write too. A whole author. Me—Amaya. Books with happy endings only. Fake ones, obviously. Mrs. Brown says it's not fake—it's fiction. Same thing if you ask me. If I ever wrote about my real life? They'd shelve that thing under horror. Or trauma. Or Do Not Read Before Bed.

Oh—and a boxer. Yup. You heard me right. So I can knock out creeps and keep Soledad from swinging on me ever again. One minute it's Paris Fashion Week, next minute it's Fight Night in the Bronx. I'm a mess. Whatever. Fashion designer—slash–author–slash–badass. That's the goal.

Anyway. Right now I'm stuck between school, the food market that smells like dead pigeons, our busted Section 8 apartment building with graffiti from people who can't spell, and the bodega where I gotta pick up Soledad's disgusting cigarettes because she's "too tired" from her salon job.

Every time I walk in, Pica-Pica—the bodega guy missing half a tooth—slides me a brown bag and says, "Don't open it, Amaya." Like that ever works. One time I peeked and found some paper with random numbers. Secret code? Illegal Dominican lotto? Dunno. Not my business. Well, kind of. But not really.

Mrs. Brown though? She gets me.

Soledad just sees herself. Miserable and stuck. But Mrs. Brown? She sees something else when she looks at me. Like I might actually make it out. She lets me borrow fashion magazines, travel books, fancy stuff nobody around here even talks about. She's the only adult who doesn't look at me like poor Amaya. She looks at me like, Amaya, you got this.

She said once, "You're a storyteller. You've got that spark in your writing." I think about that when I'm doodling dresses all over my English notes instead of paying attention. I know Shakespeare's important but so is this.

But I'm not just dreaming anymore. I'm planning.

One day those brown bags won't be stuffed with Soledad's cigarettes and whatever shady numbers Pica-Pica slips in. They'll be filled with fabric swatches, sketchbooks, drafts of books nobody's seen yet. And if I ever see Mrs. Brown again, I'll give her one—my kind of brown bag—with something good inside. A signed copy of my book, or my name on a runway ticket. Just so she knows she was right about me.

Okay, enough. I sound like I'm giving an Oscar speech and I'm sixteen. Watch me write a whole book before I even graduate.
'Til next time,
xoxo, Amaya

Chapter Eight

I'm gripping the broom so tight it might snap in two. My chest's tight, head crackling with static. The studio looks like a renovation graveyard—half-painted walls, exposed wires, dust layering everything like a second skin. Not just a mess—chaos. No matter how hard I work, the finish line keeps moving.

I spin in place, eyes bouncing from one half-done project to another. Every direction screams unfinished—not just the mess, but the meaning behind it. The money I've poured in. The heart. The risk.

What if this doesn't work? What if I run out of money before the paint dries? What if this dream is too big—and I'm not enough?

What if that article wasn't a celebration, but a countdown? What if the whole town's watching, waiting for me to fall flat on my face? I was so proud. So sure. And now… it feels like I invited everyone to the show before I even finished building the stage.

Tears blindside me. I swipe them away with my hoodie sleeve, but the pressure in my chest doesn't move. If Soledad were here, she'd find something cold to say. She always did. And the bills? They're stacking fast. Utilities, supplies, permits—every line item a ticking clock.

Can I even afford to keep this dream alive?

The door creaks open. I jerk upright, wiping my face, pretending I'm fine.

And there they are.

Mr. Nouel, holding a steaming cup like it's medicine he brewed himself. Esperanza, carrying a paper bag that smells like a little slice of heaven.

"Amaya, my girl," she says, walking straight toward me. Her smile fades when she sees my face. "*Ay, mija…* you okay?"

I nod too fast, forcing a smile that feels thin, brittle. "I'm fine. Just… tired."

"Tired?" she echoes, setting the bag on a dusty table. She takes the broom from my hands, props it against the wall. Then she pulls me into one of her hugs—the kind that makes everything feel okay, if only for a heartbeat.

"You're doing too much, Amaya—when was the last time you actually took a break?"

I open my mouth, but nothing comes out. Sure, I've been running in the mornings, trying to stay sane. Other than that night at Hudson River Tavern—and the annual Day of Glorious Relaxation—I've been grinding nonstop, splitting every hour between the studio and clients. I knew opening this place was a long shot, especially on a shoestring budget. No shiny remodel. No backup plan. And emotionally? I'm held together with tape.

Mr. Nouel steps closer, his tone soft but steady. "Listen to her. Esperanza always knows what's what."

Esperanza brushes a tear from my cheek, her hands as steady as her voice.

"Let it out, *mija*. You don't have to hold it all in."

"I'm fine," I whisper—but we both know I'm not.

She gently brushes my cheek. "*Dios está en ella; ella no caerá.* You're stronger than you think. And you're not alone. Marcel and I—we love you like you're ours."

Mr. Nouel nods. "You *are* ours. You're part of this family."

My throat tightens. I want to say thank you, but the words catch in my chest. I nod instead, tears rising again—softer this time. Grateful.

Esperanza claps her hands once. "Okay. Enough sadness. Marcel, grab that mop. Amaya, sit down and drink this coffee. No arguments. I'll get the *ti-ri-güi-llo*."

She raises her brows, daring me not to smile.

I laugh, the sound cracking through the weight in my chest. "Not the *tirigüillo*!"

She smirks. "Bet you haven't heard that word in a minute."

She's right. Just hearing it wraps around me like a hug from home. Suddenly I'm back in Moca, watching our neighbor Carmelita charge down the street with a *tirigüillo* in hand, chasing the kids who stole mangoes from her tree. That broom was legend. Back then, Dominican women used it for everything—sweeping, scolding, solving life's problems one swat at a time. Equal parts discipline and comedy. And always effective.

Before I can say another word, Esperanza is already unwrapping a croissant for me while Mr. Nouel rolls up his sleeves like he's auditioning for *Cleaner of the Year.*

"If Ryan were here," he says, giving me a wink, "he could use those big muscles of his to help. But you're stuck with an old man like me."

My smile slips. Ryan.

Hearing his name stings a little. Who am I kidding? A lot. He left chasing a dream that didn't include me. And what's worse? It still hurts. After all this time, part of me still burns at the mention of him. I shove half the croissant into my mouth before the emotion can settle in.

Esperanza must catch the shift, because she gracefully changes the subject.

"You know," she says, sweeping beside me, "when I first started at Maison Madeleine, it was falling apart. Madeleine had passed, and Marcel was doing everything he could to keep it afloat. On the outside and most of the inside it looked charming—but behind the scenes? Total mess. Broken ovens, crooked floors, barely enough money for paint."

Mr. Nouel laughs from the other side of the room. "Truth. I was ready to quit. But then Esperanza walked in—and somehow, everything changed."

"She brought the bakery back to life," I say, softer this time.

Esperanza smiles, resting a hand on my shoulder. "Because we didn't quit. Even when it felt impossible. Just like you won't. This studio?" She looks around. "It's already becoming something beautiful. One step at a time, *mi amor.*"

We work side by side for the next couple of hours. The space starts to shift—not just in how it looks, but how it feels. Lighter. Warmer. Esperanza hums "Bésame Mucho" while she sweeps, her voice soft and haunting, carrying all the heartbreak and hope a song like that holds. Mr. Nouel cracks jokes while he mops, pausing every few minutes to dramatically inspect his "hard labor."

By the time they leave, the chaos doesn't feel so heavy. And my heart? It doesn't either. Almost like Esperanza really did chase it all away with that invisible *tirigüillo.*

✷ ✷ ✷

I can't sleep.

It's that weird mix of exhaustion and adrenaline and… something else. Something warm and restless that won't stop spinning in my chest. The silence gets too loud, so I reach for the one thing that always listens.

The Nouels' story is still playing in my head. I've heard pieces before—but today, they gave me the full version, and it felt like getting dropped into the middle of my favorite romance novel.

I open my journal, needing to pour out what the Nouels left behind in my heart.

One breezy afternoon, a younger Esperanza (and don't even try asking her age—classified information) strolled through downtown Nyack in her signature red heels, hips swaying to a silent merengue beat. She was new in town, exploring the neighborhood, looking for work.

Then she smelled it.

Fresh coffee. Something sweet—almost exactly like the coconetes from back home. The scent stopped her in her tracks.

She looked up.

A little Parisian-style bakery stood in front of her, draped in cascading ivy and vibrant flowers, like something off a postcard. Above the door, a wooden sign read Maison Madeleine in elegant gold lettering. And in the window, a handwritten sign—

HELP WANTED / NECESITO AYUDA

That was all the invitation she needed. But first—lipstick.

She reached into her bag, touched up her lips, then caught it—her blouse button was undone. "Ay, Dios mío," she hissed to herself, fastening it quickly before her job hunt turned into a scandal.

She wasn't afraid of work—never had been. She'd scrubbed factory floors until they gleamed, baked desserts that made grown men cry, babysat half the neighborhood (until one kid named Daniel ate an entire cake meant for a special family dinner), and even tried pet-sitting—until a German Shepherd tried to turn her backside into a chew toy.

Now here she was, standing in front of a dreamy little bakery, ready to try again.

Outside, a man was sweeping the front steps like he was trying to erase more than dust. Hair wild, expression focused, completely unaware of her.

Esperanza took a deep breath, smoothed her skirt, and walked over.

"Hola, hello!" she called, voice bright, warm, full of Caribbean sunshine. "*Mi nombre es Esperanza Nouel. Mucho gusto.*"

The man paused, broom in hand, and looked up—curious eyes, a shy smile tugging at his mouth.

"Nice to mee choo," she added, just in case Spanish wasn't going to cut it.

He cleared his throat and replied with dramatic flair. "*Bonjour, Mademoiselle,*" he said in a buttery French accent. "Marcel Nouel."

She blinked. Wait—what?

"*Bon-yurr, bon-día,*" she laughed, tilting her head, both amused and confused. "Excuse me, mister, you Nouel?"

He chuckled. "*Oui,* mademoiselle. My last name is Nouel."

Her hand flew to her chest. "*No me digas*" she said a little too enthusiastically. "Me, Nouel... you, Nouel... we Nouel!", she added.

Mr. Nouel let out a warm, playful laugh, clearly charmed. "Ah, *Señorita* Nouel, I need *mucho* help—*pronto!*" He motioned toward the café, his broken Spanish drawing a playful raise of her brow.

"Pronto, huh?" she teased, her lips curving into a smile.

"Yes, yes! I need someone who is... how you say... organized. Good with the, uh... oven, croissants."

She narrowed her eyes, still smiling. "Yes, I bake. *Pan de agua.* Close enough."

Mr. Nouel's face lit up like a Christmas tree. "Fantastique!"

"But I don't know French stuff, Mister Nouel," Esperanza added quickly, not wanting to oversell herself.

"No *problema!*" he replied, waving it off. "You teach me Spanish, I teach you croissants. Deal?"

She paused, then leaned in, mock-serious. "Deal. But you must pay me on time, every week. I have to go to the salon to maintain this fabulous hair. I can't have people in Nyack thinking I bake in a tornado."

Mr. Nouel laughed, hand to his chest, clearly both entertained and captivated.

She smiled. "Okay, okay. Muy bien. I can check it out now?"

"Of course, mademoiselle," he said, motioning her inside. "After you, *Señorita* Nouel."

Esperanza stepped into the bakery, and the warmth rose around her, as if the walls themselves had been waiting for her to arrive. Soft lighting glowed over rustic wooden tables, and the air was thick with the scent of fresh bread, butter, and something comforting. Something that felt like home.

Mr. Nouel followed close behind, eyes lingering just a moment longer than they should've. There was something about her—her confidence, her light—that stirred something in him he hadn't felt since Madeleine, his late wife, last filled this space with laughter.

Esperanza turned to him, hands on her hips. "Tu-moro morr-ning?"

"Tomorrow, yes! Of course," he said quickly, clearly not concerned with résumés or references.

"Betty good," she nodded, already making herself at home.

The next morning, they dove headfirst into a whirlwind of flour, butter, and sugar. The kitchen was a beautiful disaster. Esperanza's laughter echoed through the space, and Mr. Nouel couldn't stop smiling.

"Mister Nouel, what's the secret to making these croissants so flaky?" she asked, rolling dough with the ease of an artist.

He raised a finger with mock-seriousness. "Ah, *Señorita* Nouel, it's all about the love you put in. And *mucho butter*."

The rest, as they say, is history.

Esperanza walked into Maison Madeleine that day looking for a job, but she found more than a paycheck—a second chance she never saw coming.

And Mr. Nouel? He didn't just hire a helper. He found his second chance.

Mr. and Mrs. Nouel inspire me in ways I can't explain. You don't hear stories like this every day—a love story wrapped in French pastries, Caribbean soul, and the same last name.

Maison Madeleine isn't just a bakery. It's a little sanctuary. A place where laughter floats through the smell of coffee, sugar, butter, and every customer gets a slice of the joy they built from scratch.

Watching them—Mr. Nouel fumbling through new Spanish while Esperanza rolls her eyes with a smile—is like seeing love in its purest form—messy, warm, and worth every bite.

By the time I finish, I'm smiling—the kind of smile that sneaks up on you and stays. Their story isn't perfect. It's messy. It's funny. It's dusted in flour and loud with laughter. And it's real. And if they could build a second chance from scratch… maybe I can build my first.

I close my journal and whisper into the quiet. "Dios está en ella; ella no caerá."

God is within her; she will not fall.

Chapter Nine

I'm standing in front of the mirror, caught between timelessly classy and daringly sexy. Tonight needs both.

The black dress clings like it was made for me—simple, bold, just dangerous enough. By the door, patent stilettos wait to add height, attitude, a little drama. One swipe of retro red lipstick and my mouth becomes a warning label.

It's just a casual night out. That's what I keep telling myself. But my heart's been pacing since Max texted. Why do I feel like a teenager on her first real date? There's something about him—quiet confidence, secrets in his eyes, the kind of danger that keeps my pulse unsteady.

And then there's the music. He picked a jazz bar. I've never been to one, but I grew up on brass and percussion—sounds that build slow, then break wild. Saxophones always felt like they were confessing things you didn't know you were carrying. Maybe it's the Dominican in me—raised on boleros and bachata, where instruments don't just play. They talk. They unravel you note by note.

I slip into my coat and check the mirror one last time. The girl staring back has come a long way. She's strong. Beautiful. Unstoppable.

✳ ✳ ✳

Outside, a black car waits at the curb, streetlights sliding across its paint like liquid glass. Not a taxi. A black car. With a driver.

The door opens—and Max steps out like he owns the night. Tailored black jacket, crisp white shirt undone just enough, suede boots meeting the pavement with quiet certainty. His scent drifts in—

amber, spice, and something darker—whispering you'll remember me long after I'm gone.

His gaze moves over me—unhurried, deliberate. It lingers at my mouth before rising to meet my eyes, quiet but charged, like a flame held just beneath the surface.

"You look…" His words trail, then shape into a smile. "Unforgettable."

Warmth climbs my skin, but I don't break the stare. "I could say the same about you." The words slip out softer than I meant, almost girlish, but I hold my ground. *Perfect timing to sound fifteen, Amaya.*

He steps closer, the soft crunch of his boots the only sound. His hand brushes mine—barely there—before he gestures toward the waiting car.

"Shall we?"

I glance at the driver, then back at him. "You hired a car?"

A half-smile curves his mouth. "Wanted the night smooth. No distractions. Just you… and the music."

Just you. The words settle in my chest and something inside me falters—breath, heartbeat, all of it tumbling out of rhythm.

"You're setting the bar high."

"Let's call it… intentional."

The door closes with a hush. Inside, the city lights smear across the tinted glass, blurring into streaks of gold and shadow. Max sits composed, like a man in control of more than just the evening. His scent curls into the silence between us, tempting me to rest my head against his chest. This isn't just a ride to a jazz bar. It feels like crossing a threshold into something thrilling. A little dangerous. Completely new.

"You're gonna have a good time tonight," he says, voice low and smooth. "I promise."

It isn't the words. It's the way he says them—like the ending is already written. As if music is only the beginning.

A smile slips across my lips. "I'm looking forward to it."

I try to play it cool, but inside, my body is restless, alive. He shifts slightly, like he's about to say more. But he doesn't. He just watches the road, letting the silence settle.

And then—

The hum of tires folds me into somewhere else. The George Washington Bridge. Fernando shouting. Soledad crying. My fists strangling the seatbelt, as if grip alone could save us. The car veering too close to the edge. The black water rising up to meet us. Panic splitting me open from the inside.

Memories don't ask permission. They break in, heavy-handed, louder than now.

"Amaya?" Max's voice cuts through.

The present rushes back. My hands are trembling. He's watching me, eyes softened.

"Hey." His warm hand closes over mine. "You okay?"

I nod too fast. "Yeah. Just… memories."

His thumb moves slowly over my knuckles, steady, reassuring. "You're safe," he says. "With me."

I breathe in—and let myself believe him.

✷ ✷ ✷

Velvet Noir is exactly what he said it would be—and more.

Tucked beneath a historic brownstone in the Village, its unmarked black door and discreet brass plaque give it that whispered-about vibe. The kind of place you don't find unless someone wants you to.

Inside, it glows. Candlelight. Jazz. Deep reds. Soft golds. Shadows shift across the room, slow and weightless—like they're dancing to a rhythm no one else can hear.

Velvet couches in jewel tones hug the walls. A polished black marble stage gleams under warm light. The air smells of aged wood, faint bourbon, and a trace of cigar smoke—warm, masculine, timeless.

A saxophone hums low in the background—slow, sultry, full of longing. Each note slides through the room like silk against bare skin, lingering as if it knows more than it's letting on. It isn't just music. It's foreplay.

It hits me deep, electric. A shiver wakes something I didn't realize I'd let asleep.

A hostess in a shimmering black dress greets us like she's been waiting all night. Max murmurs something low, and she leads us to a corner booth hidden in shadow. His hand brushes the small of my back. Not guiding. Just… there. We slide in. A server appears, but Max waves off the menu.

"A glass of your finest red for the lady," he says. "Macallan 25 for me."

He doesn't ask. He decides. And I hate how much I like it.

The drinks come quick. My wine is deep ruby—rich, full-bodied, like the night itself. His whiskey glows like firelight. Max leans back, arm draped behind me, settling into the moment like a man who has all night.

"You look like you've never been in a place like this before," he says.

"And you look like you own it."

He smirks. "Let's say I make myself at home."

I roll my eyes, but the smile betrays me.

Onstage, the trio starts again. The saxophone whispers low. The bass hums low, steady. The piano drifts—soft, deliberate, like a lover's hand tracing skin. Then the singer steps forward. Her voice pours out smooth and warm, like brandy in the dark.

Hold me close and whisper, let your heartbeat guide the way… In your arms, the night is endless, and the dawn feels far away.

It aches in the best way.

Max leans in, voice brushing my ear. "What do you think of the music?"

"It's beautiful," I say, sinking deeper. "It feels alive. Like it's telling a story."

"And what story's it telling you?"

I meet his eyes. Searching. Curious.

"Maybe one about a man who thinks he's got me all figured out."

His mouth curves. "Do I?"

"Not even close."

"Good," he says. "I like a challenge."

Then he stands.

"Dance with me."

My heart skips. "Here?"

He offers his hand. "Right here."

I take it.

He pulls me into the open space near the stage's shadow. There's no real dance floor, but it doesn't matter. Not with the way he's looking at me.

His hands rest at my waist. Mine at his shoulders. We move—slow and close. No steps. No plan. Just heat, rhythm, breath.

The music curls around us like silk. His cheek grazes mine. His lips brush close to my ear. He breathes me in.

"You smell like vanilla and cinnamon," he murmurs. "And something I haven't named yet."

His fingers drift down my back. My legs tingle, electric under his touch. My chest glows—alive from the inside out.

He leans in—lips brushing the curve of my neck. Just once. Soft enough to pretend it didn't happen. Strong enough to know it did.

We keep swaying. Wrapped in hush and heat. When the song ends, neither of us lets go.

We stand there a moment, holding onto the last note as if it could stop time itself. The singer's voice fades. Glasses clink. Conversations drift. None of it touches us.

Max shifts just enough to meet my eyes. His gaze dips to my mouth, then back—checking if it's okay to stay this close.

His mouth curves—more secret than smile. "You're dangerous, you know that?"

I lift an eyebrow, pulse humming. "Dangerous how?"

He leans in, breath warm against my cheek. "The kind that makes a man think twice about walking away at the end of the night."

A quiet laugh slips out. "And is that what you want? To walk away?"

His hand tightens just slightly at my waist. "Not when the night's just beginning."

My fingers brush the back of his collar, braver than I mean to be. "Good."

His hand drifts to the back of my neck, fingertips warm.

"Come on," he says, voice brushing my ear. "Let's sit before I forget how to be a gentleman."

He takes my hand, then pauses. "Hey. Back in the car… if you ever want to talk about that—"

I start to shake my head, but he squeezes my fingers.

"Just if you ever feel like it. No judgment."

Something warm flares in my chest. Not just want—trust.

He lets it go—just like that—and leads me back to the booth.

We slip back in, closer than before. The server returns, quiet as a whisper, refilling my glass and freshening his without a word.

Max lifts his drink, studying me over the rim.

"To nights that shouldn't end," he says.

I tap mine to his. "To the kind of nights that write their own songs."

We sip. The saxophone slips into another secret. His knee bumps mine beneath the table—stays there. And in that soft glow of candlelight, his eyes say it clearer than words—tonight isn't over. Not yet.

✻ ✻ ✻

We pull up in front of my apartment building. The night's cool, but my skin still carries the trace of his warmth.

Max steps out first, then circles around to open my door. He holds it, waits, like this is all part of the rhythm we've fallen into. When I stand, he doesn't back away. He steps closer instead, and everything I already know about him—the steadiness in his gaze, the calm he carries, the quiet gravity—it hits me at once. Familiar. And still enough to make my knees forget their job.

"Did you have a good time?" he asks, his voice lower now. Softer.

"Yes," I say. Barely more than breath.

He reaches for my hand, and when our fingers link, it's like my whole body pays attention.

Then he leans in and kisses me. Not fast. Not rough. Just deep and slow. Like we've been building to this all night and now it's finally allowed to happen. His lips are warm, patient. He doesn't rush—just eases in, lets the moment stretch. When his tongue brushes gently against mine, a spark shoots through me. Slow. Sure. Patient.

And I let him.

Before I can even catch my breath, he leans in again—this time kissing the corner of my mouth, softer, like a secret he wants to leave behind.

"Sweet dreams, Amaya," he whispers. Then he pulls back. Just a step.

His eyes hold mine for a second longer than they should—like he's trying to memorize something. Or maybe he already has. I don't move. I don't speak. I just watch him walk back to the car. The black door closes behind him, a final note fading into silence.

I let myself stand there a moment, heart pounding, louder than the quiet around me, lips still tingling. Every inch of me—wide awake. Then I head inside, close the door behind me, and lean against it. The quiet wraps around me, but I don't feel alone. Not with that kiss still fresh. Not with him still under my skin.

I love that he didn't ask to come up. That kind of respect is rare. But if I'm being honest? I hate it just the same.

Chapter Ten

My head is pounding like a rock concert at full volume. It's barely 5:00 a.m., and I'm clawing my way out of bed, dragging my pillow with me like it might silence the migraine drilling through my skull.

"Ughhh," I groan, shuffling to the kitchen like my bones are bricks. Café Bustelo, extra sweet cloves—my personal cure-all. Abuela always said sweet cloves chase out bad spirits and bad air—keep the body warm, the heart soft. I swallow two Advil with a glass of milk, and slather Vicks on my temples—because, duh, I'm Dominican. Then I crawl back under the covers, praying the Advil kicks in before the *greca* screams.

I shut my eyes, begging for blackout peace. But nope. My brain decides now's the perfect time to rerun Max like a late-night drama on loop.

It's been over a week since the jazz club, but that night won't leave me. The way he looked at me—like the rest of the room didn't exist. The way he ordered our drinks—zero hesitation, all confidence, no room for negotiation. That slow, dangerous smile. His hand on my lower back, warm and dragging heat up my spine… and that kiss.

But it wasn't just the kiss. It was the dance.

No spotlight. No crowd. Just the two of us. Moving like we'd done it a hundred times in another life. Every breath, every shift in weight felt like our bodies spoke a language we never had to learn. I felt seen. Desired. Anchored and undone, all at once.

He was heat wrapped in control—hands that gripped just enough to keep me there, cheek brushing mine, breath dragging slow along my neck. It woke something in me. I wanted to press my lips to the curve of his jaw. We weren't just dancing—we were the song. Moving to a rhythm only we could hear, like the music lived inside us and we were just answering its pull. And I didn't want it to stop.

It took every shred of self-control not to invite him upstairs. And now? Because my brain is a petty, chaotic traitor, it tosses me the worst kind of question. The kind that makes me cringe. Who kisses better—Max or Ryan?

Seriously?

The *greca* bubbles like it has opinions. I shoot upright—and immediately slam my shoulder into the doorframe.

"Shit. Get it together, Amaya."

I lunge for the stovetop and catch the coffee just before it floods. Eyes closed, I inhale—praying the caffeine hits my bloodstream through breath alone.

This week has been brutal—plumbing disasters, electrical drama, bills stacking up like bad news on repeat—and I've been running on fumes and maybe four and a half hours of sleep total.

But the day's finally here.

Opening day.

Through the chaos, I keep thinking about my family back on the island. Every dollar I send, every late night, every stubborn headache—this dream isn't just mine. I carry them with me. Failure's not an option.

Still, I've been lucky. Everyone's pitched in one way or another. Basha, with her chaotic motivational speeches—equal parts life coach, hype woman, and stand-up comic—and her scary-good organizational skills. Oscar, rolling in late to paint and blasting throwbacks like it was a team sport. Mr. Nouel and Esperanza, dropping by with enough spicy lattes to keep me wired for a week, plus bakery treats and stories that made me laugh, cry, and question reality—and half the time, they were scrubbing floors like it was their own place. Even Milo and Carmen dropped off *pastelitos*, still warm, before hurrying back to the bodega.

And Max.

Max has been… something else. He's there almost every night, doing the literal heavy lifting. He shows up with takeout like it's his mission to keep me upright—and honestly? It's working. A girl could get used to that—someone who stays. Someone who shows up.

He's thoughtful in a way that catches me off guard—especially for someone who walks like temptation and smells like every bad decision I swore I was done with.

But he's been consistent. And that might be the most dangerous thing. I hate how easily he's sliding into my life, how quickly I look forward to seeing him, hearing him, feeling him close. Thoughts I wasn't ready to have again.

I know his type. He doesn't chase—he gets chased. And still... a tiny, annoying voice keeps whispering—what if he's different? What if he could be more than just a beautiful distraction?

Nope. Stop it.

I lay out my grand opening outfit like it's a battle plan. My go-to SPANX Moto faux leather leggings—edgy but still polished enough to look like I have my life together. A soft off-white sweater I recently grabbed from a little boutique in Nyack—cozy but low-key fancy. And my FREEBIRD booties—broken-in, bold, totally me.

In the shower, I lean my forehead against the tile and let the water wash over me. Steam fills the room, but it can't clear the fog in my head. Max keeps showing up. Gentle. Helpful. Present. And it scares me. What's he really after? What am I to him?

I don't know. But this I do—I'm not losing myself again. Not ever again. Not for anyone.

Makeup goes on. Concealer hides most of my lack of sleep, but the exhaustion runs deeper than skin. I style my curls into something halfway decent and head to the studio early—an hour before the first guest might even think about showing up.

Sitting in my car, I whisper the words I need. *"No matter how today goes—whether one person comes or fifty—you did this. You deserve every bit of this light."*

And at this moment, I let myself believe it.

That's when I see him—Tom Riley. Leaning against the studio door like he's been there forever. Envelope in hand. That soft smile.

"Tom!" I breathe. "What are you doing here?"

He holds up the envelope. "Thought you'd want to see the article before the public does."

My heart skips. I wipe my palms on my leggings and carefully open it, already shaking.

I flip through the glossy pages, and there it is.

A REFLECTION OF RESILIENCE

Amaya Lee's Journey to Redefine Nyack's Creative Space
By Tom Riley

I suck in a breath.

The layout's beautiful—clean, bold, full of light. One of the photos he took outside—back when the inside still looked like a construction zone—sits at the top. I'm standing in front of the studio, the new Reflections sign gleaming above me, gold letters catching the sun just right.

But the words? The words nearly undo me.

"A few months ago, I met Amaya Lee in a dust-covered shell of a studio, still mid-renovation, still full of questions. Today, I walked into a space transformed—not just by paint or light or furniture—but by purpose. This studio, like its owner, is all heart."

Tears burn behind my eyes.

"Tom, this is… it's perfect."

He waves it off like it's no big deal. "It's all you, Amaya. I just wrote it down. Watching this journey—it's been an honor."

I laugh, throat tight. "I swear, if I ruin my makeup before the doors even open…"

"Oh no, no crying allowed today. You've already done the hard part. Today's just the celebration."

And then he drops it.

"This will be my last piece, Amaya. I've decided it's time to retire."

I freeze. "Wait—seriously?"

"Yup," he says, with that calm, nostalgic smile. "I'm starting a little writing workshop, traveling around the Hudson Valley. It's been a dream of mine for years—helping others learn to tell their stories."

Emotion squeezes my chest. "Tom… that's incredible. And I'm honored. Truly. That this was your final piece."

He gives me that look—the one that makes you feel completely seen. "This—your story—is what journalism should be. Hope, grit, transformation. I wanted my last piece to be something real. And this?" He gestures around. "This is as real as it gets."

And just like that, I'm crying again.

Tom's always felt like a gentle grandfather—kind, quietly wise. When he hugs me goodbye, I don't want to let go.

"Oh—one more thing," he says, handing me another envelope. "These are the photos from our first shoot. But today…" He smiles, raising his camera, clicking like he's collecting moments, not just images. "Today is the real transformation."

He captures the light, the corners, the colors—the pieces of me I poured into these walls.
It's not just a studio. Not just a dream. It's alive. It's mine.

✳ ✳ ✳

Note to self—showing up early? Best decision ever.

Because surprise photo shoots and tear-streaked cheeks do not mix. The second Tom leaves, I lock the door, bolt to the mirror, and fix my makeup like it's Fashion Week and I'm sixty seconds from the runway. Twenty minutes later, the front door bursts open like a confetti cannon.

"GIRL. THIS. PLACE. IS. A. VIBE!"

Basha storms in like she's headlining a parade, dragging balloons, a bouquet the size of my torso, and enough glitter to light up the zip code. She spins like she's the grand finale of her own confetti show. I laugh so hard I almost smear my mascara—again. I love her so much it hurts. Then she stops. Grabs my shoulders. And hits me with it—right in the soul.

"Amaya. Do you even see what you've done? You took your pain and made it into something beautiful. You turned chaos into art. You're living proof that broken doesn't mean finished. I hope you're as proud of yourself as I am of you."

And yep—tears again.

She squeezes my hand. "You fell seven times, baby. But you got up eight—and on the ninth, you crawled, mascara running, swearing in two languages. And look at you now. Keep shining, Freebird. The world needs more of you."

I swallow hard, voice barely holding. "I wouldn't have made it without you, Sunshine. My ride or die."

✶ ✶ ✶

Mr. Nouel and Esperanza walk through the doors, beaming like proud parents.

"Oh, I wish you endless blessings, my beautiful Amaya," Esperanza says, pulling me into a hug that smells like Caribbean spices and home.

"You've built something amazing here. *Magnifique*," Mr. Nouel adds, eyes shining like he already knew I could.

And just like that, the space comes alive.

By mid-morning, the energy is electric. My neighbor Ifetayo shows up with snacks and emergency lashes. "Amaya, you are glowing," she says, striking a red-carpet pose like she just walked off a fashion runway.

"You're a queen," I tell her, full heart, full smile.

Then the door swings open again—and to my surprise, it's Maggie. She's holding a bouquet so bold, so bursting with color, it looks like it walked in and made its own damn entrance.

"These? For the woman of the hour," she says with a wink. "Because basic blooms don't belong anywhere near a badass."

I freeze, genuinely caught off guard. We only met a couple weeks ago—first behind the bar at Hudson River Tavern, then again when I dragged my half-dead self into Nyack Urgent Care. Since then, she's become one of Basha's salon regulars. She's quick, loud, impossible to forget—and somehow, she remembered this. I didn't expect her to come. But she did. And that hits deeper than I thought it would.

We hug—quick, tight, real. "You did something really special here," she says, her voice softer than I've ever heard it.

I laugh, blinking fast. "You're ruining my mascara."

"Nope. You're ruining mine," she fires back, already dabbing her eyes with the back of her hand.

People keep coming—clients, neighbors, friends I haven't seen in years. The parents of the kids I used to babysit. Women asking about makeup sessions. Teens already dreaming about photoshoots. Strangers wander in, curious… and leave with something lit behind their eyes.

At one point, I catch a glimpse of a mother and daughter laughing near the styling station. Something sharp tugs in my chest. That should've been me and Soledad. But I let it go. Not today.

Today is about the light. About showing up, even when everything inside you wanted to disappear. About the late nights, the near-breakdowns, the scraped-up dreams that refused to die.

Today is for me. Today—I shine.

Chapter Eleven

By early evening, the crowd has thinned. The studio is a glittery, flower-and-balloon-filled disaster. My feet ache, my voice is shot, and my cheeks hurt from smiling so much.

I'd ordered a tray of *pastelitos*—just a little taste of home to mark the day. I figured it'd be more than enough. But Milo and Carmen rolled in with a second tray, plus a surprise batch of golden, crispy *quipes* that vanished in minutes. I hadn't tasted *quipes* in forever, and just the smell alone dragged me back to childhood holidays. I told Carmen to start prepping her *sazón*—because if this place really takes off, I'm putting in a big order for December.

"I'm hoping to partner with Kitchen Angels for a holiday event," I tell her. The nonprofit sits just a few blocks from her bodega—a team of volunteers feeding people all over town, no questions asked. "Still working out the details, but I want to give back before the year ends." They fed me when I had nothing. Now it's my turn.

The Nouels went full Parisian patisserie, showing up with a mountain of delicate French pastries—and later, Esperanza surprised me with *besitos de coco*. "You know I had to throw in a little Caribbean spice," she winked. Bite-sized, tender, sweet—gone before I could blink. Back home, every *colmado* or beach stall had trays of those little coconut kisses—simple, irresistible, a quick taste of island sunshine. Some village ladies made them right in their humble kitchens, selling them warm by the dozen to anyone craving a little sweetness on the walk home.

I lean against the front window, watching the sunset spill gold across the Hudson like someone tipped over a bottle of light. For a second, it's quiet. Still. And then, a tear slips down my cheek.

I think of Soledad. Her voice, sharp as ever—*Girls like you don't belong in places like Nyack.* I glance around these walls, the love poured into them today—and I think, *look at me now.*

Nyack didn't just accept me. It changed me. It rooted me.

The door chime rings, slicing through the hush. I turn, expecting another neighbor, maybe someone who forgot their phone—or a curious local peeking in to see what the buzz is about. But when I see who it is, my whole face lights up.

"Mr. Linwood!"

He steps in, holding a bouquet of fall-colored flowers, warmth written all over his face.

"Hope I'm not too late," he says.

I rush to hug him. "Never too late. But really—where am I going to put this gorgeous arrangement?"

We both laugh as I shuffle around to find a spot.

"I just wanted to stop by and show my support," he says. "You've come a long way, Amaya. I'm proud of you."

The words land like sunlight after weeks of rain. I blink fast, refusing to cry for what feels like the seventeenth time today.

"Thank you, Mr. Linwood," I whisper. "You were the first person to give me a real chance."

He smiles, and I catch the familiar light in his eyes—the same one from the day I told him I was leaving The Nyack Hideaway Bed & Breakfast. He was quiet then, a little sad, but he said something that's stayed with me ever since:

"I knew the moment you walked through my door you wouldn't stay long. Not because you weren't good—but because you were meant for more."

We talk for a bit, reminiscing about my time there. He was my first boss when I came here—a teenage girl with big dreams, an empty wallet, and no clue how to start over. He didn't know my full story, but he respected me anyway. I'll never forget that.

Just as he pulls back from hugging me goodbye, the door opens. Max steps inside—hoodie up, black joggers, carrying that quiet intensity that always seems to follow him in. And for a second, the air shifts—barely, but enough for me to feel it.

Something tightens under my ribs. Max isn't smiling. His eyes move from me to Mr. Linwood, to the bouquet he just gave me, then to the gold vase overflowing with red roses—the ones *he* had delivered earlier, impossible to ignore.

"Keep shining, Amaya," Mr. Linwood says, giving my arm a gentle squeeze. "You've come so far."

"Thank you," I say again, slower this time.

He nods at Max on his way out. "Hello there."

Max offers a faint smile. 'Good evening.' His voice smooth, polite—but the tightness at the edge of it gives him away.

The door closes behind Mr. Linwood. The room stills. Max lingers by the counter, jaw tight, eyes locked on the flowers like they're daring him. A low heat hums beneath my ribs. That old instinct, the one that used to tighten before Soledad snapped. But I won't go there. Not tonight. Not when everything else is humming with joy and magic.

I drift toward him, like something in me refuses to stay still. Like it wants the space gone.

"You okay?" I ask, voice soft.

He doesn't answer right away, but I see it—the tightness in his shoulders loosening. Then he looks at me, and the tension melts.

"I'm good," he says. His voice lowers. "You amaze me, Amaya. Everything you've been through, everything you've built... you're incredible. I need you to know that."

The knot in my chest unravels like the last chord of a song. I exhale and meet his eyes.

"Thank you, Maximiliano," I whisper, drawing it out—Maxi-mi-liano. Like saying his full name is a quiet kind of closeness—one I didn't expect, but maybe want more than I'd admit.

I see him feel it—his mouth shifts.

"I love the way you say my name—Maxi-mi-liano," he murmurs, echoing it back, that teasing softness brushing the air between us. "If I didn't know better, I'd think you were trying to seduce me."

I laugh, rolling my eyes even as my cheeks flush. "Don't flatter yourself."

He leans in, brushing his lips near my ear, his voice dropping. "Too late."

And then—he kisses me.

It's not careful. It's not polite. It's the kind of kiss that steals the air straight from my lungs, the kind that feels like a door swinging wide open. His mouth moves against mine with heat and certainty, like he's wanted this from the second he walked in and finally stopped holding back. My fingers fist into his hoodie, dragging him closer, while his hand presses firm at the small of my back, pulling me into the gravity of him.

The taste of him is fire and want, dizzying, like I could drink him in until the world blurred. His tongue finds mine, slow at first, then deeper, and I melt into it—into him—like he's the only thing holding me upright.

When he finally breaks away, his forehead rests against mine, both of us breathless, the air between us still buzzing like it refuses to let go.

"I'm so proud of you," he murmurs, voice low, rough around the edges.

And just like that, the noise of the day disappears. My aching feet, the glitter clinging to my skin, the exhaustion weighing down my bones—gone.

Right now, there's only this.

This room. This man. This moment.

And the wild, unstoppable truth of a dream that finally kissed me back.

Chapter Twelve

The glow of the grand opening still lingers—like the last note of a song hanging in the air. This whole week has felt unreal. Compliments, laughter, clients booking weeks out. More than I ever imagined. Every time I replay the smiles of my clients or hear the hum of approval in memory, it feels like a dream.

But the day after? That didn't feel real at all.

Ryan showed up.

I was sweeping glitter near the door when the chime broke the silence. I looked up—and there he was. Same soft brown eyes. Same easy smile. Just… older. Wiser. Time had added something to him. His presence didn't just stir something in me—it knocked something loose.

He carried a small bouquet—sunflowers, eucalyptus, and one random purple flower I couldn't name. It smelled like late summer. Like clean sheets and sunshine. He smelled the same too—cedar, citrus, and something warm. Like a song I hadn't heard in years but still knew every word to.

"You did it, Amaya," he said. Just that. And it nearly knocked the wind out of me.

We didn't talk long. Five minutes, maybe. But the way he looked at me—it felt like we were speaking through layers of history I hadn't touched in years. When he left, his presence lingered, like he'd quietly slipped a memory into the walls of the studio.

And then Max walked in. Right as Ryan was heading out.

Their shoulders almost brushed in the doorway. Their eyes met— brief, unreadable, like two men speaking a language I wasn't invited to. The moment was wordless but heavy. Max's eyes lingered on the bouquet in my hands before sliding back to Ryan, then me. He said nothing, but the silence was louder than any accusation.

Hours later, that moment still clings to me like smoke. Shadows stretch long across the room, but nothing feels gentle anymore.

I stand at the window, staring over Main Street. It's quiet enough to hear my own breath. Cool air seeps through the old panes—cold, not comforting. The town hums like it's holding its breath.

Barefoot, the hardwood cool beneath me, I step onto the balcony. The moon glides across the Hudson, turning it silver and alive. I should feel calm. Grateful. Triumphant. But something simmers beneath my skin.

I close my eyes, and Ryan's face surfaces—the way he looked at me, like I was someone worth coming back for. Then Max—his eyes after seeing Ryan. That look. The kind that says *you're mine* without ever asking if I wanted to be.

The front door creaks. *I hear footsteps. Heavy. Measured.* My stomach drops. I whip around, heart clawing up my throat. He's already inside—shadowed, still. Max. Had I given him a set of keys? I can't remember.

The room shrinks around him. His presence sucks the air from it—and from me. His stare doesn't blink. Doesn't soften.

I'm in a black silk camisole, barely-there fabric against bare skin. I feel exposed, too seen. His eyes don't move away. But something is wrong—he doesn't feel like him. Max always carried light. This version is darker. Closed. His jaw tight, his posture tense—like he's holding something dangerous just beneath the surface. His eyes are cold, unsettling.

He moves toward me. Not rushed. But every step lands like a fist against my chest.

"Amaya," he says. Low. Controlled. It doesn't feel like care. It feels like ownership.

Then I smell it—whiskey. Sharp. Heavy. It clings to him like a second skin. Not just alcohol—anger. Possession. It used to smell like intimacy, the kind of closeness you crave in the dark. Now it burns my throat like regret.

"You've been avoiding me," he says again, eyes locked on mine.

I swallow. My voice comes out small. "Max, what are you talking about? Please…" I don't even know what I'm asking for. Space? Time? For him to go back to the Max I know?

His hand shoots out, grabbing my arm. Too tight. His fingers dig in, making a point with pain. Panic rises fast, choking me.

"Max!" My voice is louder now. "What are you doing?"

He yanks me closer. "You think I'm blind? You think I don't see the way Ryan looks at you? The way you look back?"

The mention of Ryan is a gut punch.

"What? No—Ryan has nothing to do with—"

"Don't lie to me, Amaya." His grip shifts, clamping around my chin. He forces my face up, eyes burning into mine.

In a blink, my apartment dissolves. I'm back in Soledad's place. Low ceilings. Stained walls. The broken heater hissing like it's warning me. Her voice sharp in the next room. That same weight. That same frozen panic crawling up my spine.

I try to fight it, but my body betrays me, locking up.

"Stop," I say louder this time. My voice shakes. So does everything else.

He doesn't hear me. Or maybe he doesn't care. His other hand finds the back of my neck. His breath hot against my skin. His lips graze my cheek, slide to my jaw.

"You think you can just walk away from me?" he growls.

I freeze.

This isn't Max—it's every fear I thought I'd buried.

"I won't hurt you," he says, but his grip says otherwise.

Then his mouth is on mine—rough, claiming. Not a kiss. A theft.

"STOP!" I scream, muffled and wild.

I shove at his chest. Scratch at his arms. Fight like I'm drowning.

BANG. BANG. BANG.

The world crashes in. His hands—his voice—still echoing.

BANG. BANG. BANG.

I wake. Air rushes back. I gasp like I've broken the surface of deep water. I jolt upright, tangled in damp sheets. My body trembling. The room dark. Silent.

BANG. BANG. BANG.

I sit frozen, heart hammering. A dream. No—a nightmare. And for a moment, I don't know where it ended and reality began.

"Amaya? Amaya, are you okay?"

Ifetayo's voice slices through the dark, pulling me back.

I stumble to the door, fingers trembling on the lock. She's standing there, eyes wide, wrapped in a robe, backlit by the hallway light. "I heard you screaming."

"I…" My voice is broken. "It was just a dream."

She steps closer, hand gentle on my arm. "You sure?"

I nod, but it's a lie. My whole body is trembling beneath the surface, my chest tight. I look down, half expecting bruises on my wrist. There's nothing. Just skin. Just tension.

"Thank you," I whisper.

She hesitates, then nods. "I'm right next door if you need anything."

I close the door and lean against it, breath still shallow.

3:33 a.m. Of course it is.

I sit on the bed, arms around my knees, trying to remember how to breathe. It was just a dream. But the fear? The fear is real. Not just about Max. Or Ryan. Or even Soledad. It's the kind that lives in my bones. The kind I carry even when I'm safe. Even when the door is locked.

I stare at my hands—still now, but cold. I touch my wrist. No bruises. No marks. But I feel them anyway.

The tears slip out before I can stop them. Quiet. Relentless. I don't cry because of the dream, but because of how familiar it felt. Because no matter how far I've come, my mind still drags me back. Still convinces me I'm in danger. Still casts shadows over people who haven't earned them.

I'm tired. Soul-tired. Tired of the fear. Tired of the overthinking. Tired of bracing for impact when there's no crash coming. Even when love reaches for me, I shrink back, waiting for the hurt.

Something inside me cracks open, spilling grief I never made space for. My body folds in on itself. I bury my face in my hands and sob—deep, shuddering, uncontainable.

Because surviving takes strength. But healing—healing demands more. It asks for surrender, for trust, for battles I don't always have the heart to fight.

And tonight, I have nothing left. Only the weight of my bones, and the echo of my breath in the dark.

Chapter Thirteen

I walk down the narrow hallway, feet heavy, like I'm dragging pieces of last night behind me. Each step sinks me deeper into everything I've been avoiding. The air thickens, pressing against my chest. Even the faint buzz of the overhead lights drills into my skull.

My wrist still tingles from the dream, where Max grabbed me. Just a dream. But try telling that to my nervous system.

Why am I even doing this? I don't want to be here. But my legs keep moving, dragging me toward the one place where hiding won't work.

My breath stutters as I reach the door. I hover, hand shaking above the handle. Every instinct says run. I shouldn't have to dig this stuff up again. Shouldn't have to say it out loud. But it's there anyway—alive inside me. Growing.

I grip the handle and push it open.

The waiting room feels unreal. I sit, still thinking about leaving, like it's the smarter choice.

"Amaya Lee?"

I don't move. For a second, it's like the name belongs to someone else. Then it hits—my whole body stiffens, like my name just pressed on a bruise I've been hiding. I'm not ready. Probably never will be. I look up. Crystal Bianchi—my therapist. The one I'm supposed to tell everything to. She says my name like there's anyone else it could've been—like the waiting room is packed with people dying to unpack trauma before breakfast.

She looks… normal. No white coat. No clipboard. Her hair's in a bun, and she's wearing a soft navy blazer—something you'd see in a J.Crew window, not a therapist's office. But it's her eyes that hold me.

Warm. Calm. Like she's already decided not to treat me as broken, or as a project.

"That's me," I manage, my voice too quiet. My legs feel like overcooked spaghetti. But I walk in anyway.

The office smells like lavender and vanilla. A diffuser, maybe. Or a fancy overpriced candle. Everything's soft. Warm light spills through the windows onto neat, book-filled walls. And the couch? Massive. Swallow-me-whole massive. Honestly, I kind of want it to.

I sink into it. Or try to.

There's a little fountain in the corner, bubbling like it's trying to be soothing. All it does is make me feel like I need to pee. I shift in my seat, crossing and uncrossing my legs, pretending I'm not already calculating the fastest way out.

Crystal sits across from me, notepad in her lap, pen untouched.

"Thank you for coming," she says, her voice gentle, practiced. Like she's done this a thousand times.

"How are you feeling?"

How am I feeling? Like I might throw up any second. But I say, "Nervous."

My voice shakes. So do my hands.

She smiles—not too big, just enough to let me breathe. "That's okay. Most people are during their first session. It's normal to feel unsure, even overwhelmed. This is your space, Amaya. We'll take it at your pace."

Somehow, the tightness in my chest loosens. Just a little. "Okay," I whisper.

She shifts, posture open but not polished, like she actually means it.

"I know starting therapy can feel like a big step. What brought you here today?"

The question hangs heavy. I stare down at my lap, twisting the hem of my sweater. Why am I here? Because last night I woke up choking on air? Because I can't keep pretending I'm fine when I'm not?

"A nightmare," I say finally. The word feels foreign. Fragile. "It freaked me out."

She nods slowly. "Nightmares can be deeply unsettling, especially when they feel real. Would you like to talk about it?"

I hesitate, heart thudding so loud it fills the silence. But I force the words out. "It was about Max. He's… someone I've been seeing. I don't even know what we are yet, but it feels like it could be something. Like he could be someone really important."

Crystal doesn't move. Just listens, her eyes steady.

"In the nightmare, he wasn't himself. He was angry. Controlling. I felt trapped—like I couldn't breathe." I pause. Swallow. "It didn't feel like just a bad dream. It felt like a warning."

She tilts her head. "You said it felt like a warning. Do you think there's something about Max—or the way you two relate—that might've stirred those feelings?"

That question slices deeper than I expect. My first instinct is to say no. To defend him. But the words don't come.

"I don't know," I whisper. "Max isn't like that in real life. He's not perfect, but… he makes me feel seen. Like he actually gets me."

She stays quiet, giving me space I don't even know how to use.

"But then… there are moments," I say, quieter now. "Like when Max walked in on me hugging my old boss, Mr. Linwood. He didn't say anything—but I felt it. This tension. I told myself I was imagining it. That I was just reading into things."

I pause. "But now… I don't know. It's like my body remembers something my brain doesn't want to admit."

Crystal's voice stays soft. "How did that moment make you feel?"

"Uncomfortable." It slips out before I can stop it. "But I didn't say anything. I just let it go."

"Why do you think that is?"

I exhale slowly. "Because it felt familiar," I whisper. "Like when I was younger, always trying not to set my mom off. It was easier to keep the peace than deal with the explosion."

Crystal leans in slightly, elbows on her knees. Not pushing, just present.

My hands won't stop shaking. They never do. Like my body panics before I even know why. And the pressure in my chest is back—the twisting, crushing kind that once had me convinced something was wrong with my heart. But the cardiologist said everything was normal.

They called it anxiety. Just anxiety. But when it's happening, it never feels small.

"Amaya." Crystal's voice is steady. "You're not in that place anymore."

She waits. Patient. And for once, the silence doesn't feel dangerous—it feels like breathing.

"From what you've shared, you've survived so much—but you don't have to keep living like you're still in survival mode. In a healthy relationship, it's okay to speak up. It's okay to be heard."

My throat tightens. I blink fast. "What if I can't trust my instincts? What if I don't know the difference between a red flag and my own fear? What if I walk away from something good… because my past won't let me trust it?"

"Your instincts aren't broken. They're protective. They've kept you safe. But part of healing is learning to tell the difference between real danger… and fear that belongs to someone else's story."

I nod, slow. A lump rises in my throat.

"Relationships thrive on honesty, respect, and boundaries," she says. "From what you've shared so far, I'm not hearing a crossed boundary yet. But if anything ever feels off, you're allowed to name it—and how he responds is information."

Something in me loosens. Not completely, but enough to breathe deeper.

"And remember," she adds gently, "you don't have to have all the answers today. This is about learning to listen to yourself again. One step at a time."

When I stand, I notice my hands. Still—not perfectly steady, but not shaking like before. Even the air feels different, like I can finally take it in without it catching in my chest.

I leave her office lighter—not fixed, not whole—but maybe, just maybe, I'm letting a little light in.

My fear has a history. It didn't start with Max.

Her words follow me out—steady as a metronome—while my body hums with old alarms.

✷ ✷ ✷

Back at my apartment, I don't even turn on music. I drop my bag, sink into the couch, and sit there in the quiet—just me and the shoebox. I'm not planning to read anything, but my hand moves on its own, pulling out one of the older pages like it already knows.

Hey Sofia,
I freaking HATE when this happens.
We were supposed to go see Abuela in Haverstraw today, but of course, it turned into a fight. It always does.
I wore this cute dress my cousin gave me, with a pair of black booties the Salvation Army donated to Soledad. They're too big, but they look mad cute—and I'm sure I'll grow into them. I was lowkey hoping to see that boy I told you about—the one who just moved into the apartment next to Abuela's.
Tía Lola says he might be deaf, but Abuela swears she just makes stuff up to have something to gossip about. Either way, I don't care. He's fine. Curly hair. Cinnamon skin. Smile that makes you forget your boots don't even fit right. Honestly, if he is deaf, maybe it's a blessing. At least he wouldn't have to hear Soledad yelling 24/7.
Anyway. We were about to leave when Soledad told me to grab her keys and wait in the car. I didn't ask questions—I already knew better.
I sat there forever. Watching the usual crew outside the bodega. Same loud laughs. Same side comments. Same clowns acting like it's their block. One of them waved but stayed put. They all know better than to get too close. Fernando doesn't play.
After like forever (okay, probably 45 minutes), my chest started to feel tight. You know that feeling when your body knows before your brain does? I just knew something was wrong. I didn't want to go upstairs. I really didn't.
But I went anyway.
My boots felt heavy—like I was dragging sacks of rice up a hill I didn't choose. My stomach was already twisted. I got to the door and froze. I heard yelling. No, screaming. Fernando's deep, angry voice, and Soledad shouting back like her throat was on fire. I stood there, paralyzed, heart pounding like it was trying to warn me. I couldn't knock. I knew better than to get in the

middle. Last time I tried, I was the one with the red mark on my face.

So I turned around. Almost took the stairs, but the boots are too damn big—I would've probably fallen and broken a rib. I took the elevator instead, holding back the tears crawling up my throat. When I got outside, I sat on the steps, knees to my chest, trying to breathe. Just breathe. I hate them. I hate them for doing this to me over and over. Why can't they just be normal for *one* day?

After forever, Soledad called. Told me to come back up. I didn't want to. Every part of me said *don't.* But I went. Because of course I did. Like always.

The air in the apartment felt thick. Not from her nasty cigarettes. From something worse. Fernando was in the shower. Soledad sat at the table, silent.

"We're not going to Abuela's anymore," she said. That's it. No explanation.

Then I saw it.

A knife on the chair by the window. A small, rusty stain on the cushion. Her ankle wrapped in a strip of a white T-shirt. My white T-shirt. Of course.

My stomach dropped. My hands shook. I lit her cigarette like she asked—like it was just another regular day. I didn't ask anything. Couldn't. Wouldn't. Soledad's made it clear. I'm not allowed to have opinions. And if I ever call the cops or tell anyone? She said I won't survive it. So yeah. I'm writing you instead. Because you are the only safe place I have.

I'm tired, Sofia. So tired. Of the yelling. Of the pretending. Of all of it.

'Til next time,

xoxo, Amaya

As if that wasn't enough, the next entry stares back at me like it's been waiting all this time to be read again.

Hey Sofia,
Soledad beat me with a broomstick. Yeah. A broomstick. Why? Because I did my hair "too cute."

I swear, every time I think she's done finding new reasons to come at me, she proves me wrong.

I always walk home with Basha—my ride or die. Takes us like forty-five minutes, but I don't care. Better than the bus. Better than getting home early. Those walks are the only time I feel normal. We laugh, talk trash, dream like maybe we'll actually get out one day.

She's the only Polish girl on our block, pale like milk, with that braid that never moves no matter what. Meanwhile I'm out here sweating, fighting humidity, trying to keep my curls together with edge control and an old toothbrush.

Basha's family? Different. They don't really mix in with people here, but you can tell they love her. Her dad hugs her right in front of everybody at the bodega like it's nothing. Papi hugs me like that too. But he lives in DR. And Soledad? All I get from her is smoke in my face and attitude. Her mom's always in the window, watching. Probably praying for us in Polish. Strict, yeah. But not violent. Not cruel.

Last Friday I came home feeling fly. Baggy jeans Soledad got from donations, a tank top I fixed up myself, big gold hoops. Hair up in a high ponytail, baby hairs laid flat. Left hand on my backpack, right hand holding a sour apple Blow Pop. I looked cute.

Then boom—Soledad was home early. Bad sign.

She gave me that sideways look. The one that makes my stomach drop before she even says anything.

She told me only "loose women" wear their hair like mine. That no real man would marry a girl who looked "fast." That I'd end up with a thug.

I didn't say it out loud, but honestly? I wouldn't mind a thug. At least he might protect me from her.

Before I could even blink, she grabbed the broom and swung it at me. First my back. Hard.

I shut my eyes and tried to picture her getting hit instead. Someone bigger, stronger, finally giving her what she gives me. In my head, she was the one crying. Screaming. Scared.

Reading these again reminds me—I've come far. But damn. Some of it still feels fresh, like it just happened. I shove the pages back in the box, like I can hide the cuts they left. Maybe I'm finally ready to hear the girl who wrote them.

I was just a kid trying to survive a house that felt like a battlefield. No wonder my hands still shake, like they're warning me it's not over. But maybe now, I'm ready to let someone in.

Chapter Fourteen

I hang up with Basha, still laughing at her last words. "Don't do anything I wouldn't do—which, let's be real, doesn't leave you much room to mess up."

"Crazy woman," I say, tossing my phone onto the bed, smiling.

Tonight feels… different. Lighter, maybe. Or maybe that's just me, trying to believe it can be. I closed the studio today—no appointments, no emails, no distractions. Just stillness. It felt indulgent, like skipping school when you already know you're going to ace the final.

Or maybe it's Max.

The way he looks at me—like I'm made of something rare. Like he's studying me, but without rushing it. There's something in his eyes that undoes me.

His skin still clings to mine. Warm, like sunlight on bare shoulders. His kiss lingers too—unhurried, deliberate. Like he's tracing the shape of my mouth without saying a word. Like he's asking a question only my body knows how to answer.

And somehow, it does—before I can even think.

I spritz on my favorite perfume. Wrists, behind the ears… ankles too. Just because. In the mirror, I catch my reflection and pause.

High pineapple puff. Curls tilted just enough to look effortless— even though I spent half an hour making sure they tilted the right way. Coral off-shoulder sweater—cozy but slightly flirty. High-waisted black jeans. High heel ankle boots that add the right kind of edge.

"You're glowing, Amaya," I whisper. And the mirror doesn't argue back.

Max opens the door before I can knock.

He's in a fitted black tee and dark jeans. Simple. Clean. Devastating. The sleeves cling to his arms like they were made to test every boundary I've drawn. If I choke tonight, please let it be dramatically into his arms.

"You look stunning," he says, stepping aside.

His voice is that deep, slow burn that melts knees like butter.

"You clean up pretty okay yourself," I say, slipping past him—and stopping.

The entire back wall is glass, revealing the Hudson glittering like a shaken snow globe. Inside, it's sleek—black leather furniture, brushed chrome, a massive gray rug spreading across the floor like it owns the place. A hoodie's draped over a chair, books stacked like Jenga blocks, a half-drunk glass of something dark glowing in the corner. Lived-in. Intimate.

"This is not what I imagined."

"What, no LED lights? No neon sign that says, *Work Hard, Play Harder?*"

"I was expecting at least one poster of a Lamborghini."

His laugh is low and warm—the kind that doesn't just echo, it settles in you.

In the kitchen, he uncorks a bottle of red and holds it up like a trophy.

"Chianti Classico. Smooth. Bold. A little stubborn." He lifts an eyebrow. "Reminded me of someone."

"I'll take that as a compliment," I say, trying not to smile too big.

He raises his glass. "To unforgettable dinners—and even better company."

"To dangerously good food. Cheers."

The wine is lush—dark cherry, a little smoke, a whisper of spice. It lingers on my tongue, warming everything inside.

He pulls out a leather stool at the island. I slide into it; the stool's way too comfortable. Of course it is. He moves through the kitchen like water finding its course—completely in his element.

Watching him feels… intimate. Like I'm seeing something most people don't.

"So," I ask, chin resting in my hand, "do you cook like this for other people often?"

He glances over his shoulder. "Only for people who matter."

I swallow. The air feels warmer now.

"So what's on the menu tonight, Chef Max?"

"You'll see," he says, easy, like he already knows he's going to blow my mind.

"What's your favorite photo you've ever taken?" he asks, not looking up.

I pause. Not sure anyone's ever asked me that. Most people just want to know what camera I use. Not what I see. I glance at the wine. Then at him.

"A little girl at a party last summer. Her face was covered in blue cotton candy, eyes lit up with pure, messy joy. It wasn't posed—it was freedom. I think I loved it because she looked how I wanted to feel."

He nods like he gets it. "I love that. Most people just try to capture what's in front of them. You captured something inside her. The thing I love about photography is that you freeze feelings. That's rare."

I smile—slow, full. "Yes. That's exactly why I do it. It's not about the shot—it's about the pause. That split-second where everything— light, emotion, truth—just holds its breath. I don't just capture how something looks… I capture feelings before they disappear. Little pieces of truth."

A quiet settles between us as the kitchen fills with the scent of garlic, lemon, butter.

And just like that, Ryan crashes in. Uninvited.

Suddenly, I'm barefoot in my old apartment, humming to some song I can't even place, while filet mignon sizzled in butter. To this day, I haven't tasted mashed potatoes that good. I surprised him with *flan*—Abuela's recipe, the one she swore could fix a broken heart, as long as I didn't burn the caramel. He said it tasted like home.

He didn't just cook. He noticed things. He made me feel seen. And when he left, it cracked something open in me I've been trying to seal shut ever since.

I blink again, back in Max's kitchen. But Max is nothing like Ryan. And maybe that's what scares me. I push the memory aside, focusing on the now.

Dinner is unreal.

The first course is an arugula salad with roasted cherry tomatoes, shaved parmesan, balsamic glaze. Light. Fresh. Perfect.

"This is insane," I say. "Like… five-star restaurant-level insane." Okay, maybe I've been to one five-star. Once. Still counts.

"We haven't even hit the main event," he says, setting down the next course with quiet pride.

Scallops—perfectly golden—on a bed of lemon risotto. Roasted asparagus with just the right whisper of char.

I take one bite and moan. "This is offensive," I declare, dropping my fork. "You should be arrested."

"For what—seasoning crimes?"

"For hiding this talent. Who taught you to cook like this?"

"Glad you like it. Let's just say I learned out of survival. Milania once burned mac and cheese. After that, I took over."

We laugh. Then he tells me about Milania—how she lives in Miami, designing interiors for people with too much money and not enough taste. How he practically raised her. How most days growing up felt like keeping their world from falling apart.

"She deserved to feel free," he says, mostly to himself.

There's a weight in his voice, and I feel it—but he doesn't go deeper.

"You've got this... protector heart," I say softly.

He keeps his eyes on mine. Then just... nods. But he doesn't stay there.

"Your turn—what's the weirdest client request you've ever gotten?"

"Oh, easy," I say, leaning in. "A woman once hired me to help her find the perfect outfit for a funeral."

His brow lifts. "What?"

"No, seriously." I hold up a hand. "She was very specific. Wanted something *tastefully sultry.* Her words, not mine. Not too much cleavage, but just enough to make her ex's new girlfriend sweat."

He laughs, full and unfiltered. "You're making that up."

"I wish. She told me funerals are basically high-stakes high school reunions. And I quote: *'If I have to mourn, I'm gonna mourn in Chanel.'*"

"That's either genius or slightly unhinged."

"Honestly? Bit of both. But she didn't just want to wear black— she wanted to wear power."

I pause. "Somewhere between the black midi dress and the veiled fascinator, we had this raw conversation about loss and starting over. She didn't just want to look good. She wanted to feel like herself again. Like she hadn't disappeared."

He doesn't respond right away. Just exhales—the laughter still in the air, but softer now.

"People are wild," he says.

"They are," I nod. "Wild and unpredictable. But if you really listen, you always walk away with something. About them. About yourself. Sometimes both."

The quiet that follows isn't empty. It's steady, heavy with things unsaid—warm, like light that doesn't want to leave.

He pours more wine, then leans across the counter. "Tell me something you've never told anyone."

I stall, tracing the rim of my glass. "When I was thirteen, I shoplifted a pair of sparkly hoop earrings. I panicked and returned them in a tissue two hours later."

He laughs. "Criminal."

"Mastermind, clearly."

His smile fades, like he's carrying something heavy. "I've never been in love."

The words land quietly between us.

"Like… ever?"

"Technically, I have. But not the kind that changes the way you see the world."

I nod slowly. "I've known that kind. And I've spent a long time trying not to."

His eyes never leave mine. We drift to the windows, wine in hand. The view is unreal.

"You're quiet," he says.

"I'm just… taking it in."

"I'm glad you came tonight," his voice drops, barely above a breath.

"So am I." The words slip out softer than I mean them to.

He walks to the speaker and presses play. Soft jazz fills the room. I don't say anything right away. Just let myself feel it—the calm, the quiet, the thing that feels a little too close to safety.

"Velvet Noir vibes?" I tease.

"I remember you liked that song. I pay attention."

He holds out a hand. "Dance with me."

I hesitate—just a beat. Then slide my fingers into his.

He pulls me in—one hand low on my back, the other steady in mine. We move like we're inside the song—like the night doesn't want to end. He smells like sun-warmed skin and something rich—amber, coconut, maybe dark rum. It's heady, warm, pulling me under. He feels like comfort and danger, all in one heartbeat.

I close my eyes for a second, just breathing him in. The music hums low, the room folds in around us. For a moment, there's nothing else—no past, no fear. Just this. He pulls back just enough to look at me. His eyes move over my face, deliberate. Like he's undressing me without touching a single button.

"You move like the music was made for you," he murmurs, voice low against my cheek.

I don't know what to do with that. So I breathe. A slow, shaky inhale. I smile into his shoulder, heart stupid and loud. And I keep moving. One step, one breath.

"You don't have to go," he says. "Stay. If you want to."

I don't move right away. My heart answers before I do.

We settle on the couch. A blanket draped across both of us. My legs curl beneath me. His hand finds my thigh.

We talk. A little. Sip the rest of the wine. Then comes the silence. Not awkward—just waiting to become more.

He brushes a curl from my cheek. I trace the edge of his jaw. It does something to me—his closeness, his calm. I tilt my face toward his. He meets me halfway.

Our kiss is slow. Intentional. Like he's learning me, one breath at a time. My fingers slip beneath his shirt. He exhales against my mouth. We don't talk—but every touch says enough.

When we finally pause, foreheads pressed together, he whispers, barely above a breath—"I want you, Amaya. But only if you want this too."

I don't answer. I just close the space between us.

Chapter Fifteen

Morning light spills through the floor-to-ceiling windows, painting the room in gold and soft blue. I blink, then blink again, sinking deeper into the ridiculous, cloudlike comfort beneath me.

Max's bed is… criminally comfortable. King-sized. A thick comforter. A battalion of pillows—just one goose short of a full scandal. It's the kind of bed that spoils you, whispers you deserve better. My own bed—with its cheap cotton sheets—keeps me humble. Grounded. Productive. This one? This one ruins you for real life.

I stretch with a soft groan and glance at the clock. 5:35 a.m. What kind of masochist chooses this hour on purpose? Right. Max.

Somewhere in the apartment, the faint clink of cups. The scent of espresso sneaks in like a bribe. I bury my face in the pillow one last time.

"This bed should be illegal," I mumble. "How do you ever leave it and still function?"

Eventually, caffeine wins. I pad out of the bedroom, tugging the hem of Max's T-shirt a little lower. The espresso trail pulls me forward, impossible to resist.

Then I see him—and it's like the world forgets to keep spinning.

Shirtless. Barefoot. Silk pajama pants slung low—criminal or intentional, I can't decide. He moves with that quiet morning ease some people are just born with—casual but deliberate. At home in his body in a way that feels almost unfair.

Light slides over his back, tracing the curve of his shoulders. I stop in the doorway, forgetting why I came in here. He's dictionary-entry fine—frame-it-on-the-wall fine.

This is the kind of moment you want to bottle. Or stretch. Or live inside a little longer.

"How is this even fair?" I whisper.

He turns, catching me mid-stare. That look—half lazy, half lethal—spreads across his face. "Morning, sleepyhead." His voice is all rough edges wrapped in warmth.

"You've been up for hours, haven't you?" I ask, leaning into the doorframe like I haven't already surrendered to the view.

"Long enough to ruin the first batch of eggs," he says, holding up a pan like a confession. "So, no. I'm not perfect, in case you were wondering."

I lift a brow. "Good. I was starting to worry."

He steps closer. When he hands me the cup, our fingers brush— and that single touch crackles louder than anything we've said all morning. I hold on like the cup is holding me back, because if I let go, I might kiss him without thinking twice.

The espresso is rich—dark, sinful. I close my eyes as warmth slides through me, a sound slipping out before I can stop it.

"Okay. Yeah. Forgiven."

We stand there in the quiet, balanced on the edge of something we're not ready to name. His eyes stay on mine over the rim of his cup, like he's reading whatever's hiding just under my skin.

"Seriously… how do you leave that bed in the morning?" My voice comes out softer than I mean it to.

He doesn't answer right away. Just studies me, weighing how honest to be.

"Discipline," he says. "And maybe a little motivation—and caffeine."

He turns back to the counter. That's when I spot the spread.

Croissants. Still warm. Edges golden. The smell is unmistakable— Maison Madeleine. My stomach pulls tight. I don't ask if he went this morning or last night. If he knew, or just guessed. It shouldn't matter. But it does.

Beside them, fruit gleams under the light. A glossy swirl of preserves next to a curl of butter. Scrambled eggs—redemption batch—fluffy and golden. A pitcher of orange juice glows like it's been kissed by the sun.

It's simple. But it doesn't feel casual.

"You put this together?" I ask, raising a brow.

He shrugs, setting a plate in front of me. "Didn't seem right to let you wake up to nothing."

I slide into the seat. The hem of his T-shirt skims my thighs when I cross my legs. I reach for a croissant and tear off a piece. It flakes apart under my fingers, delicate layers scattering across the plate like gold dust. One bite, and I forget how to be cool.

Across from me, Max sips his espresso, watching me the way someone does when they already know how this plays out—but want to savor it anyway.

"Wanted you to wake up to something warm," he says. No teasing. No performance. Just presence.

When I smile—small, unguarded—he does too. Then he steps around the island and stops behind me.

He slides his arms around my shoulders and presses a soft kiss to the top of my head. I lean back without thinking. His warmth folds over me like a second skin.

One hand rests across my stomach. The other drifts lower settling at the curve of my hip.

"You look ridiculous in my shirt," he murmurs, voice low and scratchy.

I tilt my head up, teasing. "Ridiculous good or ridiculous bad?"

He leans in closer, lips brushing the shell of my ear. "Sexy. Distracting. Can't think straight."

My breath catches hard. I feel the curve of his smile against my skin. His hand skims the top of my thigh, tracing lazy circles.

"And your curls—" his voice dips lower, "messy. Wild. Perfect."

I turn just enough to rest my hand over his. "You're really leaning into the romance this morning, huh?"

He kisses the side of my neck. "Not romance. Just facts."

We stay like that a while—his chest against my back, his touch unhurried, the world outside still hushed.

And just like that, last night rewinds itself. Soft around the edges, sharp where it matters. His mouth on mine—slow, quiet, like a secret I didn't know I was keeping. His hand at my waist. The way he asked before taking. The way I answered without words. Nothing rushed. Just two people moving toward each other like it was always supposed to happen. Somewhere between the silence and the softness, he let me in.

The words come back now—fragments of what he told me in the dark, the moment he let his guard down.

"My mom," he'd said, voice rough. Like the words cost him. "She drank. A lot. After my dad left…"

I hadn't said a word. Just listened. Let him carve his way through the hard parts.

"She broke. I think she was already broken, but that made it worse. Milania was nine. She didn't understand. Hell, I didn't either. I just knew I had to take care of her."

His eyes had stayed on the ceiling, but his fingers had found mine. "She keeps in touch with our dad now. I don't. Not sure I ever will."

That was the version of Max most people don't get. The one who doesn't ask to be seen.

And now—here in this golden morning light—even the way he moves feels different.

Not just Max with the arms and the effortless cool. But Max who's carried other people's survival on his back. Quiet when the world's loud. Loyal when it's hard. Steady when it counts.

Watching him in his kitchen, something stirs in my chest. Maybe it's joy. Maybe it's the ache of safety that feels too good to trust.

I promised myself I'd take it slow this time. Learn how to trust the quiet. Let the bruised parts breathe. And yet here I am—wrapped in his T-shirt, inhaling his scent, sipping espresso beside my favorite croissants—falling for a man who touches me like he wants to heal everything that came before.

Am I falling too fast? Maybe. But right now? I don't want to stop.

Eventually, I pull away and exhale. "I should get ready. Big day."

He watches from the doorway, arms crossed. Still shirtless. Still unfair. "What's on the agenda?"

"A few styling sessions. One client's doing a full style reset—her ex told her she looked 'washed out,' and now she's out for fashion-fueled revenge. She's on a mission to make him regret everything."

"Sounds like she came to the right woman."

"She did." I smile, grabbing my phone. "What about you? Morning class? Rescue missions?"

"Couple new clients. Testing some equipment. Might stop by your studio—make sure no one gets too friendly."

His eyes spark as he adds, "Any male clients today?"

"A few," I say, matching his energy.

He steps closer, lowering his voice. "Good. I'll drop by. Flash a little bicep. Let 'em know."

I laugh, dragging my fingers down his arm like that's going to stop him. "You're ridiculous."

"Still gonna do it."

At the door, he catches me again. "Wait," he murmurs, dipping his head. "One more."

And then he kisses me—soft, slow, like he's memorizing the morning on my lips. When we part, his thumb lingers at my hip, holding me there like he's not ready to let go.

He leans in, voice low, teasing. "Debating whether to shower… or walk around smelling like you all day."

I don't answer. Just leave him with a smile—lit with fire. And walk out knowing I'll be on his mind.

✷ ✷ ✷

The door clicks shut behind me. Cool air brushes my skin, steadying me—just enough to feel everything again.

My phone buzzes as I step onto the sidewalk.

> **Basha:** Girl, I need every detail of last night. ALL OF IT.
> Also, I have news. You're gonna die. But first, SPILL.

I smile. What do I even say? That I woke up in a bed softer than my doubts? That Max made breakfast like a love letter? That he opened up in a way I never expected—and now I want more? That I might be falling… and I'm not sure if that's brave or reckless.

> **Me:** Coffee. Croissants. Silk pajamas. The abs? Unfair.
> Might need therapy. Can't wait to hear your news.

Pause. Then I add—

> **Me:** Also… remind me to ask if I'm losing my damn mind.

Chapter Sixteen

The studio is quiet—the kind of still that feels earned after a packed day. I've just wrapped up with a client, a lively woman who spent half the session ranting about her ex-husband while I styled her final look.

"I'll show that bastard I can still turn heads," she said, beaming at her reflection.

Now, with the place to myself, I grab the broom and blast some music—Celia Cruz's *"La Vida Es Un Carnaval"* floods the air.

"*¡Azúcar!*" I yell, shaking invisible maracas as I sweep.

When I push open the door to shake the dustpan, the scent of back home hits me. Fried dough, garlic, something sweet underneath—like love wearing an apron.

Milo's walking toward me, smiling like he's delivering treasure, a brown paper bag in hand.

"*Pastelitos de yuca*, Amaya," he says, his accent thick and proud. "Carmen made them this morning. Says you've been working too much. And you need a little meat on your bones."

He presses the bag into my hands, still warm.

"Of course she did," I laugh, heart tugging. "Tell her she's starting to sound like my *Abuela*."

Dominican women don't whisper their concern. They fry it in oil, wrap it in wax paper, and push it into your hands. You're not truly loved until someone calls you *flaca* while insisting you eat.

The smell carries me straight back to Moca—to Saturday mornings with my cousins, sweeping the patio while Juan Luis Guerra blasted from a neighbor's speaker. We'd pretend the broom was a mic, dancing like backup singers in a music video. The whole block smelled like bleach, fried plantains, and pride. Cleaning in the DR was never quiet—it was rhythm, neighbors shouting across *galerías*, someone calling, "¡*Buen día, vecina*!" It wasn't unusual for a neighbor to snatch the broom from your hand or ask if you had a second one so they could help sweep up the patio leaves.

I blink back to the present, smiling as I balance the warm bag in one hand and the broom in the other.

"*Gracias*, Milo. You two are unreal. Tell Carmen I'll swing by later to thank her."

Of course she thinks I'm too skinny. Dominicans don't believe in filters or portion control. If you're not holding a plate and working on a second chin, something's wrong. Reminds me of *Abuela*, always calling me *palo flaco* while piling rice and beans like I hadn't eaten in days. Love, to her, always meant seconds—and thirds.

Milo tips his Yankees cap, already heading back to the bodega, mumbling about bringing more next week. His shoulders are curved from decades of lifting crates and working hard—just like Papi.

Watching him walk away, something catches in my chest. People like Milo and Carmen remind me why I love this town—and how good God's been to me. And just like that, for a second, my whole studio smells like Moca. Like home. Like I never left.

I bite into the *pastelito*—flaky, warm, beef hitting all the right notes—and let out an embarrassing happy moan. Broom in one hand, bag in the other, I'm half-dancing, half-sweeping, letting Celia carry me away.

Someone pounds on the door and the music slices off in my head.

I spin around, still chewing—and freeze.

Ramona.

Standing in front of me in all her over-the-top glory—lipstick too bright, smile too wide, leopard-print leggings clashing with a red leather jacket trimmed in pink fur. Gold boots sparkle under the studio lights like they wandered in from a bad music video. She looks like chaos and home all at once.

"Amaya, *mamita*, are you okay? Don't die on me now—I didn't take the damn bus from the Heights just to watch you choke!"

I cough, swallowing what's left in my mouth, eyes wide. Joy and panic hit me at the same time. "Ramona?"

She beams, arms flung wide like she's onstage. "In the flesh, *mamita*! What, no hug?"

Before I can answer, she crushes me in a hug. Her coat scratches my cheek, her laugh rattles the walls, and I'm drowned in menthol, hairspray, and cheap perfume.

"You're alone, right?" I ask, glancing over her shoulder—half-expecting Soledad to come storming in, *chancletas* in one hand, a kitchen knife in the other.

Ramona throws her head back laughing, her gold tooth catching the light.

"Relax. Soledad's too busy keeping Fernando from flirting with the salon girls to bother with me. These days, the only time she cares where I am is when Fernando gets on her nerves and she needs someone to trash-talk him with."

I exhale—sharp, shaky—but my hand still tightens around the broom handle. Just in case.

Ramona spins slowly, taking it all in. "Damn, *mamita*. I always knew you'd do something big, but this? *Divino.* You made it."

The pride in her voice is the real kind. It lands in my chest and stays there.

"Thanks, Ramona." My throat tightens. "How'd you even find me?"

She whips out her phone like she's pulling out evidence, screen already lit up. "Instagram, *mamita*! Look—there you were, looking all fancy and grown. I said, No way that's my little Amaya! Then I see this post about your studio, and boom—the address was right there on the flyer, like you wanted me to show up."

She zooms in on the photo, shoving it practically in my face. "Tell me that's not destiny."

Damn social media. Great for business. Terrible for staying hidden.

She shrugs, lowering her phone with that same unbothered, unapologetic grin. "I said, why not? It's been a minute since I came to *el campo.* You know how long it's been since I breathed air that didn't smell like bus fumes and hot dog water? Soledad used to drag me up here when she visited family in Haverstraw."

El campo. She says it like it's a hike through the jungle. But that's how city Dominicans talk about Rockland—including Soledad. Only Ramona could make it sound like both an insult and a hug.

Ramona plops into one of the salon chairs like she owns the deed, crossing her legs and tugging her too-tight jacket down like she's settling in for hours of *chisme*.

"So? You seeing anyone? Don't you dare lie to me. A woman like you should have *papi chulos* lined up around the damn block." She waves that diamond-studded nail like a lie detector I'm already failing.

Before I can open my mouth, she's off again.

"Wait—how did you even get here?"

"Took the Coach bus. Driver didn't even charge me—guess he liked what he saw." She winks. "And *muñeca*—I met this fine white man on the way. Smelled like a million bucks, not like Dominican pesos. I might just give him a call."

I shake my head, laughing. "Ramona, you are too much."

She squints at me. "Wait, wait, wait—did you say you have a boyfriend? Lover? Significant other?"

I pause, eyes dropping to the floor. "I'm… figuring things out."

Ramona studies me for a second, like she's trying to read my mind. When she finally speaks, her voice is softer.

"Well, don't drag your feet, *mamita*. You deserve the kind of love that doesn't make you second-guess yourself. The kind that shows up, takes the bus if it has to, and smells like peace—not drama."

I blink at her, totally thrown by the sudden switch from stand-up comedian to motivational speaker.

Then she winks, sprays herself with way-too-strong perfume, and whips out a tube of red lipstick—same shade, fresh coat—gliding it on like she's filming a TikTok ad. "*Tesoro*, life's too short to keep wrestling with these Caribbean men and their side chicks. Time to diversify, you know?"

And just like that, she flips again. Her eyes sharpen, her voice drops. "But for real, Amaya…I'm so proud of you. I always knew you'd make something of yourself. Even that night you showed up at my door, shaking like a leaf—I saw it."

The memory sucker-punches me. I'm seventeen again, cold, starving, hand trembling as I knocked, terrified Soledad would find me. Ramona swung the door open, eyes wide, already launching into a blur of questions—what happened, why are you here, did that crazy woman put her hands on you again—but she didn't wait for answers. She just pulled me inside, shoved food in my hands, wrapped me in a blanket that smelled like coffee and menthol, and made space for me on her couch like it was always meant to be mine.

And I'll never forget what she said—dead serious, frying pan in hand like she was about to headline a WWE match.

"Don't worry, *mamita*. Soledad may be my friend, but if she shows up here acting crazy, I'm clocking her with this pan and blaming menopause."

I laugh at the memory, even as my throat tightens.

"Why were you even friends with Soledad?" I ask. I've never said it out loud before. Never understood how someone so full of life could stand being around her.

Ramona shrugs, leaning back like she's digging through memory. "Your mom… she's complicated. We met bartending at Salsa Heights. She was tough—fierce—in a way that drew people in. Not many were crazy enough to mess with her. She saved my ass once in a bar fight. After that? We were tight."

She pauses, eyes narrowing. Choosing her words. "She's got a good heart, Amaya. But that temper? Lethal. That's why they call her *La Loca*."

I go still. *A good heart?*

If she had a good heart, why did she laugh when I cried? Why did she take pleasure in watching me shrink? My jaw locks, heat crawling up my neck. I don't say it—but it burns anyway.

"She almost killed me, Ramona." My voice cuts sharper than I expected. "I can't forget that."

Ramona exhales slowly, her tone softening. "I know, *tesoro*. And I'm not asking you to. But you're doing so damn good now. Don't let her steal your shine—not even in memory."

She presses on before I can argue, like she's been waiting years to say this.

"She's a complicated woman. I'm part of that same generation— the ones raised in poor Dominican homes where nobody had time, money, or words for things like mental health. *Psiquiatra?* Please. That was for rich or crazy people. We just… got through however we could."

Her face shifts, equal parts pity and annoyance. "I think your mom wanted to protect you, in her own twisted way. But she didn't know how to do it without tearing you down. That's her tragedy."

My fists clench. Jaw tight. "Tragedy or not, I'm done."

Ramona squeezes my shoulder—steady, grounding. "Good. You don't owe her a damn thing. You built this life from scratch. Just don't let the broken parts make you forget how strong and rare you are."

Then she pops up, fluffing that ridiculous pink fur collar like she's walking along the runway. "Alright, *mamita*, I've taken up enough of your time. I gotta catch the bus back to the Heights—and trust me, these heels weren't made for chasing one down."

I watch her head for the door, a knot of gratitude and grief tightening in my chest.

She winks before stepping outside. "But listen—if you ever need to disappear again, my couch is still yours. Not that you'd ever leave this beautiful place," she says, flashing her gold tooth with a proud smile.

I open my mouth, a dozen things I want to say caught in my throat. "You were the first person who made me feel safe, Ramona. I'll never forget that," is all I manage before I start sobbing.

For the briefest second, her eyes soften—like she heard me deeper than she wanted to. Then, just as quick, she masks it with a laugh, blows me a kiss, and struts off like the whole sidewalk was built for her.

I stand there, broom still in hand, chest tight with gratitude and grief braided together. The studio feels too quiet without her laugh rattling the walls.

✳ ✳ ✳

Back at my apartment, I drop my keys on the counter and sink into the hush, Ramona's perfume and laughter still clinging to me. I grab my phone and do what I always do when the past gets too loud.

"*Hola*, Papi," I say, trying to lace my voice with a smile.

"¡*Mi niña*!" he answers, warm as ever. Just hearing him makes my shoulders drop an inch. "How are you?"

We talk about crops. The weather. Tía's bad knee. Tío's latest scheme to trap the neighbor's rooster that keeps waking him up at five. He tells me the plantains are doing well this season and that the nights have started getting cooler in the *campo*.

I tell him about Ramona. About the visit. About the fear that still curls in my gut like smoke that won't clear. "She said not to worry," I whisper. "That Soledad isn't coming here. But what if she does?"

There's a pause. The kind that says he's weighing his words. "Amaya, *mi niña*," he says gently. "I know seeing Ramona brought a lot back. But fear can't guide you anymore. You've already carried enough. Let God protect you. You are stronger now. If Soledad ever shows up… meet her with that strength. Not with the fear she left behind."

His words settle over me like warm soup on a cold day. Comforting, but not enough to quiet the doubt. Everyone says I'm strong. But what if they're wrong? What if she still has the power to break me?

"*Gracias*, Papi," I whisper, wiping away a tear before it can fall.

"Always, *mi amor.*"

We hang up, and I stare at the screen, my reflection faint against the glass—caught between the woman I am and the girl I used to be.

The day's weight settles on my chest, heavy and familiar. And for the first time in a while, I feel the crack of something old trying to surface.

No sooner do I hang up than my phone lights up again. Basha. I let out a breath I didn't know I was holding.

The weight on my chest loosens, just a little. I answer on the second ring, managing a smile.

"Don't tell me you're calling to plan the wedding. I've only slept over once."

"Wedding? Pfft. Who said anything about that?" she snaps, voice sharp as ever. "Just get your ass over here. It's important."

I pause. "What's so important you can't tell me over the phone?"

"Just come, Amaya. *Pronto*. And don't take forever like you usually do!"

I grab my keys and slide into sneakers without bothering to change. When Basha says *now*, she means ten minutes ago.

✷ ✷ ✷

By the time I get to her place, the door swings open before I can even knock.

"Took you long enough!" she says, yanking me inside. "I was two seconds from calling the funeral home myself."

"Please," I shoot back. "If you're gonna die, at least let me pick the casket. Something glittery to match your dramatic ass."

She rolls her eyes and waves me toward the kitchen like she's unveiling a grand surprise.
"Come on. I have something for you."

On the table sits a box from Vilma's Bakery in Haverstraw—the holy grail. The scent alone could make grown men weep. Inside is an obscenely thick slice of pineapple Dominican cake and mini guava-and-cheese empanadas. Heaven, basically.

I clutch my chest like she just betrayed me. "When the hell did you go to Vilma's without me?"

"Focus, Amaya!" she snaps, but the smirk tugging at her lips gives her away.

She hands me a fork. I don't even try to resist. One bite and I melt. The icing's thick like whipped clouds, the pineapple tangy and rich— like vacation in a forkful. Coconut trees. Warm breeze. Childhood summers in DR. My shoulders drop as if sugar alone could undo a lifetime of tension.

But before I can ask what the hell this is all about, she flashes her hand in front of my face.

A ring.

For a second, my brain refuses to process. Then I scream.

"Oh my GOSH!" I yell, nearly knocking the chair over as I jump up. "Oscar proposed?!"

"Yep. Last night," she says, voice trembling with that kind of joy that makes your chest swell too fast for your ribs.

We jump like kids chasing the *frío frío* cart in July—laughing, spinning, breathless by the time we collapse onto the couch, glowing like fools in love.

"Wait," I pant, still catching my breath. "Oscar proposed… with cake and all?"

She scoffs. "No, girl. The cake's from a client. But listen—this man really outdid himself. Gave me a freaking memory box."

I blink. "A what now?"

"A box full of ticket stubs from every concert, little notes, even that napkin with my lipstick from our first date."

She throws her arms like she's conducting an orchestra—loud, dramatic, perfectly offbeat.

My jaw drops. "No. He. Did. Not."

"At first I'm like, what is all this sentimental mess? But then I see the ring, sitting at the bottom like it's been waiting this whole time—and girl, I let out a scream that probably traumatized the neighbor's cat."

I slap a hand over my mouth, already tearing up. "Stop. That's… literally perfect. Did you scream?"

"Please. You know me—I cried, tackled him, and said yes before he could even finish."

We lose it, laughing until she shoves her hand in my face. A radiant-cut diamond sits loud and proud on a chunky gold band, flanked by two side stones sparkling like they're in a competition. It's bold. Extra. Borderline dramatic. In other words—totally Basha.

"Now you know why I dragged your behind over here," she says, eyes shining. "This is huge, girl."

I pull her into another hug, tighter this time. "Sunshine, that's not just huge. That's everything."

"Damn right it is," she says, flipping her hair like she's auditioning for a shampoo ad. "Spill it. What's up with you and Hot Max?"

I groan. "Here we go…"

"Don't even start," she cuts in, jabbing that ring-covered finger at me like I'm on trial and she's Judge Judy. "I fed you cake. I earned this gossip."

"Fine," I groan. "You've been itching to grill me anyway."

And yeah, I cave—because I always do with her.

"He made me breakfast," I say.

Her eyes go wide. "… Okay, and??"

"Croissants from Maison Madeleine. Fresh fruit. Scrambled eggs. Espresso. Shirtless."

Her hands fly into the air. "Girl, this man is a walking romance novel. Keep talking."

I smile, heat creeping into my cheeks. "He cooked barefoot. In silk pajama pants. It was almost rude."

"You didn't even stand a chance," she says, scandalized. Then her eyes narrow, playful and wicked. "So how is he in—"

"Not going there," I cut in, holding up a hand.

She grins like a cat who already stole the fish. "That good, huh?"

I roll my eyes. "I said I'm not going there."

"We ate. Talked. Kissed…" I trail off, biting my lip. "And the night before? He played jazz and pulled me into a slow dance—like we'd done it a hundred times."

Her eyes widen. "Wait. Dinner too?"

"Yeah," I nod. "Scallops, risotto, Chianti. The whole scene. Candles. Conversation. That man really said, *let me ruin her standards.*"

"That's it. I hate him."

I laugh, warmth blooming in my chest. "I think I'm getting used to him."

She leans in, eyes narrowed like she smells confirmation. "And?"

I pause, fingers curling around the edge of my fork. "And… I think I'm falling for him."

She falls back like she just hit bingo, arms in the air. "Told you! The ones who make you roll your eyes the hardest always end up stealing your heart."

I roll mine again. "Okay, okay. You get this one. Don't let it go to your head."

"Too late."

She lifts an invisible glass. "To love. To cake. And to fine-ass men who cook."

I tap my fork to hers like it's a toast. "To besties who bring the real—and men who bring the heat."

We collapse deeper into the couch, sugar crash creeping in, laughter softening into smiles.

That's when I tell her about Ramona. The visit. The memories. The name that still slices like broken glass—Soledad.

"She almost killed me, Basha," I whisper. "She broke me in ways I still can't name. What if she shows up and ruins everything I've built?"

Basha straightens, her hand finding mine. "Listen to me. That woman doesn't get to control your life anymore. You've built something real, Amaya. Something beautiful. You are in control now."

Her eyebrow lifts, her voice edged with that sharp, no-nonsense tone I've loved since high school. "And if she does show up? I'll grab a hot comb and handle it."

I laugh so hard a tear slips out. Because I had that same ridiculous thought earlier—Basha storming in with a hot comb and no patience. Great minds think alike.

A protector. My ride or die.

Chapter Seventeen

I wake up feeling like I ran an emotional marathon in my sleep. No finish line—no medal. Just exhaustion. And questions that won't leave me alone.

Sunlight slices across my face like a spotlight I never auditioned for—warm, too honest, and way too early. I'm still in my old T-shirt. The one that's survived breakups, breakdowns, and maybe one or two breakthroughs. It smells like sleep and last night's ice cream. I don't even remember putting it on.

My thoughts won't shut up. They're already spiraling—every glance, every almost, every conversation I didn't ask for but now can't stop replaying.

And Ramona—man, Ramona. She stormed in full of truths I didn't want but maybe needed. Her laughter still echoes—defiant, infectious. Her words linger too, bold as lipstick on a wine glass. She makes me feel like I'm still figuring out how to live in a body that's both soft and scarred.

And then there's Basha. My safe space. My sister by soul. She's glowing with ring-light joy. Meanwhile, I'm over here wondering if I've done enough healing to even deserve a love story. I'm so happy for her. But her happiness holds up a mirror—and I don't always like what I see.

And Max. Oh gosh, Max. He's temptation in silk pajama pants. There's danger in the softness of his hands, the teasing edge of his tongue, the way his mouth undoes me before I even know I'm lost. His kisses don't just melt me—they rearrange something deep inside.

Am I falling too fast? Or did I already fall that night at the jazz club, when he pulled me close—like we were the only ones alive between the saxophone's moan, the shimmer of low light, and the heat of his hand on my back?

I groan, dragging both hands down my face. "Too much," I whisper to no one but my plants. It's not even 7 a.m., and my emotions are already doing Zumba in stilettos.

✳ ✳ ✳

Maison Madeleine smells like Sunday mornings and second chances. Warm bread, cinnamon, and chocolate. It's a hug I didn't know I needed.

"Amaya, *ma chérie!*" Mr. Nouel lights up behind the counter, all warmth and old-school charm.

I place a package in his hands, wrapped in faded sheet music, every fold pressed with care. "Happy birthday. Found this and immediately thought of you."

He unwraps it slowly. When the vintage "La Vie en Rose" vinyl appears, his hands go still. "Madeleine's favorite," he says softly. "She played it every Sunday. Used to drive Ryan insane."

I feel a tug in my chest, but my face stays calm. "I figured you'd like it," I say, skipping over Ryan's name like a crack in the sidewalk.

He hugs the record like it's made of memory. "*Merci*, Amaya. You've given me a piece of her."

"So glad you like it. Enjoy it in good health. Where's Esperanza?"

"At a hair appointment," he says, puffing up with pride. "Wants to look her best—even if it's just for me."

I smile. "She always does. Tell her I said hi."

Esperanza makes aging look like an art form. Always polished. Always radiant. The kind of woman who wears lipstick like legacy and tucks wisdom and grace behind every gold earring. If I'm even half that put-together at her age, I'll call it a win.

As I head for the door, I hear him humming "La Vie en Rose". The sound trails behind me—low, like a secret only the heart can hear. Not a memory. Just a reminder that some love doesn't fade. It just changes shape.

"Amaya!"

My heart slams into my ribs. "*¡Ven acá!*"

I stop cold. The voice tears through the calm like a fire alarm in a church.

Every instinct screams—*run*.

I turn, breath caught—and see Carmen, waving a brown paper bag like it holds the cure for heartbreak.

"The Dominican *aguacates* you wanted! Straight from the Bronx! I saved you two!"

Relief floods me so fast my knees nearly give out. "Carmen!" I clutch my chest. "You almost gave me a heart attack!"

She throws her head back and laughs—loud, carefree, all hips and humor. "¡*Ay, mija, perdóname*! Next time I'll whisper it like I'm confessing a crime—'A-M-A-Y-A… I have your avocados.'"

We both crack up. My breath's still catching up, but this time it's adrenaline and gratitude.

"You're too much."

"Too much," she says, handing me the bag, "but I bring you the good stuff."

"No one else saves me the good stuff like you do."

"You're not just anyone, Amaya. Don't forget that."

✳ ✳ ✳

I carry Ramona's words with me all the way to Crystal's office. The second I step inside, my shoulders drop an inch.

The office smells like herbal tea and quiet bravery. I sink into the couch and glance at the pillows she keeps waiting—bright colors, soft fabric, each word stitched like it's trying to help. *Joy. Hope. Breathe.* I reach for *Breathe*. Hug it to my chest like it might hold me together while I talk. The fabric's warm under my fingers.

Crystal watches me, not rushing me. I tell her all about Ramona's visit.

"Ramona's visit cracked something open," I say. "And then today, I thought I heard Soledad on the street. It was just Carmen… but for a second, I was back on Ramona's doorstep at seventeen."

Crystal leans in, voice calm as a pulse. "What's the worst thing that could happen if Soledad showed up?"

I hesitate.

"She could try to hurt me again. Humiliate me. Burn down everything I've built."

"And what would you do?"

I swallow hard, my throat tight. The words stall, almost choking me before they come. "I… I'd protect myself."

"You're not that girl anymore. You've got tools. Boundaries. People. Power."

When she says *tools*, I picture Basha storming into my studio with a hot comb in one hand and murder in her eyes—ready to straighten more than just hair if Soledad even thinks about stepping close. *This baby heats to 450 degrees—and I'm not afraid to use it.*

I laugh. Not the polite kind. The real kind.

"Sorry," I say, catching my breath. "When you said *tools*, I pictured my best friend threatening someone with a hot comb. Let's say she's… very passionate."

Crystal smiles. "Laughter's a great tool too. Sometimes the best kind."

She slides a small lavender notebook across the table, still wrapped in plastic. "I want you to try something. Write down every fear you have about her showing up. And next to each one, write how you'd handle it. Sometimes, seeing your strength on paper makes it feel more real."

I tuck the notebook into my bag, unsure if I'll actually use it.

✳ ✳ ✳

Reflections Studio is quiet, bathed in golden afternoon light. The kind of stillness that feels like a reward.

The lavender diffuser hums like a lullaby. I water my plants, straighten a few props, and look around the studio—the business I built from pain and persistence. Every corner whispers the same thing. *You did this. You survived.*

Eventually, I sit. The notebook waits—patient, blank, gentle. Crystal's voice floats back. *"Seeing your strength on paper makes it feel more real."*

I stare at the cover, still sealed in clear plastic, the lavender underneath looking soft, like it's trying to be gentle with me. What if writing it all down makes it too real? What if it opens a door I've been holding shut with my whole body?

But then again… What do I really have to lose?

I peel the plastic off, open it slowly, and let the first page stare back at me.

What if Soledad shows up?

She might scream. Volume has always been her favorite weapon.

She might try to humiliate me. Emotional terrorism is her love language.

She could hurt me—physically, emotionally. Been there, done that, still have the emotional receipts.

She could bring her chaos into my world. This place is mine. She has no freaking right.

She might guilt me into letting her back in. Classic Soledad. Guilt-trip with a side of gaslight and a sprinkle of fake tears.

I breathe. Flip to a clean page.

What will I do?

If she screams, I'll stay calm. She feeds off reactions—and I'm off the menu.

If she tries to humiliate me, I'll remind myself her words don't define me. They used to. Not anymore.

If she tries to hurt me, I'll call the police. This time, I have a voice. And backup.

If she threatens my business, I'll lock the door, blast some merengue, and water my plants. This is a no-chaos zone. Not her stage.

If she guilts me, I'll remind myself I don't owe her anything. I don't do emotional blackmail anymore.

I close the notebook. It hums with quiet power. My hands don't shake. Not anymore.

Maybe she'll always be a shadow. But I'm done living in the dark.

✳ ✳ ✳

My phone lights up.

I stare at the screen, heart doing something strange in my chest. Even from a distance, he still manages to show up in my life.

I click the link. My mouth falls open.

Words upon words about Ryan's booming tech empire. Photos of him at global charity events. Details about the schools—plural—he's helped build.

Ryan Nouel. The man who once held my hand like he was afraid to lose it. But he did.

Now he's out here changing the world.

Once upon a time, I thought I'd never get over him. Now? I don't even blink.

My phone buzzes again.

Max.

"Hey," I answer.

"Hey, beautiful," he says, voice smooth enough to sip. "Hope you're not too busy tonight. I'm craving steak… and the way you taste."

I laugh. "And you think leading with steak is how you seduce me?"

"Oh no, that was just the appetizer," he says. "The main course is me, ruining your lipstick tonight. Blackstone Steakhouse. Seven. Wear something I'll want to take off. And trust me—"

We both say it at the same time: *"You won't regret it."*

We laugh—low, knowing. Like we've already undressed the evening.

I hate that it works. Hate that his voice knows exactly where to land. Hate that I'm already picking out the perfect dress in my head.

Chapter Eighteen

Max pulls up to a red light and gives me that wicked smile that makes my heart do a little salsa in my chest. He leans in, breath warm against my neck, lips brushing just beneath my ear—light as a whisper.

"I love this perfume on you," he says, voice low. "Sexy. Just like you."

I bite my lip, trying not to melt. "Careful, Maximiliano. Keep this up, and we'll miss our dinner reservation."

He laughs, hand grazing my knee as he leans back. "Wouldn't be the worst thing, would it?"

The light turns green. He eases forward, smile still tugging at his mouth.

When we pull up to Blackstone Steakhouse, he turns to me. "Babe, I'll drop you off while I park."

The way he says babe loosens something deep in me I didn't realize was tight.

"What about valet?" I ask, eyeing the sleek coupe up ahead.

He shrugs. "I don't trust anyone with my car. Valet's a last resort."

I roll my eyes but smile as I step out, smoothing my coat. "Fine, go park your precious car."

He drives off. I turn toward the entrance—

And freeze. Silence rushes in, loud as a siren only I can hear.

No. It can't be.

But it is.

Ryan.

My past, standing there like it owns space in my present. Like the ache never left. He's beside Esperanza and Mr. Nouel, all three laughing like heartbreak's a foreign language.

Esperanza spots me first. Her face lights up like a merengue song just walked in the door.

"Amaya, *mi cielo*!" she calls, practically bouncing over. Her curls bounce too—full Dolly Parton volume, Celia Cruz flair.

"*Hola*, Esperanza," I say, leaning into her hug. Her warmth feels like home, even as my thoughts spin like a slot machine.

Mr. Nouel follows with a bright smile. I hug him too.

"Looking sharp, handsome birthday man," I tease.

He laughs, deep and delighted.

"And you, *ma chérie*, look radiant. As always." He kisses both cheeks, with that unmistakably French charm. I've always loved that about him.

And then Ryan steps closer. His cologne finds me before he does—clean, sharp, carrying pieces of nights I thought I'd forgotten. He leans in, kisses my cheek. For a heartbeat, I think he'll kiss the other too—like he used to. But he hesitates. Pulls back instead.

"Amaya," he says, voice still carrying the ache of things unsaid.

"Ryan," I reply, spine straight. My tone is neutral. My pulse? Anything but.

He looks…good. Too good. *Not that I care.* His coat fits too well. Same eyes. Same quiet confidence that once undid me. His presence is overwhelming—the way only someone who once knew every version of you can be.

My first instinct is to tilt my chin, let him see exactly what he gave up. But I don't. I'm not here to perform heartbreak in lipstick and heels. I don't dress for regret. And I'm freezing. But more importantly—I have nothing to prove. I'm with Max now. Max, who pulls everything into his orbit.

Esperanza's voice snaps me back. "Ryan surprised us for Marcel's birthday! Isn't that sweet?"

"Very sweet," I say, polite and clipped.

After a few pleasantries, Mr. Nouel ushers them inside. Ryan lingers. His attention shifts to the street—already locked on Max before I even turn.

Ryan's jaw tightens—barely, but I catch it. His expression holds a beat too long. Like something in him just… recalibrated. A silent acknowledgment.

"See you around, Amaya," Ryan says, unreadable, before walking inside.

Max strides up, confidence like a second skin. He kisses my lips, then my hand.

"Ready for some steak, beautiful?"

I nod. Grateful for him. For the way he wraps the moment in comfort and light. I hate how much I need it. Especially with Ryan nearby.

✳ ✳ ✳

The restaurant hums with low conversation, clinking silverware, smooth jazz. Dim lights and polished wood make everything glow. Blackstone doesn't try too hard—it just gets it right.

Max waves off the wine list, names some fancy Cabernet without blinking. I pretend not to see the price. Still, I can't help smiling.

"You do realize you just ordered a mortgage payment in a bottle, right?"

He shrugs. "It's a celebration."

"Of what?"

"You. Dressed like that. Sitting across from me."

So simple, so confident it steals my breath.

Then I hear it—Esperanza's contagious laugh.

I turn instinctively, but my eyes never make it to her. They land on him instead. Ryan. Still perfect. Still infuriating. I drop my eyes fast, pretending to study the menu, but the words blur.

Max notices. "You seem miles away, babe. You okay?"

"Oh, yeah," I say too fast, throwing on a smile that screams *see? Totally chill.*

I think Max picks up on it. His eyes shift toward Ryan's table. He doesn't say a word. Just watches a beat too long. Then he turns back, calm but tighter. He reaches across, takes my hand, and kisses it. Slow. Deliberate. Like punctuation—like a warning.

I smile and sip my water.

"You look very... focused," Max says.

"I'm just making a very serious steak decision. No pressure."

He laughs. "You sound like Milania. Menus sent her into crisis mode. Once made a waiter describe every single cut of steak. And then still made me choose for her, just so she wouldn't regret it later."

I smile, grateful for the shift. "Honestly? Relatable. Ordering food feels like a personality test."

"She swore the wrong entrée could ruin her whole night."

"I get it. Safe choice and you miss out. Risky choice and you regret it. It's not dinner—it's destiny."

He laughs, eyes lighting up. "She once faked a stomachache so I'd cook. Then, like clockwork, she 'recovered' just in time for dessert."

"Classic. Dessert commitment is a power move."

"She'd say the same thing. Except she always pushed me to commit."

I laugh, shaking my head. "Smart girl. Skipped the risk, kept the reward."

We're laughing before I even realize it—the kind of laugh that sneaks up and sticks around.

"Okay, random question," I say, leaning in like it's a secret. "If you could hop on a plane right now, no responsibilities, no schedule, where would you go?"

"Japan," he says, no hesitation. "Food. Design. Discipline. I've always wanted to immerse myself there—train in the martial arts, study the philosophy, the way discipline is part of everything."

"That's so you," I say. "You'd crush it there—the precision, the mindset. You'd probably come back with a dozen new ideas for your gym classes."

His mouth curves. "Of course I'd come back with new ideas. Can't let you think I'm only good for lifting weights and opening wine bottles. What about you?" he asks.

"Italy or Paris," I say without missing a beat. "Fashion. Architecture. Fresh pasta. Bookstores. Heaven basically. I want to wake up to cobblestones and espresso, and end the day with wine-stained lips and music drifting in from the street."

His smile deepens. "Then let's do both. Japan first. Then Italy. Paris. I'll train, you'll style, and we'll eat our way through it."

The word lands heavier than it should. *We.* Not him, not me. *Us.* Like he's already sketching out his future with me in it, without asking if I want in. And the worst part? A part of me already does.

"Deal," I say, pointing my spoon at him. "But only if we make pasta from scratch in Tuscany and you let me dress you in linen."

He groans, laughing. "Linen? That's a big ask."

"So is mastering chopsticks etiquette. But hey—if we can survive that, we can survive anything."

✳ ✳ ✳

We start with Wagyu tartare and heirloom tomato salad—rich, fresh, like every flavor is showing off. Max orders Kobe. I stick to filet mignon.

The food is amazing, but it's his velvet-smooth voice that keeps pulling me back. He talks expansion like he's already halfway there and just needs the world to catch up. His spark is magnetic. I could listen to him talk all night.

"I've been scouting spaces for a second MAX Fitness location," he says between sips of wine. "The studio's already packed—waitlists for most classes. I'm thinking of adding more specialty training. Maybe a women's strength series. Reformer Pilates. Mobility flow."

"That's incredible, Max," I say. And I mean it.

He shrugs. "It's not easy. But I love it. Helping people feel strong? That's what it's about."

Warmth blooms in my chest. "I get that. My studio's the same. Every night when I lock up, I whisper goodbye to my little creative sanctuary. Sounds silly, but it feels like home. Like I built a piece of myself into those walls."

He doesn't laugh. Just looks at me like I've said something sacred. "It doesn't sound silly," he says. "It sounds like you're exactly where you're meant to be."

His words settle softly, but they stay—pressed to the center of my chest.

Dessert comes. Chocolate Double Sin Cake.

"We'll only need one," Max says, handing back a spoon without breaking eye contact.

He feeds me the first bite. Chocolate melts on my tongue, heat in his stare making it taste richer. His fingers lace with mine. The wine buzzes in my veins. I sink into it. Into him. The restaurant murmurs around us, but it might as well not exist. Max is everything I didn't think I'd find. He doesn't just show up. He chooses to. He pours the last sip of wine into my glass, brushing my hand. I let myself believe in this. In him. In us.

Maybe—just maybe—I can let the past stay buried.

But deep down, that quiet voice whispers what I don't want to hear—some things don't stay buried. I hear it. I just pretend I don't.

Chapter Nineteen

A low tide of voices ripples through the room—glass against glass, silver against porcelain, the buttery warmth of garlic and wine softening the air.

Max's hand brushes mine as he tops off my glass, his laugh low, confident, easy. That smile could light up the whole town. How did I get so lucky?

The server arrives with a polished smile. "Would you like our signature espresso or coffee?"

Before I can answer, Max waves her off, charm dialed all the way up. "No, thanks. Another bottle of wine's perfect."

His voice is smooth—and a little too loud. He lifts his glass and clinks it against mine. "To us."

We slip back into conversation—his dreams beyond MAX Fitness, my hopes for Reflections Studio. It flows like bachata. Fluid, flirtatious, perfectly in sync. His smile feels like sunlight after rain. Warm. Disarming.

And then—something shifts. His voice sharpens—too loud, too sharp.

When the server takes too long with the wine, he throws up his hands. "What's she doing, planting the vineyard?" His voice has an edge now, more bite than charm.

The couple at the next table glances over. Heat climbs my neck, that awful kind of flush you get when strangers are watching. I press my napkin into my lap. Breathe. Even. Controlled.

The cork finally pops, but I barely hear it.

I'm too busy calculating how much this dinner's costing—or worse, how much more he plans to drink. Before she walks away, I jump in—too fast:

"Could we get some water with lemon, please?"

She nods, but her smile falters. A tiny crease forms between her brows. And for a split second, I wonder if she sees what I'm trying not to.

Max grabs the bottle and pours again, unfazed.

And just like that, the warmth of the evening evaporates. What was cozy now feels tight, suffocating—like I'm trapped inside something beautiful, already starting to crack.

I force a smile. "Hey," I say lightly, "maybe we slow down on the wine?"

He laughs it off. "Relax, babe. We're celebrating—your success, my success, our success."

I nod. I bite my tongue, but something inside me twists.

And suddenly, the past crashes in—Fernando drunk behind the wheel, Soledad screaming, the GW Bridge flying past. The panic. The chaos that followed. I force a breath. Try to stay here. But the now feels slippery.

"Bathroom," I say, too quick, too quiet. The chair scrapes loudly. I don't look back. I just move.

✳ ✳ ✳

I nearly walk into the men's room. A guy pushes the door open at the same time I reach for it. We both freeze, then part.

"Oops—sorry!" I blurt, stepping back like I touched something electric. He gives me a weird look but walks off.

I stand there too long. Then I catch my reflection. Washed out. Off. Like I'm wearing a face that isn't mine. I reach for my lipstick—not because I care, but because I need something to do with my hands. Swipe. Inhale. Exhale. Shoulders back. Pretend you're okay.

I step into the hallway—and stop. The air feels heavier, charged.

I see Ryan leaning against the wall like he's been there all along. Hands in his pockets.

"Amaya."

He says my name like it's a memory he never let go of.

"I'm fine," I snap, too fast, too brittle, my voice splintering on the last word.

He doesn't move. Just tilts his head slightly, reading everything I'm not saying.

"You don't look fine."

I should walk past him. Roll my eyes. Go back to Max. But I don't. I just stand there, the knot in my chest pulling tighter.

Ryan steps forward. Lifts my chin with two fingers—gentle, careful; like he knows I might shatter.

"Amaya," he says again, quieter this time. "Are you okay?"

I want to lie. Want to pretend I've got it together. But nothing comes out.

His eyes drop to my mouth. I look away.

"I don't need saving," I whisper. "And I definitely don't need your pity."

His hand falls. But he stays rooted.

"I'm not here to save you," he says. "I know how strong you are. I always have. Just… be careful with this guy. Promise me you won't ignore the warning signs."

My jaw locks. "I don't have to promise you anything." The words come out hotter than I mean, but I don't take them back. "And *that guy*—" I snap, "is my date. He has a name. He's not some random I picked up."

Ryan nods. "Fair enough. But don't lie to yourself. Don't ignore what's right in front of you."

Heat rushes up my neck. My pulse hammers so loud I swear he can hear it.

"You're one to talk," I shoot back. "You walked away from me for your grand adventure, remember? I can handle Max. I've handled worse."

I don't wait for a response. I turn and walk away.

✳ ✳ ✳

I chug my water too fast and end up coughing. Loud. Awkward. A chorus of heads turn. Great.

Max laughs. "Slow down, babe. It's water, not tequila."

I try to laugh too. It comes out hollow.

"Maybe we should take a break. Get some air," I say. "Or at least grab another glass of water before we go."

His smile thins. He takes another sip of wine.

We're halfway through our second bottle, and somehow, he still thinks I'm overreacting.

"I'm fine, babe. Stop worrying."

I hate how he says *babe* now. A leash made of sugar.

"I'm not trying to babysit. I just… I don't think you should drive."

His jaw tightens. "You think I'm drunk?"

"I think you've had too much to drive safely. That's all."

He lets out a dry laugh. "I drive better than most people sober."

But I see it—the glassiness in his eyes. The slack in his shoulders.

"Max, please," I say, voice steady. "Let me drive."

"No," he snaps, rising from the table. "I'm getting my car."

And he storms off.

Cold air smacks me the second I step outside, a faint trace of salt from the river threading the wind. I pull my coat tighter. Of course he parked somewhere far. I hover near the restaurant entrance, arms crossed against the chill, staring into the dark.

And for the first time tonight, I don't know what I'm waiting for—him, or the version of him I'm scared I already lost.

My phone's already in my hand. Do I call an Uber? Basha? Just go?

Then headlights slice the night. Max's car screeches around the corner, too fast, too loud. My chest locks up, breath sticking in my throat. My body remembers even when I don't want it to. He slams the door. Storms toward me.

"Max," I say, hands up. "Listen to me. Just wait. Drink some water. Breathe—"

"Enough, Amaya!" His shout cracks the air open. "I'm fine! Stop treating me like I'm some drunk!"

His steps stutter once on the curb. Mine don't. Then he grabs my wrist. Too tight. And suddenly I'm eleven again. Soledad's grip. Adrian's breath. Fernando's rage. The shame. The fear.

"Max," I whisper. "Let go."

"Just get in the car," he growls, yanking me closer.

"Let go of her." The words hit like a bullet. I turn, and there he is—Ryan. Fire in his eyes. Stepping out of a sleek black car.

Max freezes. His grip loosens. Then—he lets go.

"Mind your own fucking business," Max spits.

Ryan steps forward. "Amaya. Are you okay?"

I nod—barely.

Ryan turns to Max. His voice? Ice. "She's not going anywhere with you."

Max barks. "You think you're some kind of hero? Back the hell off."

Then a car door opens, and Mr. Nouel steps out.

My hands won't stay still. I shove them inside my coat pockets, hoping no one notices. But the nerves won't let me hide—I pull them back out a second later, fingers twitching in the cold air. My body's all static, buzzing, like it doesn't know where to put the fear.

"Is there a problem here?" His voice is calm. Nothing like the storm inside me. His eyes are sharp, though. Sharper than I've ever seen them.

And in that second, I realize—Ryan got this from him. That same unshakable calm under pressure.

Max barks a bitter laugh. "Yeah. Mind your own fucking business, old man."

Ryan's fist curls. But he stays still. "She's not going home with you. Walk away."

Max's eyes shift between us. "Oh, I get it. You wanna be the big man tonight," he snaps. "How convenient."

Ryan doesn't answer. Just looks at me. "Amaya. Please. Come with us."

And then—Esperanza. She walks out like thunder wrapped in silk, heels striking the pavement with purpose, eyes locked on Max.

"Amaya, *mi tesoro*," she says. "Get in the car. Now."

Her voice is pure fire. I swear she might slap him. Her fingers twitch. "You've done enough," she tells Max. "Leave her alone."

He stares her down—but it's useless. She's immovable.

"You think this is over?" Max spits. "You'll regret this."

Tears spill down my cheeks. But I find my voice.

"Fuck off, Max. We're done. I'm done."

I pause. Swallow. "I'm going with them." I choose the word *them* on purpose. Not Ryan. Saying his name might throw gasoline on whatever fire's still burning behind Max's eyes.

Max points at Ryan. "You'll regret this," he repeats.

Then he storms to his car. But before he opens the door, he pauses—then looks at me like the street just tilted. Everything stills. There's still rage. But under it—something like disbelief. Like he's losing something he never knew how to hold. Then it's gone.

He slams the door. Tires screech. And he's gone. The silence rushes in like a wave. The sidewalk tilts. I don't even realize I'm falling until Ryan catches me. His arms wrap around me—strong. Safe. I hate how small I feel. Embarrassed. Exposed. Like the past just swallowed me whole.

"You're gonna be okay, Amaya," he whispers. "I promise."

I bury my face in his shoulder, and the tears come—hard, fast, relentless.

Esperanza's hand finds my back. "Shh, *mija*," she says. "You're safe now."

Mr. Nouel's voice carries the kind of authority that feels like shelter. "No one will touch you while we're here."

And that's what undoes me. Not the adrenaline. Not Max.

This.

This gentle kindness that cracks something open. Because right now, more than anything—I wish my dad were here. His voice. His arms. The way he could hold the broken parts of me without asking for an explanation.

A memory rushes in. I was seven. Crying under our mango tree after a fall. It wasn't the blood that scared me, it was the fall. Papi scooped me up like gravity didn't apply to him. Kissed my head. Told a dumb joke about the mango being jealous. I laughed so hard I forgot why I was crying. Right now, I'd give anything to feel that kind of safety again.

"That's enough for tonight," Mr. Nouel says softly. "Let's get her home."

Ryan's arms gently tighten around me, and for once, I don't run.

I just let myself feel. All of it.

Chapter Twenty

The car ride is quiet—not the peaceful kind. It clings like fog, thick with everything we're not saying. Every bump in the road sends a dull throb through my wrist, and the rest of me feels like lead.

I glance at the rearview mirror. Ryan's eyes find mine—not invasive, just searching, like he's trying to measure the damage. I look away.

My hands lie useless in my lap. I stare at them, trying to make them feel like mine.

Mr. Nouel clears his throat. "Ryan, take us home first," he says, firm but gentle. "Then take *ma fille* home. Stay with her for a while. Make sure that Max guy doesn't show up. If anything happens, call me, son."

Ma fille. My girl. He's said it before, but tonight it lands different. Heavy. Soft. Like balm over bruised skin.

"Of course, Dad," Ryan replies without hesitation. No questions. No second-guessing. "I'll stay with her."

I should say something. I should remind them I've been handling myself my whole life. But the words don't come. They sit in my throat, heavy and sharp. All I can do is exhale—shaky, quiet—and sink deeper into the seat.

When we pull up to their house, Esperanza turns toward me. Her eyes hold mine like she's trying to speak straight to my soul.

"*Mija,*" she says gently, "Promise me you'll rest tonight. You're safe now."

Her words crack something in me. She reaches for my hand and pulls me into a hug that smells like jasmine and honey, like the gentleness I always wanted from Soledad.

It's not the kind of hug you expect from someone who isn't blood. It's the kind that says—*you're not alone anymore.*

"You're safe now," she whispers again. And I want—no, need—to believe her.

Mr. Nouel pulls me into a hug. "Amaya, *ma fille*, don't hesitate to call us. For anything."

I nod, but I can't speak. There's a lump lodged in my throat that refuses to move. I watch them walk inside, their warmth trailing behind like something I want to believe belongs to me.

Back in the car, the silence returns—but this time it doesn't feel so heavy. It settles between us, soft around the edges.

When we pull up to my building, Ryan shifts toward me.

"Let me walk you up."

I start to shake my head. "You don't have to—"

"I know," he says, cutting me off gently, eyes locked on mine. "But I want to."

Something about the way he says it makes it impossible to argue. I let out a slow breath and nod.

"Okay."

✳ ✳ ✳

Inside my apartment, everything feels off. Too still. Too quiet. Like it doesn't belong to me anymore. I drop onto the couch—it feels like the only thing holding me together.

Ryan doesn't say much. He just moves quietly, grabs the blanket off the back of the couch, and lays it over me. His hands are careful, like I might break.

I hate that he's seeing me like this. Raw. Messy. I pull the blanket tighter, trying to bury the shame crawling under my skin. I hate how gentle he is. I hate that he's here—because he's the last person I want witnessing this. And yet… part of me doesn't want him to leave.

I don't react when he moves closer. His scent lingers in the air, tugging at me. Part of me wants to lean in, breathe it deeper, let it quiet everything rattling inside me. The other part knows that's dangerous.

"I'll make you some tea," he says, voice low.

"No. Bustelo," I mumble into the blanket, a bitter laugh almost slipping out. Chamomile can't fix this. I should've said whiskey.

Something that scorches instead of soothes—burns through the humiliation and anger. But I already know how that ends: a splitting headache, regret knotted in my chest. Like I need another reason to feel weak.

He doesn't argue; just quietly moves toward the kitchen like he remembers where everything is.

The soft clack of the *greca* on the burner breaks the silence. A low hiss follows, steady, patient. I glance over. He's there—watching me. At first, his expression is unreadable. Then his eyes soften, and something in my chest pulls tight.

I look away, yank the blanket closer, like it might shield me from whatever that look means—or from what it's undoing in me.

The dark and earthy scent finds me next. It seeps through the room, grounding and alive all at once. The sound of him in my kitchen feels wrong—too intimate, like he belongs here.

I don't want him here. But being alone feels worse.

He comes back with two mugs. One of them is my favorite—black, heavy, the word WORTHY glinting in gold across the front like it's daring me to believe it.

"Here," he says softly.

I take it without looking. The aroma blooms in my chest, gentle and insistent, like it's daring me to breathe a little deeper. I take a sip. It tastes like *the before*—safety with something sharp underneath.

"You remembered," I say, too quickly, too sharp.

He doesn't blink. He just nods, gives me a quiet, sad smile. "Just like you taught me. I couldn't forget even if I tried."

The words hit somewhere I don't want them to. Part of me wants to spit back that anyone can learn how to make coffee, and remembering doesn't mean he stayed. But I don't. I swallow it, look away, and take another sip—pretending it's the coffee that makes my throat tight.

My chest starts to tighten. The warmth of the drink curdles into something sour. I can feel my pulse rising in my throat, that familiar sting behind my eyes—the one that comes before I say something I'll regret. My fingers drum against the mug, restless, searching for an anchor that isn't there.

Then I set the mug down—too hard. Ceramic knocks against the table, loud in the silence.

"You don't get to do this," I say, voice low, shaking.

He blinks. "Do what?"

"This." I gesture between us. "Act like it's nothing. Like you can just show up and remember how I like my coffee, like it doesn't—" I stop, bite it back—doesn't still hurt.

He doesn't rush to speak. Just lets the weight of my words hang between us, and it makes me feel exposed, like I've already said too much.

I press my palms into my knees, trying to keep myself anchored. "We're not the same people anymore," I say, softer this time. "You chose your life. Your work. All the traveling. And I…" The rest catches in my throat. He says nothing—only the muscle in his jaw moves.

"I don't know what you're trying to do here," I say, louder now. "But I don't need you to save me, Ryan. I've been saving myself my whole damn life. While you were off chasing dreams and disappearing without a word, I was learning how to patch myself up alone. So don't show up now like you suddenly care."

There it is—the fire I've been swallowing since he walked back into my life. It cuts through the numbness, hot and sharp, burning a hole in the quiet. And suddenly I wish I could take my words back.

Ryan leans forward, elbows on his knees. "I'm not trying to save you, Amaya," he says, calm but clear. "I just want to be here."

The words land soft, but they stay. I hate how real they sound. How some part of me wants to let them in.

Silence falls again—heavier this time, weighted with everything we don't say.

He notices my wrist. Something shifts in his expression. Before I can react, he reaches—fingertips grazing, careful. I want to pull away. But I stay. Still. My hands tremble, but it's not fear of him; it's the echo of every hurt I've endured. And beneath that, deeper, heavier—the ache of missing what I swore I'd stopped needing.

"Amaya," he says softly, pulling me back. "Please. Look at me."

I hesitate. Everything in me wants to curl up, disappear. But I lift my eyes. Just enough.

"You don't have to let anyone treat you like this," he says. "Not with their words. Not with their hands. You deserve better than that. You deserve to feel safe. And respected."

His voice doesn't shake, but it's thick with something I can feel.

"Max?" he says quietly. "He's the one who should feel ashamed—not you."

The words crash over me like a wave, and the walls I've been holding up all night begin to crack. A tear slips down my cheek before I can stop it. I reach up fast to wipe it away, but Ryan gets there first—his hand brushing mine aside, thumb catching the tear.

His touch lingers, and suddenly breathing feels like effort.

"It's okay," he whispers. "Let yourself feel it. You're allowed."

I squeeze my eyes shut. His words cut through every defense I've built. And for the first time tonight, I fully let go.

The tears come hard. Messy. A storm I've kept locked inside too long. And I don't stop them. I don't try.

Ryan doesn't move. Doesn't talk. He just stays—quiet, solid. Here, in it with me.

By the time the sobs slow, I'm drained. But my mind won't quit. Everything plays on a loop—words, moments, touches I wish I could erase. Pain carved into me.

Ryan's still here.

When is he going to leave? Do I want him to?

I should tell him it's fine. That he can go. Say thanks. Let him off the hook. But the words don't come. They're stuck somewhere between my pride and this heavy comfort I didn't expect.

His presence is infuriating. And it's the only thing keeping me grounded. I hate that. But I don't hate him being here. I lean my head back against the cushion, eyes on the ceiling—blank, hollow. My limbs too heavy to move, too drained to carry the weight of tonight. Ryan doesn't speak. Doesn't press. He just stays quiet like he knows silence is the only language I can understand right now.

Without thinking, my head tilts to the side—and rests against his shoulder. I don't pull back. I'm too tired to overthink it. His arm shifts around me. Both strong and gentle. His touch doesn't ask anything of me—doesn't demand or invade. It just… holds. And somehow, that's the scariest part.

Why does this feel like peace?

"I've got you," he whispers, and it's too gentle, too close—like something I shouldn't let myself keep.

The words sink in deeper than I want to admit. They slip through the cracks—past the fear, past the exhaustion—landing somewhere I thought was sealed off for good.

I close my eyes. Just for a second. Just to rest.

Somewhere in the apartment, the pipes tick and the air settles.

And in the quiet, Esperanza's voice echoes softly in my mind—"*El amor verdadero no sólo cura las heridas… también te enseña a confiar de nuevo.*"

I want to believe her. I want to believe that true love doesn't just heal wounds. It teaches you how to trust again.

Chapter Twenty-One

I wake to warmth draped over me, limbs tangled on the couch like I passed out mid-fight. Every joint aches. My jaw is tight. My shoulders hum with soreness. My body feels like it spent the night fighting memories.

The apartment is dim. A narrow slice of morning light slips through the blinds—soft, shy.

My stomach twists—heavy and sour. I don't need to remember last night. My body already does.

I reach for my phone. It's 6:05 a.m. Of course it is—like my body's still on disaster time.

Max. Ryan. The way Ryan sat—silent, steady as a heartbeat I could borrow. The way I fell apart and he stayed.

That silence still echoes in my chest. I shift to sit up—and everything stills. There are two blankets. One is my throw. The other, my bedroom comforter. I didn't get it. I know I didn't. My stomach tightens.

Ryan must've—

Nope. Not going there. I shut the thought like a door I refuse to open. I don't want to picture his hands tucking it over me. I don't want to feel what that would mean—seen, cared for. I rub my face, trying to lodge the feeling back where it can't reach me.

The apartment is too quiet. The bathroom—empty. The kitchen, too. The bedroom—empty. No trace of him anywhere. Relief slips out. Right behind it comes disappointment—sharp, unwelcome. They knot in my chest—tight, messy, impossible to separate.

I look toward the balcony, half-expecting him to be there, watching the sunrise like something out of a movie. Empty. Still gone. Good. Right?

I sigh and move to the kitchen for the *greca* by habit. A folded note near the stove catches my eye. My name in that sharp, precise handwriting. My fingers hesitate. Then I pick it up. I don't want to read it. But I do.

Amaya, I didn't want to wake you—you need the rest. Your Bustelo is waiting, just how you like it. Please try to take it slow today. I know that's hard for you. Just… try. I'm leaving tonight. Call or text—anytime. I mean that.

—Ryan
P.S. Canela, nutmeg, sweet cloves. I remembered.

I sink onto the barstool and read it again. Then again.

Canela. He wrote cinnamon in Spanish. He never used to do that.

I remember teaching him—how his lips shaped the word, how he repeated it just to make me laugh. The way he used to tease me—said my skin reminded him of cinnamon kissed by golden dusk.

The *greca* waits silently. The jars of *canela*, nutmeg, sweet cloves sit where he left them. The kitchen remembers him—like his hands never really left. I reach for the knob. My fingers linger. Then I finally turn it.

The smell blooms—warm, spiced, more him than it should be. It rises like a memory I wasn't ready to breathe. I pour slowly, careful as if rushing might split something open. It's perfect. I know this flavor by heart. But today it tastes like the past. Today it tastes like him.

I carry the mug back to the couch, holding it with both hands as if it might fall apart. I sink into the cushions and, for a long beat, just sit—listening to the quiet. Letting it ache.

I don't want to do this. But I do.

The Sofia shoebox waits, heavier than it looks. I dig past last winter, past heartbreaks I already know too well. This time I am not flipping aimlessly. I know what I'm looking for.

There it is—the entry I wrote the day Ryan left for California. I was twenty. I thought I knew heartbreak.

Hey Sofia,

I don't know why I thought we'd make it. Maybe I just wanted something good. Something real. But now? I can't stop crying. My chest feels tight—like I'm choking on all the things we were supposed to be.

Ryan's gone. Not a little gone. Not "maybe we'll work it out" gone. Gone. Off to California chasing dreams I was never going to be part of.

And yeah, I saw it coming. He always talked like the world owed him an open sky. San Francisco. Singapore. London. Always somewhere else. And me? I just wanted roots. A little peace. Music. Trees. The same bakery on Sundays. A place where my name meant something.

We fought last night. Dumb fight. He said, "I need to see it all, Amaya. Build something that matters." And I snapped back, "What about here? What about me?"

The look he gave me… I knew right then. I wasn't part of the plan. Just a stop. A memory. A story for later.

He said he loved me. That I'd always have a place in his heart. What the hell does that even mean? You can't live in someone's heart. You can't crash on its couch or call it when your world is falling apart. It's just words people say when they're already halfway out the door.

And he never really got it. He doesn't know what it's like to grow up in chaos, always waiting for the slam of a door, watching faces to see if the bomb's about to drop. I used to dream about peace. About belonging. Nyack gave me that. Cobblestone streets. Bookstores that smell like dust and old love stories. Music drifting from windows. Artists with paint on their hands, sipping coffee at the corner café.

He wanted freedom. I wanted home.

And I'm mad. Mad he left. Mad I loved him that hard. But honestly? I'm even more mad at myself—for thinking he might stay. For thinking I'd be the one he chose. For believing I'd be enough.

I hate how much I miss him. I fucking hate it.

I hear his laugh in my head. I see his stupid face every time I close my eyes. I want to scream. Smash plates. Throw his *passport into the Hudson. But I won't chase him. I'm not that girl anymore. I deserve someone who doesn't need convincing.*

So yeah. It's me now. Maybe that's a good thing. Time to focus. Load up on FIT classes, try to graduate faster. My dream's screaming at me. I thought I wanted to be a designer, but maybe I was wrong. What I love is styling people. Photographing them. Helping them see themselves the way I see them. That's mine. My thing. And I'm gonna chase it until it's real.

And Sof? Fuck him. For real. What do guys even do but take and disappear?

He got my time. My loyalty. My heart. I got... a goodbye. Nah. I'm done. Let him take his carry-on and go be "global." I'll be here—building something real. Creating joy. Putting down roots. I've survived worse than a guy with good cologne and a boarding pass. I survived Soledad.

Let them keep their empty I love yous. From now on, it's me. All in. All heart. All rise. And when I do? He'll wish he stayed. He'll wish he chose this life—me.

Damn it hurts. Hurts like hell. But someday, this burn's gonna turn into something else. Power. Drive. Maybe even gratitude.

But today? I want to launch his damn suitcase into the Hudson. Maybe I'll mail him a postcard: Wish you were here— drowning with your dreams.

I'll get through this. Right after I Google how to curse someone in seventy-seven languages.

'Til next time,

xoxo, Amaya

I exhale, sip, then set the cup down, still half full.
Because if I finish it, it's over.
And I'm not ready for it to be over.

✷ ✷ ✷

The drive to therapy is a blur. Thoughts scatter like broken beads—rolling in every direction, impossible to collect.

"El Perdedor" by Aventura plays through the speakers. Of course it does.

El Perdedor. The loser. Is that what I am? A loser stuck in limbo—half a heart in the past, half gasping for a future? *Un perdedor. Un soñador.* A loser. A dreamer. The lyrics land harder than they should. Is this who I'll always be? A girl with one foot in heartbreak and the other clinging to something that barely exists?

I don't skip the song. I let it play. I let it hurt. The cup in the console has gone cold, but it still tastes like him.

I hate him. And I miss him. Gosh, I hate that I miss him. He doesn't deserve me. Correction—neither of them do. A tear slips down. I swipe it away and grip the wheel tighter.

✳ ✳ ✳

Crystal's office is warm, the air different today—coconut and jasmine instead of lavender. Why do I notice these things? I sit stiff, every muscle locked like I'm trying not to feel too much.

"Talk to me, Amaya," she says gently. "Rough night?"

A dry laugh slips out. "You could say that."

"Take your time. You're safe here."

Her words splinter in my throat. I could swallow them down, but I don't. Not today. I tell her everything. The fight with Max. The alcohol. The way he grabbed my wrist. How I begged him not to drive. How he looked at me like I was the problem. My hands still shaking. How familiar it all felt.

And then Ryan—stepping in. A shield. Solid. Unshakable. Mr. Nouel—calm, composed. Made me feel safe without saying a word. Esperanza—pulling me in like she wouldn't let me break. And Ryan again. That look. Like I mattered.

Her face tightens a fraction, but her voice stays steady.

"Amaya, Max's behavior wasn't just wrong. It was dangerous. It was abusive."

I blink. "I mean… yeah, it was bad. But abusive? That's a strong word. It was the alcohol—"

"No." Her voice cuts clean. "He crossed every boundary. He put your safety at risk. He grabbed you. That is not okay."

My throat tightens.

"You know this pattern, don't you? The anger. The drinking. The control." She leans in.

I do know it. All too well. It's not just Max. It's Fernando. It's Adrian. It's Soledad. Every slammed door, every slammed bottle, every night I lay awake waiting for the storm. They taught me what it means to live in fear. To shrink. To obey. To survive.

Fernando's voice cuts through my thoughts. *Shh, bonita... you don't want to make a scene, do you?* His sour breath hot against my ear. Soledad's voice too—sharp, cold. *Cry one more time and see what happens.* My shoulders tighten. My whole body remembers.

She doesn't push. "I know this is hard, Amaya. But do you see the connection?"

Panic spikes. I know what she's saying. I know she's right. I can't take it.

"Max is NOT Fernando," I snap—too loud, too fast.

My voice fractures. The words explode out of me before I can stop them.

"Fernando was an alcoholic. A criminal. That bastard—" I choke on the word. My hands tremble. I press them to my thighs, trying to steady myself, but it's useless.

The silence after feels like punishment.

"You've been through hell, Amaya," she says. "But you don't have to repeat it. You don't have to explain it away."

I look down at my fingers digging into my jeans. I'm trying to hold it together. To be okay. I'm not.

"And Soledad forgave him," I whisper. "In less than twenty-four hours."

Rage lights up in me like a match to dry wood.

Her face softens. "That wasn't love, Amaya. That was betrayal."

I laugh—brittle and small. "I was her daughter. Her own blood. And she still chose him."

"She always chose him," I repeat. "Every. Single. Time."

She listens like she can feel the weight I've been carrying all this time. "You don't have to repeat history."

Those words cut into me. They terrify me because part of me knows she's right. I shut down. The door slams—loud, final, protective. I can't go there. Not yet. If I do, I might not come back.

My breath thins. My leg bounces. Vision blurs at the edges. I grip the cushion as if it will hold me still.

She doesn't rush. She just shifts slightly, like she sees the fracture and makes space for me to breathe through it. Her eyes soften. She doesn't speak, but I hear her anyway—*I see you.*

"And Ryan?" she asks gently. "How did it feel... having him there?"

His presence felt like safety.

"I don't even know what I feel," I admit. "It's like I hate him. Like something cracked open I thought I buried. Like I was holding my breath the whole time he was near—and when I woke up, the silence he left behind was louder than anything. Like I shouldn't have let him be there for me."

She nods. "You trusted him."

The truth settles under my ribs. "I did. Makes me feel weak."

"That's not weakness, Amaya."

I twist my hands in my lap. Weakness feels right. I should've been stronger. I should've handled Max on my own. I don't say it out loud.

"Be mindful," she says. "Old wounds make us vulnerable to the wrong kind of love."

Her words hang. Heavy. Humid. I nod even though I'm still lost.

"It wasn't your fault," she says.

"Then why does it still feel like it was?" I whisper.

"Because trauma remembers," she says. "It waits. And when something echoes the pain—it floods back. Even when your mind can't make sense of it."

"So what do I do?"

"You heal. Slowly. Messily. But you heal."

I exhale and sink into the chair.

She tilts her head. "Can I ask you something?"

I nod.

"Why didn't you reach out to your father when you were younger?"

The truth lodges like a stone in my throat. "I... I couldn't. Soledad was always watching. Listening. If I even hinted at the truth, she'd find a way to punish me. She'd beat me. Hard."

She stays quiet.

"My dad wouldn't have let it happen. If he'd known, he would've stopped it. He would've moved mountains to get a visa just to come and get me. He would've come here illegally if he had to. But he didn't know. And now he carries that guilt like it's his own."

"Does he know now?"

I nod. "Not everything. But enough. And it eats him up. He thought sending me here would give me opportunities. He didn't realize he was handing me over to a monster."

"Do you resent him for not knowing?"

I pause. "I don't know. Maybe. Sometimes. I wonder if he should've asked more. Looked closer. I know he loved me—but love doesn't always equal protection. I wish he'd seen through the lies. Just once."

I breathe out, soft. Like release.

"By the time I ran for the last time, I was seventeen," I say. "I'd learned the language. I had dreams—big ones. FIT wasn't just a school—it was my way out. Going back to DR would have meant giving it all up. Starting over. Handing my life back to the people who decided what was best for me. Maybe that sounds selfish, but after everything—I couldn't do it. I couldn't hand my future back."

"That wasn't selfish," she says. "That was survival. Survival isn't a flaw—it's how we keep going when we've been failed by the people meant to protect us."

She pauses, letting it land.

"It's okay to wish he'd seen more. To carry both love and hurt in the same breath. But none of this was your fault. You did the best you could—with what little you had. And no child should ever have to choose between safety and silence."

A breath slips out—uneven, but it feels like release.

"You've carried this for so long on your own," she says, her voice softer now. "But you don't have to anymore."

Her words settle in my chest like the first sip of coffee after a long night. Maybe the bravest thing I'll ever do is believe her. To speak. To let go of silence before it becomes me.

✳ ✳ ✳

I run on caffeine and fumes. Full schedule. Zero energy. But I can't fall apart. So I do what I do best—fake it.

I erase the wreckage under my eyes with concealer, resurrect my lashes, and swipe on lipstick loud enough to lie for me—because sometimes survival looks like glamour with a side of denial.

My phone buzzes—Basha. Relentless. I call. She picks up on the first ring.

"Girl, don't play. I need details."

I open my mouth.

"Wait. First. One of my clients came in all 'highlights, highlights,' then broke down mid-process because she meant lowlights. Lowlights, Amaya."

"You're lying."

"Full-on ugly crying. I had to pat her head like I'm certified in grief counseling."

A shaky laugh escapes me. "Basha, you out here doing charity work now?"

"Please. Emotional support ain't free—I better get a tax write-off." She shifts gears. "But enough about my tragic life as a hairdresser-slash-therapist. Let's talk about you and Mr. MAX Fitness. Did he open the door like a gentleman, pull out your chair, order for you in that Denzel voice? Or did dinner come with… an after-hours training session? You know—dim lights, no witnesses, all cardio, no clothes?"

I close my eyes. "Basha—"

"Why do you sound like that?" she presses.

"Like what?"

"Like you aged ten years overnight."

I stay quiet.

"Oh, hell no." I hear her pacing. "Start talking—now—or I swear on my imaginary patience, I will show up at your studio yelling like I'm on reality TV."

I inhale. "Max got drunk. And then everything went downhill." I swallow. "Ryan was there."

Silence. Then Basha drops into a tone that makes the hair on my arms rise. "Why the hell didn't you call me?"

"It was too much," I lie to her and to myself. "I can't even—my first client's due any minute."

"Nope. Not doing this. You don't go through this kind of shit alone." She breathes out heavy. "Tonight. My place. Takeout. No excuses."

"Basha—"

Click.

The silence that follows is too loud. I sit with it, heart racing, hands still, pretending everything's fine.

Beneath the concealer, mascara, lipstick that lies—something shifts. Not enough to rewrite the story. But enough to prove it's not over.

Chapter Twenty-Two

Basha's apartment smells like buttered popcorn and vanilla candles. The second I walk in, she announces she lit an extra one for me—praying for peace, clarity, and a fine-ass man who won't stress me out.

Only Basha.

We curl up on her sectional, blankets pulled to our chins, legs tangled like teenagers again. She squints at me. "How bad is it?"

The answer sticks in my chest like a stone.

By the time I finish telling her everything, I feel hollow—like I spilled every messy thought out but somehow, the weight still lingers. Basha doesn't interrupt, except two or three times when she really can't help herself, which is saying a lot. For her, that's restraint.

When I finally stop talking, the room goes still. She exhales long and slow—then launches into a full-blown multilingual roast of Max. A hundred years of curses in three languages, fired like a one-woman army.

"I swear," she says, halfway through a handful of popcorn, "we're an endangered species. The good men? Extinct. Fossils. The ones left? Evolution failed them. Fine—Oscar gets a hall pass. Temporary. Renewable yearly."

A weak laugh slips out of me. "Then why do we keep falling for them?"

She flops dramatically against the cushions. "Because the bastards are charming. They make us laugh, say the right thing at the right time—and then bam. You're emotionally invested. Rocking matching pajamas. Swimming in red flags like it's a damn waterpark ride."

I shake my head. "You're not wrong."

My eyes drop to my phone—just long enough to give me away. The screen lights up before I can look away.

Basha tilts her head. "Amaya Lee."

I drag a hand down my face. "Max texted me."

She groans and reaches for my phone like it personally betrayed her. I pull it back.

"Relax—I didn't answer."

Her glare softens—barely. "Well? What's he sending—an essay on *Why I Suck 101?*"

I stare at the screen. The message is long—longer than I expected. My thumb hovers, almost setting it down.

"I'm not sure I'm ready to read this," I admit. But I clear my throat and read it aloud:

> **Max:** Amaya, I need to say this clearly. I was fucking wrong. I should never have grabbed you. I should've listened when you told me not to drive after drinking too much. I acted like a complete asshole.
>
> **Max:** I made you feel unsafe and that's something I'll never forgive myself for. You didn't deserve any of it. I let my anger and my own issues bleed into us and hurt you. That's on me. I take full responsibility. I don't expect you to fix me. I need to fix myself. And I will.
>
> **Max:** No matter what happens between us, I want you to know I see what I did. I just hope, one day, I can prove I've changed. Please, babe. Just let me say this to your face. Let me apologize in person.

The words hang in the air, thick and suffocating.

Basha lets out a sharp breath. "Oh, hell no."

I shake my head. "Basha, it's—"

"Nope. Not today. Not ever." She sits up, suddenly all focus. "Let me explain something."

She points at my phone as if it threatened my peace. "That text? That is a perfectly crafted trap. It's pretending to be deep, all broken-man-on-a-healing-journey. And you, my beautiful, big-hearted, fix-everything Dominican queen, are two seconds away from falling into the oldest trick in the book."

My jaw tightens. "He's not—"

She grabs my chin, turns my face to hers. "Let me finish, Freebird. You are NOT his therapist. You are NOT his emotional support animal. You are NOT his damn rehab center. This man needs prayers, therapy, and maybe an exorcism."

I choke on a laugh. "Basha."

"I'm serious." She steps back, shaking her head. "Men like Max? They don't need love. They need healing. And you are not a hospital."

The words hit hard. Because the truth is… she's right.

If I text him back—if I let him speak—I know exactly how it goes. He'll say the right things. He'll cry. He'll look at me like I'm his peace. And before I know it, I'll be holding all his shattered pieces while mine keep getting ignored.

I groan and press my palms to my face. "Ugh, I don't know, Basha. I'm not saying I'm gonna text him back—not today. Maybe not ever. But part of me wonders if I'll regret not hearing him out. When I'm stronger. When I'm not this hurt."

My voice cracks—angry, raw, confused. One part of me wants to scream. One part wants to cry. One part—gosh I need help—wants to type, send, fix.

Basha laughs—ninety percent judgment, ten percent concern. "Did he, though? Did he actually say 'I'm sorry'? Or did he just trauma-dump to justify what he did?"

I start to answer, then stop. She lifts an eyebrow. "Exactly."

She studies me. "Wait. You're not still in love with him, are you?"

The look she gives is full-on horror, like I just confessed to keeping his hoodie under my pillow and whispering affirmations into it.

"No, no, no." She shakes her head hard. "You're supposed to hate him. Be allergic to his entire existence. Wish him nothing but weak Wi-Fi. If his shadow even *thinks* about your personal space, you better launch a green plantain at his chest. Unripe, girl—the kind that hits like a bad decision and leaves a bruise shaped like accountability."

She pauses, lowers her voice, and taps her temple. "And if you ever run out of plantains? Don't worry. I got a frozen pizza with crust sharp enough to cut through generational trauma. It's basically therapy in triangle form—with extra pepperoni and emotional damage."

Only Basha.

My phone buzzes again. Another message.

> **Max:** I'm really sorry for last night. For the drinking. For grabbing your wrist. I hope you're not hurt.

I stare at the words, my stomach tightening. I tap the message field. The keyboard pops up. My thumb hovers—just hovers. For one second, I almost type something. Almost. But then I remember the way his grip clamped on my wrist. The way I froze.

A dry, humorless laugh slips out. "Right. Like a text is going to undo all that."

Basha tilts her head. "Exactly. This man bruised you—physically and emotionally. And now he thinks a sad little text is enough?" She throws a hand up, exasperated. "If men put half as much effort into therapy as they do into regret-texting, the world would be healed and moisturized by now."

I set the phone down, but the memories rise anyway.

The night he stayed at the studio until midnight, scrubbing dried paint off the floor. The times he brought me food when I was too overwhelmed to eat—without me asking. The way one kiss from him could make everything else disappear. His voice when he whispered my name—low, warm, like honey poured over heat.

He made me feel wanted. Like I was the only thing in the room worth looking at.

And I miss that. I miss *him*.

But then I remember the flash in his eyes. The way his fingers dug into my wrist. The sharp edge in his voice when I told him no. My body didn't respond with love. It responded with fear. I suck in a sharp breath. My stomach knots tight.

Basha cuts me a look. "What?"

"I just…" My throat closes. Then, quieter: "I don't want to be like my mother."

Her face shifts. "What do you mean? Like her?"

She doesn't say the name. She doesn't have to. The silence fills it in. Soledad.

I nod slowly. "She stayed. For years. And I used to think—how could she not see it? But now…" My voice falters. I shake my head. "I'm scared that one day I won't see it either. That I'll make excuses for someone who hurts me. That I'll start believing love means endless second chances—even when it keeps breaking me."

I press my hand to my chest like I can quiet the tremor beneath my ribs. "My heart's too soft, Basha. And I don't know if that's a blessing or a liability."

Her face softens—less tough love, more tenderness. "You're not her, Amaya. You saw it. You walked away. That counts for something." She reaches for my hand. "And the fact that you're afraid of becoming her? That's proof you won't. You're not walking through this blind— you're walking through it awake. And that takes strength, not softness."

Her words settle, but doubt still hums through my bones like static. "Then why does it still feel like I'm about to fall right back in?" I whisper.

Basha sighs and grabs her phone. "Hold up. I need to text someone."

"Who?" I narrow my eyes.

"The CIA. The FBI. NASA. Maybe even the Pope. Because clearly, divine intervention's the only thing keeping you from texting him back."

A laugh bursts out of me—sharp and unfiltered. "You're the worst."

She points both thumbs at herself. "Incorrect. I'm the best."

DING-DONG. The buzzer shatters the quiet.

My heart jumps, like someone yanked the beat out of it. I sit up straight, frozen, breath stuck somewhere between chest and throat. Basha's head snaps toward the door. We lock eyes—wide, startled.

My brain spirals fast. *What if it's him? What if he's standing there with that same sorry face and a box of apology pastries?*

For a beat, neither of us moves. Then her expression shifts. She blinks. "Wait—" A pause. "Shoot. It's Wok & Roll," she breathes, pressing a hand to her chest like she just survived a horror movie. "Damn, girl. You got me out here thinking all kinds of crazy. Don't play with my blood pressure like that."

She exhales hard; the tension snaps like a rubber band. I sag back against the cushions, my body finally unclenching. My lungs remember how to work.

She stands, half-cursing under her breath as she storms to the door. "Girl, we out here jumping like it's a thriller. For what? Some emotionally constipated… protein-powder philosopher?"

She swings the door open like she's ready to press charges. "Sir," she deadpans to the delivery guy, "please tell me you're not Max."

He blinks. "Uh… no?"

"Good. Because I was two seconds from ruining your whole week."

He nods slowly, completely unbothered, like he's seen way worse on the job. "Uh. Your food?"

Basha snatches the bag and slaps a tip into his hand. "Thank you, kind sir. You've officially saved yourself from the wrath of a woman ready to set men on fire tonight."

He blinks, already backing away. "Uh… okay, okay. Bye-bye."

She slams the door shut with her hip and tosses me a look. "See? If anyone's getting past me tonight, it better be Denzel Washington—and even he needs to knock first."

The tension in my chest finally loosens. I laugh.

"You're ridiculous."

"You love it."

She drops onto the couch and tears open the bag. "Now let's eat our weight in carbs while we psychoanalyze your tragic love life. Shall we?"

I grab my container and chopsticks. The second I lift the lid, my stomach hums in gratitude.

Basha moans over her sesame chicken. "Food is my soulmate. Men? Just background noise with good biceps."

I laugh and dip a dumpling in sauce. The warmth spreads through me—not like medicine, but like sunlight through stained glass. Gentle. Restorative. Almost holy.

She digs through the bag and gasps. "Oh, hell yes." She pulls out two fortune

cookies like they're final exam results for our love lives.

"Fate has spoken."

I roll my eyes but take one. Crack it open. Pull out the tiny slip of paper.

Healing is messy, but staying the same is worse.

I stare at it. Too long.

Basha snatches it, reads it, and whistles. "Damn. That basically translates to 'get your life together.'"

She cracks hers, crunching loud and unbothered.

A closed door is sometimes protection.

Mid-chew, she side-eyes me. "Girl. If this isn't about Max, I'll eat the damn paper."

Then, dramatic as ever, she stands, pokes her head behind the couch, and whispers, "There better not be a tiny writer hiding back here typing metaphors for our emotional destruction."

She pops back up, hands on her hips. "Nope. Just dust and my dignity."

I laugh—soft, breathless—but it catches in my chest like a held note. Because she's right. These messages aren't even pretending to be subtle.

I stare down at the slip in my hand. This flimsy thing that somehow knows too much. And maybe it's silly—letting a fortune cookie whisper truth to me. But there's something real in it.

Healing isn't graceful. It's raw. Uneven. Tender in all the places I'd rather build walls. I've never been good at sitting in the ache. I'd rather smooth it over. Patch it up. Pretend I'm fine until the cracks vanish.

But maybe tonight… I let the crack show.

Still, I can't stop thinking about Max's text.

That part of me still wants to believe him. Before I can talk myself out of it, I grab my phone and scroll to the last message.

> **Max:** I'm laying off the expensive wine. It's not worth the hangover or the heartbreak.

I fight it, but a smile slips out before I can stop it.

Basha clocks it instantly and launches a pillow at my head. "STOP. Do not romanticize his jokes. He is not funny. He's a rerun of bad reality TV—predictable, messy, and never worth the rewatch."

It smacks me square in the face. I laugh anyway, then sigh, biting my lip. "He's kind of funny."

I hate that I mean it. I hate that even now—with everything that's happened—my heart softens more at his sadness than it clings to my anger. I hate that forgiveness comes too easily. Like a reflex. Like muscle memory.

And the worst part? I don't know if that's something beautiful in me… or the thing that will break me over and over again.

Max is trying. He's apologizing. He's reflecting. And that's what makes it so damn hard to walk away. For a second, I wish I could believe him. That he'll change. That he'll be better—for me. But love doesn't work like that. I press delete.

Because wanting it to be true doesn't make it safe. And knowing better doesn't make it easier.

Maybe I forgive too easily.

Or maybe… I'm still unlearning what I thought love was.

Chapter Twenty-Three

The slap of my jump rope echoes against the mall floor, steady and sharp. My breath finds a rhythm. My feet barely touch the tile.

I spot sneakers out of the corner of my eye—Maria and Joyce gliding toward me, their usual warm smiles in place. Richard and Paul trail behind, casual but observant.

"Good morning, guys," I say, flashing a small smile, still jumping. I'm hoping they'll take the hint and keep moving. I love them, I do. But today I'm carrying a quiet ache I can't shake, and cheerful feels impossible.

Maria slows, planting her hands on her hips. She tilts her head like she's trying to solve me. "You're not yourself today, Amaya."

Richard steps beside her, adjusting his Yankees cap. "You okay?"

Joyce edges closer. Her fingers brush my wrist, and I pull back without meaning to.

She catches it. Her eyes drop to the faint bruise. "And this?"

I swallow. I didn't think anyone would notice.

Paul doesn't say much. He just quietly watches, reading more than I'm saying. Then, completely serious, he says, "Want me to fight someone?" He cracks his knuckles. "I'll stretch first."

I almost laugh, but the sound dies halfway. What comes out instead is a smile—thin, unsteady. I wish I didn't feel the hollowness sitting beneath it. I hate showing people my pain, but sometimes it leaks through the cracks no matter how hard I try to hide it.

And because awkward moments come in bulk, more people show up—smiling, waving—like this is a chill morning meetup, not an emotional ambush. I open my mouth, then shut it again when another familiar face appears. From where, the ceiling? Wouldn't even be surprised.

Okay. Can the floor just swallow me now?

"It's a long story," I say, giving a tired shake of my head. "But it's nothing to worry about."

Their eyes stay on me like they don't believe that for a second. I feel peeled open.

Maria's expression softens. "I'll be praying for you."

"Oh, me too," Joyce adds, hand to her heart. "We love you, Amaya. You're usually glowing. But today… you've got that look."

"What look?" I ask, trying to keep it light.

"That look. The one behind your eyes. We don't like it."

I draw in a slow breath. "Thanks. I'm okay. Had better days, had worse. Today's… in between."

Richard arches a brow. "Promise?"

"Promise." I scrunch my face into something goofy. It works, a little. The tension lifts just enough.

Maria and Joyce exchange one of their knowing glances before Joyce steps in again. She touches my cheek gently—so gently it stings a little, like kindness I used to crave from Soledad when I had a bad day at school.

"Just take care of yourself, okay?"

I nod. A lump builds in my throat, but I swallow it down and keep jumping.

The second they walk away, the tears come. No warning. No buildup. Just spill over, hot and fast.

✳ ✳ ✳

Throwing myself into work is the only way I know how to keep from unraveling. I move through the studio like I'm on autopilot—setting up for the afternoon clients, adjusting the lights for the next photo session, reorganizing my makeup kits with the kind of focus that borders on obsessive. I sort through the stacks of fabric swatches I use for color analysis—rich jewel tones, muted earth shades, soft pastels. If my hands are busy, maybe my heart won't spiral. That's the plan, anyway.

The chime of the studio door breaks through my thoughts.

"Maggie!" My face breaks into a genuine smile as she walks in, her energy as radiant as ever.

"Girl, tell me why I'm finally embracing my inner diva and booking a full-on birthday shoot," she says, tossing her beautiful red curls like she's auditioning for a hair commercial.

I laugh, the heaviness lifting just a little. "Please. You've *been* a diva. Now you're just giving the moment the glam it deserves—and the photos to match that cover-girl energy."

She smirks. "Exactly. This face needs high-quality documentation while I'm still in my prime."

Then she leans in, stage-whisper serious. "Also, I fully expect to look like I belong in a luxury perfume ad—hair blowing, face glowing and I don't mean greasy-glowing by the way, everything on point. No pressure."

I shake my head. "Maggie, you could roll out of bed and still shut down the town."

"Facts," she says with a wink. "But let's still use the soft-focus filter. Just in case."

We both crack up. And for the first time all day, I forget. Forget Max. Forget the ache. Just… breathe. As she wraps up booking her appointment, the door chimes again.

Ifetayo walks in, glowing in that way she always does. There's something about her presence that calms the room without trying.

"Ifetayo, hey!"

Maggie tosses a look over her shoulder. "Don't forget—nothing less than greatness."

I laugh. "Nothing less."

She points her finger at me like she's handing over an oath. "I'll see you on shoot day. I'm expecting full red carpet energy."

And just like that, Maggie's gone—leaving behind the scent of citrus and sass—right as Ifetayo steps further in, already scanning the space with those candlelit, observant eyes.

The laughter lingers for a beat, but as the door clicks shut, the ache slides back in like it was waiting for me. I press it down, straighten my shoulders, and meet Ifetayo with a smile that says I got you—even if I'm not sure I've got myself.

"Amaya." She smiles. "I need a personal color analysis. I'm done wasting money on shades that make me look like I've been hiding in a basement with no sunlight and bad decisions."

I breathe into the shift, pull my focus tight, and motion toward the styling chair. "You came to the right place, beautiful queen. Let's free your closet from beige crimes and figure out what tones were actually made for you. Your new wardrobe will make your melanin sing."

She laughs, and the sound cuts through the heaviness like a breeze.

I love this work. I get to help women see themselves—*really* see themselves. To play with color and texture, bring visions to life, send people out of here standing a little taller. It keeps the lights on, keeps my heart busy, and keeps my sanity mostly intact. Even when I feel scrambled inside, this work still gives me purpose.

I start draping fabrics—sage, wine, blush, saffron. When her eyes drop to my wrist, I tug my sleeve down on instinct. Too late.

Her voice softens. "How are you doing, Amaya?"

I keep it light, professional. "I'm good. Staying busy."

She doesn't push. Just tilts her head like she's tucking the answer away for later.

"If you ever need anything," she says, gentle but steady, "say the word."

My throat tightens. I grab my water, take a sip, nod. "Thank you."

By the time we finish, she's glowing—spinning in the chair like she just discovered she's royalty. Marigold lights her up. Deep teal clings to her, not like fabric but like recognition—like seeing herself for the first time. She brushes her fingertips over the fabrics again and again, like they've been hiding her reflection all this time

"I can't believe no one told me color could do this," she says. "You're coming with me on my next shopping trip. Strictly for emotional support—and to slap my hand if I even glance at another beige blazer."

I smile. I love that I can still help women feel beautiful—even when I'm struggling to feel it myself.

Before she leaves, she gives me a hug that lingers for an extra second and says more than words do. Her joy hangs in the air after the door clicks shut.

Then it swings right back open.

A guy walks in, barely visible behind a mountain of flowers.

"Uh, where should I put these?" he asks, catching his breath.

I blink. The arrangement is unreal—sun-warmed dahlias, burnt-orange calla lilies, deep plum ranunculus, olive sprigs curling like they're trying to calm me down. And in the center, one oversized sunflower. Bold, bright, unapologetically hopeful.

A small envelope peeks out from the bouquet like it's trying not to look guilty. I reach for it slowly, like lifting something heavier than it looks. Max. Of course. And I stare at the note with the weight of everything I haven't said.

"I sold all my stocks in *Bad Decisions Unlimited* and reinvested in *Do Better Co. and Second Chances Ltd.* Fingers crossed for a good return. Forgive me? —Max"

I let out a laugh I didn't ask for. Damn him. Of course he'd try to make me smile with a joke. And worse? It worked. Basha would actually murder me if she caught me smiling at his note.

I set the note down and take a step back—from the flowers, from the memories, from the part of me that still wants to forgive too easily. Max has been trying. The missed calls. The voice messages full of regret. The texts—pleading for a chance to apologize in person. I haven't answered any of them. Because I know myself. The second I see him—those stupidly beautiful eyes locking on mine—I'll start convincing myself maybe he can change.

But I don't need to fix him. I need to protect and heal me.

I grab my phone and scroll to his last message. My thumb starts typing thank you, then freezes. I delete it before I can make it real.

Just one reply wouldn't hurt, right? Just a "thanks for the beautiful flowers." A simple "it means a lot to me." But then I remember the grip on my wrist. The way my body didn't feel safe.

I press delete.

Then I grab my keys, flip the sign to *CLOSED*, and walk out.

✶ ✶ ✶

The scent of *arroz con pollo* fills my cozy kitchen, the rich aroma of *sofrito* and simmering spices carrying the island straight to me.

I open YouTube and hover over the playlist. No *bachata*. No *boleros*. Aventura? Absolutely not. I know better than to let Romeo mess with my feelings tonight. I scroll past the sad stuff and tap on some *merengue* instead. Let the rhythm do the heavy lifting.

I move around the kitchen, pretending—just for tonight—that I'm back in Moca. Before heartbreak. Before complicated men with even more complicated apologies. Back when I was just a girl, chasing chickens in flip-flops, playing under mango trees, begging my *abuela* to let me stir the pot on the stove. Back when love was just something you saw in *telenovelas*, not something you had to survive.

After plating my food, I drop into my seat and pull out an old journal.

My handwriting stares back at me—messy, raw, packed with dreams, regrets, and all the versions of myself I've tried to be.

One entry stops me cold. Just one line, standing alone on the page like it had been waiting for me.

Love should never make you feel small.

I set the journal down and just stare at the words, letting them settle into my chest.

I miss Max. Gosh, I hate that I do. But missing someone isn't a reason to go back. I take a slow, calming breath. Close the journal. Pick up my fork. Tonight, I choose me. And for now, that has to be enough.

Even if my heart hasn't figured out what to do with that—yet.

Chapter Twenty-Four

I stumble across the finish line at the Rockland Lake Turkey Trot—lungs burning, sides aching, legs screaming betrayal. Cardio has once again humbled me.

And yet… I absolutely love this tradition. Every year, I show up without training, and every year, I somehow survive. There's something about it—the crisp November air that stings your lungs, the swish of tutus against tights, the goofy turkey hats bobbing in the crowd. A sea of strangers, running together for something bigger than themselves.

It's all for childhood cancer awareness, and that part hits me every time. These kids fight battles no one should face. And as always, I remind myself: if they can face cancer with courage, I can survive five miles with my ridiculous, perfect friends.

Behind me, Basha staggers across the line like she just ran barefoot through a blizzard. Her turkey hat's sliding down her forehead like it barely survived the finish line, and her voice is pure outrage.

"You! Are! Evil!" she wheezes, pointing at me like she's about to file a lawsuit. "Why do I let you talk me into this? Every. Single. Year."

I'm wheezing too, but from laughing. My tutu catches the wind like it's celebrating solo—bouncing and swaying like it finished the race without me. Basha's tutu rides up in all the wrong places—betraying her dramatic meltdown.

"Because it's for a good cause, you love me, and… I bribed you with an obscene stack of blueberry pancakes and mimosas?" I say, still catching my breath.

"Never again!"

"You say that every year."

She glares, tutu migrating north. "Because every year your bad influence ruins my hair."

And yet—she still shows up. She always does. For all her theatrics, Basha has a heart of gold. She'd give you the clothes off her back if you needed them. Sure, she'll complain about the cold every second of this race… but deep down, she loves it as much as I do.

Oscar, who finished long before us looking like a Thanksgiving fashion emergency, is already waiting at the sidelines, phone in hand. He's rocking turkey socks, clashing plaid shorts, and a too-tight hat slouched on his head like it's given up on life.

"Oh, this is absolutely going on Instagram," he says, grinning like someone just stole the last slice of pumpkin pie.

"Smile, ladies—let the world witness this athletic excellence."

I'm tempted to curse at him in both English and Spanish, but I settle for, "Post that, and I'm unfriending you in real life."

"You'll thank me when this goes viral," he fires back, already recording like a documentary filmmaker.

I narrow my eyes. "I hope you step on a Lego. Barefoot."

The crowd buzzes around us—laughing kids, volunteers in neon vests, the smell of cider and cinnamon sugar drifting over from the snack tents. That's when I spot Sana—the world's most patient pharmacist—rocking matching fleece jackets with her husband. She waves like we planned it, though I had no clue she'd be here. I limp over for a sweaty hug.

"So nice to see you, Sana! I didn't know you were running!" I say, breathless.

She laughs. "First year. I feel like I ran thirty miles. And I see you're torturing your friend."

"Tradition," I admit, smirking.

"Tradition sucks," Basha groans.

We all laugh, arms tangled around each other like we just survived something far more dramatic than five miles in turkey hats.

"I'll see you at the pharmacy," I tell Sana, squeezing her one more time.

"You better. I'll have Advil waiting."

We wave goodbye, and I fall back in step with Basha and Oscar. Our post-run ritual is already calling.

"Diner?" Oscar asks, strutting ahead like he wasn't just roasting us minutes ago.

"A stack of pancakes taller than my trauma," Basha groans. "That was the deal."

"And mimosas," I add. "Don't think I forgot the bubbly part of this bribe."

We limp off together toward our favorite greasy spoon—laughing, aching, and more than ready to drown our sore muscles in maple syrup.

I think back to the laughter at the race and then at the diner—Basha threatening to Google *"how to fake your own death before next year's Turkey Trot,"* Oscar documenting our misery like he'd been hired by the History Channel, and the three of us limping out like we'd just survived some epic battle instead of five miles. It was ridiculous. And honestly? Kind of perfect.

By the time I head out again, my legs feel like cement blocks, but I've still managed to pull off my signature pumpkin pie—heavy on the cinnamon and nutmeg, made with fresh sugar pumpkins from the Nyack Farmers Market. Esperanza had one very specific request: *"Make sure the whipped cream is extra creamy, not that light nonsense."*

Basha isn't with me this year. Her parents are in Poland, visiting her grandparents, and she's spending Thanksgiving with Oscar's family in Westchester. I picture her surrounded by his loud, affectionate relatives—already on her second round of turkey and pie, already three opinions deep into a debate she didn't even start, while Oscar's grandmother throws in unsolicited commentary about her hair, her shoes, her life choices. I smile. She's exactly where she wants to be.

Me? I would've been fine alone—just me, my couch, and a marathon of holiday movies where everyone magically finds love in a small town surrounded by pine trees and unrealistic expectations. But the Nouels didn't let that happen. Ryan couldn't make it home, so it's just the two of them tonight, and when Esperanza called, she didn't ask. She said, *"Dinner is at six. Wear stretchy pants, mi cielo."*

She always calls me things like that—*mi cielo, mi tesoro, mi reina.* Each one lands soft and warm, like a hug in word form. She reminds me of my *abuela*, who could turn even a grocery list into poetry if she sprinkled in enough endearments.

Before I even reach the door, the smell hits me—roasted turkey, garlic, citrus, and whatever Esperanza adds that can't be found in cookbooks. Pure magic.

The door bursts open before I can knock. "¡*Mi amor*! You made it!" Esperanza pulls me into a hug that squeezes the air out of my lungs, then immediately zeroes in on my hands.

"Is that my pumpkin pie?"

"Yes, your pie," I say, rolling my eyes. "Because clearly I spent all afternoon baking just for you."

She inhales like she's judging a baking competition. "Good girl. Now let me see the whipped cream. If it's that light nonsense—"

"It's full-fat," I cut in, lifting the container. "I know better."

She beams, victorious. "That's my girl."

Inside, the dining table looks like something out of a magazine—burnt orange and deep red accents, flickering candles, soft music humming underneath it all. The whole house smells like Thanksgiving and love.

Mr. Nouel is at the stove, stirring something rich and velvety. He wipes his hands and greets me with a quick hug. "*Bonsoir, ma fille*," he says warmly, eyes already drifting toward the pie. "Esperanza's been talking about this all day."

"As I should," Esperanza declares, chin high.

Later, we settle at the table, candles flickering, and Esperanza takes Mr. Nouel's hand, then mine, her eyes closing with quiet purpose.

"Yes, Lord, we thank you for this feast, for our health, and for the good people in our lives who remind us that love and laughter are the best side dishes to any meal. We pray for those in need around the world, Marcel's family in France, my family in DR—even the ones who think the shoes I send are too small and the coffee's too bitter. Bless them, Lord. Give them gratitude—or at least better taste buds."

I bite back a laugh, the warmth of it bubbling up anyway.

She pauses for dramatic effect, then smirks. "And Lord, bless Amaya here, who came bearing the world's best pumpkin pie, and help her remember that no matter how creamy the whipped cream is, it's still no match for the sweetness she brings to this table. And bless our

Ryan, wherever he is—hopefully eating something half as good as this. Amen."

My cheeks burn.

Mr. Nouel lets out a soft chuckle, lifting his glass. "Amen to that."

"Amen," I mumble, hiding the stupid grin tugging at my mouth behind my napkin.

Dinner is everything. The turkey, marinated with Dominican *naranja agria*, bursts with citrus and spice. The *arroz con gandules*—lined with plantain leaves the way Esperanza's grandmother taught her—has this subtle touch of coconut that makes me want to smuggle out leftovers. Esperanza even sneaks plantain into her stuffing, like only she can. And Mr. Nouel's mashed potatoes? Silky, indulgent, laced with Gruyère and roasted garlic. Basically, sin on a plate.

Halfway through the meal, Mr. Nouel lifts his glass of *vin chaud*. The air swirls with cloves, cinnamon, and warm red wine, the kind of scent that feels like it could stitch a family together.

"To gratitude," he says. "For health. For laughter. For the people at this table. For what we had, what we hold, and what's coming."

We clink glasses. For a moment, it's all warmth and candlelight, laughter and love.

Esperanza smiles at him, then winks at me. "And for pumpkin pie, because apparently I'm not the only one obsessed with it."

We laugh, glasses raised, and I take a sip. The spiced wine blooms warm in my chest, but it's more than that. It's the way his words linger, wrapping around me like something I didn't know I was still missing—a seat at a table that feels like home.

Mr. Nouel clears his throat, as if shaking off the weight of his own words.

"Ryan's company is doing well," he says casually, like he's just giving the weather.

I nod along, grateful for a full mouth.

He takes a slow sip of wine and sets the glass down.

"He's buying property in Nyack."

The words land heavy, louder than the clink of silverware.

The table seems to exhale. My fork freezes midair. "Wait, what?"

Esperanza sips her wine, watching me over the rim of her glass. Her look is smug and soft all at once. "I told Marcel—he'll be back the second he realizes what he left behind."

It hits me like a match to dry sugarcane—fast, hot, impossible to ignore.

Ryan's coming back? Why didn't I know this? *Why do I care?*

Mr. Nouel lowers his glass; his tone drops. "Ryan's heart has always been good, Amaya. When his mother passed... he buried himself in work. I prayed God would protect him. And He did."

That lump rises in my throat before I can stop it.

He hesitates, then adds, "I know you two were close. And I never wanted to meddle. But I'll admit... I always hoped you and Ryan would end up together. Maybe even give me grandbabies."

I nearly choke on my drink.

Mr. Nouel isn't usually the type to say things like this out loud. How many glasses of *vin chaud* does it take for confessions like that to slip out?

Esperanza jumps in without missing a beat. "Of course he regrets leaving, Marcel. What's not to regret about this beautiful, hardworking Latina? You think he wakes up every morning happy with his choices? *Por favor.* Men are stubborn."

I let out a soft laugh, the kind that tries to sound casual but doesn't quite stick. Esperanza's words don't slide off me the way they usually do. They settle—low, heavy—like they've just been waiting for their turn.

Maybe it's the wine. Maybe they're just being sweet. They can't seriously think Ryan regrets leaving... right?

Mr. Nouel sighs, swirling his glass like it holds the kind of wisdom you only get after decades of heartbreak and hope. "He built that company from the ground up. But I've always wondered if he regrets what he left behind. I saw the way he looked at you that night, *ma fille.* I may be old, but I'm not stupid—I know love when I see it."

Something knots in my ribs. Five more miles in a tutu would almost be easier than sitting through this.

Before I can answer, Esperanza refills my glass and changes lanes entirely. "Marcel had a health scare recently. A small one. But there was talk of a 'peace-maker.'"

I freeze. "Wait—what? You mean a pacemaker? Why am I just now hearing this?"

Mr. Nouel waves it off like he's brushing crumbs from his sweater. "Just a scare. Nothing serious."

Esperanza exhales so dramatically she could blow the whipped cream off a pie. "That's what he says. But Ryan was worried sick. And you know how men are—they think ignoring things makes them disappear."

And suddenly, it clicks. Maybe that's why Ryan's coming back. Not just for work. Not just for appearances. Because of this. Because of his dad.

I reach across the table and place a hand over Mr. Nouel's. "I'm so sorry. If you need anything—a ride to the doctor, help at the bakery— just say the word."

He smiles softly. "You're too good to us, *ma fille.*" He pats his chest with mock pride. "Look at me—I'm still standing, still handsome, and I've got at least thirty more good years left. Maybe forty, if Esperanza keeps feeding me like this."

Laughter ripples around the table, the tension momentarily eased. He shifts the conversation to my studio, asks about my family in DR, and I nod and answer, but my thoughts are somewhere else entirely, turning and turning, restless as a dryer drum.

Ryan is coming back. Not just for business. Not just to check in. And I have no idea what to do with that.

✷ ✷ ✷

I'm home now, but part of me is still at their table.

I hang my coat on the hook and let silence settle. My stomach is full, my cheeks still warm from Esperanza's kisses and Mr. Nouel's soft smile. And yet… the quiet stretches too wide. It always does. Holidays have a way of sending silence hunting for me afterward.

Thanksgiving is the worst offender.

I close my eyes, and just like that—I'm back in Haverstraw. Somebody's yelling over the blender. Tíos arguing about who's buying the next bottle. Tías locked in a lifelong rivalry over whose seasoning reigns supreme—each one secretly convinced it's theirs. And always, without fail, someone sneaking crispy skin off the *pernil* before it even hits the table.

Because it wouldn't be a Dominican Thanksgiving without *pernil.* And turkey. And at least three versions of chicken—*guisado, roasted, chicharrón-style.* Add *chivo, longaniza* sausage, beef (no cut specified, just

The Last Time I Run | **177**

carne de res), *pastelón, moro, arroz con gandules,* and enough *ensalada rusa* to dye your soul pink. And don't even ask why it's called Russian salad. I asked Abuela once. She looked me dead in the eye and said, *"Porque sí."* Because yes. Translation? Mind your business. Eat and be grateful.

Dominicans don't do "just turkey." We turn Thanksgiving into a block party. Somehow, there's always a random neighbor claiming to be *primo de concón.* No one remembers inviting him, but he still leaves with three to-go plates like it's his constitutional right.

I miss it.

The music. The dancing. The terrible karaoke that turns into bachata circles by 1 a.m. and merengue battles by 4. Cousins too cool to dance—until the rum kicks in. Then it's elbows, hips, regret. Always one tío or tía who swears they can take on the teenagers when the *dembow* drops. The knees never win. But the confidence? Bulletproof.

I miss the noise. The love. The everything. And most of all… I miss them.

Even the ones who gossip louder than the music. The ones who hug like they're checking you for broken ribs. The ones who call me *flaquita* like it's both a compliment and a diagnosis. I miss them because they were mine. Because they were the soundtrack to every holiday I ever loved—before Soledad turned the volume down on that part of my life.

She didn't just hurt me. She stole those moments too. And I hate her for that. I really do.

I open my eyes and swallow the ache. It's been years since I danced with my cousins until sunrise. But I still feel the music in my bones.

I sink into the couch, still full—but it's not just the food. It's the memories pressing against my ribs. My journal waits on my lap, pen hovering like it's daring me to tell the truth. I take a breath and begin.

> Hey Sofia,
> It's Thanksgiving night, and I can't stop thinking about what I've lost—and what I still hold.
> Gratitude is strange. It settles beside heartbreak, walks with longing. It doesn't erase the ache—it only softens the edges.
> Tonight I sat at the Nouels' table. Candles, laughter, food that tasted like love. For a few hours, I felt safe. I felt loved. I felt… like I belonged.

The words hum on the page like a door left half open.

The room exhales. My phone doesn't.

I close the journal and reach for my phone, planning to scroll the studio's Instagram. First, I clear out texts—promo codes from stores I never unsubscribed from. Then Basha. A string of goofy selfies with Oscar across a Thanksgiving table one dish away from collapse. I smile.

And then…Ryan.

Ryan: Happy Thanksgiving, Amaya.

That's it. Two words. No emoji. No question mark. No pressure. And yet, it lands like a soft knock on a door I thought I'd locked.

I don't respond. Not yet. But my eyes don't leave the screen.

He's coming back—to buy property—after all this time away. And something about that feels different. Maybe it's because he left right after we fell apart—when I still believed we were forever. I hope he knows the version of me he left isn't the version he'll find.

I set the phone down and exhale slowly.

The room is warm, the lights soft—but the ache finds me anyway. I thought I'd already made peace with missing my family in Haverstraw. So why do the memories rise again—louder this time, like my heart isn't finished saying goodbye?

I remember the exact day I stopped going back. Not because I stopped loving them, but because I finally started loving myself. I chose peace over proximity.

They meant well. They always did. But the few times I tried to speak my truth, someone would smile gently and say, *"Amaya, just let it go. Life's too short. That's still your mother."*

As if letting go were a switch you flip when the noise inside gets too loud.

Maybe they were right, in their way. But I couldn't keep showing up where my silence was more welcome than my healing. Peace isn't something you buy. It isn't something you fake. It's something you seek, something you fight for. And sometimes, it costs everything. Even the people you miss most.

In a perfect world, I'd go back. Pop in for *café con leche*. Laugh with my tías. Dance with my tíos. Hug my cousins until they complain. But the fear of running into Soledad… of seeing Fernando again… is heavier than the ache I carry now.

So I love them from here. From memory. From peace.

I glance back at my phone. Ryan's message glows on the screen, patient. Waiting. And I hate it—how no matter how much time passes, no matter how far I've come—his name still knows exactly where the softest parts of me live.

I shut the thought down. Hard. He's not back. This isn't about me. He's just… looking at properties. A maybe. A someday. Not a return. Mr. Nouel's health scare rattled him—how could it not?

I tap out a reply.

Me: Thx—Happy Thanksgiving to you, too.

I hit send before I can change my mind.

Life isn't about forgetting what broke you. It's about guarding the peace you fought for.

Chapter Twenty-Five

I walk down the narrow hallway toward Crystal's office, each step heavier than the last. The air shifts—dense, unwelcoming—like it knows I've been avoiding this. *Why am I even doing this?* The question won't quit; it grows louder with every step. I want to turn around. To run. To disappear back into the silence that's kept me safe for years. But my body keeps going.

At the door I stop. My hand hovers above the handle. Fingers trembling.

This is a mistake. Too late. Too hard. I'm not ready.

Maybe that's just fear wearing different masks—logic, doubt, anger. Whatever makes it easier to stay stuck.

The truth is, I'm already unraveling. Like a rope fraying strand by strand until there's nothing left to hold. And I know the only way out is through. So I take a breath and open the door.

Inside, everything is the same. Soft lighting. Muted tones. A room built to feel safe. But none of it touches the ache today. Everything here whispers, *"You can let go now."* But I can't. Not yet.

I feel like one of those faceless Dominican dolls—painted bright, dressed pretty, meant to sit still and look perfect. No voice. No expression. Just silence, molded into every curve. People think those dolls are beautiful. I used to think so, too. But they're breakable. Beneath the surface, fine fractures creep through the porcelain—lines no one sees until it's too late. And I'm already cracking in places even I can't see.

Crystal looks up. She doesn't rush. Just offers a quiet smile—the kind that says, take your time. I'm not going anywhere.

"Hi, Amaya," she says gently. "You made it. That's enough. You don't have to rush. This space is yours."

Does she know how much it took to get here? How every step down that hallway felt like dragging a thousand-pound weight?

I nod but don't sit. My grip tightens on the strap of my bag like it's the only thing keeping me from floating away. My heart pounds so loud it drowns out thought. Every instinct screams—Leave. Get out. You're not ready. But I stay.

One step at a time I cross the room and lower myself onto the couch, moving as if I might break if I go too fast. *One wrong move and I'll shatter.*

My eyes land on the pillows. I reach for the one that says *Breathe*. Right now, that word feels like oxygen. Beside it: *Joy*—bright and bold—and *Hope*—soft and patient. Today, both feel too far away.

The windowsill catches me. Tall plants reach toward the light like it's the easiest thing in the world. There's one in the corner I always notice—steady, green, fearless. I don't feel like that plant. I feel wilted. Folded in. Hiding in plain sight.

"I…" My voice cracks. I bite my lip to trap the sob clawing up. "I don't even know where to start."

Crystal leans forward. "Start wherever it feels right. There's no wrong way."

I hug the pillow tighter. "I've been carrying this for so long… and I—" My voice gives out. "I don't know if I can do it."

"You already are," she says. "You don't have to carry it alone anymore."

I swallow. My throat burns.

"Crystal, there's something I need to say."

"Go ahead."

I stare at the floor. Can't look up.

"His name is Adrian Contreras."

The second I say it my stomach turns. My hands go cold. I squeeze the pillow until my knuckles ache. Saying his name feels like lighting a match inside my body.

"He was Fernando's best friend. And when I was still a child… he hurt me." A tear slips down my cheek.

"I was eleven, at most. He touched me. Did things I won't describe. In ways I didn't understand—ways no one should ever touch a child."

Silence stretches. Only the ticking clock dares to move. Shame crawls up my spine like cold water.

"Adrian was around the apartment a lot. He and Fernando were like brothers—inseparable, loyal to a fault. Back then, I didn't know about their drug business. That came later. I was still young. Innocent. Just a kid trying to make sense of a world that never made space for her."

I draw a breath. "We all lived in the same building in the Dyckman neighborhood, before we moved to Inwood. Adrian's place was a few floors below ours. One night—for reasons I still don't understand—Soledad, Fernando, and I stayed at his apartment. It wasn't a holiday. No party. No family thing. Just… a night."

I pause. "Adrian lived there with his girlfriend. She was beautiful—magazine-cover kind of beautiful. She was kind to me. But even then I noticed the sadness in her eyes."

My grip tightens. "That night I slept in the living room on one of those old folding cots with a thin, creaky mattress. Even now I don't know why we didn't go home."

I swallow. "Soledad was the kind of mother who'd leave me alone to go clubbing with Fernando. She'd hand me a few dollars for snacks from the corner bodega, then disappear until sunrise. I was used to it. But that night she stayed."

My voice shakes. "And then… in the middle of the night, after everything had gone quiet, I felt a hand press hard over my mouth."

I close my eyes. "I opened them. And I froze." The words tremble in my throat. "It was Adrian."

Crystal's voice stays low. "I'm right here, Amaya."

"He touched me. Violated me. And something in me never came back. I didn't have words for what was happening—I just knew it was wrong."

My vision blurs. "I wanted to cry. But I was terrified. Terrified that if I made a sound, Soledad would hear—and twist it into my fault. That she'd storm out furious—not at him, but at me."

My jaw locks. "So I stayed still. I shut my eyes and let him hurt me." My voice drops to a whisper. "I let him—because I didn't know how not to. I didn't fight. I didn't scream. I was too small. Too scared."

"When children are terrified, they don't always fight or scream. Sometimes they go still, because it's the safest thing they can do. You weren't weak, Amaya—your body chose the only way it knew to keep you safe."

I stare at the floor. "I just lay there, praying. Praying I could disappear. That maybe if I died right then, I'd go to heaven and finally be safe."

My breath is slow and shallow. "I didn't know what to call it then. But my body knew. It was bad. It was dark. It was evil. I shook the rest of the night, silent and afraid."

My eyes drift back to the plant in the corner, reaching for the sun. "I buried it so deep I convinced myself it was gone. But it never left. It stayed with me—like a shadow behind everything I tried to build."

"The next morning, I woke with a pounding in my skull—so sharp it made me squint at the light. I thought it was just the crying or the way I clenched my jaw all night, trying not to make a sound—but the pain didn't leave. Not that day. Not the week after. I didn't know it then, but now I do. That was my first migraine. The first of many."

"I dragged myself to the kitchen and tried to pour cereal, hands still trembling. I spilled a few drops of milk. Just a few. But it was enough. Soledad slapped the bowl off the table and screamed like I'd ruined her whole life. I stayed quiet. Pretended I was fine. Cleaned up with shaking hands while she lit a cigarette and cursed. And underneath it all, I was terrified of her—terrified in a way that went deeper than the slap, deeper than the yelling. Even after all this time, the part of me that fears Soledad never left. Seven years since I last saw her, and she still lives in my chest like a shadow I can't shake."

My grip tightens around the pillow. "It's haunted me, Crystal. All these years. I still can't shake it."

"You were a child, Amaya. You didn't let it happen. You survived in the only way you knew how."

"I never told a soul. I thought no one would believe me. Especially not Soledad. She'd say I made it up. Or worse—beat me for it."

Crystal stays quiet, giving me space. Time slips. The clock hands move; we don't. The room feels suspended, like time has paused so I can finally speak what's been unspeakable.

"After that night I went silent. Shut down. Like I was back inside that tiny body, trying to survive all over again."

My hands tremble in my lap.

"You deserved to be protected, Amaya. You deserved to be believed. The way you were hurt—and then ignored—was wrong, and I'm so, so sorry."

She reaches for a tissue and sets it in my hands. "You did what you had to do to survive. That was not your burden to carry. You carried it alone for far too long, and I want you to know I see you now."

I take the tissue with shaking fingers and try to breathe.

She waits. "Would you like to pause here and take a slow breath, or do you want to keep going? Either way, we'll stay with this together."

I shake my head slowly. "Keep going."

"I didn't want to be a burden," I whisper. "I just wanted someone to see the storm… and not treat me like the rain was my fault."

My fingers tighten around the tissue. "I remember the night I told Soledad about how Fernando tried to kiss me—cornered me in the Inwood bathroom, towel hanging too slow on his hips. It wasn't just a kiss; there was a look in his eyes that promised more. I had rehearsed the words a thousand times, wondering if they would even matter. I had nothing left to lose. Adrian had already broken something in me— I couldn't let Fernando finish the job. At first she acted like she cared. She screamed at him. Threw something. Called him a sick bastard. For a second I believed her. I thought maybe this was it—the moment everything would change. I let myself believe she'd be softer. Like a real mom."

I squeeze the pillow. "I believed I mattered enough for her to choose me over a man," I say, and it hurts to say.

"But the next day… everything changed. I was washing the dishes, listening for every creak in the floor, still on edge—like any second he'd sneak up behind me. I kept my back straight, my breath tight, still scared he'd be right there—silent, grinning, waiting."

I pause. "Then I heard Soledad scream. I didn't know what it meant—if he'd hurt her, or if something worse had happened. I panicked. Grabbed a knife from the rack and slid it into my pocket. I didn't even know what I was going to do with it. I just needed to feel like I had something. Some kind of defense. Some way out."

My heart kicks against my ribs.

"I wanted to run. To scream for help. But I didn't even know what kind of help I was looking for. Instead, I slowly walked toward her bedroom. My shirt trembled with me."

The memory takes the air from my lungs.

"The screaming didn't stop. I knocked… but I didn't wait. I opened the door slowly, terrified. She was on her knees by the bed, crying so hard her whole body shook. Fernando was there too—sitting, stunned, like the world had just tilted sideways. And Soledad… she was screaming Adrian's name. Over and over."

I look past Crystal, watching it happen all over again.

"For a split second I thought maybe she'd found out about Adrian. Maybe she knew what he did to me years ago. Maybe she was screaming for me. Then she turned to me—eyes wild, like she'd seen death itself— and said my name. Then she told me. He was dead."

I let the silence breathe.

"Shot. Killed. Gone."

My throat burns as I try to swallow the tears, but they break loose anyway. Grief and fury braided together—too tangled to pull apart. "I didn't feel anything. Not grief. Not even relief—at first. Just numb. I remember staring at them while they cried—and feeling nothing. Later, alone in my room, I exhaled. That's when it hit me: a quiet, deep relief. I was glad he was dead. Glad the bastard was gone for good. Glad he'd never touch me again. But I couldn't show it. I swallowed that relief like poison and wore a mask of silence while they mourned him like a saint."

I shake my head slowly. "The sobbing continued from Soledad. I went to her. Knelt beside her. Put my hand on her back. Not because I wanted to. Not because I cared. Because it felt like duty—the kind you perform out of fear, not love."

"Fernando helped her up. They held each other, cried, fell apart— together."

I stare at the floor, back in that spinning room. "And I just stood there. Empty. Erased."

I look at Crystal. My voice barely rises above a whisper, but it carries everything. "She forgot. Just like that. Like Adrian's death erased my words too. She pushed me closer to Fernando, like standing near him could stitch our 'family' back together. What I'd told her about Fernando the night before—gone. Maybe that was her twisted version of moving on. Or maybe it was easier for her to pretend she never heard it at all. That the man she chose again and again, was ready to abuse me. But all it did was prove what I already knew—she'd choose silence, choose him, choose anyone… before she'd ever choose me."

"She still seemed angry at Fernando, but all her grief—every last tear—was for Adrian. The man who stole something from me I'll never get back."

I inhale raggedly, breath catching like barbed wire. "I felt betrayed. Alone. And instead of being comforted, I had to watch Soledad mourn the man who violated me… and hug the man who tried to do the same."

I press the pillow to my chest. "I wanted to scream. To tell her how wrong it was. But I couldn't. I couldn't move."

My voice drops, hollow. "I felt invisible. Like I didn't matter. I just wanted to disappear."

She nods, eyes steady. "I'm so sorry that happened to you. You're not invisible anymore. You're here. Your pain matters."

I lower my voice. "I just wanted someone to see me."

"What you just shared… that takes enormous courage, Amaya. To speak such painful truth is no small thing. I want you to know—I see your strength, even in the hurt. And I'm grateful you trusted me with it."

I nod, a tremor running through my fingers.

"You're not alone in this anymore," she continues. "Healing begins with being seen, and you're doing that—right now."

The tears come again, but this time I don't fight them. I don't hold them back.

Crystal leans in. "It makes sense that you feel this way. When your pain is ignored—when no one stops to ask what hurt you—it leaves a wound deeper than the harm itself. But Amaya… your hurt is real. Your feelings matter. Just because no one named your pain doesn't mean it wasn't there."

Her words hit slow and deep, like rain soaking dry plantain fields after a long drought—the kind my father used to pray for.

"I wish she could understand," I whisper. "To know what it's like to be standing there, screaming without sound—right in front of someone who never sees you."

Her expression softens into a quiet sorrow—the kind that says, *I hear you. I believe you.*

"Remember, healing isn't a straight path," she says. "It's messy. It's slow. It asks you to sit with what you've lost—and what you never received. You're allowed to grieve that. You're allowed to want recognition, even if it never comes from the one person who should have given it. That doesn't make you weak. It makes you human."

Her words settle in my chest like warm light breaking through fog.

And for the first time, I begin to understand that letting yourself feel isn't weakness. It's the first stitch in healing.

Chapter Twenty-Six

Part of me almost didn't show up.

I'd left Crystal's office earlier feeling cracked wide open, like I'd spilled something I could never take back. I sat in my car for a long time debating whether to drive home and disappear under the covers.

But life isn't just about what you feel—it's about showing up anyway. Because no matter how heavy your story seems, someone else is carrying something too. Sometimes worse.

As soon as I walk in, Elana catches my eye and flashes a warm smile. Across the room, Caty is already delegating tasks to a circle of eager volunteers. They run this place like a well-oiled machine—every person who walks through the door receives more than a hot meal. They receive dignity. Care.

Volunteer chefs from local restaurants rotate in and out, turning donated ingredients into something extraordinary. The scent of fresh bread and simmering soup drapes over the room like a quilt stitched with memory.

I've been coming here for years, slipping into the rhythm whenever I can. The clang of pots, the hum of conversation, the bursts of laughter—it all blends into a comforting kind of chaos.

Peadar, an Irishman with a thousand jokes etched into the lines of a face mapped by time and laughter, bumps me with his elbow as he pulls plates from the dishwasher for me to dry.

"What's got ya lookin' so serious today, lass? Lose a bet, or just thinkin' too hard?"

I smile, shaking my head. "Just thinking, Peadar. Now mind those hot dishes."

He smirks, stacking plates like he's racing the clock. "Ah, thinking's dangerous. Leads to all sorts of trouble. Best stick to scrubbing—when that goes wrong, you don't get heartbreak. Just soap bubbles."

I laugh, handing him a towel. "How do you move so fast? Did they plug you into the coffee machine again?"

"Nah, lass. Just built different. Old bones, high speed."

"More like adrenaline and Irish coffee."

He winks. "That too."

He passes me a pan still steaming from the rinse. "Careful there. You drying dishes or givin' 'em a massage?"

I roll my eyes. "Shh, we're having a moment."

His laugh rumbles through the kitchen—and, like always, it's contagious. The other volunteers crack up too. From beyond the doorway, I catch faint echoes of the dining room—voices rising, chairs scraping, a burst of laughter spilling over the clatter of dishes.

Funny how life throws you from one place to another without warning. A few hours ago, I was breaking down in Crystal's office. Now I'm here, gripping a dish towel like it might soak up more than just water.

I pause and take it all in—the clatter and chatter, the gentle kindness carried across bowls of soup, the gratitude in the guests' eyes met with smiles free of judgment.

This place reminds me that no matter how lost I feel, I can still show up. Still be of use.

I say my goodbyes and promise to return soon.

✳ ✳ ✳

I step out of the car, and the cold air hits my face like a reset button.

I'm still carrying the weight of therapy—everything I said, everything I let rise to the surface—but out here, beneath the open night sky, there's space to breathe again.

Nyack's village center glows in soft golds and icy blues, like something pulled from a snow globe. Cobblestone streets glisten with frost. Wreaths crown every lamppost. Candlelight spills behind frosted windows. Holiday carols drift from the shops, stitched into the air like memory.

It's beautiful. Quietly magical. And it presses something raw in me—a bruise I'd forgotten was there.

The Christmas Market hums with life—locals, tourists, children bundled like tiny marshmallows, couples holding hands beneath the lights. I wave at a few familiar faces. Nod at others. The scent of roasted chestnuts and cinnamon curls through the air, warm and sweet, softening December's sharp edge.

Then another scent cuts through everything. And it stops me cold. *Plátanos al caldero.*

I inhale. Deep. Slow. My breath clouds in front of me. And suddenly, I'm not in Nyack anymore.

I'm a child again, barefoot in my grandmother's kitchen, watching Abuela stir her *caldero* like it was a sacred ritual. Sweet plantains sizzle in brown sugar, caramelizing into deep amber.

"Don't you ever use white sugar for this dish, my beautiful Amaya," she'd say, lifting her spoon like she was passing down more than a recipe. "*Solo azúcar prieta.*"

She never explained why, only that it was the way she'd been taught. Maybe it was her mother's rule. Maybe her grandmother's before that. Maybe tradition didn't need a reason—just devotion. She'd drop in a few cinnamon sticks to steady the sweetness—though I always sensed she longed to add more. But when you grow up counting sticks, you learn to stretch flavor like faith. And always, a pinch of salt—tossed like a blessing.

That tiny kitchen, worn and holy in its own way, would fill with the scent of her—of home. Her *calderos* weren't just pots. They were history, blackened by years of feeding generations, carrying stories, holding together what life tried to break apart.

I can still see her hips swaying, gently, to music stitched into her soul. *Boleros* that made her eyes shine with memory. Songs of praise rising like prayer from the radio. Her hands moved with grace, adding a pinch of this, a splash of that—never measuring, always knowing. Recipes written in her bones.

It wasn't cooking. It was worship. It was poetry.

My chest aches with longing. I miss her. I miss how she could turn an ordinary meal into something holy. I miss my father. My cousins.

The way my name used to sound—soft, safe, spoken in voices that held love. I miss a life that feels out of reach now, like a story I once knew by heart but can't quite recite anymore.

Christmas has always been complicated. Bittersweet.

Memories rise like steam—faint moments with Soledad that weren't all bad. *Té de jengibre* steeping in the air. Ginger and cinnamon clinging to my skin. She'd stand by the window, cigarette in one hand, steaming mug in the other. *"It soothes the stomach and cleanses bad luck,"* she'd say, to no one in particular.

But nostalgia is cruel. It clings to the warmth and blurs the rest.

I've said this before—thought it, written it, even spoken it out loud in therapy. But some truths don't fade after one telling. They circle back, louder with each season, demanding to be felt again.

Because the truth is, when I ran from Soledad, I didn't just run from pain. I ran from every version of family that should've protected me. My father's people—still on the island, too far to save me. My mother's family in Haverstraw—too close to help, too quiet to question.

I love them. I do. But seven years later, I still keep my distance.

I can't risk bumping into Soledad… or enduring another gentle-but-persistent push to forgive from relatives who only know the watered-down version of my life. The highlights—not the hurt. The echo—not the scream. Their hearts are in the right place. But they never had to live inside the wreckage. They know a sprinkle of truth. Not the storm.

How do you forgive someone who's never admitted what they did? Soledad never said sorry. Never named the damage. But somehow, my family expected me to move on. As if forgetting were healing. As if silence could stand in for forgiveness. It's always the ones who never stood inside your pain who preach the loudest about letting go.

A heaviness settles in my throat. The wind snaps me back to the present. Above me, strings of lights crisscross the market like constellations. I tug my scarf tighter and shove my hands into my pockets. I should've brought gloves. But I hate gloves. They make my hands feel trapped.

I walk on. Past Milo's Bodega—the only Dominican spot in the village—where soft Christmas *merengue* drifts into the street, alive with the same joy that once filled my grandmother's kitchen. The rhythm carries the island in its bones, and for a moment, it carries me too. It stirs something in me I can't quite resist.

And with it comes another memory. Soledad. Again.

It was one of the few times a year she seemed… softer. Holidays rounded her edges, if only for a moment. I'd catch her dancing, half-smiling, stirring a pot of whatever she felt like making. Maybe the music reminded her of my father. Or maybe of someone else. I push the thought away. I don't have memories of them together. And I don't want them. Easier to pretend the lyrics belonged to someone else.

I stop at a booth selling handcrafted ornaments—tiny painted scenes of Hudson Valley winters. Snow-covered bridges, glowing farmhouses, cottages wrapped in garlands. One catches my eye. A delicate glass French bulldog in a Santa hat. I pick it up, its surface cold and smooth against my palm. Maybe I'll get a Frenchie next year. The thought makes me smile—then I shake my head. Maybe someday.

A child tugs at his mother's sleeve, eyes wide with wonder. She bends low, smiling like he's just handed her the world. And for the briefest second—barely a breath—something tugs inside me too. Not envy. Not longing. Just… a sting. The kind that whispers, *you were never held like that.*

"Perfect night for cider, huh?"

The words pull me back. I blink, turning toward the voice.

A vendor stands behind a steaming pot of spiced cider, smiling as he ladles the drink into a paper cup. Cinnamon and cloves rise with the steam, curling around me like a hymn from childhood—warm, familiar, threaded with a sorrow I never learned to outgrow.

The perfect night for everything, I think. But I just nod and keep walking.

Carolers carry *"O Holy Night"* into the air, their voices drift like prayer. A Salvation Army bell rings somewhere in the distance, echoing hope across the cold.

At a small jewelry booth, I run my fingers over a silver bracelet engraved with soft words: *Courage grows here.*

I don't buy it. But I whisper the phrase anyway. Tuck it into the stillness like a seed.

At the end of the market, I pause. Take it all in—the lights, the music, the way strangers and families and couples move together through the night, as if they've found what I've spent my whole life aching for.

Maybe showing up here is a kind of prayer too.

For a moment, it feels like peace. I inhale. Let it settle in my chest. The weight doesn't disappear. But right now, it loosens.

Maybe this year will be different.

I turn the corner toward my car—and everything in me stops.

Max.

He's only a few feet away, hands buried in his coat pockets. His dark eyes lock onto mine like he's been standing there—waiting.

The market lights slide across his face, catching the stubble on his jaw, the sharp edges that used to make me stare longer than I should have.

My heart kicks hard against my ribs, torn between running and staying. I didn't expect this. I didn't plan for him.

"Max." My breath fogs between us.

His voice is low, uncertain, like he's not sure he has the right to say my name. "Amaya."

I fold my arms across my chest. The air thickens between us— heavy with everything we never said. Everything I'm not ready to feel.

"I stopped by your studio earlier," he says, stepping closer. "You were already closed."

His voice is low. Gentle. Dangerous in the way it reaches places I don't want touched.

"I've been busy," I answer—too quick, too flat.

He nods, eyes searching mine. "I've been trying to reach you. Calls. Texts." He pauses. "But you know that."

Before I can reply, someone bumps into me from behind. "Sorry!" a teen calls out, already disappearing into the crowd.

I stumble, thrown off balance—and Max moves fast. His hands close around my arms, with a heat I wish I couldn't feel, one that remembers every version of us I tried to bury.

And suddenly, it's too much. His touch. His scent. The way he doesn't let go right away.

Our eyes meet, and in that instant, the past presses hard against the present—the grief, the pull, the old version of me colliding with this one, the one who swore she was done with him.

"Are you okay?" he asks.

I nod. Step back. Break the contact.

"There's nothing to talk about, Max."

Something shifts across his face—hurt, maybe. Regret. But I don't let myself look too long.

This isn't over.

Chapter Twenty-Seven

I should've left a damn minute earlier.

That's the thought pulsing through me as I stand frozen at the edge of the Christmas market, heart still pounding from the way his hands steadied me—like they remembered what it felt like to hold me. His grip had been warm, solid, achingly familiar in a way I didn't want to admit.

Max hasn't moved.

He's just a few steps behind, watching me like he's searching for the words I refused to let him say.

String lights scatter gold across his face, catching on the stubble I used to trace with my fingers when everything felt safer. He's let it grow out a bit. Makes him look… rougher. Sharper. Tiny flecks of snow cling to his coat; his hair's a little windblown.

But it's not the looks that get me. It's his eyes. They hold something I'm not ready to look at—regret. Maybe more.

He closes the distance slowly, careful not to startle me. "Amaya," he says, voice low. "You look beautiful."

I fold my arms. "Max."

The space between us tightens. Something unsaid swells in the silence.

He nods toward the cider stand. "Two, please."

The vendor raises an eyebrow. "Man—either you're in trouble or in love."

He lets out a soft, dry laugh. "Maybe both."

I roll my eyes. My mouth almost betrays me with a twitch. Almost. He hands me a paper cup and our fingers brush. I hesitate. He feels it.

"Thought it might keep you from freezing before you tell me how much you hate me," he says.

I take the cup. "It's gonna take more than cider."

His smile fades. "I know."

We stand quiet again. I sip the cider—perfectly warm and spicy. I hate that it tastes so good—that it makes me want to sigh like nothing ever broke. I hate even more that I'm still listening. That some part of me hasn't slammed the door shut for good.

"Can we talk?" he asks. "Not here. My place?"

"Not your place," I say too fast. "And not mine."

He nods slowly. "Okay. So... where?"

I scan the edge of the market. It's quieter here—less music, fewer people. There's a row of benches near a café firepit, soft orange light flickering behind a screen of smoke.

I tilt my head toward it. "There. If you want to talk—really talk— then it's on my terms."

He doesn't argue. He just follows.

We sit, the fire spits softly behind us. The warmth cuts through the cold, but not the space between us. For a second it feels like we're in an in-between place. Not past. Not future. Just this strange little pause.

He looks at me like he's searching for the right door to open. I let him sit with it. Let the silence press in. Then he finally says it.

"I messed up."

"You did."

"I was drunk," he says. "That night at the steakhouse. I wasn't thinking. Everything got too loud in my head and I..." He exhales. "I was an asshole."

"You were worse than that." I don't say it to be cruel. Just honest.

He nods, jaw clenched. "I'm not here to defend it. I've been trying to figure out why I acted that way."

"So why did you?"

He rubs his hands together, like he's trying to warm something that isn't just skin. "Because there are things I buried so deep, I forgot they were still bleeding. But that doesn't make it okay."

"No. It doesn't."

Silence stretches. Now, down the street, carolers have begun singing "*Silent Night*", like the world isn't broken at all.

"You're not the only one who's been hurt, Amaya," he says. "But I know that's not an excuse."

I stare into my cup, watching the steam curl like breath I haven't released yet.

"I'm not here to bleed for you, Max. I've done enough bleeding."

"I know."

"Words don't hold much with me anymore," I say, low. "Not after everything."

He doesn't argue. Doesn't try to defend himself. Just waits. I let the words sit there, heavy, before I breathe in.

"I've got scars," I say, voice calm but clear. "Ones I don't hand out like souvenirs. So if I ever let you in again…" I look up. Lock eyes with him. "You better know what the hell you're holding."

The firelight flickers across his face. His eyes shine, but he doesn't blink. "I do."

"Good."

He takes a breath like he's carrying something heavier than words. But all he says is, "I'm sorry."

I want him to sit with the silence. To feel it like a weight his apology can't lift. But my heart, reckless, stupid thing, still remembers. His taste when he kissed me. The warmth of his touch. The sound of his breathing in the dark. The way he once made me feel like the safest kind of risk.

"I know," is all I give him.

He notices my hands. Trembling. Reaches for one.

And I let him. Just for a second.

His palm is warm. Not possessive. Just… present. Even that feels like a danger I'm not sure I'm ready for. I pull back gently. Not to punish. Just to draw a line.

"I've missed you," he says, barely above a whisper.

I don't respond.

He hesitates, then gestures toward the market. "Maybe sometime I could cook for you. Just dinner. Space to talk. Without all this."

I don't say yes. I don't say no. I just stand and tighten my scarf.

"I'll let you know."

If I stayed another second, I might start believing him again. I can't afford that. So I leave.

I take one last sip of cider, toss the cup, and step back into the street. The wind catches my coat. A child laughs somewhere, cutting through the falling snow and soft glow of lights. I don't look back. Not broken. Not bitter. Just… still here. Still choosing, even if I don't yet know what that means.

I walk. Not far. Just far enough. Away from the fire pit. Away from him. I move through the night like the wind is carrying me along, faster than I mean to, weaving through the thinning crowd, chasing distance. Until something stops me.

A vendor hums softly in her booth, following the carolers' tune, hands busy arranging rows of ornaments. My eyes drift past a tiny wooden dove, then catch on the star hanging crooked beside it—simple, hand-carved, too close to the ones from home.

How simple life was when I was wrapped in innocence and the future felt as far away as the stars themselves.

She keeps humming, caught in her own rhythm, unaware she's brushing against a wound I carry. I keep walking. The market blurs, like a dream slipping out of reach just before I wake.

"Amaya?" I stop. My name again—louder this time. "Amaya!"

I turn. And there she is. Xiomara. Bundled in a puffer coat, curls spilling from beneath her beanie, scarf looped twice around her neck. Her eyes—wide, warm, and stitched with memories of who I used to be—lock onto mine like she's seeing a ghost.

Something inside me folds. Like a part of me I thought I'd locked away just blinked back to life.

"Xio," I breathe.

Just saying her name feels like unlocking a room I'd closed the door on years ago—and finding that everything I left behind is still waiting for me.

She steps closer—cautious, gentle. "Wow. You look… like you. Just older. Braver. Like someone who's been through fire but didn't let it burn her down."

I cover my mouth like it might hold back the tears—or the truth—pressing hard at my throat.

"It's been a long time."

She nods. "I know." Her eyes drop. "Way too long."

We stand there in the hush of flurries, the sidewalk quiet around us. The market crowd drifts past with shopping bags and cider cups, but we don't move.

It's like we've been dropped inside a snow globe—delicate. Once ours. A little cracked.

"I almost didn't say anything," she admits. "Didn't wanna make it weird. But then I thought… screw that. You were my ride-or-die before I even knew what that meant."

A shaky laugh slips out. "Yeah. We really were."

Her eyes shine. So do mine. We don't name it.

"I always understood why you pulled away," she says, quieter now. "From the family. From everything. From me."

She breathes in deep, like she's storing up courage in her ribs. "My aunt didn't just make it hard to breathe, Amaya. She didn't just cause drama. She hurt you. Over and over. And I saw more than anyone thought I did."

She pauses, jaw tense. "When you left, I hated her. I knew exactly why. Every family gathering after that? I acted like she didn't exist. I couldn't even call her *Tía* anymore—not after she blamed you. Like it was your fault for finally leaving. Like you didn't have the right to protect yourself."

Her voice catches, but she doesn't stop. "And when she laughed—actually laughed—about cutting off your phone so no one could reach you…" She swallows hard. "That was the moment I knew I couldn't forgive her. Not then. Maybe not ever."

My throat tightens. My eyes sting. A tear escapes before I can stop it.

"I wish I'd done more," she whispers. "I wish I'd dragged you out of that house myself. But I was just a kid."

Another tear. I wipe it fast, but she sees. Now she's crying too—quiet, but real.

"I hated that you were gone," she says, brushing beneath her lashes. "Some of the family took it personal. Thought you didn't care anymore. But I knew it wasn't about caring. It was about surviving. I never blamed you. I just… missed you."

Something inside me cracks wide open. Again.

She pulls a crumpled receipt from her coat pocket, scribbles something on the back, and folds it slow, careful, like it matters.

She hands it to me. Our fingers brush—and it's like touching a thread I thought had snapped, pulling me back not just to her face but her voice, her laugh, the way she used to smell faintly of coconut oil and cheap vanilla body spray. Tiny things I thought I'd forgotten press in sharp and sudden, like they never left.

"I'm not trying to rush you," she says. "Or fix everything. I just… if you ever wanna talk. Or sit in silence. Or throw a *chancleta* at me like you used to—" She laughs through tears. "—or roast me for still wearing socks with sandals… call me. Please. I miss you."

I take the paper gently.

"I never stopped loving you, Xio. Not even when it hurt to remember you."

She blinks. Her face crumples. And we fall into each other. No hesitation. No pride. Just arms and tears and seven years collapsing between us. We hold on like we used to—tight, messy, all heart. Cry into scarves and sleeves and silence. When we finally let go, it's slow. Reluctant. Like neither of us is ready.

But we both know we have to be.

She looks at me one last time, and I swear the girls we used to be pass between us—just long enough to break my heart.

I nod.

She turns, eyes shining, and walks away—slow, quiet, disappearing into the hum of cider and carols.

By the time I reach my car, my cheeks are frozen. My tears might as well be ice. I slide into the driver's seat and close the door. Everything feels too still. Too loud.

I pull the receipt from my pocket—Xiomara's number. Her handwriting hasn't changed—curved, hurried, like the kid who scribbled *love yous* in the margins of my notebooks.

I stare at it for a long time. Then fold it. Carefully.

And tuck it back into my coat pocket—like something precious I'm not ready to touch again, but don't want to lose.

My hands fall into my lap.

I breathe.

Then lean forward, forehead resting against the steering wheel, and let myself feel it all—the weight. The guilt. The ache of seeing her. The memory of who I used to be.

***

I turn off the kitchen light and drift to the couch, too tired to do anything but fall into it. The cushions catch me. I lie back slowly—coat still on, scarf loosened. Everything aches, but not in a way I can name.

I close my eyes. Suddenly I hear her. Xiomara. Still soft, still bright. Still sounding like the barefoot girl who swore she wasn't afraid of anything. The way she said my name—like it still meant me. Like she never stopped believing it did. The way we held each other, cried into the quiet like it was the only language we had left.

Then Max—his voice low, careful, his apology heavy, firelight on his face like a wish I once whispered into my pillow.

My phone vibrates again. I reach for it this time.

> **Max:** Glad you're home. I meant what I said. All of it. Sleep warm, Amaya. Tonight I'll be praying. For you. For a miracle. For the chance to see you again soon.

I don't respond. Not because I don't want to. But because I don't know how to answer someone who's starting to feel like a memory and a possibility at the same time.

I set the phone down gently on the arm of the couch, pull the blanket over my chest, and let the quiet stretch around me—not heavy, not hollow—just enough to hold me.

Chapter Twenty-Eight

Six days.

That's how long it's been since the cider. Since Xiomara. Since Max. Since everything cracked open and left me standing in the middle of it, unsure what to pick up first.

So I did the only thing I know how to do—I worked.

Back-to-back shoots. Styling racks. Makeup brushes lined up like little soldiers, waiting for orders. I packed my schedule so tight there wasn't room to breathe—color consults, emergency client calls, even a last-minute bridal session that left my shoulders burning and my hands trembling by the end.

I haven't let myself slow down. Because if I do, I'll have to feel it all.

Reflections Studio is thriving—booked out for weeks, word-of-mouth spreading faster than I can keep up. I should be proud. I *am* proud. But busy isn't the same as healing. Or okay. Or anything close.

When I got home tonight, I dropped my bag, kicked off my boots—started to slip off my coat. Then stopped. I don't know why. I unwrapped my scarf, loosened it just enough to breathe, and walked straight to the balcony.

Maybe I needed the air. Or the view. I don't know. I've photographed the Hudson River thousands of times, but always in daylight. Always when the light was kind and the water still. Tonight, I raised the camera and took one shot. Just one.

The river glowed with that bruised kind of blue that only appears just before night falls. I stood there for a while, staring through the lens.

I haven't answered any of his messages. Not because I don't feel anything. But because I feel too much.

Tonight, he doesn't just send words. He sends a link.

Max: *Late Night Blue – Jazz for Slow Minds*

Thought this might match your thoughts today. It matches mine.

I stare at it for a full minute before pressing play.

It moves through me—slow, like a fingertip tracing something tender. Sound slips through the apartment like it's always belonged here. Low trumpet. Slow piano. A saxophone lingering on one aching note too long—like it's apologizing and asking a question I'm not ready to answer. It doesn't just fill the room. It presses closer, like it knows something I haven't said out loud.

I curl up on the couch, coat still on, scarf loosened, legs tucked beneath me as I watch the Hudson glide past like it has somewhere to be. I don't.

My phone buzzes.

Basha: Oscar's picking me up in fifteen. Red dress or black jumpsuit? Also—please say you're alive. And drinking water.

I smile. Barely.

Me: Alive. Sort of. Go with the red Sunshine. Enjoy! xoxo. Call me tomorrow.

I set the phone aside and close my eyes. Sink deeper into the cushions, letting the memories slip in with the sound.

Somewhere in the middle of the trumpet solo, the doorbell rings. I don't move. Not right away.

It's not Basha. It's not delivery. I didn't order anything.

After a long moment, I push myself up. Maybe it's Ifetayo. But when I open the door, the hallway is empty—except for a paper bag hanging quietly from the doorknob.

I glance down the corridor. Nothing. No footsteps. No doors creaking shut. Whoever left it is already gone.

I bring the bag inside and set it down carefully, staring at it like it might shift on its own.

My fingers tremble as I reach inside—and find a small white box, tied neatly with twine. No label. No note. I undo the knot slowly, my heartbeat ticking louder with every pull.

Inside are four delicate pastries that look more like art than food. Glossed. Dusted. Filled with things I can't pronounce but instantly recognize as expensive. Resting on top is a napkin. My name written across it in Max's handwriting. Just *Amaya*—with a tiny red heart drawn beside it.

No *From Max*. No *Thinking of you*. No apologies. Just the simplest thing—like that alone is the message.

I stare. Then lift the box and turn it over. The logo glints in gold: a French name I don't recognize. I look it up.

It leads me to a small patisserie in Manhattan—just a few doors down from Velvet Noir. The jazz club he took me to. The one with the low lighting and slow songs. The one with the booth I can still feel beneath me.

Did he go all the way there just for these? Or was he already at the club? Was he with someone else? Did she laugh at the same song he once said reminded him of me?

I hate that I wonder. I hate that I care. But I do.

I lean in and breathe the pastries in—sugar, citrus, and something floral. But somehow… it smells like him. Or maybe just what I remember of him—warmth, hunger, ache.

I close the box and place it gently on the coffee table, as if it might bruise if I set it down too hard. Then I sink back into the couch.

The music keeps playing, trumpet notes drifting through the room like smoke that doesn't know where to settle. The river outside doesn't pause. It just keeps going. But inside me, the current has gone quiet.

I stare at the pastries, untouched. At my keys beside them. And for a long time, I do nothing.

I think of Xiomara. Her soft, truth-telling eyes, the way she looked at me tonight like she saw everything I'd tried to bury and didn't turn away. Seven years apart, and still no judgment in her face. Just that quiet, familiar understanding she's always carried.

I never told her everything. But I told her more than I've told anyone. She knew where the cracks were and never mistook them for weakness. She didn't look away. She held my half-spoken truths like they were something sacred. She didn't ask why I stayed away. She just looked at me like she always had. Like I was still her cousin. Still hers. Like love doesn't vanish just because you needed space to survive.

I think of Max. And the silence between us that somehow still feels full.

My coat's still on. Half unzipped. Like even my body can't decide. I tug at the scarf, suddenly too hot, but I don't take the coat off. It's holding me together. Or maybe holding me back.

The music makes it worse. The trumpet curves like a hand around my waist, and I remember how he held me—firm, tender… until that night. Until his grip turned into something I had to pull away from. But I still miss him. The taste of him. The weight of him. The way my name sounded in his mouth—like it meant something. And Gosh, I hate that my skin still remembers.

The apartment glows with that amber kind of evening light that makes everything look softer than it is.

My phone rests in my lap. His name glowing quietly on the screen. I don't know what it means—that he keeps showing up like this. Offering small things instead of asking for big ones.

But I think about him. About the way he looked at me under the firelight tonight—like I was something he'd never stopped reaching for. Like he was afraid I'd vanish if he blinked.

It took everything in me not to close the space between us. Not to bury my face in his chest, breathe in the smell of cologne and soap and memory. Not to say yes to something I still don't fully trust.

I'm tired of things breaking. Tired of starting over. Tired of wanting something that might undo me all over again.

But I can't lie to myself—he's still in me. In the music. In the stillness. In the ache I carry like a second skin.

Maybe healing doesn't arrive like a wave. Maybe it drips in—slow and unassuming.

A jazz track. A box of pastries. A name scribbled in familiar handwriting. A memory of someone who reminded you how to be seen.

I don't text Max back. Not yet. But I let the music keep playing. I whisper his name this time. "Maximiliano." Soft. Like a truth I'm still learning how to live with.

I close my eyes again—just for a moment. Long enough to know what I need to do.

I move—like maybe the music will lead the way.

The door clicks behind me. The music follows.

Chapter Twenty-Nine

The playlist carries on, each song blurring into the next, like it knows I'm not ready for quiet yet.

I don't remember deciding to come here. But somehow, I'm parked outside his building, fingers locked around the steering wheel, staring up at the windows like they might confess what I'm too afraid to say out loud.

I told myself I just needed air. A drive to quiet the restlessness. But here I am—still trying to decide if showing up is the same as forgiving.

Eventually, I cut the engine. Grab my keys. Inhale. Exhale. Step out of the car.

His apartment is exactly as I remember it. Clean. Precise. Curated. Like a showroom pretending to be lived in—if you ignore the tension humming beneath the surface.

Everything in its place. Except for the books. They're lined neatly across a shelf by the couch—*Atomic Habits, Can't Hurt Me, The Subtle Art of Not Giving a F*ck*. Books on healing. Discipline. Control. Self-improvement stacked like scaffolding over the cracks.

Were these always here? Or are they part of the new Max—the one trying to rebuild himself from the inside out?

I haven't looked him in the eyes since I walked in. Because the moment I do, the weight of his attention settles on me. Not just watching. Undoing me, thread by thread. Like he could strip away more than clothes.

He's watching me—quiet, searching, like he's trying to read what I won't say.

"You've been busy," I say, nodding toward the shelf.

He exhales. "Trying."

I sink into the couch, arms crossing like armor. "So talk."

Max drags a hand through his hair. "Like I told you at the Christmas Market, I fucked up. That night at the steakhouse. I was drunk. I was out of line. I was a fucking idiot." He stops. Meets my eyes. "But you already knew that."

A bitter laugh slips out. "You're not wrong."

"I'm not here to defend myself. Or make excuses. Just to explain… if you'll let me."

"Explain what?"

He hesitates. "The drinking. The control. The anger."

"I don't need explanations," I snap. "I need to know it won't happen again. That you'll never grab me in anger. That you'll never make me feel unsafe in my own skin."

His jaw locks. "Amaya, I hear you more than you'll ever know."

"Do you?" My voice sharpens, edged with everything I've been swallowing. "Because I don't think you do. I don't think you realize how much that night reminded me of—"

I stop. Breath catching.

Max's expression darkens. "Of what?"

I shake my head. "Forget it. Doesn't matter."

"It does." His voice drops. "Please tell me."

My jaw clenches. I want to look away. To change the subject. To swallow it down like I always do. But the words claw their way up anyway.

"Of my stepfather. Of every man who ever made me feel powerless."

Silence stretches between us, heavy and unrelenting.

Max inhales slowly. "I never wanted to make you feel that way," he says, "I never wanted to be one of them."

"Well," I whisper. "You were."

His shoulders lift with a breath he holds too long, like releasing it might make everything too real. Then he lowers himself beside me, hands clasped between his knees. For a moment, he just sits there, the silence stretching, heavy. When he finally speaks, his voice doesn't sound the same.

"I started drinking when I was a kid." He pauses. "My mom was an alcoholic. My uncle was into harder stuff. I didn't know what drugs were at the time, but I knew what alcohol did. I knew it made people forget."

I hold my breath.

"I'd sneak leftover bottles after parties. Drink whatever was left. Just enough to feel… different." A short, bitter sound escapes him. "Messed up, right?"

I stay silent.

His hands curl into fists. "I've never told anyone what I'm about to say."

Something tightens in my chest—because I think I already know. And I'm not sure I'm ready to hear it.

"My uncle," he says, his voice trembling. "He… he did things to me. When I was little. And no one noticed. No one ever asked."

He swallows hard. "My mother was drowning in her own pain. My father was more absent than present—alive, but never really there."

His voice hardens. "That bastard hurt me in ways I wouldn't wish on anyone. Drinking numbed it. Control kept me from falling apart."

Tears sting behind my eyes. I reach for his hands, gently loosening the fists. My fingers trace the ridge of his knuckle, something steady in the storm. Nothing comes out when I open my mouth. The words are there, pressing against my ribs, but I can't pull them free without coming apart.

His eyes meet mine—as though holding the wreckage of something too fragile to survive. And I understand. Because I've lived inside that silence too.

So I do the only thing I can. I breathe for both of us.

"You're not broken," I whisper. "You were just trying to survive the only way you knew how." It's what Crystal told me once. What I've been trying to tell myself. Saying it to him now feels like testing a truth I'm still learning to hold.

He doesn't respond. His eyes drop to our hands, still tangled—like he's searching for something steady in the mess. Or maybe ashamed to let me see how much it hurts.

My voice barely makes it out. "I was molested too," I whisper, my words trembling like his.

His whole body stills.

"My stepfather's best friend. When I was eleven." I swallow hard. "He died later. Shot in a drug deal. My mother cried for him like she'd lost some kind of saint. To this day, she doesn't know what happened to me—and I don't think she would've cared for more than a day."

A sharp, aching breath slips out. "And when he died, I had to fake sadness. Pretend it was a loss—so my mother wouldn't ask questions. So she wouldn't see the truth written all over my silence."

My voice cracks. "Because if she did… I think she would've chosen him anyway."

Max stares at me like he's seeing me for the first time. Not the polished parts—me. The scarred parts. The stories I never say out loud. And he doesn't look away. Doesn't blink. Just watches me like he finally understands what it costs to carry silence.

Then he pulls me in. I don't resist. I melt—slow, heavy—like something inside me finally exhales. We sit like that for a long time. No words. Just his breath against my hair. My fingers clench in his shirt like I'll come apart if I let go.

It's not comfort. Not exactly. It's recognition—ache meeting ache. Two people realizing they weren't the only ones. And I know this doesn't erase the past. It's not forgiveness. It's just my choice, right now, to stay.

Then his lips graze my cheek. My jaw. My throat. Each touch soft, careful. Like a prayer. Like a question I'm already answering without words.

His voice breaks at the edges. "Let me make this right, Amaya. Please. I swear—whatever it takes… we'll find a way through."

I nod. Barely. There's too much in my throat to speak. His breath is warm against my neck. Ragged. Wanting. Not just of me—of something whole.

"Let me love you the way I should have." His hands tighten. His next breath lands on my collarbone. "I can't stop thinking about you. You're everywhere. Day. Night. You're… in me."

My fingers twitch. Wanting to move. Wanting to trust. But I stay still. Every nerve pulled tight like a breath I haven't exhaled in years.

Then his lips brush my ear. "You're the only one I've ever wanted like this."

And when he kisses me, it's not a demand. It's a question. One I've been aching to answer.

I should stop him. I should walk away. But I don't. Because I know exactly what this is. Not healing. Not forgiveness. Escape. And for tonight, I choose it.

His hands are on me. His mouth finds mine—slow at first, then searching. We fall into that familiar language of grief and longing, want and memory.

The air thickens. Pain and desire pressing into the spaces between what we don't say.

When he carries me to the bedroom—when he moves like I'm something he's afraid to shatter—I let myself believe. Just for now. That maybe love is enough.

✷ ✷ ✷

The sound of the doorbell cuts through sleep. I blink, disoriented.

The last thing I remember was his fingers tracing slow circles on my back, his breath warm against my neck, his heartbeat steady beneath my palm—an anchor I didn't know I needed.

He's already up, moving like he never really slept. He pulls on sweatpants from the floor, stretches, yawns—as if the night never touched him.

I narrow my eyes. "Were you even asleep?"

He smirks. "Nope, watching you sleep. Almost made me behave."

I groan, dragging the sheet over my head. "So you just watched me drool?"

His grin is wicked and unapologetic. "Highlight of my night."

"Creep."

He presses a kiss to my shoulder. "Get up. I ordered food."

I reach out to swat him, too slow to land it. He laughs, already heading for the door.

I stay tangled in the warmth, too content to move. And then it clicks—he ordered food.

"Wait—seriously?" I call, voice still heavy with sleep.

From the kitchen, his voice drifts back—cocky and smooth, the kind of tone that gets under my skin. "Of course, babe. What kind of man would I be if I didn't? Options are limited for night owls, though."

Bags rustle in the distance, followed by the soft clink of takeout containers on the counter. Then silence. A silence long enough to pull me upright.

Moments later, his footsteps draw closer. And then he's there—framed in the doorway, arriving like a slow exhale.

He leans against the frame, that smirk curling where it always lands. "Get your ass up, Amaya."

His voice is low. Playful. Just dangerous enough to make me want to obey.

I groan, dragging the pillow over my face. "Five more minutes."

He walks over, peels the pillow from my hands, presses a kiss to my forehead. "You've got seventeen seconds before I come back in here and carry you to the kitchen."

I peek up at him, smirking. "You wouldn't dare."

He flashes a daring smile. "Try me."

A moment later, he's at the counter, opening containers like he's unveiling a five-course meal. His movements are smooth, confident. His sweatpants ride low on his hips, muscles flexing as he reaches and shifts, as if gravity itself bends for him without effort.

I linger in the doorway, quiet, still, watching the moment unfold like I could fold it small and keep it in my pocket. He glances back at me, eyes trailing over the hem of his shirt draped across my body. His smirk deepens, sharp and knowing. I pretend not to notice, reaching for a pair of chopsticks instead.

"Eat," he says, handing me one.

I reach for it, but before I can take a bite, he slips in behind me.

The warmth of his breath brushes my neck, close enough to raise every fine hair along my skin. His lips graze the curve where shoulder meets throat. I forget to breathe, eyes falling shut, the weight of it sinking deep.

"You keep doing that," I whisper, "and I might start thinking you actually missed me."

He smiles—the kind that barely breaks the surface but says everything without words. His hands linger at my shoulders, grounding me, steady and sure. Holding me like he's afraid to let go. Holding something we both feel but don't dare name.

And then, just like that, he steps back—quietly, as if each inch costs him. He grabs his pepper steak and digs in, like a man starving for more than food. I reach for a fortune cookie.

Max side-eyes me. "Babe, fortune cookies only work if you read them after stuffing yourself."

I smirk, cracking it open anyway. "Maybe I'm starting a new tradition—skip the belly, save the fortune."

He laughs, but his eyes stay on me as I unfold the tiny slip of paper.

A bright flame may burn out before it ever warms the heart.

The words hit harder than they should, sinking like a stone in my chest. I stare at the message, fingers gripping the delicate paper too tight. *Is that what we are? A flash fire—bright, fast, too intense to last?*

I set the cookie down. Quietly.

He picks up the slip, reads it, then lets out a low whistle. "Damn. That's deep for a cookie. I'm officially protesting by not reading mine." But his hand still hovers, restless, near his own.

I smirk. "You're such a rebel."

He taps my nose. "You love it."

I'm about to roll my eyes when I take a bite of shrimp—too fast— and choke mid-laugh. The spice hits the wrong way, sharp and sudden. I cough hard, one hand waving him off, the other gripping the counter.

His eyes widen. "Babe?! You okay?"

Still coughing, I nod, eyes watering. Then a laugh bursts out of me. He watches me, and then he's laughing too—deep and unguarded, the kind of laugh that shakes something loose in me I didn't realize I'd been holding.

For a moment, that's all there is. Not the past. Not the weight we carry. Not the questions waiting. Just this.

Laughter echoing off the walls. The smell of takeout in the air. The memory of last night still soft against my skin.

His laughter fades first. The quiet stretches between us. I glance at him, still smiling, but something tugs at the edge of my chest—a fragile thread of hope I don't know if I can trust.

Because even now, with his hand brushing mine, I can't help but wonder how long something this gentle is allowed to exist.

Chapter Thirty

I sink into the couch; hands curled around the warm cup of chamomile tea.

Crystal offered it a few sessions in—chamomile, she'd said, because some people find it calming. Now it's part of the ritual.

The scent rises—soft, floral, familiar. It reminds me of my grandmother's kitchen at night. The kind of comfort that soothed scraped knees and quieted storms.

Today the tea isn't comforting—it's steeped in truth. And truth doesn't soothe. It stirs everything up.

Crystal shifts in her chair, crossing one leg over the other. She doesn't speak, just waits—steady, patient, watching me with those calm eyes that never rush me.

I take a breath.

"Max and I are back together."

The words slip out before I even realize I've said them.

Crystal doesn't react. No sharp intake of breath. No judgment. No *Are you serious?* Just a blink, and silence.

"Before you say anything, just—just hear me out." I lean forward. "We talked. Really talked. He opened up about his whole past. About everything. And it makes sense now."

She tilts her head slightly. "What feels different for you this time? What makes sense?"

"Why he drank that night at Blackstone. Why he lost control." My chest tightens. "And I get it. The trauma. The anger. The fear. I've been there too. We… we understand each other in ways no one else could."

The story spills out of me in jagged pieces—his mom's depression, her drinking, her death. His father disappearing. His uncle's abuse.

I expect her to nod. To say she gets it. To confirm what I already believe. But she doesn't.

Instead, she exhales slowly, thoughtful. "Amaya," she says gently, "I hear how deeply you care for him. And I also need you to be careful."

The edge in her voice catches me off guard.

Careful? Heat crawls up my neck, my fingers death-grip the mug as if it might steady me. What does she think—that I'm naïve? That I can't tell the difference between love and something toxic?

My jaw tightens. "What exactly are you trying to say?"

She leans forward, resting her elbows on her knees. Her voice stays calm, measured. "Sometimes, when we meet someone who shares our wounds, it feels like love. It feels safe. Familiar. But familiarity isn't always the same as healthy. When both people are still healing, it can slip into something else—dependence, even codependency. That kind of bond can feel powerful… but it can also be dangerous."

My throat tightens. "I don't *need* him to survive, Crystal. I just… I love him."

She nods once. "I believe you. But I also want you to ask yourself— if Max wasn't hurting, if he didn't need saving, would you feel the same pull toward him?"

The question hits something soft and raw. Would I? If he were whole—steady, unbroken—would I still feel this magnetic need to hold him together? Or do I only know how to love what's cracked? Maybe that's why it feels so familiar. Because it's the same pattern—me reaching, him unraveling, both of us mistaking rescue for love.

A knot forms in my stomach. "That's not fair."

She doesn't look away. "It's not about fair. It's about clarity. And about safety—yours and his. Has anything really changed when it comes to the drinking?"

I open my mouth to defend him—to defend us—but the words catch. Because what if she's right? What if nothing's really changed? Nothing comes out.

Crystal rises, walks to the bookshelf, and runs her fingers along the spines until she pulls out a worn hardcover. She turns toward me, her voice gentler now.

"I want you to read something."

She hands it over. *Codependent No More.* Melody Beattie. She presses it into my hands like it might hold the answer to the question I won't say out loud.

"I've shared this with a lot of clients," she says. "Some put it aside. Some skim a few chapters and never touch it again. But a few…"—she pauses, looking right at me—"…a few find themselves in its pages."

I stare down at the cover, my fingers tightening around the edges. This isn't how I thought today would go. I expected a nod. Reassurance. Something soft. I thought she'd say Max and I were soulmates stitched together by survival, and love could patch the rest.

Instead, she's asking me to sit with the questions.

She never gives me what I want—only what I need. Maybe that's why I keep coming back, even when I swear I won't. Not for comfort—the tea never really helps—but for the truth I don't want and can't seem to stop chasing.

Even if part of me still wonders if she'll ever fully understand the whole picture—me, Max, all the tangled pieces we're both trying to hold together.

Even if I don't understand it all either.

✳ ✳ ✳

I barely have time to exhale before Basha storms into the studio like she's on a damn mission, holding two spicy lattes like caffeine is a matter of life-or-death.

"Wake up, Sleeping Beauty. Your long-suffering bestie brings caffeine and judgment."

I shake my head, accepting the cup she basically smacks into my hand. "I was very awake, thank you very much."

She narrows her eyes. "You had that *I'm overthinking my entire life again* face. Start talking. I brought caffeine for a reason."

I hesitate, take a slow sip.

"Max and I are back together."

There's a pause. Her lashes flutter once like her brain's buffering. Then her eyes go wide.

"Tell me you did not just re-enroll in Tragedy 101. Girl, if this is a joke, I'll nominate you for an Oscar."

The latte scorches my tongue. Perfect. My mouth's on fire—and so is my love life.

"Jeez, Basha!"

She points a dramatic finger at me, her voice climbing like she's about to deliver a TED Talk titled *You Said You Were Done.*

"*YOU* ignored his calls. *YOU* said you were done. *YOU* swore up and down you were finally free. And now you're just… what? Wrapped up in his big, sexy arms again—like those same arms didn't leave bruises on your wrist? Like none of that happened?"

She exhales, softer. "I'm scared for you, that's all."

For a second, I hear Crystal's voice in hers—different tone, same warning.

I swallow hard, throat tight. "We talked first! It wasn't like before. He… he opened up. It wasn't just me running back, okay? It felt different. He's different. I'm different." My voice comes out sharper than I mean.

She crosses her arms. "And then?"

"And then we… worked things out."

"Worked things out, or worked each other over?"

I groan. "Why are you like this?"

"Because someone has to keep you from self-destructing," she says, throwing her hands up like it's obvious.

I roll my eyes, but a smile tugs at my lips.

"Look, I was avoiding him because I knew the second I saw him, I'd give in. And… yeah, I did. But not like you think."

Her arms stay crossed, foot tapping, waiting me out.

"It wasn't just some hot reunion," I say, tightening my grip on the cup. "It was hard. Messy. Honest. We didn't fall into bed. We fell into truth. And that scared me more."

She tilts her head, watching me like she's trying to decide if I'm insane or just hopelessly in love. Honestly, she might be right on both counts.

I exhale. "I ran into him at the Christmas Market. It wasn't planned. Not some big romantic moment. Honestly, it was awkward as hell. But then we talked. Like, *really* talked. It was raw. Intense. Necessary. And—Basha, I felt it. I know he means what he says."

She doesn't respond right away. Just studies me. Which says a lot, considering this is the same woman who once interrupted my heartbreak to critique my eyebrows.

Finally, she sighs, shaking her head. "Amaya, my way-too-kind, soft-hearted Freebird …"

I already know what's coming. And yep, there it is.

"I get it. I get that you love him. I get that he's hot. I get that when you look at him, your brain does that thing where it forgets math, common sense, and every tear you've ever cried. But—" her voice drops lower now—"he grabbed your wrist. He drove drunk. He scared you. You cried over him. And not just once. I watched you fall apart day after day. You said you were done."

My throat tightens. "I know. I know what I said."

"So what changed?"

I take a breath. "He did."

Her eyebrow shoots up, the word *Really?* Practically stamped on her face.

"Basha, he's been through some real shit. Stuff he never told me before. His mom, trauma, his whole past. It's a lot. I didn't know how much he was carrying. And yeah, he messed up—big fucking time. But I shut him out before I even gave him a chance to explain. I was so focused on me, I didn't let him speak."

Basha rubs her temples. "So what—he gets a free pass because life's been hard? Amaya, you've been through hell too. That doesn't excuse his choices."

"He doesn't get a pass." I bite my lip. "He knows he messed up. He's not blaming the trauma. He's owning it. And that matters to me."

She stares for another beat, then groans and throws her head back.

"Damn Freebird, you're really in this, huh?"

"Yeah," I whisper. "I wish I wasn't, but I am." The words stick in my throat, but they come out anyway, like they've been waiting there all along. I let out a shaky laugh. "Don't judge me, but I think I'm actually falling in love with that stupid bastard."

"Judge you? Please. I live to judge you." Her expression loses the edge. "But I also love you. Which is why, if he makes you cry again, I will personally march into MAX Fitness, pretend to sign up for a membership, and when he least expects it—BAM. Right hook to the face. That sexy but emotionally stunted mule won't even see it coming."

I burst out laughing. "You'd get arrested."

She shrugs. "Worth it."

I sip my latte, not sure if the warmth in my chest is hope… or denial disguised as cream and cinnamon.

"I really believe he won't mess up again. I just… I do."

Basha sighs, dramatic. "Fine. I'll forgive him too. For now. But just so you know—I already ordered binoculars and a drone to keep tabs on him."

I throw my head back, laughing. Basha may be extra, but she's the kind of extra I need.

She sips her latte, side-eyes me. "Just hope Max knows I'm watching. And if he even thinks about stepping out of line? Let's just say—drone footage plays really well in court."

I nearly spit out my drink, laughing so hard my stomach hurts.

Basha laughs too, eyes shining with that kind of loyalty that never asks for credit. The kind that's carried every one of my breakdowns without complaint. And even now—under all the caffeine-fueled threats and killer one-liners—she's still here. Still watching. Still ready.

Chapter Thirty-One

The studio is alive.

Hairdryers roar, brushes sweep, merengue thumps low beneath the chaos.

The air smells like setting spray, hairspray, and coffee someone reheated one too many times. I barely have time to think, let alone breathe—and honestly? I wouldn't want it any other way.

It's Beauty Angels Day. The day that means everything—a celebration of a dream finally made real, and a chance to give back to Kitchen Angels, the same nonprofit that once fed me when I had nothing.

When I first came to Nyack, I did whatever I could—cleaning rooms at The Nyack Hideaway B&B, walking dogs, washing greasy hair—until I found Maison Madeleine. No family. No backup plan. Just me, hustling like my life depended on it.

Now I'm here. In my own space. Watching women look in the mirror and light up.

For the first time in forever, it actually feels like I made it. Like something finally came full circle. And yet—even with all the noise and laughter—there's still a quiet place inside me where fear waits, patient and familiar, like it's not ready to let go.

Across the street, Basha's salon—Beets Beauty Box—is just as wild. Women go there first for their hair, then they come to me for styling, makeup, and a quick photo shoot. Volunteers from Kitchen Angels are posted up in both spots—sweeping hair, folding towels, washing bowls. We're all sweaty and tired, but no one's complaining.

It's beautiful. It's chaos. It's everything.

Colleen, one of the volunteers—and a kind soul I met my first week at the soup kitchen—passes me with a stack of towels. Back then, we were both waiting for a hot plate. Now she's here, helping.

She pauses just long enough to smirk. "Look at you now, Amaya. A boss lady."

I laugh softly. "And look at you—Colleen with the secured government job, all official and everything."

She lets out a small laugh, her eyes going soft. "Can you believe that? From Kitchen Angels to payroll and pensions." She shakes her head, then her voice softens. "You know, I still remember the first day I saw you there. You were sitting in the corner, writing in that beat-up notebook while everyone else was watching the clock, hoping it would slow down a little."

I pause, surprised she remembers. "You remember that?"

"Of course I do. I asked what you were writing, trying not to feel like I didn't belong there myself." Her smile curves, tender now. "And you said, *'My future.'* I thought, *damn, this girl's either crazy or she's onto something.*"

I laugh, but my throat burns—the kind of laugh you use to keep words from turning into tears. "Guess I was a little of both."

She nudges my arm. "Well, looks like you wrote it into existence. I'm proud of you, Amaya. We both made it out—and now we get to give back."

She glances around the studio—at the mirrors, the light, the chatter and hum of women everywhere. "You know," she says, "I love the name—*Reflections.* It fits you. You used to sit and dream about who you'd become, and now you've built a place that helps other women see themselves, too."

I swallow hard, smiling through it. "Guess it came full circle. And if you keep talking like that, you're gonna make me cry—and then *you'll* be the one fixing my makeup."

She laughs, wiping at the corner of her own eye. "Fair enough— but trust me, nobody wants that. I can barely draw a straight line with eyeliner."

We both laugh. "Duly noted."

She winks and disappears into the back, and for a moment, I just stand there—letting gratitude settle deep and real, like something I can finally touch.

And then there's Basha, of course. Set up camp right next to me like she owns the place. Typical. Zero boundaries, all attitude. And I love her for it.

"My team's got Beets handled," she says, snapping on gloves like she's about to do surgery. "Besides, I couldn't let you have all the fun. Let's be real—I mainly came to drive you absolutely insane."

We barely pause all day, except for a few stolen bites of Carmen and Milo's *pastelitos* and a box of Maison Madeleine pastries. My feet are screaming, but I don't care. Every woman who walks out of here standing taller, smiling wider—worth it.

The studio door chimes, and in floats Willow, my old landlord. She's wrapped in a knee-length knit coat the color of every autumn leaf at once—rust, mustard, and forest green—and her curls are doing their usual thing, wild, unapologetic, free-range.

She's holding a mason jar stuffed with dry twigs, sprigs of winterberry with red berries still clinging, a few curls of pine, and something that looks suspiciously like she pulled straight off a rock.

"I made you an arrangement," she says proudly. "Everything's from the neighborhood. Ethically gathered. Full of happy energy."

I blink. "Oh—thank you, Willow. How thoughtful of you. It's got that natural, happy vibe."

"Exactly," she beams, setting it beside the register. "Beauty from the land for Beauty Angels."

"Thanks, Willow," I say, genuinely smiling. "It's perfect."

Before I can say more, she hugs me, leaves a faint trace of patchouli and wild herbs in her wake, and twirls out the door like a colorful gust of fall.

Midway through the day, a woman in her early thirties settles into my chair—quiet, tense, hands hooked tight around the strap of her bag.

"Thank you for doing this," she says softly as I start her foundation. "I've been struggling. Rent's behind, cable's off… but I've got a job interview this afternoon." She exhales like the weight of that sentence alone could fold her in half.

"Someone at Kitchen Angels told me about this, and honestly? I saw it as a sign. Haven't been able to afford hair or nails in forever. Made a LinkedIn account last night. Figured if I could at least look put together in the photo, maybe someone'll take a chance. If not this job, then the next."

I pause, meeting her eyes in the mirror. In her reflection, I see the girl who came to Nyack at seventeen—hungry, scared, pretending she wasn't desperate to be seen.

"Hey," I say. "You don't need perfect. You just need to be seen. And showing up? That's strength. Way more than you realize."

She nods, eyes shining.

After her makeover, I walk her over to the photo setup by the front window and snap a few quick shots—simple, clean, confident.

When I show her the final photo, she covers her mouth. "Is that really me?"

"That's you," I say. "And you look ready."

She hugs me tight and walks out a little taller than she came in. Gratitude and pride bloom deep and warm, enough to drown out the ache in my feet. This. This is why I built this place.

I'm about to grab my next client when the door opens—and my stomach flips.

Big black-and-gold sunglasses. Loud red hair. Denim jumpsuit hugging every curve. Nails like claws. Rings on every finger. Perfume so strong I swear I could taste it. Flashy as hell.

She pushes the sunglasses onto her head, and relief hits hard—I can breathe again. She's not Soledad. But for a second, she looked like her. And that's enough. Even the thought of running into her again still has me twisted up.

"Well, well, well! Look at all these stunning divas in here!" she announces, loud as a marching band. "Just came from Beets Beauty Box. My hair is SNATCHED—but this face?" She fans her nails like she's revealing a masterpiece. "This face needs drama. I want GLOW. I wanna look like I just stepped off a Glam-Vogue cover. Who's making that happen?"

Basha, mid-sip of her iced coffee, nearly chokes. She coughs into her elbow and shoots me a look that basically says, *Girl, what in the reality-TV hell is happening right now?* I bite down a smile.

Basha shifts her weight, arms crossed, and gives the woman a full up-down. Then leans toward me and murmurs, "Don't worry, babe. I got this one."

I smile at the woman. "Alright then, let's make you even more fabulous."

Before I can shake off the leftover nerves, the door swings open again.

A delivery guy walks in holding a bouquet—bright orange birds of paradise, purple orchids, and jungle-green leaves. Like something stolen straight out of an island dream—loud, wild, and alive.

I stop short. How. Freaking. Beautiful.

There's a little card tucked between the stems.

For the girl who always saw the light, even when it was dim.

The message is printed in simple script. I don't need to read the name. I already know.

Ryan.

For a second, I just stare.

They take me right back to that night—when we sat on a worn bench under a flickering streetlight, the air cold and quiet. I told him everything. About Soledad. About running away barefoot. About Fernando. About that night I still can't say out loud without my throat closing. He didn't pity me. He just stayed—solid as the ground beneath my shaking hands—while I came undone. And when I couldn't even look at myself, he looked at me like I was still a story worth reading—not just torn pages.

And the next morning, he showed up—with a bouquet like this and that exact same note.

I trace the edge of the card, pulse quickening, warmth blooming slow and dangerous in my chest—memory tangled with something I shouldn't still feel.

I wonder if he still writes these words to anyone else—or if he even remembers what they meant.

"Daaamn," Basha says. "Somebody's trying to impress."

I don't even need to look—of course she's smirking.

"Okay," she says, arms crossed. "Who sent you this exotic declaration of passion and petals?"

I clear my throat and slide the flowers to the side. "Just a friend."

She doesn't buy it for a second. "Uh-huh. And does this 'friend' have a name?"

I pretend to focus on my client's blush. "Ryan."

"OHHH. RYAN."

She drags out his name like she's tasting gossip for dessert. I instantly regret saying anything.

"Don't," I warn, pointing at her with my setting spray.

"What? I'm just saying—this amount of flowers ain't cheap. And that note? That sounds like a man who's still thinking about you."

I roll my eyes and clip the card back on the arrangement, like tucking the whole moment out of sight. "It's not like that. He's just… being nice."

"Mmhmm," she hums, turning back to her client. "And I'm just here to do hair and makeup, not stir the pot."

The denim diva chimes in from her chair like she's narrating an episode of *Love & Lashes*.

"Well, I don't know who this Ryan is, but if he's sending flowers like that? Honeyyyy. If men like that came with the lash package, I'd be here twice a week, no questions asked. I hope he got a brother. Or a fine-ass cousin."

She lets out a loud "Mmm-MMM!", grabs one of the event flyers from the counter, and fans herself like the bouquet just turned up the heat.

"A man who sends orchids and believes in your dreams? That's husband material, baby."

I drop my brush. Basha loses it—laughs so hard half the room turns.

I glare at both of them like I'm two seconds from assigning time-outs. But there's no daycare for grown women—so I shake my head and keep working.

✳ ✳ ✳

By the time we're wrapping up, I feel like I've been hit by a truck. My hands ache, my back's shot, and I'm pretty sure I've inhaled half a bottle of setting spray. But I'm glowing. Today was everything.

Then the door opens again.

He walks in like temptation dressed down—no effort, all impact. Black coat. Soft sweater. Jeans that fit like a memory I'm not ready to unpack. He's not trying to make an entrance—but the whole room shifts.

"Well, well, well," Basha says, spinning around. "If it isn't Mr. Nouel himself." She air-kisses both his cheeks like they're at Paris

Fashion Week. "Look at you, back in Nyack acting like you don't know you're fine."

"Good to see you too, Basha," he says with a soft smile.

Then his eyes find mine. "Congratulations, Amaya. I heard about today. I'm really proud of you."

I try to keep my face neutral, but my body remembers before I do—old heat, old ache—flaring up like they never left.

"Thanks for the flowers," I manage. "They were… really thoughtful."

He smiles again, small, like he's trying not to make it a moment. "Of course. My pleasure."

The word *pleasure* hits somewhere low in my chest—quick, uninvited. I blame it on exhaustion. His eyes look tired, like he hasn't slept much. I hate that I notice. But they're still warm. Still soft. Still… Ryan.

"You just get in?"

"Straight from the airport. Landed a couple hours ago."

My chest tightens. "You came here first?"

He nods. "Didn't want to miss it."

Before I can find words, he pulls out a check. And it's not small.

"Oh. OH," Basha says, eyes wide. "This man really said, 'Fund the whole nonprofit and sponsor the Olympics.'"

I swear I'm going to kill her. Right here. In front of witnesses.

Ryan laughs. "It's a good cause."

"Ryan, are you sure? Every little bit helps. This is… a lot. You don't have to—"

"I want to," he says. "Simple as that."

He pulls out a card and scribbles something on the back. "Just in case," he says, handing it to me. Our fingers brush—barely—and a current runs up my arm, sharp and alive, like static that remembers.

I glance down. It's his business card—but on the back, in his handwriting, is his personal number. The same number I could still dial from memory.

For the girl who always saw the light, even when it was dim.

The same words from the bouquet—and from that night years ago when he first wrote them. Funny how something can stay the same, even when everything else doesn't.

"I already have your number," I say, the words coming out softer than I meant.

"Yeah," he says, smiling just a little. "But maybe you forgot."

I laugh—soft and kind of stupid. For a heartbeat, I want to step closer. But that would just make things weird. So I stay still.

I tuck the card away, and that's when the door opens again.

Max. Because of course he'd walk in now.

The air shifts.

Ryan doesn't look at him. Doesn't need to. He just slips out—quiet, controlled, leaving the air heavy enough to choke on.

I finally breathe.

"Hello, beautiful ladies," Max says.

I don't look at Basha. I know she's looking at me.

He walks over. His eyes land on the bouquet. Shit. The note.

His jaw tightens. Just a little. I pretend not to notice. Pretend I'm adjusting a brush that doesn't need adjusting.

He doesn't say anything. Just steps closer, presses his hand to my lower back. Warm. Steady. Claiming. Like he's reminding me who's here—and who's not.

"Babe," he says low. "What do you need help with?"

"Nothing. I'll come in early tomorrow to finish cleaning."

Basha throws up a hand. "Girl, you better hire somebody. My feet? DONE."

Max laughs a little, but he doesn't let go. He leans in, kisses my temple. Then my lips—slow, deliberate, like he wants to erase every trace of Ryan before it can linger. For a heartbeat, I want to melt into it, to believe this warmth could quiet everything else inside me. But something in me stays still—watching from a distance, waiting for my heart to catch up.

Maybe that's the worst part—how easy it is to pretend the ache isn't there when someone's holding you close. How the right touch can quiet the noise but never the silence underneath. Max feels like safety, like the life I built after the storm. But Ryan... Ryan was the storm. And sometimes, I wonder if I ever really learned how to stop chasing the thunder.

He doesn't ask. He just finds the thread and pulls—until there's nothing left but want.

"I'm so proud of you," he whispers.

"You mean proud of *us*, right?" Basha says, crossing her arms. "Because I'm out here with setting spray in my bloodstream and traumatized cuticles."

He laughs. "Of course. This wouldn't have been a success without you, Basha."

"Damn right," she says, flipping her hair like she just won an award.

I laugh—because she's not wrong. We did this. Together.

"Okay, beautiful ladies," he says. "Bar Barazo. Drinks on me."

"Aww, thank you… but I need to go freshen up," I say.

"Same," Basha adds. "Oscar can't see me looking like I just lost a street fight with a can of hairspray."

"He'd still think you're fire," Max says.

"Let me have my standards, Maximiliano."

"We'll meet you there, Sunshine," I say, still laughing at the image of Basha post–hairspray battle.

Basha struts out like the undisputed queen of drama and beauty.

The door clicks shut, and the room goes still. Laughter fades, replaced by the hum of lights and the thud of my heartbeat.

Max pulls me closer; his hand slides down. Heat shoots through me.

"You good?" he whispers.

I nod, even though I'm spinning—caught between past and present, between what's safe and what still burns.

He studies me, then kisses me again—deep, claiming, like he's reminding me where I belong.

"I meant it," he says. "So damn proud of you, Amaya."

I nod again, because sometimes, movement is easier than honesty.

I glance back—at the bouquet, the brushes, the mirror smudged with fingerprints. At the dream that finally came true, and the feelings I still can't name.

Ryan.

Max.

The past pressing in.

The present pulling forward.

And me—caught in the ache, still chasing clarity I'm not even sure I want.

Chapter Thirty-Two

The second we step into my apartment, Max spins me around, pressing me against the door, his mouth already on mine—hungry, urgent, like he's been starving all night. His hands grip my waist, pulling me close like the inches between us are somehow disrespectful. I melt into him, warm and weightless.

"Damn," he breathes against my lips, voice low and gritty as his hands slide down my sides. "You're the sexiest stylist, photographer, and Latina entrepreneur on this planet."

I giggle, dizzy with adrenaline. "Oh yeah?"

He trails kisses down my neck. "You're everything, Amaya. You drive me crazy."

It hits somewhere soft in my chest. The way we move together—the fire, the rhythm—it's easy to believe this is love. That heat like this could rewrite history, drown out doubt. Maybe that's what scares me most.

Max leans back slightly. "What?"

I shake my head. "Just… you."

His eyes lock on mine, heavy with heat. "You keep looking at me like that, and I'm gonna have to handle it."

I laugh, pushing lightly at his chest. "Control yourself, Maximiliano. Basha's showing up in five and will drag me out by the lashes like she's on a mission."

He groans, dramatic. "I thought we were meeting her there?"

"We are," I say, grinning. "Just trying to scare you off before we're late for all the wrong reasons."

He smirks. "One more kiss and Basha's going to have to drag us out herself."

"Exactly. And I'm not explaining to her why my lipstick's on your neck instead of my face."

"Fine. But only because I love you. And because if I hold you one more second, I might explode into a million damn pieces."

It's not the kiss that steals my breath—it's the words. *Because I love you.*

The air changes—too warm, too still. I don't say anything. Just nod, turning toward the hallway.

The strap of my purse slips, and everything spills across the floor—lip gloss, gum, pens, keys, a journal. Chaos.

"Shit." I drop down, sweeping things up.

Max drops down beside me, picking up glosses like they're hot merchandise. "Damn, babe. This is a whole beauty supply store."

I smirk. "Don't judge my emergency stash."

"This many glosses should be illegal," he says, lining them up like evidence.

I wave him off, still laughing. "Back in a sec. A Dominican sec."

"So… next week?" he calls after me.

✳ ✳ ✳

When I step back into the living room, I'm still riding the high.

Beauty Angels was everything—one of those days that stitches itself into your soul. I pulled it off. We pulled it off. The women. The light in their eyes. The way we turned pain into beauty, grief into glow.

I start dancing through the apartment—barefoot, beaming—like joy is moving through me and I can't hold it in.

But Max isn't dancing. He's standing still—one hand in his pocket, the other holding a glass.

My eyes land on the bottle on the table—Hudson Valley Reserve. The whiskey. The expensive one. From our night at Hudson River Tavern. The one he gave me after that night, wrapped in a ribbon. The one I never opened—saving it for us. For a night we could sip slow, laugh too loud, and just breathe together. But not tonight.

Shit. If we don't leave now, we're not leaving at all—and Basha's gonna show up banging like NYPD.

He pours himself a drink, movements steady and way too calm. Too smooth. Like he's still burning from earlier—still turned on and ready to prove it. One more second of this and he's going to rip my clothes off—and this whole night will shift into something else entirely.

I try to keep it light. "Celebrating already?"

He doesn't answer me.

I do a little playful spin, still barefoot. "Come on," I say gently. "Let's go before Basha comes looking for us with backup."

He's holding something. That's when I see it—a black business card between his fingers. Matte. Gold lettering. My lungs forget how to work.

Ryan.

I already know what's written on the back.

For the girl who always saw the light, even when it was dim.

Max lifts the card, thumb brushing the handwriting like it stung him.

"What is this, Amaya?"

His voice is too calm. Too controlled. Like he's holding something in.

I swallow. "It's just a business card."

A sound escapes him—not quite a laugh, more like disbelief.

"Yeah? People just write sweet little messages on their business cards now?"

"Max—"

"No, please. Help me understand. He just happened to show up? With flowers? And leave you a note that sounds like a damn love letter?"

"Are you serious right now? It wasn't like that."

He steps closer. "Then what was it?"

"It was a donation," I say. "He came to support the event. That's all."

He lets out a bitter laugh. "That message doesn't read like a business transaction."

"You're twisting it."

"Then untwist it."

"I don't owe you an explanation," I snap.

His jaw tightens. His grip on the glass shifts, like he's deciding whether to throw it or drink it.

"So I'm just supposed to stand here while you defend him?"

"Do you trust me or not?"

The space between us stretches—quiet, charged, like a fuse waiting to snap. Then he turns and pours another drink.

"Don't." My voice slices through the air.

He raises the glass.

"Max. Please. I said don't."

He drinks anyway. And something inside me splits—not from what he did, but from what it confirms.

"How long have you two been talking?" he asks.

"Are you serious now? We haven't *been talking*."

He holds up the card again. "Then what the fuck is this?"

"It's an old quote."

"From the guy who walked away from you?"

My jaw tightens. "At least he was honest. He told me the truth, even when it hurt. He didn't lie to keep me close. He didn't make promises he couldn't keep. That's more than I can say for you."

He steps closer. "You told me he crushed you. Now he sends flowers and you're acting like it means nothing?"

"He's visiting family. He came by the studio. He's not here for me."

"Oh, so you know his whole schedule now?"

That's it. The last thread snaps. The part of me still trying to explain—gone.

"You know what, Max? I was stupid to think we'd ever work."

He throws his hands up. "What the hell does that mean?"

His voice hangs in the air—tight, bitter. He looks at me like he's daring me to answer, like he still expects me to fix this.

Then he adds, quieter but sharper—"You're walking away again?"

"No." I motion between us. "I'm walking away from this."

He laughs once—a hollow, humorless sound. "So you can run to him?"

I break. Fury tears through me like a live wire—hot, electric, unstoppable.

"Fuck you," I whisper, then louder, clearer. "Fuck your anger. Fuck your drinking. And fuck me—for thinking this was something I could save."

"Amaya—"

And then it hits me. The dream. The whiskey. His grip. The panic. The way I couldn't breathe. It all comes rushing back—not like memory, but like warning. Like I already survived it once, and I'm about to fail the test again. It wasn't a dream. It was my body remembering before I did.

My whole body locks. Chest tightens. Vision narrows.

My phone buzzes. I glance at it. It's Basha. My finger hovers. I send it to voicemail.

"Get out," I whisper.

He doesn't move.

"Max." My voice trembles. "Get out."

"Just listen—"

"No!" My voice breaks, rising like a wave. "After everything? After you—"

He slams the glass down, the sound cracking through the room. His jaw clenches like he's holding back a scream.

"How the hell am I supposed to feel, Amaya? Tell me."

"I already did. You just didn't listen."

"I love you," he says. "I'm confused. Can't you just—"

"No." I cut him off. "We're done."

He draws in a sharp breath. Then, quieter—almost daring me to answer—

"If Ryan asked for you back right now, would you still be standing here?"

The question hits my chest before I can even process it. A slow, crushing ache blooms where my breath should be.

"Don't turn this on me," I say, voice shaking. "You crossed the line."

"And you keep crossing it with him." His tone darkens, thick with jealousy. "Always defending him."

"This isn't about Ryan," I snap. "It's about how you don't trust me. How you drink when I begged you not to. How you lose control. Twist everything until I barely recognize the version of you I'm trying to love."

His eyes go flat. Cold. The kind of cold that doesn't yell—it just kills the room.

"Maybe I don't know if I can trust you."

The words land like a punch to the gut. A blow to the hope I was still foolish enough to hold onto.

"Max," I whisper. "Get the fuck out."

He doesn't move.

I grab my keys, my hands shaking.

He grabs my arm—too tight. His fingers dig in. Panic detonates in my chest like a siren.

"Let. Me. Go."

I yank away—hard—as I reach for the doorknob. Max moves at the same time—reaching to shut it—too fast, too hard. The edge of the door slams into my face. Pain erupts under my cheekbone—white-hot, metallic, blinding. The world spins. My knees buckle. I go down. A cry bursts out of me—raw, broken loose from somewhere deep. I hold my cheek, gasping. My breath fractures into jagged pieces. My hands won't stop trembling. My wrist burns where he grabbed me—like his fingers left a brand behind.

Max reels back, both hands on his head like he's trying to hold himself together.

"Amaya—shit—I didn't mean to—"

I push myself up. Slowly. My body feels like a collapsed building.

"Just stop."

He doesn't move. Doesn't speak. Just stands there—like he's crumbling from the inside. Guilt spills across his face, but it doesn't matter. Nothing does now.

Then—quietly, bitterly, like the words cost him blood—

"You always run, Amaya. That's all you know how to do."

I don't respond. I don't scream. I don't crumble. Instead, I lift my hand and point to the door.

He stares for a long moment. Then something in him folds. He grabs his coat and walks out.

The door slams behind him—hard enough to make my ears ring. The sound echoes through the apartment, then disappears.

Silence rushes in—thick, merciless. Not the peaceful kind. The sharp, echoing, brutal kind.

I slide down, back against the door. My cheek throbs, but it's nothing compared to the hollow rupture inside me.

I curl in—not just crying for tonight.

I'm crying for every version of me that made excuses.

That believed love was a project.

That thought I could fix someone if I just loved them hard enough.

I was wrong. So heartbreakingly wrong.

My eyes land on the bottle. Still half full.

I push myself to stand. My body feels heavy—like it's made of grief and glass.

I pour a glass. The amber liquid catches the lamplight—bold, unbothered, like it knows it's not the answer but dares me anyway. I should throw it. Smash the bottle. Burn the memory. But I don't.

I grab my phone and open YouTube—not for clarity, not for comfort, just for something that knows how to bleed.

"The Trouble with Love Is" by Kelly Clarkson.

The music starts—soft piano, every note heavy with regret.

I sink to the floor. Take a sip. It burns going down. Not enough to numb. Just enough to remind me I'm still here.

I curl tighter—knees pulled in, arms wrapped around my chest. The ache doesn't quiet. It swells. Expands. Finds every corner of me.

The lyrics sting like she's singing my life back to me.

Another sip.

Then another.

But the pain won't drown.

It floats. Rises. Cracks me open.

I press my forehead to the floor and sob—loud, uncontrollable, like a storm that refuses to pass.

The screen lights up—Basha again. I silence it. Start the song over. Let it wreck me.

The music plays. My breath shudders. The ache keeps rising.

Then—

BAM. BAM. BAM.

"AMAYA!"

The voice slices through the fog.

More pounding.

"OPEN THE DAMN DOOR!"

I crawl. Fingers fumbling with the lock.

It takes three tries.

The door flies open.

Basha.

She freezes. Her mouth drops open. Eyes wide.

"No. No, no, no…"

Then rage overtakes her. She slams her fist into the wall. A picture frame rattles.

"That piece of shit. Where the fuck is he?"

I shake my head. Even if I tried, I know I can't speak.

She drops to her knees and pulls me into her arms.

And I break.

Sobs rip out of me. I grab fistfuls of her hoodie like it's the only thing holding me to earth.

"I got you," she whispers, shaking. "You're safe now. He's never going to fucking touch you again."

She rocks me, her voice cracking.

"If I ever see him again… I swear, Amaya. He won't walk away from it."

I bury my face in her shoulder. Her hoodie smells like vanilla, warmth, and safety.

I don't fight it.

I let her hold me.

I let the weight slip from my shoulders and fall apart—into the arms that never let go.

INTERLUDE
Seven Years Ago

I looked up what my name means the other day—Amaya. It means *Night Rain*. Or *The End*.
Figures.

Maybe that's why I like the sound of rain at night. Like the storm outside actually gets me—loud, messy, but kind of calming in a weird way. And *The End?* Sounds dramatic, but not if you live here. Here, the end is always close.

One wrong look. One word. One second where she completely loses it—and boom. I'm dead. *Punto final.* No real first love. No fashion line with my name stitched into the tag. No travel, no "I made it." Just a small, quiet death full of big, unfinished dreams.

That's what this house feels like—like the end is just waiting in the next room.

∗ ∗ ∗

I don't even know how long I've been standing here—hands deep in dishwater, arms soaked, fingers all pruney—just staring at this wall. Grease stains everywhere, like somebody tried to clean it once and gave up halfway.

I always come straight home after school. If I don't, she hits me. My body knows the routine. My mind, though? It's already gone.
Somewhere far.
Somewhere warm.
Somewhere I can breathe without asking.

Somewhere I'm not treated like trash in my own house.

And yeah… sometimes I wonder—what if I just disappeared? Walked into traffic. Never came back. Would Soledad even care?

Yeah. She'd care.

Who else would scrub her floors and write love letters to the convict she's about to marry?

Fernando Fortuna. My stepfather. I hate that word. I don't need anyone to step in for my dad. He could never compare to Papi. Fernando proposed to her from prison. Probably just trying to lock down a place to crash when he gets out.

The second *"Bidi Bidi Bom Bom"* comes on, I crank the volume and grab the big rice spoon. I spin like I'm on stage in Selena's sparkly purple jumpsuit. For a second, I'm not Amaya. Not barefoot, not washing dishes. I'm somebody. Someone who gets to dream. Who gets to create. Who finally gets to *live.*

Halfway through the chorus—

"AMAYA!"

She screams my name like she wants to rip it out of my throat. My heart drops straight into the dirty dishwater. Shit—why is she here so early?

I turn off the faucet, hands trembling. Music's still blaring. I don't even know what I did this time. She storms in like she's about to break something. Like that something is me.

"What the hell do you think you're doing?"

"I was just… washing dishes—"

Glass shatters. Loud. Close. I flinch as shards hit the tile, scattering like landmines. I don't move. Don't breathe. Just stare at the floor, hoping it swallows me whole.

"And singing?!" she yells. "You're supposed to be *grieving*, Amaya!"

Grieving? Who died?

I don't dare ask. But then I see it—the way she looks at me like I just spit on a grave.

She means *him.* Fernando. Of course.

"I didn't know I wasn't allowed to—"

She charges forward. Her eyes go wild. The air turns sharp and cold.

"*Allowed?* You think you get to be happy while he sits in prison? After everything he's done for us? You ungrateful little—"

Everything he's done for us?

Like the day he came out of the bathroom in just a towel, dripping slime, and pressed himself against me while I was washing dishes? I was fourteen. I didn't scream. Should've. But I knew she'd blame me. So I told him to wait in the bathroom. And he smiled—because somewhere in that twisted mind of his, he thought he'd already gotten away with it.

Still, I told her. I told her what he did. I thought that would be the end of him. But she stayed. Of course she did.

She always warned me not to call the cops. "If you ever call them, I'll take your life away right in front of them." Her favorite line—

"I gave you life. I can take it back."

Like she really believes that. Maybe she's talking about the other time. The Friday night he was drunk—music shaking the walls—and told me to sit on his lap. I was fifteen. Already curvy. I knew what would happen if I said no. So I sat. It still makes me sick. And yeah, as messed up as it sounds—sometimes I'd rather him be here than locked up. Because when he's gone, she needs someone else to punish. And that's always me.

My head spins. My lungs feel full of smoke. This isn't about the music. It's about *him*. It's *always* about him.

Something inside me snaps. The fear. The silence. Everything I've ever swallowed down.

It bursts.

"*¡TE ODIO!*" I scream. I mean it. It flies out of me like fire.

Louder this time—

"*¡TE ODIO!*"

For every slap. Every insult. Every time she picked him over me. I know I'll pay for it. But I say it anyway. I want her to feel it. Let it stick in her chest and burn.

But deep down, I know—she doesn't feel pain. She makes it. Feeds on it. She doesn't want love. She wants control. She never tried to know me. Never cared. All she does is shove her rage down my throat and call it motherhood.

She doesn't say anything at first. Just storms out of the kitchen, still fuming. I hear the lighter flick. The smell of her cigarette curls through the air, thick and suffocating. She's pacing. Cursing under her breath. Then louder—

"You wanna scream at me? You think that's how this works? You don't get to talk to me like that and walk away. You're gonna pay for this, *pajarita*."

Her voice claws through the walls. Then she's back—shaking, puffing like a bull, words spilling out faster than her smoke. She's yelling about how *ingrata* I am. How she barely made money at the salon today. How nobody tips anymore—like I'm supposed to live off blowouts and blessings.

How when I lived with Papi, I had it easier. How I don't know what struggle is. How she's been doing everything on her own while I "act like some Selena wannabe" and forget who feeds me.

She takes another drag.

"You wanna sing and dance like he didn't build this life for us? That's who you are now?"

She's unraveling—a lifetime of bitterness and exhaustion spilling out in my direction.
Every resentment she's ever swallowed. Every bad choice she's made but blames the world for.

I run.

Heart pounding, I rush to my bedroom. Grab my backpack. Fling it open.

Shit. Where's my Sofia box?

Where is it?

If she finds it—I'm dead.

I dig through clothes, under the bed, my hands shaking like they don't belong to me.

Then I hear her.

I hear the kitchen drawers slamming. Metal clinking.

Shit—*el cucharón*. The big rice spoon.

Not the cheap one that bends—but the heavy stainless-steel one she stole from Abuela's kitchen. The one she uses to scrape *el concón*.

Maybe she's just grabbing it to throw it at me. Maybe I've still got a second to get out.

As soon as I run out of the bedroom, I see the flash of silver. Not dull. Not round. Not *el cucharón*.

A knife.

And she's still smoking—like it's just another night.

My stomach drops straight through me. I don't wait. I run.

She's right behind me.

"*¡Ven acá, maldita!*" she screams.

"Amaya!"

I reach for the door. My hands are shaking so hard I can barely turn the knob.

But it clicks.

"¡NO!" I scream back. My voice cracks open.

"*¡Ven acá, hija de la—!*"

There's a whoosh—then CRACK. The knife slams into the door and sticks, right where my head had been.

My heart's pounding so loud it hurts. My knees almost give. But I don't scream. I just run. Down the hallway. Down five flights of stairs. Bare feet slapping the tile.

No stopping. No thinking. If I fall—if I slow down—she'll catch me. And that's it. Game over.

The second I hit the street, the cold punches me in the chest. But I don't care. I keep going. I don't feel pain. Just fire in my lungs. And her voice in my head—screaming my name like she owns it.

I cut sharp onto Broadway—lights, cars, people. But I'm not really there. I'm somewhere between fight and freeze.

The sound of that knife hitting the door won't leave me. Neither will her voice.

I keep running. Up Isham Street. Through shadows. Into Inwood Hill Park.

The trees rise up like they've been waiting for me.

I run deeper into the woods—away from people.

And then I collapse.

She tried to kill me.

She really, actually tried.

And if I hadn't moved—I'd be dead.

I curl into the dirt, sobbing so hard my throat burns. I always thought dying would be quiet like falling asleep. But this? This is loud.

I pass this park every day after school. But right now? It feels... different. Like the trees are wrapping around me. Hiding me. Keeping me safe.

I press my back against a tree and drag in the cold air, but it won't settle. My legs hurt, my feet are raw, my hands still smell like dish soap and fear. And this isn't even the first time I've done this. Twice before, I ran—thinking maybe someone would keep me safe.

The first time, I ran to Papi's sister in Washington Heights—Tía Leonor. She cried when she saw me, holding my face like she could glue me back together. She handed me one of her old *batas* and thick socks—one with a hole in the toe—so I wouldn't catch a cold. Made me *té de manzanilla* with too much honey and sat beside me while I drank every drop. She slipped her old rosary under my pillow—

"To keep the devil away," she said.

Promised she'd watch over me. Said she'd talk sense into my mother.

But when Soledad came pounding on her door—fake tears, poison dripping from every word—Tía Leonor folded like wet paper. Soledad promised I'd be treated better. She lied.

She dragged me home and beat me for the "waste of time", the "embarrassment". Made me scrub the whole apartment top to bottom—walls, floors, even hand-wash Fernando's crusty underwear. Like I was her maid. Like I asked for it.

She smoked.

Watched.

Called it "discipline."

She poured herself more Bustelo while I scrubbed the floor on my knees. Stirred it slow—one spoon for health, one for money, one for love.

"Salud, dinero, amor," she said to herself, like she was the only one worth it.

She tapped her ash into my bucket, took a sip, and tilted the cup like she could see tomorrow floating in the stain. She mumbled about how she was sick of doing other people's nappy hair for scraps. Said she'd branch out soon—maybe open a club, have a line of cute girls working the bar, liquor flowing all night.

"Liquor's where the real money is," she said. "Not washing out cheap dye jobs for women who don't tip."

She laughed once—low and mean—and said, "Money's coming for me. I see it right here."

She didn't look at me when she said it. Didn't say us. Just her.

The second time, I ran to my other aunt—Tía Claribel. She sat me down on her couch, dabbed Vicks on my forehead, and said it would help me breathe my fear away.

"You're safe now, *mi niña*," she whispered. I wanted to believe her. But I didn't.

Tía Claribel was the saint—the kind who'd jump if you sneezed too loud. Sweet as prayer, but no match for the bull waiting back home. I knew she didn't stand a chance if Soledad sniffed me out. But where else was I gonna go? No money. No plan.

She put on *Cantinflas* reruns and fed me three kinds of ice cream—said ice cream would sweeten my broken heart and comedy would sweeten my soul. What I didn't know was that she'd already called Soledad behind my back. Told her I was safe. Said she'd pray for our family.

When she confessed—hopeful, her hand resting on her worn Bible—I started shaking.

Soledad showed up in under an hour. Fake crying. Fake promises. Acting like she was auditioning for *Telemundo*. Said I was "rebelling." Said she just wanted to keep me on the right path. That she'd "talk to me gently."

And Tía Claribel—God bless her soft heart—sat beside her reading a Bible verse about forgiveness while Soledad probably sharpened her teeth right there on the couch.

She didn't just make me scrub floors this time. She made me stand in the bathtub for hours, clothes on, pouring ice water over myself to "wash the rebellion out." She'd flick her ashes into the sink while I shivered. If I stopped, she'd bang on the bathroom door. Again. *Otra vez.* By the time she let me out, my teeth were chattering so hard I thought they'd crack.

She called it cleansing. Said I asked for it.

That's when I learned my lesson—

Family can love you and still be too weak to protect you.

They can feed you and pray for you—but they won't fight for you. Not against her.

So this time, there's nobody. No aunt. No prayers. No soft hands waiting. Just me.

I grab a stick and start writing in the dirt. Fast, without thinking. *The Last Time I Run.*

I stare at it. And finally—breathe.

I don't know how long I've been lying here. But it's getting dark now, and the trees don't feel safe anymore. They feel like they're watching.

I hear movement—shapes in the dark. My brain starts freaking out. Is it someone walking their dog? Just some rando out late? Or did Soledad send somebody to find me?

My skin crawls. I start walking—slow, quiet—checking around like something might jump out at me.

Then I see him.

A man hunched on a bench, wrapped in layers. The old blanket barely covers him. His shoes are torn. His whole body looks like it's folding in on itself.

And suddenly—I see me.

That could be me. That might be me in seven days. Or seven hours. I don't know him, but tonight? We're the same. One scream. One night. One knife. That's all it takes to land here.

I cry. Not quiet tears. The kind that rip straight through you.

This park isn't just trees and benches anymore. It's a graveyard for forgotten dreams. And for the first time, I wonder if I'm one of them.

I walk past him, but I carry him with me. I grip the stick tighter, like it's a weapon. And I keep walking. Toward the edge. Toward Broadway.

Headlights cut through the dark. A cop car. I duck behind a bush and hold my breath. They don't stop. Just keep driving. I wait a few more seconds before stepping out. Still shaking. Still scared. Still here.

I don't feel strong. I don't feel brave. I feel cracked open—like the pieces of me don't fit right anymore.

I've got nowhere to go. So I just keep walking. I don't even know where.

***

Hey Sofia,

I never realized how much I actually love being alive... until the night I almost lost it.

The night I almost lost it? That was today.

Wishing for death used to feel dramatic—like something I'd whisper in my head when everything got too heavy. Like staring at a storm in the distance. You see the lightning. You feel the pull. But it's not touching you. Not really.

But when death is right there—breathing in your face, looking you dead in the eyes through your mother's rage? That's different. That's terrifying. That's real. It swallows you whole.

There were nights I thought dying might feel like relief. Like escape. But when it's that close—when a knife flies past your head and your legs are the only reason you're still breathing—all I can think is: I don't want to die. I don't want to die.

And somehow... I didn't. I don't even know how I made it out. But I did. I'm here. I'm alive.

It's almost midnight. I'm lying on this loud, floral couch wrapped in plastic—like one of those old-school Dominican living rooms where nothing ever gets dirty. Not even your feelings.

My feet hurt like hell. My curls are a mess. And my body won't stop moving, like it forgot how to shut off. No money. No plan. No home.

But I've got this moment. And I've got you, Sofia. You always show up when I'm at my worst—like a voice in the dark whispering, breathe, Amaya. Just breathe.

My hands won't stop shaking. My brain won't stop replaying it—her face, the scream, the knife, my feet slapping the stairs, my lungs begging for air.

It won't let me rest—like my body's stuck in survival mode. So I do the only thing I can.

I breathe.

In.

Hold.

Out.

Like they taught us in gym class—except this isn't about passing a mile run. This is about surviving my life.

"I can do this," I whisper out loud—like maybe if I say it enough times, I'll believe it.

Just one more night. Then I'll figure out the rest.
But I'm not going back.
Even if I sleep on concrete.
Even if I starve.
I'm not going back.
I can't.
'Til next time,
xoxo, Amaya

Chapter Thirty-Three

I slam the door behind me.

The sound cuts through the apartment—sharp, final, like it's trying to erase what just happened. My hands still shake as I grab my keys. Thoughts spin—anger, shame, confusion, regret—all tangled and pressing down on me.

I don't think. I move.

Out the door. Down the stairs. Into the car.

I start the engine. No destination. Just away. I need the motion. The sound. The wind. Something—anything—to drown out this hollow, splitting ache in my chest.

Streetlights blur past. I press harder. The road narrows. My foot stays down. A parked car flashes into view, and I swerve hard. Tires scream. My body jerks. My heart slams against my ribs like it's trying to break free.

I suck in air. Let it out. Try again. But it won't clear.

The fight loops in my head—Max's voice, the way his hand landed, the glass, his tone, his eyes. The exact moment I stopped being scared of him and started being scared of me. Of what I was turning into beside him. How easily I blurred red flags into something I kept calling love.

My hands grip the wheel tighter. My eyes sting. My chest clenches like it's bracing for impact. For a second, I forget which direction I'm even headed—until I catch the silhouette of Bear Mountain rising in the distance.

At some point, I must've veered onto the Palisades Parkway without realizing.

I pull into a narrow overlook. The kind with a jagged edge and a metal railing too rusted to trust. I get out, shut the door behind me, and walk toward the view. Below, the Hudson stretches wide and dark, barely moving. The wind hits my face like a slap. I close my eyes and breathe it in.

Somewhere in the back of my mind, I think about the people who stand in this exact spot and wonder if they should jump. And how so many don't realize they want to live until their feet have already left the ground. I wonder how many hearts are breaking right now across the world. Same ache. Different languages. Pain doesn't soften just because of the accent—it still lands where it hurts.

I grip the railing and stare out at the black water below, pretending I'm stronger than I feel. But the truth is, I don't feel strong. I feel like a scream stuck in a whisper.

Eventually, I turn back toward the car. Slide into the driver's seat. The silence presses in—thick, alive. I breathe once. Then again.

And I drive. Away from the edge. Away from the noise. But when I reach my block, I keep driving. Keep thinking.

Why did I let myself forgive him so fast?

Why did I think he'd never grab my wrist that hard again?

Why did I think he deserved a second chance so easily?

Why did I let my body betray me—confuse touch with tenderness, heat with love?

I veer onto the narrow road that hugs the river, quiet and winding, like it's thinking something over. Piermont eases into view, low and still beneath the soft light. Some shops are closing already. String lights stretch above the sidewalks, already glowing, like they're getting ready for night even if it isn't here yet. A few bars have their doors propped open, music drifting out like a memory.

For a second, I think about pulling over. Just one drink. Just enough to smooth the edge. Just enough to feel nothing at all. I picture myself hunched over a glass of something dark and bitter—eyes hollow, mascara smudged, surrounded by voices that don't even notice I'm there. Would anyone care? Or would I just be another woman carrying a storm she can't explain?

I shake it off. The light turns red. I tap the wheel. My chest won't stop rising too fast.

A door swings open. Laughter spills out. Golden light stretches across the sidewalk. People reach for each other like it's easy—like love doesn't leave bruises.

There's a man by the window. Sitting alone. Head low. Stirring his drink in slow circles, like he's been doing it for hours. His face is blank. Not sad. Just… gone. Like his body stayed but his mind walked out a long time ago. I know that look.

A horn blares behind me. Green light. I drive. A few blocks later, the road curves—and that's when I see it.

A small brick church. Tucked just past the edge of downtown. Nothing fancy. No steeple. No flashing sign. Just stillness. Like it's been waiting for someone to notice. The kind of place you don't see until your heart is in pieces. Its stained-glass windows glow—soft gold and deep blue. The doors are open. People step inside. Some holding hands. Some holding nothing. But they all walk like they belong.

A woman in a fitted coat holds her head high. A man in a dark suit walks with quiet purpose. A mom crosses the sidewalk with her kids, their fingers tangled in hers. Even in the chaos, they move like they have something I don't. Like they're not scared to be seen—or to stay.

I glance at my reflection in the rearview. Wrinkled hoodie. Swollen eyes. Hair tied up like I gave up halfway through. I look like the after of a breakdown—not someone who belongs in a place like that.

Why would God care about someone like me?

Someone raised in chaos. Someone who barely remembers how to pray. Someone who keeps mistaking pain for love. Who stayed too long. Who almost didn't make it out. Left too late. And still wonders if she deserves to heal.

I sit at the curb, frozen. Chest tight. Breath shallow. Then I hear her. Her voice. Soledad's mother. My *abuela*.

"No matter how hopeless it feels, *mi rayito de sol*, remember—God is always by our side. He never leaves us."

Her words live in my bones. Even when she couldn't protect me. Even when she stayed silent. Her love was the quiet kind—the kind that stayed, even when it couldn't save.

She saw the bruises. Felt the weight of my mother's rage. But she was tired. Fragile. Holding herself together in pieces. She used to brush my hair and whisper,

"One day, Amaya, you'll be strong enough to walk away—like a *mariposa* finding its wings."

She believed that. Even when she couldn't do it herself. And suddenly, I feel like that little girl again—waiting for someone to choose me. To fight for me. No one ever did.

I park the car and quietly step out. Every footstep toward the church drags behind it a version of me I've tried to bury. The girl who disappeared. The teen who stayed quiet. The woman who still doesn't know how to be soft and safe at the same time.

My head pulses. The migraine creeps back—slow and punishing. But I keep walking. The air smells like wax, old wood, and prayers that never left. Like time itself slowed down to breathe. Low organ notes hum through the space. Candles flicker. The pews creak softly as people shift. I slide into the back row. The wood feels solid beneath me, grounding me. There's something else in the air—a hush that feels almost alive.

The space reminds me of my other *abuela*—my father's mother. The one who raised me for a while when Soledad left to chase whatever dream had her attention back then.

She used to take me to a tiny chapel in our village. Sunlight poured through open windows, catching on the dust like it was made of gold. Hands held in prayer. Hymns in soft Spanish. Faith that stayed—even when the world fell apart. The neighbors prayed for rain so crops wouldn't die, for lights that didn't go out mid-novela. For clean water that lasted more than a day. And through it all, I can still hear Abuela's trembling voice asking God to keep her children gentle, her roof standing through hurricane season, and her knees strong enough to keep walking.

I wrap my arms around myself and breathe slow. I feel like one of her old porcelain dolls—still standing, but cracked all the way through.

A man steps forward. Brown skin. Kind face. Eyes that hold something gentle and knowing—like he's seen pain and still believes in healing. He doesn't introduce himself with a title. No "Father," no "Pastor," no "Minister." Just Ravi. Even his name sounds soft—like something meant to soothe.

"Good evening," he says. "Tonight, if all you brought with you is pain—that's enough. Let's open our hearts to the healing already waiting for us. No matter how far you've wandered," he says, "no matter how long it's been—you're not too far. You're not too late."

He pauses, like the silence is part of the message.

His accent is gentle. Maybe Indian. I'm not sure. But it makes every word feel warm.

"If your faith is small. If your hope is tired. If you barely made it here tonight—welcome."

For a second, I almost stand. Almost leave. But I stay.

"We all carry things," he continues. "Mistakes. Memories. Wounds. But God isn't waiting for us to show up perfect. He just wants us to show up."

I look down at my hands. They look like they've been through something.

"God sees the beauty under the bruises," he says. "He sees the story in your scars. He sees what's still growing—even when you feel like you've stopped."

He pauses. Then, with a small smile—

"And if you think you're too far gone, remember—Jesus built his church with doubters, outcasts, and screwups."

My lips almost twitch. Not quite a smile. But almost.

Can God really want someone like me? What if I was never meant to be whole?

"He's not waiting for you to be clean. He's just waiting for you to come home."

Something inside me cracks. Soledad. Adrián. The choice I made. The fear I'll never get it right. Max. The guilt that wraps itself around my spine and won't let go.

The tears come quietly. I wipe them—but not too fast. Not like I'm ashamed of them anymore. I cry for every piece of me I've buried. For the girl who kept hoping. For the woman still trying.

The service ends. People drift toward the exits. Soft voices. Gentle goodbyes. But I stay seated. Still. Small. Not ready to leave whatever this is I've found.

A voice breaks the quiet beside me.

"Sometimes it's the silence that tells us what we needed to hear."

I look up.

Ravi stands at the edge of the pew, hands folded, his face calm—like he's not here to fix me. Just to sit in the mess with me.

"I don't think God listens to people like me," I whisper.

He sits beside me.

"And why's that?"

"Because I'm a mess."

"You're human."

"I don't know if I belong here."

He tilts his head, like he's heard that a hundred times before but still cares.

"Do you know who Jesus spent most of his time with?"

I shake my head.

"The broken. The discarded. The ones the world gave up on. The ones who made a mess of things. The ones nobody thought deserved grace."

He lets it hang there, like truth doesn't need decoration.

"The Lord is close to the brokenhearted. He saves those crushed in spirit."

Something inside me gives. Like my heart's been waiting years to hear those words.

"You don't have to be fixed to be found," he adds. "You don't have to earn His love. It's already yours."

The tears come again. I don't wipe them this time. I don't tell him about Max. Or Ryan. Or Soledad. But I whisper, "I just want peace."

He nods. "Peace starts when we stop pretending we're not in pain." Then he stands. "The darkest nights lead to the brightest mornings." He steps away. Pauses.

"Please come back. You're always welcome here."

I just nod. That's all I've got left.

A moment later, he returns—quiet steps, steady presence. He slips a small card into my hand.

"This is the church number," he says softly. "You're not alone."

The card is warm, like it's been passed from one trembling hand to another. The ink is smudged at the corners, edges softened by touch. Beneath his name, I catch it: *Doctorate in Psychology & Counseling.*

He's not just a church man. That's why he sounded different. Why he felt different. Not just faith—but understanding. He speaks like someone who's sat with pain long enough to know its shape. Someone who doesn't try to fix it—just makes space for it.

"Thank you," I whisper. The words feel small, but heavy.

He nods once, the kind of nod that means he sees more than I've said. Then he turns and walks away, his footsteps fading into the quiet hum of the sanctuary—leaving behind the faint smell of wax, and something softer. Something like peace.

✳ ✳ ✳

Back at my apartment, I pull out one of the journals from the Sofia shoebox. My fingers hesitate. Then I open it.

I don't write about Max. I don't write about Ryan. I write about *me*. The girl who keeps getting back up. The woman I still want to become. The version of myself I finally believe might be real.

I write:

Maybe healing isn't about forgetting. Maybe it's remembering—without the fear.

Maybe it's about coming home to yourself.

I close the journal.

A card slips out and lands on my thigh—Ryan's. I pause. My heart doesn't race. It doesn't break.

It just… waits. For what, I don't know. I don't toss it. I slide it back between the pages. And before I can second-guess myself, I reach for the old journal—the one I know has what I'm really looking for. The first time Ryan stepped out of the background and into my story.

I breathe in. And begin to read.

Hey Sofia,

Okay. Breathe. I have to tell you what just happened.

Ryan—yes, that Ryan—was at the bakery today, helping out like he owns the place. He was looking all kinds of cute, moving around like it was his second home—okay, maybe it is his second home. And while I was trying not to sound like a total idiot, guess what he did?

He asked me if I wanted to go hiking with him at Nyack Beach next time we're both free.

And I said yes. Obviously.

I played it cool, like, "Yeah, that sounds fun," but inside? I was straight-up screaming. Hiking. With Ryan. RYAN.

I have no idea what I'm gonna wear, though. I need to wear something cute but outdoorsy cute, you know what I mean?

Like "accidentally adorable while walking through crunchy leaves and pretending it's not a date" energy. Wish me luck, girl!

'Til next time,

xoxo, Amaya.

I almost forgot what it felt like to want someone that purely. Before love got so complicated, so heavy. Back when wanting felt like enough.

Hey Sofia,

Remember how I told you Ryan asked me to go hiking? Well... we actually did it. And it was EVERYTHING.

The air had that perfect hoodie-weather vibe, cool but not freezing. The sky was all moody and dramatic. And the trees? Straight-up showing off. Reds, oranges, golds, like fall decided to throw us a private show. I think I fell in love with the season that day.

I *wanted* to stop every five seconds to take pictures. The view was unreal—but I didn't want to look away from him. When I finally did, Ryan goes, "What about a selfie?" like it was no big deal. I said sure and leaned in—too fast—and stepped right on his sneakers. "My bad," I blurted, dying inside. He laughed and said, "You just wanted to get closer." I rolled my eyes, but my face was already on fire. He leaned in again, and all I could think was, don't blink, don't sweat, don't breathe weird.

He told me about this new tech internship. How he wants to start his own company, travel, build something that matters. I told him about FIT, about wanting to design for girls like us and study photography. He actually listened, like, really listened. You know how rare that is? He *gets it.* We're both chasing something bigger. I swear, his voice and his laugh are my new favorite soundtrack. He could be talking about snakes (and you know how much I hate snakes), and I'd still be here for it.

Then—boom—rain. At first, just a cute drizzle. Then? Full downpour. We were soaked and miles from the car, so we ran until we found this random wooden gazebo. He checked his phone and said the storm would pass soon, so we waited. Just us. The rain pounding all around.

I was freezing—hair frizzy, jaw trembling—and Ryan, being the actual gentleman he is, asked if I was okay. I lied. He knew. He took off his jacket and wrapped it around me. And there he was—tank top, arms, chest. Sofia... those arms. I had to remind myself to *breathe*.

We talked about everything and nothing while the rain sang for us. It was easy. Natural. There was a moment when we locked eyes, he leaned in, just a little. Like maybe. Maybe he'd kiss me. But he didn't. And somehow... that made me like him even more.

I didn't want to seem too forward either, so I played it cool, like I wasn't totally dying inside.

So yeah. I like him. Like, really like him.

Wish me luck. Maybe next time, I'll get the kiss.

'Til next time,

xoxo, Amaya

Chapter Thirty-Four

Get up, Amaya.

You're not a damn *muñeca de trapo*. Rag dolls don't pick themselves up. But I do.

I squeeze my eyes shut against the thin morning light slipping through the blinds. My body feels like cement—heavy with exhaustion, heavier with grief. But the mess inside my chest weighs more.

Five days since Max stormed out. Since I sat on the floor, shaking—hollowed by fear, shame, and a pain I still don't have the words for.

"Fuck men," I whisper into the stillness, like a curse. A release. Then—not all men. Papi is good. Mr. Nouel's basically kindness with a French accent. Milo's a golden retriever in a baseball cap.

Fine. So maybe fuck some men.

Every day I drag myself to Reflections Studio—burying in clients, in color, in movement—anything that feels less wrecked. But the second I come home, the silence hits like a wave I can't outrun.

Still, I refuse to rot here.

I throw on a hoodie, a thick coat, that ridiculous scarf Ryan bought me at the Nyack Autumn Street Fair—burnt orange, mustard, deep red, even a little green, like fall stitched into wool. I've tossed it out three times. I've fished it back three times. Cursing him, myself, my stupid soft heart.

I hate gloves, but I shove an old pair into my pockets anyway.

Let's move, Amaya. Before the sadness gets too comfortable.

By the time I'm bundled up, I look like a walking comforter. Or a laundry pile with legs. But I don't care. I need the cold. I need something that shocks me back into my body.

I get in the car—no destination, no plan. Just drive. Let the wind and road decide. When the fog in my chest finally lifts, I'm pulling into Tallman Mountain State Park. The lot's almost empty. A few scattered cars. A world that feels paused.

The Hudson stretches wide and gray in the distance. The trees stand bare, skeletal, reaching for a sky that offers nothing. Maybe I'm reaching too. Reaching for quiet. For a version of myself that doesn't jump at every noise. For peace that doesn't vanish the second I start to believe I deserve it.

The air smells like an autumn goodbye—wet dirt, cracked bark, rushing wind. I zip my coat higher and start walking. Each step crunches loud beneath my boots—sharp and stubborn, like the earth is reminding me, *you're still here.*

The further I go, the quieter it gets. No cars. No voices. Just the raw breath of winter moving in, tugging at my coat. My breath fogs the air. Somewhere close, a creek whispers—clinging to motion, refusing to freeze.

My thoughts are louder out here. But less tangled. More honest.

I think of Ravi. His voice, like quiet water. *"God isn't asking for perfection. He just wants presence."* The way he looked at me—not like I was damaged. Just… human. *"The Lord is close to the brokenhearted. He saves those crushed in spirit."* Maybe he's right. Maybe I want to believe it.

I hike higher, until the trees open up and the Hudson comes into full view—still, silvered, waiting for no one. I breathe in deep. The cold grabs my lungs like a fist. I close my eyes and whisper into the air—like a prayer, like a dare—

"I'm still here."

✷ ✷ ✷

I'm halfway home when my phone buzzes against the seat.

Esperanza.

I exhale and swipe to answer.

"*Hola*, Esperanza."

"Hello, *amorcito!*" she practically sings. "*¡Escúchame, mi niña!* I have fantastic news!"

I wait, a reluctant smile tugging at my mouth.

"Ryan is finally coming home tonight! *¡Por fin!*" she gasps dramatically. "Marcel and I are throwing him a little welcome dinner. Nothing big, you know. *Muy casual.*"

"Esperanza, there's literally nothing casual about anything you do."

"*¡Ay, qué exagerada!*" she cries. "It's just a little food, a little *vino*, some pastries, maybe *pastelitos*, music, *cafecito… ya tú sabes*—low key."

I can't help but smile.

"Super low key," I tease. "What's next, a roasted pig?"

She laughs like she might actually consider it.

"No *lechon*, but that actually sounds amazing! Oh, and you better bring Basha. You girls are part of the family."

My smile fades. The bruise. The shame.

"I'm not sure I can go," I say quietly. "Things have been… rough."

She softens right away.

"*Ay, mi amor.* You don't have to stay long. Just pass by. Ryan gets in at eight. We'll be waiting."

Before I can respond, she hangs up.

I stare at the screen.

The bruise might be fading. But the scar underneath? Still raw.

✷ ✷ ✷

I pull up to Beets Beauty Box and push the door open like a survivor crawling into shelter.

"Hello, beautiful ladies," I call out weakly, giving a half-wave.

Basha's mid-flip with her blow-dryer, perfecting a client's honey-blonde waves. Without missing a beat, she shouts across the room, "Hello, Freebird!" in that big, loud, Basha-brand way that somehow makes everything feel a little lighter.

Without even looking up, she goes, "Girl, with that hair? People gonna stop you like, 'Excuse me ma'am, are you famous?'"

Her client laughs, flipping her head in the mirror.

"Okay, girl, you're good to go. Don't let the wind disrespect my art," Basha says, dramatically dropping her brush.

Once the client leaves, she finally turns to me—and fully clocks the damage. Hands to her hips. Brows practically climbing into the ceiling.

"What in the tragic, dehydrated-curl nation is happening on your head?" she demands, hands on hips, scandalized enough to wake the dead.

I groan. "Girl, I know, okay? I could scrub pots with this hair. I'm in desperate need of a gloss, a trim—possibly a whole new identity."

She marches over, lifts a limp curl like it just committed a felony.

"This is curl abuse, Amaya. Starvation. Your coils are filing complaints. Honestly, I should call the authorities."

A laugh rips out of me—loud, real, deep. The first one in days that doesn't feel forced.

Basha smirks, victorious. "Still got it."

I sink into the chair, surrendering.

By the time she's done—glossed, trimmed, straightened—I barely recognize myself. Sleek sheets of cinnamon caramel frame my face like captured sunlight. I look different. I feel lighter. Like maybe I've finally shed a layer of grief.

"Esperanza invited us to dinner tonight," I say, watching her in the mirror. "For Ryan."

She lifts a brow, smirking. "Ohhh, now it makes sense. Trying to look extra fine for Mr. Still-Sexy, Stupid-for-Leaving, and Suddenly-Back Ryan?"

I groan. "Don't start."

"Mmhmm. Getting your hair all shiny and dangerously fine-y just to pretend you don't care when he falls at your feet? Iconic behavior, Freebird."

"Please. I'm getting my hair done for me. Not for any man."

"Yeah, yeah. Tell it to the mirror, baby. So what are you wearing?"

"Nothing. Because I'm not going."

She gasps like I kicked her puppy. "And why not?"

I point at my face. "Hellooo? Looks like I lost a fight. I don't need the questions or the pity."

She waves it off. "Slap on some concealer and say you took a boxing class. Tell 'em the other girl looks worse."

I shake my head. "I'm serious."

"So am I." She plops down in the chair across from me like a toddler on strike. "If you're not going, I'm not going either. I'll chill with Oscar, eat all his snacks, and watch trash TV."

"Sunshine, I love you, and I know you're my ride-or-die, but tonight I just need quiet and sleep."

She softens right away. "Promise me you'll call if you need anything."

I pinky swear. She kisses my finger like we're six years old.

"Sealed."

✶ ✶ ✶

I leave Beets Beauty Box feeling lighter—like I let go of a weight I didn't know I'd been dragging around.

For a second, I think about swinging by my studio Maybe to check on my plants. Maybe just to breathe in the scent of lavender and dreams made real.

But I don't.

My hands are full enough tonight—with myself. Besides, my plants are probably thriving better than I am. I hate that, somewhere in the back of my mind, I already picked out the perfect outfit—like part of me still wants to show up tonight.

Instead, I head straight home, scrolling through Instagram as I walk up the stairs to my apartment.

Clients have been tagging the studio—smiley selfies, glowing thank-you posts—and for a second, the pride outweighs the ache.

I'm still smiling at a post when I look up—and my stomach drops straight through the floor.

Max.

Leaning against my apartment door like he never shattered a single thing. Shoulders slumped. Hoodie low. Hair a mess. Eyes red-rimmed, heavy with something that looks a lot like regret. He looks like a ghost. A haunted version of the man I once thought could be my forever future.

"Amaya," he says, voice rough. "Can we talk?"

Every cell in my body screams no. Run. Slam the door. Save yourself. But my body betrays me—caught between fear and something softer I don't trust anymore. I cross my arms, holding myself still.

"What's left to say, Max?"

He shifts, stepping closer, voice cracking. "I need to apologize. Please. Just let me in."

And against every instinct—against everything I know—I let him inside. Because I'm tired. Because the neighbors might be watching. Because a small, bruised part of me still remembers when he made me feel like I was enough. Because something is seriously wrong with me.

The second he steps in, I smell it. Alcohol. Not enough to knock me over, just enough to raise every wall inside me.

He moves like he's dragging every bad decision behind him.

"I never wanted to hurt you," he says, voice wrecked. "I love you, Amaya. I've never loved anyone like you."

I step back. Fast. "Love isn't bruises, Max."

"It was an accident," he pleads.

"You slammed the door in my face...*hard*," I snap. "You hurt me. Whether you meant to or not, you did."

His face twists. He sinks onto the couch, hands dragging down his skin like he's trying to pull himself together.

"I'll get help. Therapy. I'll fix this. Just... give me another chance."

I swallow hard. "I cared about you," I say quietly. "A part of me still does. And it hurts. But I'm not drowning with you."

He lifts his head, eyes burning.

"I've been trying. MAX Fitness keeps me grounded, but falling for you..." He trails off, his voice cracking. "It brought out stuff I didn't even know I carried. Jealousy. Fear. Losing you... I thought we were building something real."

I believe him. I hate that I do.

"I thought we were building something real," he says again, softer this time.

I take a breath. "I'm not going backward," I whisper. "I grew up in chaos, Max. I'm not living in it again. You have to fix yourself. Without me."

The warmth drains from his face in an instant. "You'll never find someone who loves you like I do. I'd give my life for you."

I lift my chin. "I don't want love like this, Max."

His hands ball into fists—shaking, like he's trying to hold himself together and failing.

"Whatever we were... whatever we could've been—it's gone. Because *you* destroyed it."

He stares at me, like he doesn't recognize the girl standing in front of him. Because I don't sound scared anymore. I sound like someone who finally knows her worth—and refuses to shrink for anyone.

"Love isn't supposed to hurt," I tell him. "And yes, Maximiliano. I *will* find someone who loves me one day. Not like you did—better."

He draws in a shaky breath, like the words punched the air right out of him.

"So that's it?" he chokes. "You're just throwing us away?"

I laugh—low, bitter. "No, Max. *You* threw us away."

He scrubs a hand down his face, bitterness crawling into his voice. "Right. So what now? You're running back to *him?*"

Before I can answer a knock slices through the tension.

My heart jumps.

Basha.

Shit. I thought she was going to hang out with Oscar. What is she doing here? If she sees Max, she might punch him. Or launch whatever she's holding. Or grab the closest kitchen knife and tell him to start running.

Please don't let it be Basha.

I crack the door—and the world tilts.

Ryan.

Standing there with an enormous paper bag. Warm smile. Tired eyes.

Shit. Not him. Not now.

"Hey," he says, voice soft. A little teasing. "Uh… bad time?"

He glances behind me, completely unaware of the storm waiting on the other side of the door.

"My dad and Esperanza thought you might need some comfort food. They might've gone a little overboard."

Understatement of the year. Try worst timing in human history.

"I thought you were Basha," I whisper.

Ryan smirks. "Disappointed?"

I try to laugh. Try to act normal. But when I reach for the bag and turn my face—he sees it.

The bruise.

His entire body stiffens. Smile vanishes. Eyes darken. Shoulders square. His mouth tightens, like he's holding back something sharp.

"Amaya…" His voice drops low, breaking apart. He steps closer, hand lifting like he wants to trace the hurt—but stops short. His fist curls tight instead.

"What happened to you?"

I step back fast. Panic flares in my chest, hot and immediate.

"I'm fine," I blurt. "I'm handling it. I'm actually really busy and—"

He hesitates—just long enough for me to hope he'll stay outside. Then he doesn't.

He steps inside, slow, deliberate, like he's done waiting for permission.

Kill me now.

The air shifts. His presence fills the room before his words do. His eyes find Max—and the temperature drops twenty degrees. Max straightens. The slumped regret disappears, replaced by raw voltage.

Ryan doesn't move at first. His silence lands harder than anger ever could.

"Was this you?" His voice is low. Controlled. Cold enough to draw blood.

"It was an accident," Max spits.

Ryan steps forward, fists flexing once at his sides.

"I don't need every detail to understand one thing. You fucking hurt her. That's enough."

Ryan never curses. He's always so controlled—too controlled sometimes. I used to love that about him. If he's swearing now, it's not to scare Max—it's because he can't stand the sight of me hurt.

Max lets out a hollow laugh. "Here comes the hero routine."

"I'm here because I care about her," Ryan snaps. "That's not a routine."

His voice is so steady it almost hurts. *Care about me?* After everything? Now? The words scrape across something I thought had scarred over.

"You don't get to play the hero," he growls. "You left her once for your precious career. You think you can just walk back in and fix what you broke?"

"You're right. I made mistakes. Mistakes I regret. But I never laid a fucking hand on her."

Regret. Easy word to say after the damage's done. Does he regret leaving… or does he just regret losing me?

Max lunges—shoulders slamming into Ryan.

Ryan barely moves. It's like watching force hit stone.

"Walk out, Max," he says, voice low, controlled. "Before you do something you can't take back."

Max shoves him again. Ryan grabs his shirt, slamming him into the doorframe. The sound thunders through the apartment.

"Stop!" I cry, the word tearing out of me.

Max yanks free and swings—a wild, reckless punch meant for Ryan, but it misses and connects with the wall. The drywall caves with a sickening crunch, a jagged hole splitting open, edges dusted white. My breath catches. For a moment, I'm not here—I'm back there. Fernando's voice breaking through the walls, Soledad screaming, the sound of fists and plaster and fear. The holes that stayed long after they left. Holes we learned to pretend weren't there.

I stumble back, heart hammering so hard it hurts. The air thickens—rage and panic twisting into something feral. For a second, I can almost see it—the moment these men could destroy each other.

"Max!" I shout, throat raw. "Get out. Just go!"

The room freezes. My voice slices through the chaos. It isn't begging—it's command.

I don't tell Ryan to leave. And Max sees it.

His chest heaves, eyes wild—somewhere between rage and heartbreak. He stops, really looks at me. The kind of look that feels like it's searching for something to take with him.

"You always fucking run, Amaya," he spits. "You think you're better than the mess you came from. All I wanted was a chance to make it right—to make *us* right." His voice cracks, then hardens. "I would've given you everything. But give it time… you'll drive him away too. *Again*."

His eyes cut to Ryan, venom curling his words. "Maybe he's exactly what you deserve—a man who already chose something else over you once."

Ryan's jaw tightens. He doesn't move, doesn't rise to it—just stands there, breathing hard, choosing restraint over ruin. But I feel it—the tremor in him, the storm he's holding back just for me.

Max storms out, slamming the door so hard the walls tremble, the air rushing through the cracks he left behind. The silence that follows isn't peace—it's the kind that hums in your ears after a bomb goes off. I sink to the floor, shaking, arms wrapped around myself. Not collapsing—anchoring. Holding what's left of me still after the breaking.

Ryan drops beside me, hands hovering, unsure. "Amaya," he says, barely above a whisper.

I shake my head, voice hoarse. "I don't need you to fix me, Ryan. I'm not some broken thing you can rescue."

He drags a hand through his hair, exhaling hard. There's a quiet ache in the sound, like he's been holding that breath for years. "I know," he says softly. "But please… let me be here for you."

Tears sting my eyes, spilling hot and fast. "What do you even want from me, Ryan?"

He looks at me like he's been waiting years to say it. "You."

I laugh—low, bitter, cracking in the middle. After years. He says it like it's simple. Like it's easy. I don't know what to do with it. Not now. Maybe not ever.

"I can't do this," I whisper.

He rises slowly, almost like he's hoping I'll stop him.

I don't.

Not because I want him gone. Because I'm scared of what I'd ask for if he stayed.

Chapter Thirty-Five

Ryan's heartbeat is the first thing I hear—steady, strong, and soothing, like waves folding over a familiar shore. My fingers twitch against his chest, but I don't move. I can't. The air feels fragile, as if one deep breath could shatter whatever this is between us. If I move, it might fall apart. I'm not ready for it to end.

I don't know what time it is. I don't want to know. Time doesn't belong here. All I can do is stay—curled against him, breathing in the quiet mix of cologne and soap, and that warm ache that's his alone.

His arm drapes around me, light but grounding, a gravity I still crave. I tell myself I should move. I don't. Because I feel safe—too safe.

A lump swells in my throat. I swallow it back, hard. I hate that my body remembers him even when my heart swore it wouldn't.

So I focus on the rise and fall of his chest, the soft pull of fabric under my fingers. Just a little longer, I whisper. One more heartbeat. For a few stolen breaths, I let the world shrink to this—his warmth, my silence, the lie that this is still ours.

Pretend it's real. Pretend he's still mine. Pretend the hurt never happened.

But it did. And it always will.

* * *

When I stir again, he's gone.

The blanket around me is neatly tucked—too careful, too deliberate. He must've done it before he left.

I sit up slowly, pressing my fingertips to my temples. My eyes feel swollen, my skin oddly soft—the small mercy heartbreak leaves behind. I move like I'm underwater, suspended between dream and daylight, still trying to decide if last night was real—if I really let myself need him, even for a stolen breath.

Then I see it: a folded napkin beside the empty mug on the table. My chest tightens. I pick it up with unsteady hands. His handwriting— small, slanted, careful: heartbreak written in lowercase.

"Didn't want to wake you. You looked peaceful. I'm still here—just not pushing."

That's it. No promises. No over-explaining. Just… him.

I run my thumb along the napkin's edge, tracing the letters like they might bleed out a hidden truth—something he couldn't bring himself to say aloud. I hate that it gets to me. Maybe because it's quiet. Because it's honest in a way words rarely are.

I'm still here. What does that even mean?

Like I'm supposed to forget he left. Forget that he chose his future over me—and now he's back with gentle words and quiet regret, as if that's enough to rewrite the past. Nope. Not this time.

Anger hits hard and fast, scorching through the ache he left behind. I shouldn't have let him hold me. Shouldn't have given in to that pull—or let myself feel anything. That was weak. Foolish.

And yet—beneath the anger, something else moves. Softer. Wilder. Alive. Something that won't die no matter how hard I try to bury it.

Because his words… they still find me. And I hate that I don't know what to do with them.

I push off the couch and head for the bathroom, splashing cold water onto my face, avoiding the mirror like it's something dangerous. When I finally look, the truth stares back—swollen eyes, tear-streaked cheeks, and that faint, yellowing bruise. My fingers brush over it gently. Still tender. Still healing. Like the rest of me.

Max's voice. Ryan's quiet steadiness. My own doubts. They echo inside my skull, overlapping until they're just noise—loud and relentless.

The bathroom light is too harsh—every line sharper, every flaw louder. For a heartbeat, I hate the fractured girl in the mirror.

I grip the sink until my knuckles are pale. Breathe deeper.

You're not broken, I whisper. *You're just healing.*

✳ ✳ ✳

I grab my coffee, Ryan's note still folded in one hand, and sink into the couch.

I should rip it up, block his number, and be done with it—but instead I just stare, letting the anger simmer. At him, at Max, at myself.

My phone lights up, cutting through the silence.

> **Basha:** Don't make me come over there to drag you out of the pit of despair. Also, I heard crying makes your skin glow, so I expect you to look like a freshly Botoxed celebrity by the time I see you next.

A tired, fragile laugh escapes me. Only Basha could turn heartbreak into skincare advice.

> **Ryan:** I didn't want to leave without making sure you were okay. I'd like to talk when you're ready. Hopefully today. Please let me know.

My stomach twists. I set the phone down like it's hot to the touch, heart tightening.

Then another notification lights up the screen.

> **Max:** Sorry about everything. I feel terrible, Amaya. So, so terrible...

I don't open it. I just let it sit there—heavy, unanswered. A wound I refuse to touch.

Then—one last ping.

A client confirming our session for Friday. Relief slices through the noise. Work. Something steady. Something clean. Something that doesn't make my heart ache.

I pull in a shaky breath, still drowning under everything I can't name. I need a voice that doesn't break me. A voice that reminds me who I am.

I need *home*.

"Amaya, *mi niña!* This is a rare treat. You just made my day," Papi says, his voice bubbling with joy.

A smile tugs at my lips, fragile but real. "I know. Sorry, Papi. I haven't called lately."

"Don't be sorry, *mi hija*. Just tell me how you are."

I pause, tracing the rim of my coffee cup, stalling. "*Más o menos*. I've... been better."

His voice softens. "Life throws us curves, *mi niña linda*. The trick is deciding which ones to swing at, and which to let pass."

A soft, broken laugh slips out. "Feels like I keep swinging at the wrong pitches, Papi."

He listens as I unravel—more than I planned to. About Ryan. About Max. About the ache that keeps finding new ways to live inside me.

When he finally speaks, his voice is calm, steady, filled with that quiet kind of wisdom that never tries too hard.

"You're not a problem, Amaya. Sometimes we carry things from our past without realizing it. Those things make us scared—to trust, to believe we deserve good love. But that doesn't make you broken. It just means you're still learning. We all are. Every day."

His words sink deep, warm and grounding. Papi never finished high school—he chose the land over the classroom. Said books could wait, but the *campo* couldn't. And yet, he's the wisest man I know. The kind of wise that doesn't need big words—just heart.

I press my eyes shut, breathing him in through the static. His words settle inside me like medicine.

"I don't think I'm built for love, Papi," I whisper. My voice feels small. "It always starts out sweet... and then it just hurts. It always hurts."

"Don't be so hard on yourself," he says gently. "Healing doesn't happen overnight. And remember, *Amaya*—you're worthy of love. The kind that lifts you up, not the kind that drags you down."

My throat burns. I blink fast, refusing to cry.

"Come visit," he adds after a beat. "Clear your head. We'll cook your favorite—*sancocho* with rice, and a side of crispy *concón* and *aguacate*."

A choked laugh bubbles out. "Papi, you had me at *sancocho.* I'll come by soon, I promise."

"I'll hold you to that," he says, his voice all warmth—safe, the kind that roots me like home.

Papi's voice lingers in my ear long after the call ends. The apartment feels too still, too heavy with what I haven't said.

By afternoon, I've packed a bag and booked the first flight out. I don't need answers—I need home.

I wake to the comforting sounds of home.

A rooster's crow cuts through the heavy morning air, carrying the smoky scent of wood fires and the bittersweet perfume of coffee brewing somewhere close. The mix wraps around me like a memory I didn't know I missed.

I stretch, sinking into the quiet warmth of my childhood room. Papi's house hasn't changed much—the same faded turquoise walls, the same threadbare curtains that flutter lazily in the breeze, like they've got nowhere better to be.

There are only a few upgrades now. Running water, a real bathroom, and a washing machine that sounds like it's trying to break out and run away. Judging by the sea of clothes strung across the yard, I'm guessing it doesn't always win the fight.

Barefoot, I step outside. The packed earth is cool beneath my feet, grounding me in a way New York floors never could.

The roads I once ran wild on are paved now, but the houses—small, proud, and loud with color—still stand like they're holding their breath in the heat. Coral pink. Sea blue. Sunflower yellow. Lime green. It's like the whole village made a pact that no two homes could wear the same skin.

As I walk down the familiar path, the past greets me in bursts.

"¡Amaya, *mi niña*! Look how grown you are!"

Doña Lidia's voice cuts through the morning, and before I can even smile, I'm wrapped in her sturdy arms. Her hug is as fierce and warm as I remember, though her face now wears a few more laugh lines—like time's been sketching quietly while I was gone.

Don Félix waves from his rocking chair, tipping his hat.

"*Mija*, it's been too long! Don't be a stranger!"

And then—Carmelita.

I barely have time to breathe before she comes flying toward me like I've come back from the dead. Her dramatic ass hasn't changed a bit.

"*¡Dios mío*, Amaya!" she cries, clutching my face between her hands like I'm some long-lost saint.

Her jet-black hair gleams in the sunlight—clearly dyed, probably with shoe polish or straight-up coal. In the span of three breathless minutes, she unleashes every ounce of town gossip, her words tumbling over each other so fast the air itself can't keep up.

"Did you hear about Don Rafa's new wife? *Ay, muchacha*, she's twenty-three—*TWENTY-THREE!* And she already thinks she owns the whole village! Also, you won't believe what happened at the *colmado* last week—some drunk tried to pay for beer with *plátanos*! Oh, and Chacha finally fixed that lazy eye, but now she looks surprised all the time!"

I blink, stunned by the flood of words and energy.

"Carmelita, please—" I start, but she cuts me off with a dramatic wave of her hand.

"No, no, let me finish! And you better sit down for this one— Doña Milagros' son? The one we all thought was studying medicine? Turns out he's in Santo Domingo selling hair extensions! Hair extensions, *mi amor!* You can't make this up!"

That's it. I lose it. I laugh until my stomach aches and tears spill down my cheeks. For the first time in what feels like forever, I let myself *really* laugh—loud and unfiltered, until my body remembers what joy feels like.

Same Carmelita. Same wild energy. Same over-the-top storytelling.

When I finally catch my breath, she grips my shoulders and shakes her head like I'm her biggest heartbreak.

"*Ay*, Amaya, you need to visit more! I have too much *chisme* and not enough people to tell it to!"

Carmelita throws the words over her shoulder as she spins on her heel, shouting after her runaway chickens like they've betrayed her personally. Her voice trails after them across the yard, sharp and loving all at once.

A couple of barefoot kids race past me, kicking up dust, their laughter spilling into the air like sunlight. For a fleeting second, I see *her*—the girl I used to be. Wild. Untamed. Free. A lump rises in my throat. I should come home more often. I should've never let so much time slip through my fingers.

I blink back the sudden sting in my eyes and keep walking, letting my feet remember the way on their own until the path opens into Papi's farm.

It's just how I remember it—rows upon rows of tall, green plantain trees stretching their arms toward the sky, their broad leaves whispering to one another in the wind. Some bend low under the weight of heavy bunches, the fruit still green, still waiting for their time. Mango trees are scattered like golden confetti, their branches heavy with fruit—some so ripe they've surrendered to the ground in sweet, sticky splatters. Near the edge of the property, the guava tree stands proud, perfuming the air with that soft, pink sweetness that clings to my childhood memories.

And there's Papi. Just like always. Hat tilted low against the sun. Hands dark with soil. Moving between the rows as if every leaf is a conversation he's still having. It wouldn't surprise me if he's whispering to the plantains again—the way he used to when he thought no one was listening.

When he spots me, his whole face lights up. That smile. The one that makes me feel ten years old again—barefoot, fearless, untouched by the world.

His voice carries pride and peace, roughened by years of sun and wind. And for a heartbeat, I forget every reason I ever had to leave.

I watch him, steady and content, and I wonder—how can someone do the same thing their whole life and still love it with every fiber of their being? Maybe that's the difference between us. I run from things. He finds peace in them.

I turn—and there it is.

Our *charamico* tree—our Dominican version of a Christmas tree, minus the pine—stands tall and proud, its dry branches wrapped in mismatched vintage lights and covered in wooden ornaments that still smell faintly of cinnamon and dust.

A memory floods through me so vivid it knocks the breath from my chest.

Papi and I riding our old donkey up the hill to my grandparents' house, gathering dry branches for our Christmas tree. It was our tradition—our kind of magic. He'd shape the branches, paint them white by hand, then leave them to dry for a day or two. By the end of the week, the tree would glow—handmade wooden ornaments, tangled strings of colored lights that blinked unevenly but somehow still felt perfect.

And the best part—the night we lit it up.

Papi playing his guitar under the mango tree, all of us singing until the stars felt close enough to touch. Until the whole world felt small enough to hold in our hands.

For a little while, everything had been simple. Good. Enough.

I swallow hard, blinking against the sudden shimmer in my eyes. I smile, running my fingers over one of the ornaments—a tiny wooden star, chipped on one side, my initial carved carefully into the back.

A laugh escapes me as another memory flashes bright and fast— the year a mango fell right on Papi's head mid-song. Then another. His face went so red he looked like he might curse, but he wouldn't—not in front of us. That second mango sealed his fate. We laughed until we couldn't breathe, gasping between wheezes and tears. I shake my head, still smiling. Some things don't change. And some things do.

Like me.

I thought I came here to run from the noise. To breathe. But maybe… I came to remember. To reclaim something I lost. Maybe the hardest journeys aren't the ones that take us far—but the ones that bring us back. Back to what we lost. Back to who we were, before the breaking.

Down the street, nearly every house has its own *charamico* tree standing proudly—rustic branches painted white, red, or green, dressed in wooden ornaments and tangled lights waiting for nightfall to bring them to life. Some neighbors get creative—twisting branches into stars, angels, even donkeys—each one a handmade testament to love, tradition, and lives stitched together with hope and laughter.

I stand there for a long moment, letting it all sink into my bones.

The sun warms my skin. The scent of guava and woodsmoke hangs heavy in the air. From *el colmado* down the street, merengue and bachata spill out in warm, familiar waves—blending with the neighbor's crackling radio, distant laughter, the hum of everyday life.

It's all so alive. So real. So stubbornly, beautifully unchanging.

I close my eyes and breathe deep, like I can trap it all inside me—keep it for the days when this place feels far away, like a dream I once had and almost forgot.

I don't want to forget any of it.

The colors. The music. The warm kiss of the sun on my skin. The way the trees sway—lazy, content, unbothered.

I don't know when I'm coming back. But when I leave, I'll carry this with me—whole, untouched, fiercely alive. A piece of home I refuse to ever let go.

By the time I shower and get dressed, the house is packed.

"Oh my gosh," I whisper under my breath.

I step into the patio—and get ambushed. Kisses on my cheeks, arms wrapping around me, hands ruffling my hair like I'm still ten years old. The air fills with laughter, stories, and voices all tumbling over each other in welcome.

"¡Amaya *llegó*!"

The shout ripples through the house, and suddenly there's clapping—loud and bright, like fireworks going off in the middle of the patio. For a second, it feels like I've just won a trophy for finding my way back home.

Tío Niel's smile stretches ear to ear as he lifts a sagging sack in both hands.

"¡*Mira, mi niña*! Look what I brought from my piece of dirt!"

I peek inside—enough avocados to feed the entire village.

"Tío… you brought the whole tree."

He throws his head back, laughing loud and full.

"¡*Pa' que no te falte aguacate, muchachita*!"

Marisol places a massive pot of white rice on the table, and the smoky aroma hits instantly—*concón*, that perfect, crispy, golden layer at the bottom.

Then comes Papi—beaming, hauling out the biggest *caldero* of *sancocho* I've ever seen. The pot's blackened edges tell its own history—decades of meals, laughter, and love. It smells like *leña*, earth, and home.

Marisol wipes her hands on her apron and announces proudly,

"Today's *sancocho* was made *al fogón*! So Amaya doesn't forget her roots."

The room erupts in cheers and clapping, loud and proud, like remembering where you come from deserves a standing ovation.

Papi winks. "Save me the *patas de gallina!*"

I roll my eyes, laughing. Only my father could get excited about chicken feet.

From across the room, Tío Lito yells, "Whoever takes the neck—we're fighting!"

Tía Ariana fires back, "No problem, *cara de burro*—I'm here for the pork!"

I lose it—laughing so hard my stomach aches, tears streaming down my face.

God, I love my family.

The noise, the teasing, the endless food, the stubborn love stitched into every hug and joke—it's everything I didn't know I was starving for.

This. This is what I needed.

And quietly, stubbornly, I promise myself—I'm coming back more often.

✶ ✶ ✶

The flight back is chaos.

People dressed like they're headed straight to the club—tight jumpsuits, fur jackets, fresh blowouts, and enough perfume to choke the air. Old men shout across aisles like they're back in the *campo*, carrying full conversations with someone three rows away. A baby screams like it just found out milk isn't free anymore. I tighten my seatbelt. We're not even off the ground yet, and I already feel like I need another vacation.

The speakers crackle, and the pilot's voice fills the cabin—smooth, practiced, switching effortlessly between English and Spanish.

"Ladies and gentlemen, welcome aboard Flight 774 with service to New York City. Please fasten your seatbelts as we prepare for takeoff."

"*Damas y caballeros, bienvenidos al vuelo setecientos setenta y cuatro con destino a Nueva York. Por favor, abróchense los cinturones mientras nos preparamos para el despegue.*"

Flight attendants move down the aisle, doing final checks, pretending not to see the woman two rows up still FaceTiming like she's hosting a live show for the whole island.

The engines roar. The plane starts to roll, picking up speed, the windows trembling with momentum. I sink into my seat and rest my forehead against the cold glass.

Below, the palm trees stretch endlessly toward the horizon, their green fading into the deep, endless blue of the ocean. The sun bounces off the water—warm, golden—as if it's trying to press this moment into memory so I won't forget.

I reach into my bag and pull out the rosary Marisol pressed into my hand at the airport.

I whisper a quiet prayer. Not because I'm afraid of flying—because it roots me, lets me hold on a little longer: to the people, the land, the parts of me I keep losing and finding again.

The wheels lift. My stomach rises with the plane. And I watch as my beautiful island shrinks beneath me, slowly swallowed by clouds and distance.

A tear slips down my cheek. I don't wipe it away.

I just hold the rosary tighter—the beads digging gently into my palm, small, steady reminders of peace. Of home. Of healing.

My chest tightens. *Soledad.*

I don't know why she comes to me now. Maybe because she never prayed—not that I ever saw. Maybe because peace always felt like something she had to fight against, something she never allowed herself to hold. She wore her wounds like armor, her anger like a second skin—never softening, never letting go.

I blink hard, exhaling slowly as I swallow the ache rising in my throat. But I know now—I can't keep avoiding this. I pull out my journal and flip to a blank page, my hand trembling—just slightly. The pen presses down.

And I begin.

Soledad, I'm writing this letter as part of my journey toward healing...

The words spill from me like water cracking through stone.

Some wounds aren't meant to be buried. They bloom—painful and raw—so something new can grow.

I set the pen down, staring at the ink bleeding through the thin paper. I don't know if I'll ever send it. But it's out of me now.

I read the letter once more, then tear the page carefully from my journal and fold it—once, twice. I slip it back between the journal's pages, where the words can rest until I'm ready to face them again. Outside the window, clouds drift past in slow procession, the sky opening and closing like it's learning how to breathe again. I close my eyes and let the hum of the engines steady my breath.

For the first time in a long time, the quiet inside me doesn't scare me. It feels like peace.

Chapter Thirty-Six

I almost don't text him back. Because love shouldn't feel like a bruise you can't explain. Maybe Soledad didn't just curse my name—maybe she cursed my heart too.

Those library romances I used to devour? The perfect timing, the sweeping gestures, the kind of love that never fractures? Maybe they're real—for someone else. Not for me. Happily-ever-afters feel like someone else's dream. And love—love can be cruel. Especially when your own mother might've prayed harder for your downfall than your joy.

Even after everything—Papi's voice in my ear, the air thick with plantains, standing barefoot on the dirt roads of my childhood, trying to remember what home was supposed to feel like—I almost let his message sit there. Maybe because I'd just spent days pretending distance didn't hurt, and I wasn't ready to feel it again.

But I'm tired. Tired of pretending his name doesn't split something open in me every single time. Because Ryan was never just a chapter. He was home before I even knew I was looking for one. The quiet steadiness that pulled me in without even trying—the way his eyes could find mine and make everything else go still.

Max was fire—loud, consuming. Ryan was gravity—quiet, steady, the force that keeps you from drifting. And that's what scares me most—how part of me still remembers how to breathe easier when he's near. So I text him back. His reply comes fast. Like he never put the phone down.

Now I'm standing outside my apartment—arms crossed, stomach tight—watching his car pull up like my world doesn't tilt a little every time I see him.

The second he steps out, I feel it. That shift. Not loud or dramatic—just the kind that moves through the air, then your lungs. Gosh, I hate how this man makes me feel. Like I'm one exhale away from falling back into something I barely survived the first time.

He holds out a Maison Madeleine bag and a steaming cup, that infuriating half-smile already forming.

"Peace offering," he says, shaking the bag. "Fresh croissant. And your favorite spicy latte. My dad swears he baked this one himself with extra butter—just for you."

I can't help the laugh that slips out. "Liar."

"Hey, if it's burnt, blame the old man."

"You're ridiculous."

"Still got you to smile, though."

Damn him.

I slide into the passenger seat and take a sip, the spices blooming on my tongue. How many nights at Maison Madeleine, this exact latte on my break while he mapped out dreams too big for this town? How many 2 a.m. texts about college deadlines, his replies coming two minutes later—like he was waiting for me to need him?

The silence in the car is heavy. I feel his eyes on me, but I pretend not to notice.

At a red light, his hand brushes mine. I look up, and he gently tilts my chin toward him—fingers soft, not like Papi's rough ones or Soledad's sharp ones.

"I just want you to know," he says quietly, "you're going to be okay, Amaya. Not because of me. Not because of anyone else. But because of you."

The words land softly, like prayer. The light changes, the world moves—but something in me doesn't.

He waits a beat before speaking again, voice lower this time. "You've been carrying storms on your own for too long. Even mountains lean on something, Amaya. It's okay to let someone stand in the rain with you."

It isn't the words—it's how he believes them for me.

I want to say something. Anything. But my voice catches behind my ribs. So I stay still. Let the silence speak for me. Believe him—just for a second.

By the time we reach Nyack Beach, the river glints through the trees like something half-remembered. The world feels quieter here, suspended. He parks facing the water. I stare out at the Hudson. Same river, same current. But the girl in this seat isn't.

My name drifts through my mind—Amaya. *Night Rain. The End.* It follows me like a prophecy I never asked for. Maybe it was always written for me—storms, endings, and the space between heartbreak and healing.

Ryan was my storm—the kind that tears everything loose, forces you to rebuild. Max might've been the ending I didn't see coming. Or maybe… I was just ready to stop pretending broken things could hold me together.

I exhale. "Why did you bring me here?"

"Because you used to love it. You told me once it gave you peace. I thought maybe you could use some again."

"I still do," I whisper.

I grip my cup tighter. "Ryan, you don't need to show up like this. This isn't your mess to clean up. You don't owe me anything. And you can't expect anything from me. My heart… it's not letting anyone else in. Not right now. I'm grateful for the Beauty Angels donation, I mean it. But beyond that?" I look down at my hands. "I'm focused on work. Just like you were."

When I finally meet his eyes, I expect disappointment. Maybe hurt. But all I find is patience.

"I hear you," he says quietly. "And I respect that. But maybe… you're misunderstanding something."

I look at him sideways. "Like what?"

He presses his lips together before he speaks. "The donation wasn't a play. It wasn't strategy. It was just… what felt right. For a cause I believe in. For someone I believe in. I didn't come here to save you, Amaya. I just want to stand beside you."

His voice roughens. "I didn't leave because I stopped caring. I left because I couldn't keep pretending I didn't want more. You wanted roots; I wanted wings. You needed home; I needed movement. I couldn't ask you to follow a dream that wasn't yours." He pauses, the memory softening his tone. "After my mom died, my dad fell apart. The bakery almost went under. I had to step up. Before school, after school, weekends—whatever it took to keep us from losing everything.

I still remember the smell of burnt sugar, the flickering lights, my dad sitting in the dark pretending the silence meant nothing." He looks toward the water like it might forgive him first. "That's when it hit me—no one was coming to save us. If I wanted security, I had to build it myself. It wasn't greed; it was survival. I told myself I'd never rely on anyone again—not for money, not for stability, not even for peace. So when I left, it wasn't because I stopped loving you. It was because I'd watched love undo my father—and if I'm honest, it broke me too. I just learned to hide it better. I worked nonstop, built my businesses from the ground up, telling myself motion meant safety. But somewhere in all that building, I forgot why. Success isn't safety. You can have everything and still wake up terrified of losing the one thing that matters."

He looks at me then—really looks. And something in me falters. Because for the first time, I see it too—the boy who ran, not out of indifference, but out of fear. The same fear I carried, the kind that makes love feel like a risk you can't afford. I used to think his leaving broke me. But maybe it just revealed the cracks that were already there.

For a second, the ache in my chest becomes a pull—an urge to reach for him, to press my face into his shoulder and let the years fall away. To forgive him. To forgive myself. But I stay rooted, hands trembling in my lap, every muscle caught between wanting and restraint.

He looks down, thumb brushing the seam of the steering wheel before he speaks again. "I needed to build something bigger than grief, bigger than fear. But I think what I was really trying to build was a life that didn't hurt to remember." He lets out a long breath. "And now I see it—the only thing that ever made it bearable was you." He turns toward me. "I dated other people. Tried to move on. But no one was you." He lets that hang. "No one will ever be you, Amaya." The air tightens. He shakes his head once. "I used to think love meant choosing one life over another. But maybe it doesn't. Maybe I was just scared."

The truth sinks into the quiet between us, stirring the memory of every night I wished he'd look at me like this again. And now that he does, I don't know how to breathe around it. Every part of me wants to reach for him, to close the distance, but I keep still—afraid that if I move, everything I've rebuilt will shatter.

"I don't need you to fit into some version of my life I imagined years ago," he says quietly. "I just want you in it. However you can be."

My throat burns. I nod, barely. It feels too small for what's breaking open inside me. I tear at the croissant wrapper, pretending to focus, pretending my hands aren't shaking.

A faint smile tugs at his mouth. "You always do that when you're thinking too hard."

"Do what?" My voice comes out small.

He nods at the torn edge. "Pick at something," he says softly. "It's like your hands say what your lips won't."

I pause, the croissant half-torn, the paper crumpling between my fingers.

He smiles faintly, trying to ease the weight in the air. "Just making sure my dad's ego survives," he murmurs. "That croissant was a labor of love."

I almost smile, but the ache rises fast. "You say you didn't ask me to give anything up," I whisper. "But I still lost things, Ryan. I lost us. And maybe that's why it broke me the way it did—because I'd already lost everything else. My father. My family. Every piece of home I thought I could hold on to—even the ones that were never really safe."

My throat tightens. "You were supposed to be the one I didn't have to run from. The one who stayed." The words catch, but I don't stop. "When you left, it wasn't just heartbreak—it was the emptiness after. I'd pick up my phone expecting your name. I'd pass places we used to go and still listen for your laugh. Even silence felt like you sometimes— like it was holding its breath, waiting for you to fill it."

A tear slips down my cheek before I can wipe it away. "After Soledad, after leaving my dad, after losing the only family I had left— every goodbye started to sound the same. You leaving wasn't just love ending. It was every loss I'd ever survived coming back at once." I swallow hard. "I hated that. I kept breathing, but I didn't know how to live without you. I didn't know it then, but it wasn't just heartbreak. It was that old fear waking up again—the one that makes every goodbye feel like the end of the world."

My voice drops, soft. "So yeah, I lost things. I lost sleep. Laughter. The girl who believed love could last. I loved you—maybe too much— and now I don't know if I trust myself to believe again."

He lets the silence stretch, like he knows I need the space to fall apart a little before I can breathe again. "Then don't," he says softly. "Don't decide what we are or where this goes. Some things don't need answers yet—just a little time. Just… be here."

For a long moment, neither of us moves. River light flickers across his face. When he finally turns to me, his voice is quiet.

"Amaya… I never meant to make you carry that alone. I thought distance would make it easier—for both of us. That maybe letting you go was the kindest thing I could do." He exhales. "But I see now… I wasn't protecting you. I was protecting myself—from how much it would hurt to stay. It wasn't because you weren't enough. It was because I was too scared to believe I could be. I'm so sorry."

Something steadies and stings at once. I want to look away, but I don't. Part of me wants the moment to hold. But the question leaves anyway. "Why are you really back, Ryan?"

He draws in a breath. "Because I don't want to regret the things that matter. I chased the dream. Built the empire. I could live anywhere. None of it meant anything if it didn't lead me back to you."

His words land somewhere deep, where grief and hope blur into the same ache. The world stills for a heartbeat. I spent years convincing myself I'd stopped hoping, but maybe hope never left—maybe it just learned how to hide. I should be angry. I should tell him it's too late. But all I can think is that maybe I never stopped hoping he'd find his way back—not just to me, but to us.

He meets my eyes. "When my mom died, I learned how fast time runs out. How easy it is to lose everything that makes it mean something. I stayed away too long—from my dad. From this town. From you."

His voice softens. "I came back because love isn't something I want to leave unfinished."

Silence settles between us—thick, electric. The river moves slow and endless. Forgiving. I stare out the window, fighting the pull toward him, truth humming under my skin—he's still the only thing that's ever felt like home.

✳ ✳ ✳

Ryan flips through a few stations. A missing girl. A life insurance ad. A song trying too hard to be happy.

Then he stops.

A soft voice drifts through the speakers on K-LOVE. The host shares a story about a woman who found peace after years of grief, her words trembling as she talks about surrendering pain, about choosing hope even when it felt impossible.

Then the song begins. "My Jesus" by Anne Wilson.

The first notes are slow, haunting—the kind that don't just play; they linger. They settle where I don't look. I know this song. I always skip it. Not because it's bad—because something in her voice cuts too close, like she's singing what I've never said out loud.

But today, I don't move. I hear everything—the ache in her tone, the breath between each line, the silence right before she exhales again. My grip tightens around the coffee cup; the sleeve buckles under my fingers, soft as my chest.

It's just a song, I lie. My grip crushes the sleeve again; breath shortens on the second chorus.

But I am—coming apart, piece by piece. Each note presses harder, stirring something I thought I buried—maybe faith, maybe loss, maybe the part of me that still wants to believe in something good.

I don't want to feel this. Not now. Not here. Not with him beside me. But the song keeps playing. And I let it. Even when my vision blurs. Even when breathing turns into something I have to remember how to do.

I steal a glance at Ryan.

He's quiet. Still. Eyes forward. Hands steady on the wheel. But something in the way he's sitting—tense, but open—tells me he hears it too. Not just the music. Me. And maybe that's what undoes me most. Because he doesn't say a word. Doesn't reach for my hand. Doesn't try to fill the silence. He just lets it be. Lets me feel.

And somehow, that stillness—his restraint—is the gentlest kind of grace. The kind that breaks me open without breaking me down.

✳ ✳ ✳

At first, it's just another blur along the road. Another landmark I've trained myself to ignore.

Until it isn't.

The little white church. The same one I stumbled into after Max shattered my heart. The same pews I sat in, silent and aching, wondering if God even remembered how to find me.

Ryan eases his foot off the gas. Then, without a word, he turns into the lot.

"Why are we here?" My voice cracks.

"Thought… maybe this place might help us both."

I go still. For a second, I don't know whether to run or breathe. But instead of panic, something quiet rises in my chest. He doesn't push. Just steps out and circles around to open my door. He used to do this every time—never letting me reach for the handle first. Back then, it felt like love. Now it just feels like remembering. It lands somewhere deep. I step out, wordless, the cold brushing my skin.

We fall into step in silence, gravel crunching beneath our feet.

Inside, the church is dimly lit, stained-glass colors bleeding soft blues and reds across the pews. The air feels thick—full of whispered prayers and unspoken hopes. We slip into a pew near the back.

Up front, Ravi's voice threads the stillness.

"Forget the former things; do not dwell on the past. See, I am doing a new thing."

The words land like a thread of light. That verse—how did he know? It feels personal. Like it was waiting for me.

Ravi continues, every word somehow finding its way through the quiet.

"Sometimes, the hardest thing to do is let go of the story we've been telling ourselves. The one where we're the failure. The one where we're not enough. The one where love always leaves."

I shift in my seat.

"It might still feel like winter—like everything's broken, or lost, or unfinished. But God is already at work. Right now. Planting something new in you. Beneath the surface. Beneath the sorrow."

My hands are knotted in my lap. My palms sting where my nails dig into skin.

"Let go of what broke you. You are not the same person who walked into the storm. And what's coming next?" He pauses, voice softening. "It's not just better. It's new."

Silence follows. But not the kind that hurts. The kind that lingers like balm. Like the hush after a deep breath.

Ravi finishes with a quiet prayer. "God, remind us we are not defined by what we've lost. Let us trust what You are growing, even when we can't yet see it. Let us step into what is new, even if our legs still tremble."

He steps down, slow and unhurried, as the congregation stirs. I should get up. But I don't. Not yet.

I look up.

Ravi's eyes catch mine—a quiet recognition warming his kind, dark eyes. I freeze. He remembers me. I was here not long ago, curled in the last pew, whispering questions I couldn't say out loud. He doesn't say anything. Just offers a quiet, knowing smile. A silent welcome back. I nod—awkward, unsure—but somehow, it feels okay. The space grows still again. The kind of peace you don't realize you're starving for until it's right in front of you.

I watch as Ryan kneels beside me, head bowed. I wonder what he's praying for. I stay seated, hands folded, unsure what I'd even ask for— peace? Forgiveness? A way forward? It all feels too big for words.

"Come on," he says quietly.

We walk in silence, his hands tucked into his jacket pockets, his pace unhurried. Instead of heading to the car, he veers toward a small white gazebo facing the river. The Hudson glows under the setting sun, long streaks of gold stretching across the water. It's quiet. Almost unreal. The kind of view that doesn't ask anything of you—just invites you to be still. Ryan exhales, glancing back toward the church. His eyes look glassy, like he's holding back something heavy.

"I used to sit in those pews every Sunday morning with my parents." His jaw tightens. "My mom was the one who kept us grounded. She was… everything." He pauses, breath catching slightly. "After she passed, my dad stopped coming. Said he couldn't understand how someone that good, that selfless, could be taken like that. I guess… I didn't understand either."

The honesty in his voice pulls something loose in me. "So, I stopped too," he adds quietly. "It was easier to throw myself into work. To focus on something I could control."

I nod slightly. I know that feeling—how stillness turns into suffocation, how motion feels like survival.

His voice drops again, rough and quiet. "Now… I think maybe I wasn't just running from the pain." He pauses. "I think I was running from hope too. Because hope means believing you can lose again."

The words land deep. Hope is dangerous. It asks you to believe in things that can break you—but also to stay open, to let light find its way back in.

I take a shaky breath and reach for his hands. They're soft and warm—the opposite of what's trembling inside me. He meets my eyes. No pressure. No fixing. Just presence.

A cold breeze sweeps in from the river, but I don't move. I trace my fingertips along the wooden railing, feeling the rough grain beneath my touch. Wind, water, breath. Long enough for the weight in my chest to settle. Long enough to realize that—for the first time in a long time—I'm not drowning anymore.

We don't speak. We just breathe. Watch the water. Let it all be.

✳ ✳ ✳

His fingers tap lightly against the steering wheel. Minutes later, we pull into a familiar driveway. Ryan puts the car in park and unbuckles his seatbelt. I go still.

A laugh slips out—short, disbelieving. I can't help it.

I glance at the house through the window. My stomach flips. No. It can't be.

It's *the* house. Our house.

The one we used to drive past late at night, windows down, arguing about which one of us would have to sell an organ to afford it. He'd always say he'd give up a lung. I offered a kidney.

What are we doing here?

"Ryan?… What are we doing here?"

He shrugs, casual as ever. "Thought we could stop by."

I laugh—a sharp, unfiltered burst of disbelief. "What, you think the owners are just gonna let us in? Maybe pour us a glass of wine while we tour their living room?"

The sarcasm drips off every word—but he just smirks like this is all perfectly reasonable.

"Worth a shot," he says.

I shake my head. "Absolutely not. You're crazy. I'm not. Well… mostly not. And I am *not* embarrassing myself."

I turn, ready to head straight back to the car—"Hey, Amaya," he calls, cracking up. I stop. Turn slowly. And there he is. Ryan, just casually holding up a key. A freaking key.

No. Freaking. Way.

He doesn't say a word. Just walks up to the door, slips in the key, and opens it—like he's done it a hundred times.

And suddenly—it hits me. The property. The one Mr. Nouel mentioned back at Thanksgiving. I felt it then, but I buried it. Pretended it didn't matter. But this… this is it.

The porch light snaps on. The door swings open, slow—like it knows this moment matters. Some places don't need introductions; they remember you. And the moment stills—like even time is holding its breath.

The inside is… unreal.

High ceilings with thick, exposed beams stretch across the open space. A massive stone fireplace anchors the far wall. Floor-to-ceiling windows cast golden light across smooth wooden floors. Beyond them, the Hudson glows—wide and still beneath the fading sky.

There's a private deck just outside the glass doors. A fire pit. Adirondack chairs angled toward the water like they've been waiting for us. Modern and rustic. Cozy but open. A future we imagined out loud, back when forever didn't feel like a risk.

This is the part in the movie where the girl realizes she's safe. That maybe she can love again. But this isn't a movie. And if it were, I'd probably be the side character who trips right before the happy ending.

"You… bought it?"

He nods, slipping his hands into his jacket pockets. "I did."

My mouth opens. Closes. Then opens again. "It's… breathtaking. You bought it? After all this time—why this house?"

He tilts his head, watching me—calm, patient. "Some doors should be open."

I don't answer. If I do, my heart won't stay quiet.

Ryan steps closer—slow, measured. And when his eyes meet mine, it's not just eye contact. It's like he's searching for the part of me I keep hidden from everyone else.

"No expectations. If you ever need a place to think—or breathe—this door is yours."

The words land heavy in my chest. Because I know exactly what he's offering. Not just shelter—space. A beginning. A maybe. And that's what scares me. Because I don't trust myself not to walk through that door and stay.

The air thickens with everything we don't say. He's offering a home. A chance. A place where hope doesn't feel like a risk—but a return.

He doesn't push. Just a small, knowing smile. "An open door," he says, softer. He slips the keys back into his pocket. No pressure. No begging. Just letting it sit. I stand there, breath caught somewhere between awe and fear.

✳ ✳ ✳

Ryan pulls up in front of my apartment and cuts the engine. For a beat, neither of us moves.

The only sound is the quiet tick of the engine cooling. My heart feels too loud in my chest.

He shifts his weight, rubbing the side of his thigh like he's working up the nerve.

"Hey," he says, voice a little rough.

I glance at him, trying to read the lines in his face. "What's up?"

"If you're free… and feel like a change of scenery—how about a ride to the Bear Mountain ice rink?"

My mouth opens automatically, the reflex words *I don't know how to skate* already lined up and ready. But the way he's looking at me—gentle, hopeful, almost like he's asking more than he's saying—stops the words before they leave my mouth.

I sigh, dramatic and half-smiling. "Fine. But only if you promise not to laugh when I fall on my face. Because I will. Probably more than once."

He laughs under his breath, lifting a hand like he's swearing under oath. "Deal. But for the record, I might not be much better."

I narrow my eyes. "Liar. You've probably been practicing in secret just to embarrass me."

He smirks. "Damn, you caught me. I've been training with Olympic coaches just for this moment."

I roll my eyes, but a smile tugs at my mouth before I can stop it. "Sure, Mr. Ryan Nouel. We'll see about that."

✳ ✳ ✳

When I finally turn my phone back on, it floods with messages from Basha.

> **Basha**: Girl, did you run off to join the circus or what?!

> **Basha**: Answer me NOW, woman!!! I swear, if you're dead in a ditch, I'm haunting you.

> **Basha**: Also, is it bad that I want to eat the empanadas I bought for YOU?

> **Basha**: Too late. They are gone.

A laugh bursts out of me—loud and full and real. Something soft cracks open. And just like that, the storm breaks loose. My throat tightens, too full to speak. My eyes burn. And then—like rain from an overfilled sky—the tears come. Silent. Unrelenting. It's not just about Ryan. Or Max. Or my past. Or even Basha's ridiculous texts. If only it were that simple. It's the weight of everything. The exhaustion of holding it in for too long. The fear of hoping. The ache of wanting something good and not knowing if I'm allowed to trust it. So I let it rain. For what was. For what could be. For everything I've lost. For the girl still learning how to believe.

Chapter Thirty-Seven

The ice is way too smooth. That's my excuse—and I'm keeping it.

Ryan, of course, looks like he was born with skates on—gliding effortlessly, hands in pockets, like gravity personally owes him a favor. Meanwhile, I look like a newborn giraffe reconsidering all its life choices.

A little girl zips past me, tosses in a tiny, unnecessary, and deeply offensive spin, then zooms away like she owns the rink.

I narrow my eyes. "Okay, that was rude."

Ryan laughs. "She's like, five, Amaya."

"So? Maybe she needs to be humbled."

Then—bam. My skate jerks sideways, and I hit the ice like a clearance-sale mannequin—limbs everywhere, ego in critical condition.

Ryan tries not to laugh. Fails. Miserably. "Okay, okay—let me—"

Ryan reaches for my arm to help, but gravity gives us both the middle finger. We crash down together.

Frozen misery seeps through my gloves and straight into my eyebrows. Yes—my actual eyebrows. I try to push up, but my skates have declared mutiny. One slides forward, the other refuses to move, paralyzed by stage fright.

I grab Ryan's arm for support—catastrophic mistake. We go down. Again.

Now I'm half on top of him, elbow in his ribs, our faces dangerously close. The ice bites my back, but all I can focus on is the look in his eyes.

For a second, everything just…stops. No noise. No movement. Just that breathless kind of stillness that sneaks up on you.

Then Ryan cracks—full-blown, helpless laughter.

"What—what is happening?" he wheezes between laughs.

"I think my skates are oiled or something," I say, attempting to get up again because I clearly hate myself.

Terrible idea. My feet betray me instantly, shooting out like I slipped on a cartoon banana peel. Dignity? Long gone. Probably skating backward in a tutu, waving goodbye.

And just when I think it can't get worse, the same glittery five-year-old glides past again—this time with extra twirls and a look that screams *you guys are pathetic.*

That's it. We lose it. Completely. Laughing so hard I'm crying, Ryan wheezing like an old man in a Zumba class.

"We're a mess," I say, breathless.

"A complete disaster," he agrees.

Eventually, we crawl off the rink—graceless, breathless, and gasping for air. Our cheeks are red, our limbs sore, and our laughter still echoing as we stumble inside, steam curling from our mouths in tiny puffs.

Ryan tilts his head. "Hot cocoa?"

I nod like it's a medical necessity.

The laughter lingers—light. Easy.

I'd forgotten what this felt like. To laugh like this. With him. Like nothing ever broke us.

✳ ✳ ✳

The second I hear the door close, Ryan calls from the kitchen, "*Rice & Roll* is here!"

I pause mid-step. "Wait. Don't you mean *Wok & Roll?*"

He pokes his head around the corner, smirking. "Nope. *Rice & Roll.* Just opened."

I narrow my eyes. "That sounds suspiciously close to *Wok & Roll.*"

"Right? Turns out it's the same family. Expanding their empire."

I burst out laughing. "So what's next—*Egg & Roll? Chop & Roll?*"

Ryan taps his chin like he's brainstorming a billion-dollar idea. "*Grill & Roll.*"

I gasp. "Oh my gosh—*Spring & Roll.*"

"*Dumpling & Roll,*" he adds.

I nod solemnly. *"Pork Bun & Roll."*

We fall apart laughing—the kind that comes from somewhere deep, that makes you forget the past existed. Like kids again. Unfiltered. Unworried. I lean back on the couch, smiling. Something warm blooms in my chest—like joy finally remembered my name. It feels easy. Like we never lost this. Like we're still… us.

Then I notice his eyes drift to the Sofia shoebox on the bookshelf. My body tenses—old reflex. He notices, of course, but instead of asking anything heavy, he just raises an eyebrow, a crooked smile tugging at his lips.

"So…did I make it into one of those entries?"

"Oh, definitely. You've got your own dedicated section."

Ryan gasps. "In the good journal or the one all the way at the bottom left—for villains?"

"Depends on the day."

We crack up again, dumplings steaming between us, the laughter chasing away everything that ever hurt us.

"Oh my gosh," I groan. "I could live on dumplings."

Ryan watches me, grinning. "You realize you just moaned over dumplings, right?"

I shrug. "If I die right now, just know I died happy."

But when I open my eyes again, the air shifts. Ryan's not smiling anymore. He's staring at his plate, pushing a dumpling around like it wronged him. My stomach tightens. I know that look.

"Okay," I say—too lightly. "What's going on?"

He hesitates. Then sets his chopsticks down. The soft click lands heavier than it should.

"There's something I need to tell you."

The words hit before he even finishes them. My chest locks. My heart drops—fast, heavy.

He's still talking—something about Tanzania, finishing a project—but it all fades, muffled, like I'm underwater.

Because all I hear is that he's leaving. Again.

And suddenly, nothing tastes right. I want to be calm. Stay. Pretend it doesn't matter. But one look at his face—and I can't breathe.

"I—I can't do this right now," I whisper, grabbing my coat.

"Amaya—"

But I'm already gone. Out the door. Running down the stairs.

✳ ✳ ✳

I drive without thinking. Just motion. Just breathing.

The town sleeps around me. Streetlights stretch shadows across the pavement. Everything feels suspended—including me.

My hands tighten on the wheel. My heart pounds like it's looking for somewhere to land. I don't know if I want to turn back or keep driving until the road runs out and the ache goes numb.

Ryan's leaving. Again. And the worst part? I should've seen it coming.

A memory crashes in—loud, sharp. The last time he left. The silence. The shattering behind a closed door.

The road curves, trees flashing past in streaks of shadow and light. I spot the small gravel pull-off near the Long Path trailhead sign and ease in, tires crunching to a stop.

I kill the engine. The silence hits first. Then the stillness.

Below, the Hudson stretches wide and dark, moonlight skimming its surface in broken silver trails. Across the water, faint lights flicker along the far shore—tiny, distant lives still moving while mine feels frozen.

The cliffs drop away beneath me, sheer and black, their edges catching just enough light to show how far I could fall. The trees crowd close, rustling softly, as if the whole mountain's holding its breath.

I've never made this drive so late. But something pulled me here. Closer to the cliffs. Closer to the water. Somewhere the noise can't reach.

I rest my hands on the steering wheel, knuckles white, gripping something I can't name. Because I know—if I let go, everything else might fall with it.

Then it does.

My forehead drops to the wheel. A sob cracks loose. Then another. And another. Until there's nothing left to hold in.

I push the door open and step into the cold. The air outside is biting, sharp enough to hurt—but I barely feel it. The wind claws at my coat and hair, but I just stand there—staring at a world too beautiful and too cruel all at once.

The Hudson stretches wide beneath the cliffs, moonlight gliding across its surface. This river has seen centuries—love and loss, war and mercy. I wonder if it's ever watched someone fall apart and find their way back in the same breath.

I press my palms to my face. My shoulders shake. I breathe once. Then again.

And then—the air shifts, like a memory brushing past my skin. I don't have to turn around. I know he's there.

A car door closes behind me. Footsteps crunch over gravel and dead leaves.

"Amaya?" His voice is soft. Careful.

I lower my hands, heart lodged somewhere between relief and fear.

Ryan steps beside me, hands in his pockets, eyes full of sadness—and something else. Something fragile.

"You… followed me?" My voice splinters.

He nods once. "Yeah." A beat. "I had to."

He takes a breath, steadying himself. "When I left before…I thought I was doing the right thing. Chasing a dream. Trying to become someone who mattered. I thought everything would make sense once I made it."

I keep my eyes on the water.

"But the truth?" His voice roughens. "The second I left, I knew I was losing something I'd never get back."

A tear burns its way down my cheek.

"I didn't leave because I stopped caring," he whispers. "I left because I didn't know how to love you without losing myself. Because I was scared—of choosing wrong. Of being wrong."

His voice breaks. "But this time? I don't want to chase anything if you're not beside me."

"I love you, Amaya. More than I can ever put into words."

The words hit like a wave. My vision blurs. I open my mouth, but nothing comes. There's too much—too many years between us, too much unsaid.

He pulls out his phone. For a second, I think he's checking the time—maybe it's too late for all of this. But then he holds it out. I hesitate. Then take it.

On the screen—a half-built school: beams, dust, sunlight threading through the gaps.

"Swipe," he says.

I do.

The next photo is full of children—some barefoot, some missing teeth, all grinning like joy is something you carry in your pocket, not your wallet. A warmth blooms where the ache usually lives. The simplicity. The light in their faces. Their innocence.

"They're beautiful," I whisper. "And they look so happy."

"They have nothing," he says softly. "But look at them."

And I do.

And I see it—joy that has nothing to do with having, and everything to do with being. That same kind of joy I used to feel sprinting barefoot through the dirt roads of Moca—dust kicking up behind me, mango trees casting long shadows, the smell of *café colado* drifting from someone's porch, gravel biting into my feet. Wild. Free. Like nothing was missing.

He's close enough that his breath mixes with mine.

"Come with me. Not to visit—to be part of it."

His hand finds my face, thumb catching a tear. "No expectations. Just an open door."

I don't speak. I just reach for his hand—and hold it. Not tightly. Just enough to let him know I haven't walked away. When our eyes meet, it feels like remembering and beginning all at once.

At the boy I once loved.

At the man I tried to forget.

At the future I convinced myself I didn't need—because I was too scared to want it.

He steps even closer, slow, like he's afraid to break the moment. And then—he pulls me in. The world narrows to the sound of the river and the steady beat of his heart against mine.

I rest my head on his shoulder, exhaustion and relief colliding in a single breath. Neither of us speaks. We don't need to. The silence says everything.

✳ ✳ ✳

I lie on my bed, staring at the ceiling, replaying everything that just happened.

My heart feels like it's still catching up—like it hasn't decided if it's relieved or wrecked.

My phone buzzes on the nightstand. Just Basha being Basha. A meeting reminder. Nothing urgent. Nothing pressing.

And then—Max.

A rush of heat crawls up my spine. Seven unread messages. My thumb hovers. I could ignore them. Block his number. Pretend I never saw them. But it isn't hope that pulls me in—it's the need to face what I once mistook for love. Before I can talk myself out of it, I tap.

> **Max:** I rewrote this text at least twenty times. Maybe I shouldn't send it at all. It's long. I'm sorry. But I need you to know this.

It feels heavy before the words even begin. But I read it anyway.

> **Max:** Amaya, I am so, so sorry. For everything. For the way I made you feel. For the way I let my pain become yours. I was drowning, and instead of reaching for help, I pulled you under with me. And I hate that. I hate knowing I became someone who made you feel like you weren't enough—when you've always been more than enough.

> **Max:** I started therapy. AA meetings too. The first time I walked into that room, I almost turned around. But I stayed. And I've been staying. One day at a time. Because I don't want to be that person anymore. I don't want to be the man who hurts the people he loves.

> **Max:** I know an apology won't fix it. It won't undo the hurt. But I need you to know—I see it now. I see how I made you feel like saving me was your job. It never was. You deserved someone who lifted you up. Not someone who dragged you down. And I hate that it took me this long to realize it.

> **Max:** I see the damage I caused. And I'm working to be better. Not for you. Not even for anyone else—for me. And I guess, selfishly, I just hope… that if we ever cross paths again, you won't only remember the worst parts of me.

Max: I want you to be happy, Amaya. Truly happy. And if Ryan is that for you… I hope you let yourself have it. I hope you let yourself love without fear. You deserve that. You always have.

Max: I won't text again. I just needed you to know. Take care of yourself.

I exhale—slow, shaky.

My fingers tighten around the phone. Not out of anger. Not even sadness. But because—deep down—I believe him. The way only someone who's been broken in the same places can. And maybe that's all that's left between us now—memories and understanding.

And just when I think I've cried all the tears I had left, the sting returns. The kind that comes when you finally let go. One tear slips down. Then another. Not for Max. Not for us.

But for the girl I used to be—the one who waited nights for this version of Max to exist. The one who carried his pain like it was hers, hoping love would be enough.

I close my eyes and let it all settle. The truth is, no matter how badly I wanted him to change, he wasn't ready. And I couldn't make him ready. Some things have to fall apart before they can be rebuilt. And sometimes…by the time they are, it's too late.

I wipe my cheeks with the back of my hand. Exhale again. Slower this time. I don't reply. I don't need to. Some wounds don't get closure. They get release. And some doors? They're meant to stay closed. And this one? This one, I'm finally ready to leave behind.

I set my phone down. Roll onto my side. Close my eyes.

It's the lightest I've felt in years. I don't know what tomorrow looks like. But tonight—I feel free. Light—like laughter on ice.

Chapter Thirty-Eight

The camera clicks, sealing the last frame of my client—a beautiful woman with soft curls, warm brown skin, and hazel eyes that shimmer like honey in the light. I lower the lens and nod.

"That's the one," I say, scrolling through the preview. "You killed it."

She leans over to peek. "Damn, I do look good." Her voice softens, like she's seeing herself clearly for the first time in a long while.

I smile, warmth spreading through my chest. This is why I do what I do. When someone finally sees what I see through my lens—it hits different.

The photo shoot went smoothly—but my brain? Not so much. Every photo came out crisp and clear, and yet I felt like I was walking through fog. Ryan. The future. Max's texts… it's like I'm being pulled in a dozen directions, none of them clear.

As soon as she walks out, I pack up quickly, sling my bag over my shoulder, and head to the car. No music. No podcasts. Just me and the noise in my head that won't shut off.

By the time I pull into the lot, my chest is tight—like I've been holding a breath I forgot to release.

Crystal gives me her usual soft smile as I sink into the couch—legs tucked beneath me, like always. I booked a double session. Honestly, at this point, I should just move into the corner.

"Rough week?" she asks, voice gentle.

I let out a dry laugh. "Try rough decade."

Without thinking, I grab the HOPE pillow and hug it a little too hard.

She doesn't push, just waits—like always—quiet, present, letting me find the thread.

I finally breathe. "I've been thinking about stability. And love. Not the kind that's about fixing each other or clinging on out of survival. I mean love that… just is."

Crystal nods. "And what does that look like to you?"

I hesitate. My throat tightens. "Ryan," I say softly.

Just saying his name… it shifts something inside me—like he's gravity, and I didn't realize I'd been floating until I said it.

"I think about him a lot. About us." I pause. "For the first time, I don't feel like I have to earn someone's love. It just… exists. Effortless. Easy. He makes me feel safe. Like I can finally breathe without bracing for the floor to disappear."

Crystal watches me with that calm, open stillness she does so well. "That's a huge realization, Amaya. Safety and love aren't supposed to be separate. You're allowing yourself to want more than survival."

Her words settle into me—deep—like they reach parts I didn't realize were still locked away.

I nod slowly, eyes fixed on my hands. "I never thought I'd be capable of this. Of wanting more. I think part of me thought love had to be hard. That it only counted if you had to fight for it."

She tilts her head. "And now?"

I breathe in, deeper this time. "Now… I think maybe I deserve love that doesn't hurt."

Crystal smiles, nodding softly. "You do."

I let that sit for a second—let it breathe in me. Then, without thinking, I ask, "Do you think I could be a mother one day?" The words catch me off guard. I've never asked anyone that before. Maybe I've never even let myself wonder.

Her expression shifts—tender. "Absolutely. And I think you'd be an amazing one."

Something shifts in me—not pain, not longing. Just… a question I didn't know was mine. Like brushing past a door I didn't mean to open. I don't linger. I reach into my bag and pull out my phone.

"Max texted me."

Crystal stays calm. Just gives a small nod. "And?"

I scroll, then stop. "He apologized. Said he's in AA. Started therapy. That he hopes I find happiness. That maybe one day we'll reconnect."

Crystal's expression doesn't shift. "How did that make you feel?"

I let out a slow breath. "I don't know how to explain it. I think part of me hoped I'd feel something—relief, maybe. Or closure. But it's just… calm." I pause. "I don't want to reconnect." I shake my head as the words leave my mouth. "But I do want him to be okay. I mean, I really do. He has good in him. Even if I can't be the one to help him anymore."

Crystal nods, her expression softening. "That's a very kind way to let someone go." A quiet beat. "Have you responded?"

I shake my head again. My grip tightens.

"I don't know what to say. And I'm scared it'll open something I've already closed."

She leans in slightly. "Closure isn't always about replying. Sometimes, it's just a decision you make for yourself. If answering would pull you back into something you've already fought your way out of, then no—he doesn't need a response. But if writing back helps you feel at peace, a short reply is okay too."

Her words land and keep sinking; I nod slowly. Maybe closure isn't something you get from a conversation—maybe it's just the moment you stop looking over your shoulder.

My hands tremble slightly as I set the phone down. Then I reach into my bag again and pull out a folded piece of paper. The edges are worn—creased and softened by time, by hesitation, by all the moments I almost threw it away.

"I wrote something," I say quietly. "For Soledad. Like you suggested… weeks ago."

I run my fingers along the frayed edge. It's been through a lot—just like me: held, reread, nearly torn to pieces. But it's still here. I guess I needed it to be.

"I wrote it in Spanish for her. But I translated it… so I could read it to you." My voice comes out shaky. "I'm not sending it. I just… needed to get it out."

Crystal doesn't say a word. She watches me, patient and still, like she understands exactly how much it's taking for me to say this out loud.

My hands tremble—like they always do when I talk about her. I hate that. Every time I say her name, drag those memories back into the light, my body reacts. My fingers twitch like they're still stuck in that apartment, waiting for the next slam of a door or crack in her voice—like they haven't caught up to the fact that I'm no longer there.

I slowly unfold the page; the paper quivers between my fingers. There's a faint scent of lavender on it—something that clings from my hands, as if calm could leave fingerprints.

So I breathe. And I begin to read.

Soledad,

I'm writing this letter as part of my journey toward healing. It's not easy, but it's necessary. There's so much I've carried for years—things too heavy, too painful—and it's time I let them go. Writing this is my way of confronting the past, no matter how much it hurts.

First, I want to acknowledge your decision to leave me in the care of my father when you came to the U.S. I can only imagine how difficult it must have been. And while I understand the hope you had for a better life, I wish there had been more communication between us. A simple call now and then would've meant the world. I know Papi didn't have a phone—but Abuela down the road did. You could've found a way. Instead, it often felt like I was left alone. Forgotten.

When you finally brought me to live with you and Fernando, it felt like I had stepped into a different world—one where I never truly belonged. Instead of being nurtured, I became something between a burden and a servant. Your anger, your yelling, the lessons you tried to teach through fear and fists—left me confused. Scared. I learned early to hide pieces of myself just to survive. Lipstick and different hairdos behind your back. Sketches of styles I dreamed of creating one day. Hidden friends. Silent tears behind closed doors.

Too many times your anger turned into violence, and I can still feel the sting of your blows—the way you hit harder if I cried. I stopped crying after a while. Not because it stopped hurting, but because crying only made it worse.

And then… the night in the kitchen. I was still just a child. Fernando tried to kiss me while you sat in the bedroom, glued to your novelas. My heart raced with fear. I froze—not just from terror of what he might do, but from the deeper terror of what you might say if you found out. Would you protect me? Would you blame me?

I told Fernando to wait for me in the bathroom, knowing full well I would never go. It was the only escape I could think of. When I finally gathered the courage to tell you, my voice shook, my hands trembled. You cursed him out. For one night—twenty-four hours. That's how long you defended me, Soledad.

Then the phone rang—the news that Adrian, Fernando's best friend, had been killed in a drug deal gone wrong. You wept nonstop for Adrian. You grieved for a man you barely knew. But did you ever cry for me? Did you ever mourn the child who had been violated in her own home, while you were just a room away?

After that night, Fernando stayed. And we never spoke of it again. I carried that silence like a shadow—always there, even in the light. But there's more, Soledad. There's a deeper wound I've never spoken aloud—not even now, not until this letter.

When I was about eleven years old, Adrian Contreras—the man you mourned—molested me. I was just a child. I was so terrified. And instead of running to my mother, I swallowed it whole. Because I knew I would not find safety in you.

That night, after Adrian left me broken and shaking, I remember thinking that dying would be easier than surviving that kind of fear. I didn't understand what was happening. I didn't even have the words. All I knew was that I was sick inside. And that the person who was supposed to protect me was just… unreachable. I carried that secret like a stone inside my chest for years. Years. Until now. I won't carry it anymore.

Despite everything you failed to see, despite the way you failed to protect me, I am choosing to forgive you. Not because you asked. Not because you deserve it. But because I deserve peace. I deserve to be free of the anger and shame that never belonged to me. I refuse to let resentment rot inside me any longer. I refuse to let my childhood define my future.

I forgive you, Soledad. I forgive you because I have to. Because I am choosing to heal. Because I am choosing myself.

A pastor I met recently—or priest, minister, whatever his title was—said peace sometimes begins with surrender, not silence. And I am done being silent.

He also said God is close to the brokenhearted. And I believe that's true—because how else did I survive living with you?

I hope someday you find the peace you could never give me. And even if you don't, I know this now—I'm strong enough to find it for myself.

Peace, Amaya

The letter trembles in my hands. My chest tightens, ribs straining like they're holding back something too big to name. My throat burns. My vision blurs. I try to swallow it down—but it's no use. One tear slips free. Then another. And then it breaks.

My shoulders shake as the weight of my own words settles over me—finally spoken. Finally real. Crystal presses the letter to her chest like it's more than paper—like it's truth. Testimony.

"Amaya," she says, voice thick. "This is powerful."

I wipe at my face, but the tears keep coming. A quiet sob escapes— raw, unexpected. Like something finally let go.

"I feel… lighter," I whisper. "Even if she never sees it. Even if it just stays between us."

Crystal nods, her eyes steady on mine, full of something deeper than understanding—recognition.

"That's because you just let go of something that was never yours to carry."

She reaches for my hand and gives it a soft squeeze.

"You've spent so much of your life fighting battles that weren't yours. Carrying guilt that didn't belong to you. Protecting people who never protected you."

The words hit hard. But they don't crush me. They free me. Something cracks open—not like breaking. Like a seed splitting right before it grows.

The breath I let out is shaky, but it's mine. Real. Solid. Alive.

I don't feel like a girl just trying to survive anymore.

I feel like a woman finally learning how to live.

Chapter Thirty-Nine

Basha stays behind to help me close up—even though she's got a business to run, a brand to protect, and a million hustles stacked on her plate. Time is money, and she never wastes either.

And still—she's here. Because we're hitting the mall after, and because that's just who she is. Loyal. Loud. Down for shopping, drama, and throwing hands if it ever came to that.

She wipes down the counters, humming off-key with full-blown conviction, while I sweep slow, lazy circles—dragging the broom like a reluctant dance partner. I step back, spin it dramatically, then dip low like we're at a salsa club.

Basha throws her head back. "Girl. *Dancing with the Brooms* needs to be a reality show."

I flip my hair like I'm about to take home the trophy. "Please. I'd sweep the competition."

She groans. "You did *not* just say that."

"I did," I say, proud. "Zero regrets."

She rolls her eyes, still humming, turning cleaning into a Broadway show.

For a moment, we're just two girls in an empty studio—laughing, spinning, alive. Like nothing bad ever touched us. Then the bell chimes. Sharp. Too sharp.

I freeze mid-dip, gripping the broom like it might actually be needed.

For a split second, I wonder if it's a client—maybe someone wanting lashes or a quick consultation.

But it's Ramona.

She's standing in the doorway, wide-eyed, jumpy, like she just ran from a crash and forgot how to breathe.

Something's wrong. Way wrong.

Her makeup's perfect—lashes stacked like fans, liner sharp, like she piled on seven coats of mascara and still went back for one more. But everything else? Panic. She's chewing gum way too fast, jaw clenching like it's trying to outrun something. That gold tooth flashes every time she bites down. Her hands are twitchy. She scratches her scalp. Her eyes flick to the door behind her. Her body won't stay still.

My stomach drops. *Is she running from someone?*

A slow, ugly suspicion crawls up the back of my neck. Does this have anything to do with that "rich white guy" she met on the Coach bus? I didn't press for details, but the way she told it—too fast, too loud—never sat right with me. Like she was trying to sell the story to herself as much as to me.

Before I can ask, she reaches for the broom—tries to snatch it from my hands, like busying herself might erase whatever she's running from.

"You need help?" she blurts, voice too high, too rushed.

I narrow my eyes. "Ramona... *¿qué pasa?*"

And then—the door opens again.

Like it yanks the oxygen out of the room.

Cold floods my chest.

And in walks the one and only. Soledad.

Everything stops.

The walls shrink. My lungs seize like they forgot their job. My ears ring. My heart punches against my ribs—the same way it used to when I heard her heels clicking down the hallway. My fingers twitch. My hands lock around the handle like it's the only thing anchoring me.

I feel sick.

She doesn't belong here.

Not in this studio. Not in this light. Not in this version of me.

This place—*my* place—has nothing to do with her.

Here, I'm not the girl who walked through doorways holding her breath. Here, I'm not shrinking just to survive. Here, I'm not small.

And still—she walks in like she owns the air. Like she didn't spend years choking the life out of it.

Basha freezes mid-wipe, Lysol bottle gripped like it might be needed for self-defense. Her jaw's tight. Her whole body still.

Soledad's dressed like she's on a fake runway. Too-tight jeans. Too-high stilettos. A slick ponytail extension swinging down her back. Gold dripping from her fingers, her neck, her wrists—like she ran out of places to wear her guilt. And that smirk. That same damn smirk. She hasn't changed. I swear—she even smells the same.

My throat tightens, but I shove it down. My voice slices through the air, sharp and cold.

"*Muchas gracias, Ramona.*"

Ramona stiffens. Her face falls.

"*Perdóname, Amaya. Perdóname.*"

I hold up a hand. "*No me hables.*"

As if saying sorry twice could pull the knife from my back.

How *dare* she. How dare *either* of them.

Soledad lets out a soft laugh, eyes roaming the room like she's here to rate the I.

"*¡Mira qué bonito todo!*" she says, nodding like this is a damn open house. "I always knew you'd do something with yourself."

I bark a dry laugh. "Did you?"

She exhales. Tilts her head—like *she's* the one hurting. "*Amaya, no seas así.* I came to talk."

Basha moves closer. Arms crossed. Protective. A whole warning in her stance.

I stare at Soledad. Waiting. For regret. For guilt. For something—*anything*—that looks like remorse. But her face? Still unbothered. Still rehearsed. Still her.

"I didn't come to fight," she says smoothly. Too smoothly. The kind of smooth that makes the hairs on my neck rise—like something slick is sliding toward a trap.

"I just wanted to see my daughter," she adds, all sugar and spin. "I know I was hard on you, but it was for your own good. I didn't want you making the same mistakes I did with men."

Oh. Hell no.

I laugh—bitter, sharp. "For my good? That's the story you're telling yourself now?"

She sighs, like this is exhausting for her. "You think I enjoyed it? I did what I had to do to keep a roof over your head and food on your plate."

She exhales hard, like I'm the one being dramatic. "Amaya, you always twist everything into an attack instead of giving me credit." Her mouth twists. "*Ingrata.*"

My jaw tightens. The nerve of her—turning cruelty into charity. "To help me? Or to control me? Because from where I stood, it felt a hell of a lot more like punishment than protection."

She stiffens. But I keep going.

"You're not the victim here. You're not the hero. You didn't raise me out of love—you broke me out of anger."

She tries again. "Amaya, *mi hija*, I—"

"Don't call me that."

My voice freezes the room.

"A mother doesn't do what you did. A mother protects. A mother loves. You left me. You called it sacrifice. But I call it *abandonment*."

My chest rises fast. My throat burns.

Still, I stand tall.

"When I finally came back to you—nine years later—you didn't open your arms. You made me pay for it."

My heart pounds, but I keep going.

"You say you didn't want me to make your mistakes? No. You wanted me to suffer like you did. You wanted control. And for years— you had it. But not anymore."

For a split second, her posture falters. Like the words actually hit.

"You always chose Fernando first."

My voice sharpens.

"You let me talk to my dad with you hovering over the phone like a prison guard. You knew if he ever found out the truth—he would've sent for me. He would've cursed your name."

Soledad's mouth tightens.

I step forward. My hands shake. But my voice? Steel.

"Do you even know what Adrian did to me?"

The air shifts. She goes still.

Ramona opens her mouth—then closes it. Even she knows this moment isn't hers.

I step closer.

"Yes, Soledad. Adrian. Your precious friend. He molested me."

My voice cracks—but I don't break.

"He stole my childhood. And I didn't say anything. Because I was more afraid of *you* than him."

Her lips part. Tremble.

"Amaya, I—"

"No. You don't get to cry."

She blinks. But I keep going.

"You didn't protect me. You didn't care. You didn't even *see* me."

"Do you know what it's like to be a child—and feel safer with a predator than your own mother?!"

She shakes her head, her voice barely a whisper. "I didn't know—"

"Because you didn't want to know."

"*Ay, Amaya, por favor…*"

But I don't stop.

"You didn't see what Adrian was doing—because you never wanted to look. And when Fernando pressed himself against me in the kitchen, wearing nothing but a towel, whispering things no grown man should say to a child—you forgave him anyway. And everything else in between that no one knows I survived. In our own home."

My hands tremble, but my words don't.

"Every time he drank and turned up the music, my legs would start trembling. After that, whenever he asked me to sit on his lap, my body went cold."

I stare at her—hard. My voice low, deliberate.

"Do you even understand what my father would've done if he knew Fernando tried to get me into bed? I was a teenager. A fucking child."

Ramona's arms cross over her chest, her knuckles white, eyes glassy—like she's holding in a scream she can't let out.

"*Amaya, por favor,*" she whispers. "Just take a deep breath. Please."

I don't look at her. I shake my head. "Just go."

She hesitates.

My voice rises—sharper now. "*Vete,*" I repeat.

Soledad exhales—like I'm the disappointment.

"One day, you'll regret turning your back on me," she snaps. "Blood is blood. No matter what you think—I'm still your mother."

My voice stays calm—the kind of calm that comes after you've already survived the worst.

"I don't think so."

She waits—for me to crack. To cry. To explain. To make *her* feel better.

I don't.

I turn around. And then, just as she starts to walk out, I stop her. "Wait."

She turns, expecting something sentimental. A crack she can crawl through.

Instead, I reach into my bag—hand her the letter. The original in Spanish—the one I wrote on the flight back from Moca, from the island that showed me what real love feels like. The same one I translated for Crystal when I was finally brave enough to say it out loud. I never thought I'd actually hand it to her—this ugly, honest truth she spent her whole life pretending didn't exist.

I don't explain it. Don't soften it. It's not a plea. Not a gift. It's a boundary on paper. The final page of a story I refuse to keep living.

I place it in her hand. "I forgive you," I say, my voice calm—steady in all the places she once shattered. "But that doesn't mean I want you in my life."

Her lips part. Waiting to bargain. To twist it. I don't give her the chance.

"It just means I'm done carrying what you did. You can call it cruel. I call it freedom. *Ya no te tengo miedo.*"

She says nothing. I turn and walk away.

No screaming. No apology. No collapse. Just the echo of power— finally mine.

The door slams behind her. And the second they're gone—my knees give out.

Basha catches me before I hit the floor, her arms iron-strong around my ribs.

"You did that," she whispers, her forehead pressed to mine. "You stood up to her."

And the tears come. But this time, they don't taste like weakness. They taste like truth. Like freedom.

She wipes one away with her sleeve, eyes sparkling.

"Also," she adds, lips curving through the tears, "I'm proud you didn't cry in front of that woman. She's not even worth the salt."

She squeezes my hand.

"But just so you know—we're still hitting that mall. So wipe your face. We've got clearance racks to raid."

A laugh cracks through me—raw, broken, but real.

For once, the last word is mine.

This is the last time I run.

This time, I rise.

Chapter Forty

I step outside, heart still shaking from everything I just let go, and the air smells different—like clean pavement after rain, like something has finally washed clean.

And there he is. Leaning against his car like he's been waiting forever. Hands in his pockets. A smile like safety. Like home.

As I reach him, he opens the passenger door—then leans in close. His eyes find mine like he's searching for something he already knows by heart. Time slows. My breath stills. Even my heartbeat waits.

He's going to kiss me—I feel it. I want it.

But he doesn't.

Instead, his fingers find my chin, guiding me closer. His breath grazes my neck as he whispers, "Breathtaking," in a tone that feels meant for skin, not ears.

I don't move. I just let the word sink in—warm and weightless, like heat through silk.

A slow, aching hum of music greets me as I slide into Ryan's car. It wraps around me before I can take a full breath. I recognize the song immediately. I used to play it over and over… until the day he left. But tonight, it lands differently. "Kiss Me" by Ed Sheeran.

I pause, fingers brushing the edge of the seat. The voice, the guitar, the ache in the melody—it's too much and not enough. A heartbeat I've never stopped chasing.

I glance at him, but he doesn't look over. He just taps the wheel, perfectly in rhythm, like he knows I'm already watching.

The lyrics drift, and I swear I feel them in my body. Not just the notes. The meaning.

His chest against mine. My lips on his throat. A thousand versions of almost. Of not yet. Of finally.

I sink into the leather seat, exhaling slowly as the air folds around me—his cologne, his mint, his heat still clinging to the air.

This silence feels like falling. And for once, I'm not afraid to land.

"It felt right," he says, voice barely above the hum. "The song. The moment. You."

I close my eyes—just long enough to feel everything I've ever run from settle in my chest. The longing. The safety. The surrender. This isn't background music. This is a vow.

He reaches over without a word and rests his hand on my thigh—gentle, warm, like he's anchoring us both to this exact second. His thumb draws slow, deliberate circles. Not casual. Not rushed. His touch sinks in—like honey warming over flame.

"I love this one," he says softly. "Reminds me of someone I know."

My pulse misbehaves.

I don't answer. Some moments aren't meant to be spoken into. I close my eyes again, the only way to hold it all. I press my knees together and stare out the window like it might help me breathe. But inside, I'm already coming apart.

"So where are you taking me, Mr. Romance?" My voice dips without permission—soft in a way that feels too close to wanting.

He tilts his head, amused, like he's deciding how much to give away. "It's a surprise."

I give him a slow once-over. "If this ends in drive-thru fries, I'm leaving you there."

His laugh is low, skimming my skin.

"Damn. I was going for mysterious and romantic."

"You're halfway there."

He leans in, hand still resting on my leg, the heat from his palm spreading like wildfire.

"Small update…" he says, low. "They pushed the reservation. We've got some time to kill."

I fake-gasp, pressing a dramatic hand to my chest. "You lured me out with the promise of food, only to starve me in my most vulnerable hour? Monster."

"I've seen what happens when you're hungry. I came prepared." His smile curves wider. "Wine. A view. And my company."

I pretend to weigh the offer. "Two out of three isn't bad."

The song restarts. He doesn't skip it—just lets it play, like he's giving it permission to say what we won't. And for the first time in years, I don't feel the need to fill the silence.

✳ ✳ ✳

I see this river every day from my tiny apartment—but here, it's different. Not just something I watch from a distance. It pulls me in, like it's been waiting for me to stop looking from afar and finally step closer.

Before, when Ryan showed me this place, I couldn't take it all in—too overwhelmed by him, by everything that had happened, by the surreal truth that he actually owns this home. But now? Now I feel it in my bones—I could stay here forever.

Ryan's house doesn't just stand here—it beats. A quiet rhythm beneath every beam, every windowpane. Max's apartment was sleek—a museum behind glass. But Ryan's house? It breathes. It belongs to something steadier. Truer.

The view isn't something you admire. It's something you enter. Live inside. Grow into. Sunrises spill over the water, sunsets melt into dusk. The river below keeps its own slow heartbeat. And me, watching. Rooted. Finally still.

The Hudson stretches wide in front of us, deep and dark—like it remembers everything we once tried to forget. The bridge beyond it glows gold, its reflection rippling on the surface like a promise that hasn't faded.

Beyond the glass, the patio glows—stealing my breath before I can take it back.

Lights hang from the sugar maples, strung like constellations meant only for us. They glow in cascading strands, soft and amber, scattering across the water like liquid stars. I blink. I don't remember them being here last time. Did he add them—or just keep them hidden until now?

"Ryan…" I whisper, stepping forward like the moment might dissolve if I move too fast.

He watches me from a few feet back, hands tucked in his jacket pockets, his smile soft. "Funny thing about the river," he says quietly.

"It never stays the same. The light changes, the tide shifts—but it's always here. Steady. Constant."

A lump forms in my throat. Words I never believed I could reach for—words that always felt like lies dressed as hope. But here he is, standing in front of me, saying them like a vow.

And just like that… I let myself believe him.

I turn toward him. He's already looking at me like I hung the stars.

"You look *magnifique*," he says, brushing his fingers along my jaw. The sound of it curls down my spine. Ryan rarely speaks French around me—but when he does, I melt like sugar in *café con leche*.

A slow warmth uncoils beneath my skin. "And you… you look incredible." My voice comes out soft, like the moment might shatter if I speak too loud.

His eyes drop to my mouth. Everything else fades.

There's this invisible pull between us—closer, tighter—until there's no space left between what I want and what I'm afraid to take.

His fingers twitch. His shoulders shift like he's holding something back.

"If I kiss you right now," he murmurs, voice like gravel and silk, "we're not making it to dinner."

Gosh, that voice. Deep. Sexy. The kind that finds its way into your chest and stays there, humming in your bones. A slow, delicious burn sparks beneath my skin.

"Oh?" I whisper, eyes on his. "Is that a challenge?"

I hope he takes it.

He leans in, lips brushing the corner of my mouth—soft, barely there. But it hits like gravity. Like my knees forgot how to hold me.

He pulls back, eyes dancing.

"Come outside with me," he says.

We step onto the patio.

Music drifts into the air, slow and low—like a heartbeat that's been waiting for this exact moment.

Ed Sheeran's "Perfect." Of course it is.

I've played it on long walks and early runs, heard it at weddings and in passing cars—but tonight, it feels like it's been saving itself for here. Now. For us.

I rest my hands on the railing, heart light. I'm still watching the bridge—steel and grace, suspended between two sides like my life lately—when Ryan returns with two glasses of wine. He offers one with a quiet smile and guides me toward the edge of the patio.

He lifts his glass, eyes locked on mine. "To beautiful nights and even more beautiful company."

I tap his, the soft clink landing like a secret. "To surprises I didn't see coming," I murmur, smiling against the rim.

As I lower my glass, Ryan leans in, his lips brushing just behind my ear. "Don't move. I'll be right back." He slips inside, his voice still warm against my skin.

When he returns, he's holding a gift so beautiful it feels like it shouldn't be touched. Soft pink paper with delicate gold floral accents, tied with a satin bow. A tiny gold heart charm catches the light.

I blink, thrown. "Ryan… what is this? It's not my birthday, it's not Christmas, it's not even my half-birthday."

He shakes his head, that smirk still lingering. "Do I need a reason to give something to the woman I love?"

I run my fingers along the bow, slow. "It's too pretty to open."

"Then I'll get you another pretty box," he says softly. "Just open it."

I start to unwrap it—slow, careful, like something sacred.

Inside, nestled in a velvet-lined box, is a soft pink leather journal. An embossed magnolia glows faintly across the cover, its petals opening toward me as if offering something hopeful. Engraved in gold script:

> *"For the girl who always saw the light, even when it was dim."*

And beneath that—my name.

Amaya.

"Ryan…" My voice barely makes it out, stripped bare. I've never felt so seen.

He gently takes my wine glass and sets it aside. "Open it, my love."

With trembling fingers, I flip to the first page.

"I have found the one whom my soul loves."—*Song of Solomon 3:4*

I stare at the verse, heart pounding. It's a declaration—one I never dared to believe was mine.

And then, just below:

Amaya,
Every story worth reading starts with courage, love, and hope. You've taught me all three. I want to write the rest of our story together, one page at a time.

Will you marry me?

Everything in me stills, and for a moment, it feels like the world is holding its breath with mine. These words aren't just written—they're carved into time itself, into me. Permanent. Sacred.

I press my fingers to the page, just to be sure it's real. But it doesn't fade. The ink stays. The moment holds. My heartbeat pulses beneath my skin like it's trying to find a rhythm. A thousand thoughts collide, each one louder than the last—hope, disbelief, awe. *Is this really happening? Does he truly mean forever? Am I finally ready to believe this?*

Then I look up. Ryan stands in front of me, patient. Unmoving. His hands are in his pockets, like he's anchoring himself from running toward me too soon.

Tucked beside the journal, nestled in the velvet, is a matching pink-and-gold pen. I reach for it carefully, my grip shaky, breath uneven. It's not fear. It's joy—too big for my body to hold.

I flip to the next blank page—the one we get to write together. For a second, I freeze. Not because I'm unsure—but because I've never let myself say yes to something this real. This lasting. This terrifyingly beautiful. My hand trembles. Then, with every ounce of love in my heart, I press the pen to the page and write three letters. Yes ♥

A tear slips free as I lift my eyes to his.

He's watching me like he's memorizing the moment. Like nothing else in the world matters but what I just gave him.

Ryan takes the journal, reads my response—and his smile? It's everything. Blinding. Broken open. Home. He leans in and kisses me—

unhurried, tasting of wine, mint, and something dangerously close to forever.

He pulls back just enough to whisper, "Amaya, you've made me the happiest man alive. And I swear, I will spend every day making you the happiest woman alive."

I lean in, breathless, pressing my forehead to his. "I can't wait to write our story."

Ryan smiles, eyes wet, voice thick. There's a light in his eyes I haven't seen before. "Then let's start now."

He slides his hands down my arms, tracing the fabric before settling at my waist. His touch is tender, but there's urgency beneath it—like he knows what he's holding is irreplaceable.

He draws me into a slow dance beneath the golden lights, one hand at the small of my back, the other resting above my heart like he's keeping it safe. I feel the rhythm of his chest against mine. Not rushed. Not rehearsed. Just real.

Music drapes over us, gentle and warm, like dusk settling in. And for once, there's no past pulling at my heels. No future stretched too far ahead to touch. Only this moment. Only this. Only us.

I rest my cheek against his chest, but the verse still lingers in me, shimmering like a secret I need to understand. My voice comes out softer than I mean it to.

"Ryan… why that verse—why Solomon?"

He stills for a moment, his thumb tracing slow circles at my back. When he finally answers, his voice is threaded with memory.

"My dad was the first one who mentioned King Solomon," he says softly. "I was a teenager. He told me Solomon was the wisest man who ever lived, and that stuck. I got curious and started reading—not everything, but enough. What stayed with me wasn't the wealth or the palaces. It was his prayer for wisdom—the way he used what he had to build, to give, to love well. When I started my own business, I tried to remember that. To build with honor. To give when I could. The money isn't the point—it's who you become while you're building. But what I never forgot was his poetry—the Song of Songs. For all his wisdom, all his building, what's lasted most is the kind of love his words captured—two souls choosing each other, again and again. So when I went searching for words for you—for us—I typed in Solomon's name.

That verse was the first thing I saw. And the moment I read it, I knew. That was you. That was us."

My throat tightens, the words lodging deep inside me like roots. A tear threatens but doesn't fall, shimmering at the edge of my lashes as I press my forehead to his. My voice trembles against the space between us.

"Then I'll spend forever choosing you too."

✶ ✶ ✶

Ryan drives with one hand on the wheel, the other laced through mine. The silence between us isn't empty—it hums. Like something sacred, full of everything we just said without words.

My thoughts spin, light and breathless—dancing through a life I never thought I'd get to live.

I'm engaged. To Ryan Nouel—the man who cracked open every wall I built and rewrote every love story I thought I'd lost.

My eyes drop to my hands—one still holding the soft pink journal, the other tingling from where I wrote *Yes* ♥.

My chest feels too full, joy pressing against my ribs—radiant and restless, trying to find its way out. It's the kind of love that makes you believe—just maybe—you were always meant to survive everything that came before this.

A part of me aches as Soledad drifts in, dimming the edges of the light like a cloud crossing the sun.

I hate that she's here. But she is. I wish she were someone else.

Someone I could call breathless with joy. Someone who'd say, *"mi amor, I'm so happy for you."* Someone who'd see this—see him—and know I found something rare. Someone who would've protected me well enough to believe I deserved it.

The longing rises—then passes. For the first time, it passes without taking me with it.

And just like that, Ryan's hand finds mine and squeezes gently, like he felt the ache before I even said a word.

I blink, pulled back into the car, into his warmth, into now.

He smiles without turning. "You're quiet. Thinking about backing out?"

I glance over, dry. "Oh, totally. Just realizing you tricked me into this engagement under false pretenses. Where was the overpriced steak dinner, Mr. Nouel?"

He laughs—that deep, effortless kind that sinks into my skin and stays there.

"Hey, I promised you dinner. I just had to secure the wife before the meal."

"Ohhh, so the steak is a *reward* for saying yes? What if I'd said no?"

"Then I'd be going to the restaurant alone, ordering the biggest steak they have, drowning my sorrows in mashed potatoes loaded with too much butter—and definitely dessert."

I burst out laughing. It feels real, like joy is alive in my skin. I lean closer, brushing my fingers over his.

Truthfully, I wouldn't have minded skipping dinner entirely. I could've stayed in his arms all night—just breathing. Just being. But no—we're being responsible adults. Dinner first. Celebration after.

Telling people. Basha.

Oh gosh, Basha's going to scream, spin, and probably throw a shoe into the air and then demand a dress code for every engagement-related event going forward.

I can't wait.

And Papi. I can already hear his voice, thick with emotion. He'd cry for sure—the kind of tears that catch in his throat before they ever reach his eyes. Then he'd probably turn to Marisol and say, *"Prepárate, mujer—we're roasting the biggest pig in the Caribbean."*

Ryan squeezes my thigh gently, his voice dipping low. "I'm the happiest man alive, future Mrs. Nouel."

"Then I guess we're the happiest people alive."

I bite my lip. My cheeks flush. My chest stretches—not with fear, never with him. Just joy blooming too big to stay still.

Gosh. I'm really his. His future. His forever. And he's mine.

✶ ✶ ✶

The second we pull up to Ciel d'Amour, the world softens—as if even the air knows not to speak.

The restaurant looks like it stepped out of a fairytale—an old mansion perched on a hill, its balconies wrapped in ivy, chandeliers casting a soft, golden glow through tall windows.

It's the kind of place where time slows, where every detail feels like the first line of a love story.

Ryan puts the car in park and beats the valet out by a second.

He opens my door with a quiet smile.

"Always a gentleman," I tease, stepping out.

"Only for you," he murmurs, pressing a kiss to my temple before taking my hand.

Inside, a woman greets us—a vision of Parisian grace in a fitted black dress, posture perfect, lips red as punctuation. Her accent is soft, elegant.

"*Ah! Monsieur Nouel, Madame—welcome!*" she says warmly. "*I am Geneviève. Your table is waiting.*"

Ryan smiles, his grip strong and gentle, thumb tracing the back of my hand.

"*Merci, Geneviève.* Please, call me Ryan."

I don't ask how she knows his name. I don't need to. I just follow, my pulse already skipping ahead.

At coat check, I slip mine off without hesitation—I didn't wear this dress to keep it hidden. Ryan, oddly, keeps his on. Strange—but I let it go.

Geneviève glides down a honey-lit corridor. The air is thick with red wine, warm bread, and something sweet and slow-roasted.

We're halfway down the corridor when I hear it—"Amaya?" High-pitched. Thrilled. Familiar. I turn—and there they are.

A full table of the Mall Walkers. Joyce and Paul. Maria and Richard. Billy and Marilyn. All dressed up, mid-toast, with a cluster of balloons floating above them. One reads: "*10 Years of Steps & Friendship!*"

I blink. "Oh my gosh… so nice to see you guys."

Joyce waves her napkin like she's hailing a cab. "I *knew* that was you, girl! All dolled up and strolling in here with a man who looks like he walked straight out of a cologne ad!"

Maria leans toward Joyce. She *thinks* she's whispering. She's absolutely not. "*Wait… that's not the one who made her cry, right?*"

I laugh. "No, Maria. This is Ryan. My fiancé."

The ladies erupt at once—gasps, claps, squeals—like synchronized cheerleaders at a prom.

"You hear that, Rich?" Maria nudges her husband. "Our Jumper's engaged!"

Richard gives Ryan a once-over, then nods with slow, deliberate approval. "You did good, son. Don't mess it up."

Billy lifts his glass—could be water with lemon, could be gin. "To Amaya," he says warmly. "You've earned every bit of that smile."

Maria softens, her voice gentler now. "We've seen you in all kinds of weather, sweetheart—power-walking, jump-roping, laughing… and yeah, those quiet days near the smoothie cart when we wished we could hug you without scaring you off. "But today?" Her eyes glisten. "You're glowing. And not from cardio."

Marilyn offers a smile that lands like a blessing. "That man's got kind eyes. That's the kind that lasts."

Ryan leans in, grinning. "Friends of yours, babe?"

"Mall royalty," I say, beaming.

They lift their glasses.

"To new beginnings," Joyce declares, raising hers like a crown. "To love," Paul echoes. "To happy feet and even happier hearts," Maria adds with a wink.

Ryan gives a respectful wave. "Pleasure meeting you all."

I blow them a kiss. "You'll see me soon—with my rope and a whole new reason to smile."

Their laughter lingers behind us as we walk on—my steps light, my heart full, my cheeks flushed with something deeper than joy.

Golden light brushes the walls; soft laughter drifts ahead. My heels kiss the marble; curls brush my shoulders. The dress feels like it was made for this moment. I am present. Rooted. Alive.

And then—Geneviève stops in front of a pair of ornate double doors. She meets Ryan's eyes. He gives a subtle nod. Her smile curves—and she swings the doors wide.

"SURPRISE!"

My heart jumps into my throat as the room erupts—light, sound, color spilling over me all at once.

A long table glows under a canopy of candlelight, draped in white and blush roses, flickering tea lights, and champagne flutes already half full.

And standing at the head of it all, beaming, are Basha, Esperanza, Mr. Nouel. Oscar.

I gasp, both hands flying to my face. "Oh my gosh! You guys!"

Before I can take another breath, Basha throws her arms around me.

"Girl! You took so long, I almost raided the kitchen. I was two seconds away from smuggling a baguette down my pant leg and walking out like nothing happened."

Laughter erupts. I pull back, tears stinging my eyes.

"I can't believe this," I say, turning to Esperanza, Mr. Nouel, Oscar—each one smiling at me like they see the whole journey it took to get here.

Esperanza squeezes my hands, her eyes shining. "Did you really think we'd let you get engaged without a celebration?"

"I—I didn't even know I was getting engaged tonight!" I laugh, pointing at Ryan. "He tricked me. Told me the dinner reservation got pushed back."

Ryan just smiles, wrapping an arm around my waist. "I prefer an expertly planned surprise."

Mr. Nouel laughs, clapping his son on the back. "I've gotta admit, *mon fils*—this was smooth. I'm proud of you."

"Thanks, Dad," Ryan says, like he's been waiting his whole life to hear that.

I open my mouth to speak—but then I see it.

And every word disappears.

A small velvet box in Ryan's hand. The air thickens, trembling with quiet. The room stills. The sound fades. And then—he steps forward slowly, eyes locked on mine.

"You didn't think I'd propose without a ring, did you?" he says, voice low—like this moment belongs only to us.

He opens the box. Inside sits a round-cut diamond set in white gold—or platinum—timeless, elegant, sparkling like it knows it belongs here.

"This ring belonged to the most extraordinary woman I've ever known—my mother, Madeleine." His voice trembles. "And now it belongs to my favorite love."

My heart stills, making space for the weight of his words. And then a memory flashes—that black-and-white photo of her in sunlight, hand resting on Mr. Nouel's chest, the ring catching light like it knew its future.

I remember how soft his voice went when he said, *"She always said love is like home—it should make you feel safe."*

I draw in a sharp breath, one hand covering my mouth as tears rise, fast and hot.

Ryan steps closer, cradling my trembling hand. Hands that once shook from fear now tremble for joy—for awe—for something so good it feels almost unreal.

"Amaya," he says, voice thick, "I knew the moment I found my way back to you that I never wanted to lose you again. We lost each other once. I won't let that happen again. You're my best friend. My greatest adventure. My home. You've been my what if for years—and now you're my always. I want to spend every single day proving that love can come back stronger than ever."

He swallows, his eyes holding mine like they've always known their way home.

"Will you marry me?"

I nod before I can even speak, laughter and tears tangling in my throat.

"Yes," I breathe, laughing through it. "Yes—of course, yes."

The second the ring slides onto my finger, the room explodes—applause, laughter, champagne flutes clinking, voices calling my name... our names.

I glance down. The ring fits like it's been waiting for me all along.

Then—*"¡Amaya, mira!"*

Esperanza shoves her phone into my hands. I blink, confused, and look down at the screen.

It tugs something deep inside me—like my heart is rising to meet him across oceans. Full of everything I've ever hoped he'd witness.

"My dad's on a video call?" I whisper, my throat closing. Of course Ryan would think of this.

Papi—my first love, the man who's loved me the best way he knew how—just witnessed my engagement.

His voice comes through, trembling, thick with emotion.

"Amaya, mi niña... felicidades. I'm so happy for you."

My chest caves in around the sound.

All my life, I wanted him to see me happy. To see me loved. To see me chosen.

And tonight, he does.

I press a hand to my heart, blinking hard. Overwhelmed. Anchored.

"*Papi… te amo,*" I whisper.

On the other end, I hear him call out—"*¡Marisol, ven acá! ¡Rápido!*" Then, his voice thick with joy, echoing like music through the screen: "*¡Nuestra hija se casa!*"

A beat later Marisol joins in, an apron still tied around her waist, a half-peeled green plantain in one hand and a knife in the other. She gasps, clasps her hands to her mouth, and then—tears. "*Ay, Amaya… felicidades, mi amor. Felicidades, Rayán.*" Behind her, a pot simmers on the stove, the scent of home spilling through the screen.

Her voice cracks. "We gotta celebrate this right. You better come home soon—we're roasting a pig and cooking enough *chivo* to feed the whole *campo. ¡Dios mío, qué bendición!*"

As champagne glasses clink and voices rise in celebration, I glance at Ryan—his hand still tightly wrapped around mine—and everything else fades.

Just him. His eyes. His heart. The grounding presence that changed everything.

This is it. This is home.

The night unfolds like a dream. A blur of music, laughter, and joy so big it barely fits in my chest.

Then the toasts begin, and—of course—Basha is already the most chaotic, ridiculous, and unforgettable one in the room.

She lifts her champagne flute like it's an Oscar, the other hand raised high to demand silence. "Okay, everyone, quiet down! I need absolute silence for this historic moment."

"Amaya, I have known you for… well, too long, honestly. And I just want to say—I have never seen you this happy. And I have never seen a man look at a woman the way Ryan looks at you. Like he's won the lottery and knows it. Like he's afraid one bad haircut and you'll trade him for a man with an accent and better cheekbones."

Ryan nearly chokes on his drink. I burst into laughter, shaking my head. Basha, unfazed and clearly thriving, charges on.

"But in all seriousness," she says, tone softening with graceful sincerity, "I love you, Amaya. You deserve the biggest, most ridiculous love story ever written. And I think—no, I know—you found it."

"And Ryan…" She turns to him, a small smile tugging at her mouth. "Thank you for proving me right when I told her good men still exist."

She raises her glass like it's the toast of the century.

"So congrats, you two lovebirds. Now, can we please eat before I pass out and start hallucinating?"

Laughter explodes around the table as glasses rise in salute, champagne fizzing and spilling over rims like joy too big to be contained. Oscar whistles from the back. Everyone claps. I'm laughing so hard my ribs ache.

And then—like someone just dimmed the lights—the room softens. Not silence—something quieter. Like reverence itself just pulled up a chair.

Mr. Nouel finds my eyes across the table, and the pride I see there doesn't crash over me—it settles deep, like roots in soil that finally feels like home.

"Amaya," he begins, "when you first walked into Maison Madeleine asking for a job, Esperanza and I looked at each other and knew."

He pauses, smiling gently. "You were exactly what we didn't know we needed. Full of light. Hardworking. That smile of yours could wake the dead—and it sure as hell woke up our sleepy bakery."

Laughter hums through the room.

"But it wasn't just your energy. It was the way you treated every person who walked through our doors. With kindness. With dignity. With heart. *Chérie*, you didn't just work for us. You became family."

I press my lips together, willing the tears to stay in place.

Then he turns to Ryan.

"And you, my boy," he says, voice thickening slightly, "I've been proud of you in more ways than I can count. But tonight…" He pauses, just long enough for something holy to land. "Tonight, I know your mama's smiling down. Because she always said you had a heart big enough for something extraordinary. And now, you've found it. I know she would've loved Amaya. She would've adored her."

He lifts his glass, his eyes carrying that quiet pride that settles somewhere deep.

"Marriage is the bravest, most generous kind of partnership. Love each other. Forgive quickly. Laugh often. And never stop being each other's safe place."

His voice catches—just slightly—but it's enough to crack something open in my chest.

Tears slip free—and I let them. *This is the kind of moment they're made for.*

"To Ryan and Amaya."

"*¡Salud!*" rises in a chorus—loud, joyful, unstoppable.

Glasses clink like bells, laughter bursts around us, and I blink fast, my heart aching with gratitude—so much it barely fits inside my skin.

As everyone cheers, I catch sight of two staff members standing quietly in the back corner. They're dabbing their eyes, holding hands, smiling like they just watched the final scene of their favorite romance film.

The sight undoes me.

Ryan's hand tightens around mine. When I look at him, his eyes shimmer with the same wild emotion I feel down to my bones.

Then Esperanza steps forward, calm and fire braided together in every step.

She doesn't need to raise her voice. The room just listens.

"*Mi niña,*" she begins, her voice warm as baked sugar, "you know I never had children. But the moment I saw you... I saw a younger version of myself. That same fire. That same hunger. The spirit of our island—of women who rise before dawn and never stop dreaming.

Of women who carried whole families on their backs and still managed to dance."

Her words stop time.

"And now you're here. Like me—making magic out of hard work, love, and second chances."

Only Esperanza could speak like this—like every sentence belongs stitched into a quilt or carved into stone. She doesn't just sound like poetry—she is poetry. Wears it. Breathes it. She takes my hand in hers, and the callused warmth of her palm steadies me.

"And you deserve a love that stays through every storm. One that's patient. One that sees all of who you are—and never looks away."

Then she turns to Ryan, a quiet power rising in her smile. "Take good care of her," she says. "Love her the way she deserves to be loved. Because this one?" She taps her heart. *She's pure gold.*

Emotion tangles in my throat. I throw my arms around her, burying my face in her shoulder. She strokes my hair gently, whispering something soft I don't even catch—but it stays with me anyway.

I pick up my glass and turn to face the room. But when I speak, I don't speak to them. I speak to him. I look at Ryan like the rest of the world has blurred into soft background noise. Like he's the only thing that's ever been in focus.

"Before I met you, I didn't believe in true love—not really. I believed in survival. In getting through the day. I was a kid who ran from everything she knew—putting herself through school, working two jobs while doing freelance work on my 'free' time, pretending she didn't need anyone."

"And then you walked into the bakery—all charm and confidence, looking like you'd never touched a bag of flour in your life—and suddenly, everything I thought I understood about love… cracked open."

"I didn't expect you. I didn't want to expect anyone. But you saw me—not just the loud, capable version I showed the world. You saw the quiet parts. The messy parts. The parts I didn't even know were lovable."

I pause, and he looks at me like he's holding his breath.

"And then we went our separate ways. Your dreams. My fear. Bad timing dressed up like fate. I told myself I was over you. That what we had was just a moment."

I glance down at my glass, then back at him. My voice softens.

"And then Max happened. And I tried again. But it was never you. And I knew that."

I breathe deep, my voice trembling with the truth of it.

"And just when I thought love was done with me—you came back. Not with fireworks. Not with perfect words. Just with that heart of yours, wide open. Showing up exactly when I needed someone to believe in again."

I lift my glass, my hand finally still.

"You are the calm after every storm. The *yes* I didn't even know I was still hoping for. The place I didn't think I'd get to return to—until you reminded me it was still there."

I smile, blinking back tears.

There's a beat of silence that feels suspended in gold.

"To us," I say, locking eyes with the man who made me believe in love all over again. "To every wild, beautiful moment that brought us here."

The glasses rise again—quieter this time, the candlelight catching in each one like liquid gold.

"To us."

The room exhales.

And I know, without a shadow of a doubt—*this is my beginning*. And this time, I'm writing it with love.

The first plates are being set on the table when Oscar pushes back his chair and casually rolls up his sleeves, like he's gearing up to drop wisdom—or start trouble. He lifts his glass, that signature smirk already in place.

"I just want to set the record straight," he begins. "The moment Basha and I started dating, she told me I'd always be second in her life—because her best friend comes first."

The room breaks into laughter as Basha shrugs.

"I mean… obviously," she says, grinning.

Oscar nods solemnly, still playing along. "So, Ryan, welcome to the club. You're marrying Amaya—but just know, you'll always be second in rank."

Ryan lifts his glass, a smile tugging at his mouth. "Good to know where I stand."

The laughter softens into something warmer, and when Oscar looks back at us, there's a quiet certainty in his eyes. His voice loses its playfulness, and in its place comes a quiet sincerity that hits me square in the chest.

"But in all seriousness—Amaya, Ryan—what you two have? It's rare. The way you hold space for each other, challenge each other, laugh with—never at—each other? That's the kind of love people spend their whole lives looking for. And what makes it even better… is that you found your way back."

He looks at Ryan with a smile that holds more than just friendship—it holds respect.

"You two went through fire and still chose each other. Some things are just meant to be."

He lifts his glass higher.

"To Amaya and Ryan—may your love be as strong as Basha's opinions and as smooth as the drinks at Bar Barazo."

"¡*Salud*!" echoes across the room as glasses rise and clink.

But Oscar's not done. He lifts a finger like a postscript is coming.

"Oh—and tomorrow night, drinks are on me at Bar Barazo. Come celebrate. Let me regret this in the morning."

Laughter bursts through the room, and Basha shakes her head, beaming.

"You better not regret it, babe. You said it in front of witnesses."

The food is ridiculous in the best way. Buttery lobster ravioli. Filet mignon that melts under the knife. Appetizers so pretty Basha spends five minutes taking photos and mispronouncing their names before giving up and pointing like a tourist in a foreign film.

Then comes the cake. Correction—cakes.

One is a classic French *gâteau*—light, airy, stacked in delicate layers of raspberry and cream. The other? A Dominican *bizcocho* from Vilma's Bakery, golden and fluffy with just the right kiss of guava in the center.

I take a bite of the *gâteau* first—elegant, dreamy, like silk on my tongue. Then the *bizcocho*—bright, nostalgic, like home wrapped in frosting.

I press a hand to my chest, eyes falling shut like I'm savoring a memory I never want to forget. "Ryan, I swear I just died and went to heaven." I open my eyes slowly, dramatic. "You locked this marriage in for life. This cake? Seals the deal."

He leans in, eyes dancing with a mix of sugar and mischief. "Noted. Good cake equals happy wife. I'll make a standing order, *Señora Nouel*."

His Spanish is still rough, a little off—but it gets me every time. That he tries, just for me? That's everything. And yeah—every single time, I fall a little harder.

✶ ✶ ✶

"La Vie en Rose" hums softly from the speakers. Candlelight glows, champagne shimmers—it feels like we've stepped out of time.

Then Basha's voice slices through the haze. "Ryan! What are you waiting for? Dance with your beautiful future wife!"

Ryan's mouth curves as he holds out a hand to me. Amaya. His future wife.

"May I have this dance, fiancée?"

I slide my fingers into his, my smile stretching through tears I can't quite hold back. "Always," I whisper.

The song shifts—"Bésame Mucho" spills out, smooth and sultry. He pulls me close, and I melt into him, my head finding its home on his chest. His heartbeat hums beneath the fabric—anchoring me to this moment, reminding me I'm home.

The room hushes at the edges.

It's just Ryan and me. And this moment.

Ours.

✶ ✶ ✶

Ryan drives me home, one hand on the wheel, the other threaded through mine. Neither of us talks much. We don't need to. This silence is sacred. Like the space between us is already full—with history, hope, and the echo of everything we've overcome.

When we reach my building, he shifts into park and turns to me. The town glows faintly behind him, but his eyes—his eyes hold all the light I need.

"Amaya," he says, voice low, like a vow wrapped in breath. "My best friend. My future wife. My forever love."

He leans in and brushes a kiss against my lips—tender, reverent. Then another, softer, over my ring finger. My heart skips, then settles, like it finally knows where it belongs—nothing has ever felt more certain.

He reaches into his pocket and pulls out a key ring, placing it in my palm as if handing me a pulse.

"These are for you," he says. "Not just for the house—but for every morning we'll wake up together. Every argument we'll survive. Every dance in the kitchen. Every dream."

The metal is cool against my skin, but the weight is warm—until I'm not holding keys anymore, I'm holding a thousand tomorrows. Laughter echoing in the hallway. A sink full of dishes we won't fight about. The scent of his hoodie on my skin. A love you build, brick by brick, after the world breaks you open. Tears gather. But I blink them back. I press the keys to my chest, right over the part of me that still can't believe this is real.

"Ryan…"

He cups my cheek, his thumb tracing over my skin like a prayer. "I want you there," he whispers. "Always."

I nod. No words. Just breath. Just ache. And then he kisses me.

Not gently. Not hesitantly. But fully. Deeply. His breath is warm, threaded with something sweet, as if he's pouring everything he's ever felt for me into my mouth, into my breath, into my soul.

I kiss him back. With every broken piece I've stitched together. With every inch of woman I've become. With every part of me that has waited, through pain and silence, for this kind of love.

This isn't a kiss. It's a homecoming. It's surrender. It's forever.

✳ ✳ ✳

The apartment is quiet, except for the rustle of trees outside my bedroom window. Sleep should come easy tonight. But my heart is too full. My thoughts, too bright.

I slip out of bed and drift into the living room, drawn to the faint shimmer beyond the glass.

Grabbing a blanket, I wrap it around my shoulders and step onto the balcony. The Hudson stretches beneath the moonlight—quiet as breath, silver as grace. A breeze lifts gently against my skin, carrying the scent of water, night, and something else I can't name—something that feels like peace.

I take a breath, slow and deep, and let it settle in the places where the nerves used to live.

I've stood here a thousand times. But tonight, everything feels different. The same skyline. The same river. But a new version of me. One who is loved. Chosen.

After a while, I slip back inside, still wrapped in the warmth of what this day has given me.

I don't want to sleep. Not yet. I don't want this feeling to pass without honoring it.

I sink onto the couch and reach for the journal—the soft pink leather carrying the hush of a blank chapter, ready to hold our story. I run my fingers over the gold lettering.

For the girl who always saw the light, even when it was dim.

I smile, biting my lip, breath held in a small, reverent moment. And then—I open it.

Reaching for the matching pink-and-gold pen, I press the tip to the crisp, untouched page.

And before I write a single word, I pause—grateful to God for protecting me, for never letting me give up, even when I begged to disappear. Because somehow, even when I couldn't see a future for myself, He did. He knew this day would come. He held it for me until I was strong enough to live it.

And tonight, I do.

Hey Sofia,
    You know how I used to tell you that real love—the kind that leaves you breathless, the kind that stays—only existed in stories? Well... tonight proved me wrong.
    Girl, I'm engaged. And not just engaged—chosen. Twice. Yeah, joke's on me.
    The first proposal happened under string lights, the Hudson stretched out beside us, and a love letter tucked inside this pink leather journal—the one I'm writing in now. No ring. No flash. Just him, me, and the kind of quiet love that rearranges everything. Sof, you know I've read the stories. Watched the movies. But I've never seen a proposal begin with a journal. Maybe one day someone will write it—or film it—and when they do, I'll know exactly how it feels.
    The second proposal happened at Ciel d'Amour. Candlelight. Two cakes. Champagne. Esperanza. Oscar. Mr. Nouel. Basha. And his mother's ring—something sacred, passed down, now resting

cool and certain on my hand, like it knew it belonged here all along.

And Papi? He saw it all. Not in person, but through a screen—eyes wet, voice shaking. "*Amaya, mi niña... felicidades.*" For a moment, I thought the video had cut out. But it was just his breath catching, like joy had stolen every word.

Marisol cried like I'd grown in her own womb—enough tears to water every mango tree on the island. She kept whispering thanks under her breath—"*gracias, Señor*"—like this moment had been sewn into every prayer she'd ever prayed. Before the call ended, I heard her yelling into the neighborhood, "*¡Vecina, mi hija se casa!*"

That moment rewrote something inside me. Because for so long, I didn't believe a love like this could belong to me. But tonight, I understood something I've never dared to say aloud. I didn't just run from Soledad to save myself. I ran to survive. And somewhere along the way... I kept running. From the pain. From believing I deserved more than just getting by.

Not anymore. Tonight, I stopped. I stood still. And love—real, enduring, forgiving love—found me exactly there.

So here's to the next chapter. To writing a life I no longer want to escape from. To being still. To being seen. To being chosen.

And this—this is the last time I run.

'Til next time,
xoxo, Amaya

Epilogue

The ring still catches the light when I least expect it—usually when I'm not even looking. It's not the sparkle that gets me. It's the meaning that still hums beneath it. It's been a month since the proposal, and somehow the world feels both brand-new and beautifully familiar.

One night, curled up with Ryan on the couch, watching the frozen Hudson glow like moonlight on glass, he takes my hand and says, "This ring holds my two favorites—my first love in heaven, and you… my forever love."

I kiss his hand and close my eyes. In the quiet, I thank God for this moment.

The second we step out of the airport, the island air rises to meet us, thick with heat, salt, and the sweetness of something living. Ryan takes my hand, his fingers threading through mine as he looks around, eyes wide, his hair ruffled by the breeze. And in that simple moment— his awe, my belonging—it feels like the island is welcoming us both.

Papi drives slower than usual. I think he wants Ryan to see everything—every bend in the road, every fruit tree leaning toward the sun, every chipped house still painted in the colors of hope. Bold. Weathered. Still standing.

We ride in a hush—me swallowing tears, him taking it all in like it's the first chapter of a story he's always wanted to read.

I was here not long ago, just trying to breathe, trying to stitch myself back together. But today feels different. Today, I'm home—and I've brought love with me.

When we pull up to the house, something inside me exhales. Ryan is here. With me. In the same place I once chased mangoes barefoot through the rain, curls wild, knees scraped, joy loud and easy. He looks at me like he's meeting little-girl me for the first time. And just like that, I'm eight again. Glowing.

Marisol greets us with her masterpiece—a massive pot of *sancocho* bubbling over the *fogón*, thick with garlic, cilantro, seven meats, and every root vegetable this island knows by heart. Nearby, a bowl of freshly squeezed bitter orange waits for its final tangy kiss. Papi says without *naranja agria*, the *sancocho* doesn't sing. Those who truly know the countryside wait until the very end to add it—like a secret the land keeps until the very end.

Another pot cradles a mountain of fluffy white rice. Beneath it, golden *concón* crackles like applause. Marisol makes poetry with her hands. She always has. The table's covered in avocado halves bigger than Ryan's hands, and enough *tostones* to feed a village—every single one fried in love and grown on Papi's land.

Ryan takes one bite, closes his eyes, spoon hovering midair. "This is officially my favorite stew," he says. Then adds, in his best, most painful Spanish, "*Gracias… mucho bueno…* san—CO—cho."

I nearly choke trying not to laugh.

Gosh, I love this man.

We wake up to the smell of real Dominican coffee—brewed the old-school way, with cloth, patience, and soul. The beans were roasted yesterday, straight from my grandparents' land.

Marisol laughs, hands on hips, and says, "Tell your *Americano* we have a *greca*… but today, he drinks it the way God intended."

Ryan—who's been everywhere—swears this is the only way coffee should ever be made.

She hands us a woven basket full of warm *pan de agua*—fresh off *el motor de* Pan-Cito, the neighborhood bread guy. No one remembers his real name. He's just Pan-Cito, as if the nickname were born with him.

"Just a little something to settle your stomachs," Marisol says—because in Dominican households, even *a little something* could feed twelve.

Breakfast looks like a still-life painting—pillows of buttery *mangú*, golden-fried cheese, crispy salami, eggs with yolks the color of marigolds, and caramelized red onions. (Not that I care—because I hate onions and skip them like my life depends on it.) Avocado slices, soft and salty, round it all out. Then Marisol pours us tall glasses of *morir soñando*, made with oranges from the backyard tree.

"These *plátanos* taste so fresh," I say to Papi.

He doesn't answer with words. He just lifts his callused hands and smiles.

"No one cooks like you," I tell Marisol.

Her face lights up like morning sun through lace curtains.

"The kitchen is my sanctuary," she says.

And honestly? It shows.

✷ ✷ ✷

After breakfast, Ryan collapses into the hammock, limbs loose—as if the island itself rocked him to sleep.

I head into the kitchen to help Marisol with the dishes. She waves me off, but I can't sit still.

As I'm rinsing a plate, Marisol suddenly gasps and grabs my arm. "¡Mira!" she whispers, eyes wide.

My heart leaps to my throat. Snake? Someone stealing mangoes or aguacates? Maybe even a cow breaking loose—again. I whip my head toward the window, bracing for disaster…

And then I freeze.

Out there, Papi is walking hand-in-hand with Ryan, pointing toward the plantains, waving his hands like he's narrating a whole *novela*. For a second, I forget to breathe. My two favorite men. Laughing. Talking. Together. Like they've always belonged in the same chapter.

I dry my hands and hurry outside to "rescue" Ryan—aka, translate. His Spanish is a solid three out of ten. Papi knows maybe three words in English. And yet somehow, they vibe like father and son.

Papi walks him through the land, proud as a king. *"Aquí sembré esto con mis manos,"* he says, eyes lit with pride, pointing to mango trees, avocado trees, sugarcane, and rows of tall plantains swaying in the wind—each one holding a piece of his story.

He speaks with the dignity of a man who's worked the earth and loved every inch of it.

Ryan listens as if every sentence is scripture.

Then Papi stops, places a hand over his chest, and meets Ryan's eyes. *"Los buenos se sienten de lejos."* You can feel a good man from far away.

I don't even translate. Ryan nods, eyes locked on Papi's—like he understands exactly what that moment means. Like he feels the weight of being seen not just as my partner, but as someone worthy of the most sacred part of Papi's world.

He turns to me, voice low. "I love this. All of it. Your culture. Your roots. You."

Then he leans in and kisses my forehead.

It starts small. Then neighbors show up. Then cousins. Then cousins' cousins.

Before long, our patio is alive—a *campo* celebration in full swing. Plastic chairs form loose circles. Dominoes click. Kids race barefoot through the trees. Everyone brings food. Everyone brings rhythm, laughter, and stories that shake the sky.

Tambora drums pound the earth. The *güira* slices the air. Guitars hum, accordions cry, and someone's banging out beats on a cooking pot. Even Carmelita grabs the lid of a *caldero* and taps out rhythm, hips rolling like she's leading her own carnival—wild, unstoppable, full of soul.

Ryan—bless him—survives three dance circles, four domino losses, and a surprise merengue battle. I laugh so hard I get hiccups.

The desserts are another world: *batata* pudding, *coconete* cookies, *jalao* coconut balls. One of my aunts brings a tray of something no one can name, but it's sticky, sweet, and gone in minutes. And yes—Marisol makes a huge pot of *habichuela con dulce*.

I try to give Ryan a heads-up, as gently as I can. "Okay, babe… you're about to eat red beans mixed with sweet potatoes, cinnamon, raisins, a hint of ginger, and a whole lot of sugar."

He stares at the bowl like it might bite back. "But it's… dessert?"

"It's Dominican dessert," I say. "Trust me."

He takes one bite. "Why does this taste like Christmas and confusion?"

We laugh until our stomachs hurt.

By the end of the night, we've eaten so many sweets, I swear even the mosquitoes are on a sugar high.

✱ ✱ ✱

A few hours ago, we arrived in Punta Cana to meet Basha and Oscar.

It's my first time in this part of the island—and yeah, I cry the second my feet touch that ridiculous turquoise water. The sand feels like powdered sugar; the breeze smells like papaya and salt. It's like hugging a part of myself I didn't even know I'd been missing.

The moment I spot Basha, I run to her like we haven't seen each other in ninety-nine years. There's something about seeing her here, in *my* land, that hits different. Like she's not just seeing me—she's seeing every version of me that came before. The barefoot girl perched on an old paint bucket, biting into guava straight from the tree. The ten-year-old who left with a beat-up suitcase full of innocence and hope. The one who dreamed of coming back whole.

She spins me around, laughing. "Look at you," she says. "You touch one grain of Dominican sand and suddenly you're glowing like a honeymoon ad. Meanwhile, I need SPF eighty-eight just to survive."

Oscar strolls up, shirt open like he's auditioning for a beach-romance movie.

"There they are—the chaos duo," Ryan says. "Now it's officially a party. Please tell me you brought stretchy pants—I've eaten like royalty and I'm one *mangú* away from needing a new wardrobe."

"Stretchy pants? Please. I've eaten so much I told the chef if she feeds me again, I'm proposing."

He turns to me, hand on his chest like he's serenading a bolero. "I love your country, Amaya. *Viva la D.R.*, truly. I'm considering leaving Basha for the *dulce* lady—she sells the best coconut candy rolled in every sweet thing God ever made. Says I look like I need something sweet in my life. That woman has molasses in her eyes and a tray full of reasons to stay."

I shrug. "Go ahead. I'll find Basha a Dominican farmer who builds furniture barefoot and squeezes lemons shirtless."

Basha smirks. "Fine. I'll trade him for the coconut vendor with machete arms and a twelve-pack."

We're all laughing—loud, rolling laughter that breaks like waves against the shore.

A beach vendor passes with a tray of shot glasses filled with dark amber liquid.

"*Mamajuana*," he says. "One sip, you'll feel like you can dance, propose, and fight a lion."

Basha raises a brow. "You heard him. Let's see what this *Mamajuana's* about."

We each take a shot. The burn comes slow—sweet and smoky—like swallowing the heartbeat of the island. A remedy my ancestors stitched together from bark, roots, and flame, born from the days when healing came straight from the land.

"To the land that raised me, the friends who held me, and the love that makes you believe in second chances," I say.

"To us," they echo.

The moment folds in—warm arms, laughter, and sea air. For a heartbeat, the laughter softens, the waves hush.

Ryan pulls me close. "You glow here, my love," he whispers. "Truth is, you always glow... but here? It's like the sun's not shining on you—it's shining from you."

I pretend not to tear up. I absolutely do.

Basha watches, misty-eyed. "When you two got engaged," she says softly, "it felt like the story finally found its heart."

And maybe it did. But we both know—this isn't an ending. It's just the next beginning.

We sit close in the sand, the four of us, letting the waves kiss our ankles—laughing, dreaming, leaning into the kind of peace you don't plan for. The kind that feels like family. The kind that feels like forever.

Life's funny like that. In New York, I'm always moving—one task, one hustle, one plan after the next. Even rest feels like a checkbox. But here? Time exhales. The hours stretch like hammocks between palm trees—held by nothing but peace. The ocean hums. Nobody's rushing you to be more, do more, fix more. You're just allowed to be. And somehow, that's everything.

After a while, the guys wander off toward a beach bar, still deep in conversation—business, travel, probably politics. Their voices fade into the hum of the waves.

Basha and I stay where we are, lying flat on the sand, crying from joy, laughing like kids, dreaming like our grandmothers prayed us into this moment.

We talk about weddings—maybe a double one. Barefoot, right here in Punta Cana. Simple. Organic. No centerpieces. No gifts—just donations to help families put down roots. A way to thank God for how far we've come.

Then I tell her my other dream. "I want to buy land," I say. "Not just build houses—but build hope. Real homes for families who need more than a roof over their heads."

I close my eyes and see it: mango trees shading every yard, avocados hanging low enough to reach from the porch, plantains so heavy they bend the trees with promise. Rows of herbs, not just for cooking, but for healing. Maybe even coffee plants, so every morning smells like *café* and peace.

She's smiling. I'm smiling.

"I just want to give people a place where everything around them says—you belong here," I say.

At some point, we notice a vendor passing by with fresh coconuts stacked high on his cart. The ring of his machete cuts the air like a bell. We wave him over and each grab one, sipping straight from the shell— with a spoonful of *azúcar morena*, obviously.

And because we never stop dreaming, we go bigger. I start picturing a trade school for girls.

"Makeup. Hair. Fashion. Sewing. Design," I say.

"All free," Basha adds.

"All love," I say.

A place for girls to dream in color and rise in confidence.

We get so caught up in the vision, we forget to pay the coconut vendor.

By the time we realize, he's halfway down the beach.

We scramble to our feet, laughing, waving soggy pesos, shouting, "¡*Señor, espere por favor*!"

✳ ✳ ✳

Back in New York, life flows sweet and quiet—like something I can finally hold without fear of breaking.

Ryan's IT business practically runs itself. He says his favorite office—out of all the cities he's worked in—is wherever I am.

Reflections Studio is blooming. My calendar's full. My heart's fuller.

I've been thinking it might be time to hire my first assistant—someone to keep my chaos in check and my calendar from eating me alive. Me. With an assistant. Wild.

Some days are calm. Others, chaos. And honestly? I wouldn't have it any other way.

On the days the noise gets too loud or my chest feels too full, I book a session with Crystal. Not because I'm falling apart—just to stay rooted. To keep tending the parts of me that still need light.

Sometimes, we don't rush into words. We sip tea. Let the quiet stretch out between us. It's not silence for silence's sake—it's space. Space to breathe. To feel. To be. Somehow, I always end up curled on that same couch, legs tucked under me, the JOY pillow in my lap.

Old habits. New heart.

It used to be comfort. Now it feels like gratitude—like honoring the version of me who kept going, even when she didn't know where she was headed. I don't go to look back anymore—I go to stay open. To make sure the peace I found keeps blooming.

Crystal once told me, "You don't have to disappear to heal. You can grow out loud." I think I finally am.

Next month, we fly to Tanzania. Ryan's school project got delayed a little—life things—but honestly, the timing feels perfect. He's ready to finish what he started.

I can't wait to meet the children whose stories he already carries in his heart. And me? I'm ready to plant something of my own.

When I told Papi my dream—to buy land, build homes for families who need more than shelter, and give each one soil that feeds them—he didn't just say he was proud. He spoke life into it. Named trees I hadn't even thought of. Told me where the sun hits best. That man could map out a farm in his sleep.

Lately, I've been thinking about Mr. Nouel—how he lost the love of his life but still believed in second chances. In love. In purpose. In people. And Esperanza, who never let broken English or broken systems stop her from chasing what was already hers.

They're part of this too. Their courage planted something. Now I get to help it grow.

I have a dream. A big one. And I believe it will come true.

Because I come from mango trees and rich soil. From hands with calluses that worked the Dominican land with love. From food that gathers souls around the table. From music that mends what words can't reach. From prayers whispered before sunrise. From a heart that never stopped believing. From God.

From storms that bent the branches but never broke the roots. From rain that fed the soil and sun that called me higher.

And if I come from all that—there's nothing I can't grow.

✳ ✳ ✳

Morning light slips through the curtains, brushing against the pink journal on my nightstand. It's still there—waiting, patient, part of my daily quiet. I don't open it most days—not because I feel less deeply, but because I've learned to live the peace and joy I once had to write my way toward.

Sofia's still here. Quieter now—like a soft wind at my back. I don't need her voice to survive anymore. But I'll always carry it.

I lift it, tracing the smooth leather with my thumb, the way you touch something sacred. For a moment I hold it close, breathing in the faint scent of Ryan still clinging to the cover.

Hey Sofia,
You were the voice I leaned on when mine was nothing but a whisper. You lived in the margins of every page I filled, steady in the quiet and holding space for what I couldn't say out loud. You stayed through every kind of ache, carrying the pieces I didn't know how to hold.

You helped me dream again. Breathe again. See myself when I'd gone missing. Maybe you were never standing in front of me, but you were real in every way that mattered.

Now…I'm living. I don't need you to survive anymore, but I'll always need you—like roots need earth. Anchored, unseen, but holding everything up.

Thank you for every night you stayed. For every dream you whispered back to life. For every truth you guarded until I was ready to claim it.

I'll never truly leave you, because you never left me.
Together, we rise.
Together, we build.
And like seeds in good soil, we grow.

'Til next time,
xoxo, Amaya

Dear Dreamer

If you're reading this, I hope you know dreams are meant for you, too.
This story was once just mine. A quiet hope I wasn't sure I'd ever finish.
But here you are. And here it is.
Thank you for holding my very first story.
For reading it. For feeling it.
Tell me—is there something you've been dreaming of?
Something whispering in your spirit, asking for a chance?
Listen to it.
Start in the very soil you stand on.
And when your dream comes true,
don't forget to give back—in the way only you can.
With your voice, your hands, your heart.
Tell your story. Feed someone's hope. Plant seeds where you once felt unseen.
And when they grow,
you'll know you've written your own thank-you note to heaven.

Note from the Author

When I first began writing this story, I wasn't sure I could finish it. Some days it felt like pouring salt into old wounds, and other days it felt like a hand reaching toward healing. What kept me going was the quiet conviction that this book wasn't only meant to be a story on a page—it was meant to be a vessel of hope.

Amaya's story is fictional, but it was born from the real weight of trauma, pain, and survival. Writing it meant revisiting pieces of my past—walking back into rooms I had locked long ago because the memories inside them hurt too much to touch. It was an emotional rollercoaster filled with deep pain and moments when I questioned if I was strong enough to keep going. But with every page, God reminded me that my vision was bigger than a book. This story was about reaching someone who needed to know they weren't alone.

This journey stretched me. I doubted myself more times than I can count. I questioned whether anyone would care about Amaya's story, whether my words could possibly matter. But through every tear and pause, God's unfailing love carried me forward and steadied me in ways my own strength never could.

And Amaya—she is more than a character. She was born from parts of my childhood marked by harm, confusion, and a kind of loneliness no child should ever know. The pain I carried into adulthood—the trauma, the anxiety, the constant rebuilding—shaped the woman I fought to become. Amaya carries pieces of that journey and of the women I love. She is fictional, but the roots of her pain are real. Writing her was both healing and heartbreaking—a reminder of how far grace has carried me.

If you've ever felt unseen, unloved, or trapped by pain you couldn't name—this book was written with you in mind. Amaya may be fictional, but her voice carries truth that belongs to so many.

My deepest prayer is that as you turned these pages, you found something that felt like light. Maybe a reminder of your worth. Maybe a glimpse of courage you didn't know you had. Maybe just the comfort of knowing you're not alone in your story.

I also wrote this book for dreamers. For anyone holding a story inside of them, afraid it might never see the light of day. If that's you, I hope this reminds you that your words, your art, your story matter. They can heal you, and they can heal others too.

This is only the beginning for me. I don't know all the stories I'll write in the future, but I know this: each one will carry heart, hope, and honesty. The world needs more of that—and I want to be a voice that offers it.

Thank you for giving Amaya's journey a home in your hands and your heart. Thank you for letting me share my first story with you. It is my prayer that it stays with you long after the last page—as a whisper of hope, a nudge of courage, and a reminder that even in the hardest places, love always finds its way back to you.

If this story found you, I believe it was meant to.

Acknowledgments

First and foremost, I want to thank God. This writing journey has taught me perseverance and revealed the unfailing love of Jesus—a love that carries us when our own strength runs out.

Writing the most painful parts of this story was often an emotional rollercoaster—bringing deep hurt and, at times, leaving me doubting myself and wondering whether this story could ever truly become a novel. Yet through every doubt and every tear, He gave me the strength to keep going, reminding me that my vision was always bigger than a book—it was about bringing hope, light, and restoration through storytelling.

To my past—though often painful, it taught me resilience and shaped the woman I am today. What once felt like breaking became the foundation for rebuilding, and for that, I am grateful.

To my boys—you are my world. Thank you for teaching me patience and showing me what unconditional love truly looks like. May this book be part of the legacy I leave you—a reminder to chase your dreams with everything you are.

To my family, and to the friends who stood beside me through storms and quiet seasons—your encouragement was the light I needed to keep going, to turn pain into purpose, and to believe that broken pieces can still come together to create something whole.

And to you, the reader—thank you for stepping into Amaya's world. Though this is my first story and a work of fiction, it carries the weight of real life, real trauma, and real hope. My prayer is that even one person might find healing, remember their worth, or gain the courage to keep moving forward.

If you are sitting in your own silent pain, may this story give you permission to breathe again, to feel seen, and to believe that healing is possible. You are not alone. Your story matters. And even in the hardest places, love and purpose can still be found.

About The Author

Y.A. Roman is a Dominican American writer who believes in the power of stories to heal and inspire. *The Last Time I Run* is her debut novel—a story shaped by both pain and resilience, written with the hope of offering readers courage, comfort, and the belief that healing is always possible.

She draws from the richness of both Dominican and New York cultures, writing from the in-between spaces—between languages, between experiences, between the shadows and the light.

Her writing blends heart, hope, and humor, exploring themes of trauma, renewal, and the brave everyday choice to love again. Since childhood, books have been her place to breathe and dream freely, and she continues to see storytelling as both a purpose and a path toward light.

When she isn't writing, she treasures time with her sons and parents, enjoys photography, exploring the Hudson Valley, peaceful walks in nature, and—always—chocolate. She lives in New York, where she dreams, creates, and embraces the unfolding journey of storytelling.